Apocalypsis

Book Four

Copyright © 2024 by Rachelle Storm

All rights reserved. No part of this book may be reproduced or used in any manner without written permission of the copyright owner except for the use of quotations in a book review. For more information, address: authorrachellestorm@gmail.com.

www.rachellestorm.com

For

Ezra the Demon Slayer

TABLE OF CONTENTS

	Page
PROLOGUE: Lying In Wait	1
CHAPTER 1: A Nightmare	21
CHAPTER 2: The Enemy of My Enemy	88
CHAPTER 3: Fallout	142
CHAPTER 4: Survival	248
EPILOGUE: The Fates Will Have Their Way	310

PROLOGUE

Lying In Wait

The full moon illuminated the pitch-black sky and surrounding forest where Dominic found himself in the middle of the night. He had spent the flight on the private jet blindfolded, but managed to slip the tiniest of slivers of fabric out of the periphery of his right eye to catch glimpses of the country and military base where they landed. He could discern from the language, road signs, and architecture in the small village the black vehicle sped by that they were in China. When Phillip said Dominic's expertise was needed, he didn't expect such treatment, but knew who was behind the move. While Phillip had spared his life, Trenton was not as forgiving. Dominic winced, as the handcuffs dug into his wrists while he shifted in his seat.

"Is all this really necessary, Connell?"

"Don't tell me the great Dominic Fachanko I've heard about for all these years can't even handle a twenty-minute car ride." Dominic smirked.

"The car ride is fine. The blindfolded ten-hour flight and handcuffs are not to my liking."

"Well, you should have thought about that, before you turned into a madman, betrayed the Brotherhood, and eliminated anyone in your way."

"I am aware of my misdeeds. No need for a recap."

"Then you already know the answer to your question. Is all this really necessary? Of course, it is." Dominic could practically hear Connell's smug smile. He sighed, as he rested his head against the window. It did not take much longer for the vehicle to slow to a halt and park. Dominic could hear Connell exit the vehicle, walk around to his side, and open the door. Connell jerked the blindfold off his face and Dominic squinted while his eyes adjusted and Connell grabbed his arm. He pulled him out of the vehicle and over to the edge of the water as Dominic looked around. They were in the middle of the wilderness, surrounded by trees and mountains. The moon bounced off the vast lake in front of them. In the distance, Dominic spotted a state-of-the-art trailer and a group of men packing several containers beside the building. A glimmer of light caught the corner of his eye, and he noticed dim, white lights beneath the surface of the lake.

"Where are we?"

"Nowhere."

"Come now, you cannot possibly keep me in the dark about everything. I know about the Lucis and I would not be here if…"

"You are here, because Phillip has deemed you to be useful to the cause. But let me make myself clear, Mr. Fachanko. I am not Phillip. I am not even Trenton. I owe you no explanation. For all intents and purposes, you are nowhere."

"I see you two are getting along as well as I imagined," called a familiar voice behind the two men. Dominic spun around and beamed with happiness when he saw his old friend. He sighed in relief and chuckled when the man pulled him into a warm embrace.

"Archibald, they called you in on this? It seems Trenton still has some sense after all."

"Trust me, I was as surprised as you, and even more so when Phillip was on the line and not you."

"Yes, well, I have been a bit…restricted in my capacity with the Brotherhood as of late," said Dominic. He glanced over at Connell, who continued to watch him closely but kept his distance so the two old friends could converse.

"So I've heard," said Archie.

"I assume your presence means you have been filled in on how dire the situation is."

"I understand the significance of the digs we're conducting and the discoveries, yes, but maybe you can fill in some of the blanks for me," suggested Archie, as he pulled Dominic aside. He waited as two members of his crew passed by, and gave them polite smiles, before whispering to his old friend.

"I'm not sure you realize the trouble you're in."

"You let me worry about the Brotherhood. I am aware they are not happy with how I have…"

"I was called in earlier than you may think."

"So, you were offered the job prior to a few months ago?"

"Try last year. It appears every resource and all hands are on deck now."

"Since last year?" Archie nodded.

"Then it appears I was not as inconspicuous as I presumed. I apologize if my actions mean you are here against your will in any way." Archie glanced down at the handcuffs on Dominic's wrists.

"I'm not the one in handcuffs," he reminded his friend.

"Fair enough. Speaking of which, are these handcuffs really necessary?" he called to Connell in the distance, while dramatically waving his hands in front of him. Connell simply ignored Dominic, but Archie gave the guard a kind smile.

"There's no place for him to go, Connell, your tracker assures that," Archie reminded him. Connell rolled his eyes as he approached the pair.

"Fine, but one false move and…"

"No need for threats. It is beneath a man of your status," said Dominic. Connell smirked as he removed the handcuffs.

"When it comes to you, Mr. Fachanko, I assure you such threats will be the least of your concerns, if you try to pull something. You make one move to escape, and it will be my pleasure to put you down like they should have the moment you even thought to use that tablet for personal gain. Tread lightly around him, Archie. He is not the man you remember," warned Connell, before taking his post back by the car. Dominic rubbed his wrists and looked around, as Archie let out a low whistle.

"You always did know how to piss people off," teased Archie.

4

"Apparently it is somewhat of a gift, must have inherited it from my father."

"I always thought you took far more after your mother than you realized."

"Maybe, but Connell is right. I am not the man you used to know. I have done things I am not proud of." Archie wrapped an arm around him as they walked toward the lake.

"You know, that's why I never envied you or the Brotherhood. This world is hard enough. It finds ways to harden us all. Adding the weight of being responsible for its survival? No, thank you."

"You have always been a class act. I am glad you are here, now in such a time. For all my critiques of the current state of the Brotherhood, they always provide the best of the best. What have you found? What is this place? Where are we?"

"Nowhere," called Connell from behind them, with a smug smile. Dominic rolled his eyes at the man.

"Oh good, back to this game," grumbled Dominic. Archie chuckled at his displeasure.

"It seems you've lost your virtue of patience. You certainly are not the man they chose to lead all those years ago. Although, I refuse to believe all of the rumors," said Archie. Before Dominic could respond, Connell approached again, this time giving Dominic a firm clap on the back, which made the older man wince.

"I would not be here if they were merely rumors, Archie. I am under strict orders, to not only keep an eye on *him*, but to make sure his influence does not endanger anyone else," said Connell.

"I am not a danger to anyone. I simply lost my way for a while," defended Dominic.

"Is that what you call becoming a serial killer?" challenged Connell. Dominic gritted his teeth.

"I am not a serial killer. You of all people should not judge me when you have…"

"Alright, enough, you two! Connell, Phillip didn't request his presence for you to torture him or rehash the past," reminded Archie.

"And I am not here at Phillip's request. My orders are quite clear when it comes to Mr. Fachanko. Phillip may want him here, because he believes your discovery may prove him right, but I am here because, much like Trenton, I see him for the conman he is. I understand you two are old friends, but do not forget what is at stake, or who pays you, Archie," warned Connell. Archie gave him a nod and Dominic glared at Connell as he walked over to a member of his security team to check the status of the perimeter.

"You really should not let him speak to you in such a way. His umbrage with me is warranted, but you are here as a kindness. You always did allow others to treat you well beneath your class and grace."

"I'm fine. You're the one I'm worried about. It seems my purpose is twofold. Finding the Lucis not only could help save the world but also you as well."

"They believe me to be the Ultimate Evil, but I am nothing of the sort. They are wasting their time with such notions. Its arrival is imminent. It has to be, so show me what you have found. You have always been quite good at what you do."

"Having a blank check always makes it easier. I was finishing up a dig in Pakistan when I received the call. All this time I believed the Lucis to be a myth."

"But you found one? Where are we? Come on, just tell me." Archie glanced back at Connell, who was still speaking with his team. Archie stepped closer to whisper into Dominic's ear.

"I'm sure you realize by now that you've caused quite the stir. Trenton and Phillip disagree on what to do with you, and as two of the last remaining Guardians, the choice is up to them."

"I am aware. They might as well be the last of us. The others are in hiding and have washed their hands of the situation."

"Which is why Trenton is desperate to end this. In his eyes, the Guardians are no more. However, Phillip is more hopeful, and believes, like I do, that you may be right about what's to come. My search began in ancient ruins, and I conducted digs all over the world. One led me to a map amongst the treasures of Mang Qi."

"I am not familiar with the name."

"He was an emperor of an ancient Chinese dynasty, but it was overthrown after only a few years. Mang was a paranoid man and ruled with cruelty. According to his writings, he always knew he would be betrayed by his men, so he built a fortress in a secret valley where he and his family could flee in case of a mutiny. When one did indeed occur, he managed to narrowly escape with his wife and son to the fortress to live out the rest of his life. The valley the fortress was built in eventually flooded and became this lake."

"What made you decide to search here?" asked Dominic, as he looked around again at the vast expanses of land and water.

"In his writings, he spoke twice of a light that would emit from the ground from time to time. He went in search of it and even tried to dig, but no matter how deep he searched, nothing would appear. No one believed him when he told them. Toward the end of his life, even he believed it to be a hallucination. He was right, though, a light buried so deep, and yet still shone bright."

"A Lucis," said Dominic. Archie nodded and pointed toward the lake.

"I decided to triangulate the location based on the map and found this lake. You can imagine my surprise when I realized it wasn't inhabited. It took quite some time to make the arrangements for a dive and Trenton had to call in quite a few favors with his contacts at MSS, but here we are. If anyone asks though, we aren't here, and this place doesn't exist."

"So, nowhere."

"Precisely. When the valley flooded, the entire fortress was submerged in well over six hundred meters of water. One of the divers found what we were looking for, though. It was floating inside the house. There was seismic activity in the area six months ago. We think it was knocked loose." Dominic gulped at the words.

"Six months ago? When, exactly?" Archie noticed his nervousness and gave him a sympathetic smile.

"The night you were taken into the Guardians' custody."

"You mean the night the Naturas created Absolution?" Archie nodded.

"Unfortunately, while running some tests on the artifact, it cracked and..."

"Wait, what do you mean tests? Are you out of your mind? You are playing with forces far bigger than you. The Lucis is invaluable and may be the only thing standing between us and the end of the world. Are you telling me you lost the only…"

"We found more," interrupted Archie.

"*More?* Where?"

"They're trapped under some ruins beneath the surface. The divers are preparing the equipment to free them. We've tried quite a few methods to release them already, but it seems an underwater explosive may be the best option for dislodging the structure they're trapped under."

"You already destroyed one and now you want to blow up the others? And all this time I thought you were the smartest of us all."

"I am, always have been, and you better not forget it. That's why I'm here, being paid lucratively to perhaps save the world while you're trying to stay out of handcuffs." Dominic glanced back at where Connell watched them.

"You may have a point, but you of all people must know how absurd it is to use such devices on ruins of this nature."

"We have already assured MSS that once we retrieve the Lucis, we will hand the site over to the Chinese government. The ruins they are stuck under will be nothing compared to the riches they will find inside that fortress."

"I don't care about the fortress. I care about the Lucis. If you destroy them…"

"It took a laser." Dominic frowned in confusion.

"What?"

"We were testing the Lucis we found and deemed it to be indestructible…well…until we used the third laser, the most powerful one in existence." Dominic pinched the bridge of his nose.

"You found the only artifact in the world that may be able to momentarily, I repeat, *momentarily*, harm the Ultimate Evil and you decided to see how much it would take to destroy it?" asked Dominic, incredulously. Archie gave a sheepish smile.

"In our defense, it held up really well against the first two lasers."

"Archibald, I swear to…"

"The metallic liquid inside kept its form for a moment even after the casing broke," he added. Dominic listened intently, as Archie got a faraway look in his eyes and remembered the moment the Lucis cracked.

"I saw it glow, Dominic. It was…I've never seen anything like it. All the digs, the vast ruins, and ancient civilizations, never once have I seen something so…so…"

"Otherworldly," suggested Dominic. Archie nodded.

"And there are more."

"How many more?"

"Looks like five."

"So, there were six, just like the Naturas. It cannot be a coincidence. The Ultimate Evil has to be here. Are you sure you can retrieve the Luci without destroying them?"

"We're just about to get started. I figured you would want to be the first to see them all up close together." Dominic stared out at the light peering from underneath the water again.

"This is why Phillip wanted me to come. The Seer and the Naturas are together. The Luci were unearthed the night they created Absolution. It's time. It's here."

"I thought Absolution could only be created after the Ultimate Evil was defeated, so how was it even created that night?"

"I thought the same, but I was wrong. I was wrong about so many things, more than I ever thought possible, but I cannot change that now. All I can do is try to help. The Naturas are not ready. They think it is over, but I know it is not."

"You know I want to believe you. I saw the beaming light of a Lucis up close. It didn't just radiate light, it made me feel…Hope, maybe? It was powerful. That doesn't change that the Naturas created Absolution and there are signs of it all over the world. The War on Destruction is over. Borders are coming down, people are seeing each other as human beings again, not based on man-made walls or casualties to consider in wars. The world is getting better. There are more and more stories about it every day."

"And yet other stories as well. Agencies around the world may be coming together to stop the evils of self-important men, but the gravity of all the good is masking the consequences of the world. That oil pipeline that fractured last month and contaminated land from Russia all the way to Europe…"

"That was a tragic accident, but countries are collaborating to clean up the mess and have shut down the pipeline altogether."

"The earthquake in the Philippines…"

"Earthquakes are unfortunately common there…"

"And yet it never crossed the minds of the corporations fracking there to consider that before doing so. Oh, and let us not forget the volcanic activity disrupting the lives of millions in Indonesia." Archie sighed.

"True, but you are missing the point. No more coverups or downplaying their significance. People all over the world are coming together to not only support all those people and places impacted but to think about what caused such issues in the first place. The pipeline is closed, the fracking has stopped, and new laws are being written every day to ensure it doesn't happen again. That would have never happened before." Dominic waved him off.

"Laws mean nothing to humans in the grand scheme. You cannot legislate morality."

"But you can deter and discourage more harm, even the past loopholes have been closed. You know it to be true. The world is not the same as it used to be. Don't tell me all those years in the Brotherhood have jaded you to what's right in front of you?"

"I can admit that the response has been encouraging, but that does not mean there is not still much evil in the world. It is why Trenton's decision to make me Public Enemy Number One was so ridiculous. There is obviously still much to do. Humans cannot inflict this much harm for this long and expect for it to simply not matter anymore."

"Says the man who needs that to be true," Archie reminded him. Dominic frowned.

"I do not like what you are insinuating."

"I am not insinuating anything. I am saying what we both know to be true. Your life depends on it not being over, but what if the Luci aren't really a sign, and the Naturas have already done what they set out to do by…" Archie stopped midsentence and Dominic looked down.

"By defeating me?"

"The world has been better since they stopped you, Dominic. You have to at least see that." Dominic took a deep breath to steady his nerves and slowly nodded.

"I do. I admit that, and I understand why Trenton believes it too, but you are a man of science and history. You have studied more civilizations, languages, and ways of life than anyone I know, so you of all people have to see it too."

"See what?"

"What did you say you felt when the light of the Lucis glowed? Hope? You of all people should know when great hope arrives, a desperate attempt and onslaught of hate tends to follow. If human history has proven anything, it is that hope is a threat that hate wants to bury. The Ultimate Evil has to have arrived, and those Luci are going to help us stop it." Archie eyed him curiously.

"Don't you mean the Naturas stop it?"

"I may have been wrong about a lot of things, but I know those boys. They are not ready, and if it is here, or about to be, it could be over for all of us."

"Dominic, I wasn't going to ask, because a part of me really doesn't want to know, but…"

"You want to know what the Ultimate Evil is, don't you?" Archie shook his head.

"I don't need to know *what* it is. I just wonder if you even know at this point. Is it that you are worried that the Ultimate Evil *is* coming or that it *isn't?*"

"I need you to trust me now more than ever, Archie. I know I have not given you or the others reason to, but you must believe me. The Ultimate Evil is coming. In fact, it will be here quite soon, if my suspicions are correct. For all we know, based on all these natural disasters, it may already be here. I just do not know where yet."

"Or are all these natural disasters just the earth reminding humans of our past transgressions? Maybe part of Absolution is cleaning up the messes we've made and finally putting an end to our role in them. It could all be part of the process."

"True, but the fates will always have their way, whether we want them to or not is neither here nor there. You are forgetting something quite important. Six Naturas, six Luci, and now…"

"Six months," whispered Archie, as realization dawned on him.

"Our paths cross now, six months after my mistakes, and six months after the Naturas created Absolution. I had no reason to believe such a thing could play out this way before, but if I am right, the world is still most certainly in danger."

"I hope for all our sakes you are wrong, but I'm happy I could find you the Luci, just in case you're right. Whether you'll need them or not, I guess only time will tell. I'll go finish setting everything up." Dominic gave him an appreciative smile and looked around the lake. Archie headed toward the trailer to make the final arrangements for the retrieval of the artifacts. Connell rolled his eyes at the smug smile Dominic wore as he approached the man.

"This does not mean you were right, and it most certainly does not absolve you of anything you've done," reminded Connell. Dominic gave a sly smile.

"I am aware, but we both know the moment those Luci are free, so am I."

"I am aware," Connell begrudgingly conceded, through gritted teeth.

"Which means no more handcuffs or blindfolds or distasteful remarks. Also, I need my phone back. Phillip and I have much to discuss." Connell smirked and shook his head in disbelief but pulled Dominic's phone from his pocket. He handed it to the former leader and arched an eyebrow at him.

"You're lucky, but your luck may run out soon enough." Dominic took the phone with a smile.

"But today is not that day. Now, please excuse me. I have a phone call to make." Connell rolled his eyes again, but gave a curt nod, before heading over to the lake to watch the extraction of the artifacts. Dominic immediately called Phillip and sighed in relief when the elder Guardian answered.

"Careful about being too smug with Connell. Trenton still has you on a short leash and we both know who will be more than happy to pull at that particular chain." Dominic looked up at the sky and gave a wave to the drone hovering over the lake.

"Always keeping a close eye, I see."

"Not always, just since you made it clear such a thing was necessary."

"I want the compound."

"Excuse me?"

"I know you built it, and I know you actually heeded my warning. The only question is if it is fully functional and ready."

Dominic waited for Phillip to weigh his options and sift through his thoughts.

"What you are asking…"

"The Guardians are null and void at this point. I thank you and Trenton for keeping resources in place while the others turned their backs, but my mission, the oath I took, it still matters. I have made my mistakes, but you have kept me alive for this long for a reason, Phillip. I need that compound."

"I hope for your sake, and the sake of mankind, that is not true. However, just in case it is, well…Godspeed." Dominic let out the breath he was not aware he was holding, as Phillip ended the call. Even he was surprised the elder had conceded and approved his request so quickly, which reminded him just how desperate they all were. Dominic's stomach churned, as he looked out over the lake. A sense of unease fell over him.

"Six Naturas. Six Luci. Six months. Where are you?" he wondered out loud, as he thought about the Ultimate Evil. The Luci were mostly intact. The Seer and Naturas were discovered. He knew he was running out of time, one way or another, when it came to the Ultimate Evil. Either he was wrong, about even more than he could have ever imagined, and was doomed to die known as the man who became the Ultimate Evil, or he was right and the true evil was lying in wait.

o o o o o

Scott finished setting up their gear while Jessi reinforced their expedition tent. The frigid air sliced through the first layers of protective clothing like a knife as the scientists conducted their analysis of the region. The wind and swirling snow made for almost whiteout conditions, but the harsh weather did not stop Scott from smiling. Jessi noticed and rolled her eyes.

"They aren't going to name it after us," she called out, over the loudness of the swirling wind.

"Sure, they will! It rolls off the tongue better than the new coordinates for the Northern Pole of Inaccessibility."

"They aren't going to change it to name it after us just because we think we figured out its exact location. We'll be lucky to get them to believe us in the first place, with all the conflicting reports and hypotheses."

"Trust me, they'll change it. And since you have so little faith in that, my name is definitely going first."

"Yeah, yeah, we can argue over the name *after* we collect the last of this data and get out of here. I'm not sure the tent can hold up much longer."

"We'll be back at the station before you know it. Besides, it's downright balmy out here right now. Gotta love global warming," he teased.

"Did you *really* just say that with a straight face? The fact that climate change is making it easier to access it is just another bad omen, in my book. Even with everything we brought with us, it's been hard to pinpoint this place. Maybe there's a reason for that."

"Come on, Jess, lighten up. We did it! We found the shift in coordinates. We can finally track how much it's changing based on…hey, did you see that?" Jessi frowned in confusion, when she noticed him looking behind her. Before she could ask what he saw, he was walking past her and into the distance. The swirls of windswept snow kept visibility low, but she squinted her eyes to try to keep her eyes on him as he disappeared into the white abyss.

"Scott!" she called. He didn't answer. She cursed under her breath and trekked after her colleague. The pit in her stomach grew, as she went in search of him, but she managed to ignore it the moment she spotted Scott. He was staring at something that captured his full attention and her eyes widened when it came into view. She shivered and a chill went down her spine. In front of them was a small pool of jet-black, viscous liquid that had settled over the ice. Scott knelt to get a closer look.

"What the hell is that?" he asked. Jessi peeked over his shoulder.

"Looks like oil."

"No, it can't be." He reached out to touch it, but she swatted his hand away.

"Ow!"

"Don't touch it!"

"I have on gloves and plenty of protective…"

"That doesn't mean you should touch it. Horror film 101. Don't touch things you just find out in the middle of nowhere."

"Really? Horror film 101? You're a scientist."

"And apparently, you're an idiot, but a scientist too. People can be more than one thing at once." He rolled his eyes, but nodded.

"Fine, let's get something to take a sample and…" Suddenly, the ground began to rumble and quake. In an instant, the ice beneath them crumbled and they crashed through a hole in the surface. Snow and ice showered them as they landed with a thud underground. Jessi let out a cough, as she tried to catch her breath and roll to her back.

"Scott?" she called, as the snow began to settle, and she looked around. The frozen cavern was dark, and the light peering from the hole they crashed through barely illuminated the space. As she squinted, she managed to see the shadow of Scott. He was in a pile at the bottom of the sloped plain. She winced, as she made it to her feet and limped over to him.

"Scott? Are you okay?" She managed to turn him onto his back and sighed in relief when he let out several coughs. She helped him to a seated position and inspected him for injuries.

"Are you injured?" He shook his head but then groaned as he held it.

"No…okay, maybe a little. My head is killing me. You?" She stood up and tested her left ankle by putting weight on it.

"Just a sprain. I think I can make it back up. There's an incline over there. We should be able to climb back to the top. What do you think?" she asked, as she tried to gauge the incline and its distance from the surface. Instead of answering, Scott began to cough violently. She spun back around as he grabbed at his throat, trying to feel for anything that might be constricting it. Jessi reached out for him, but he jerked back as he shook his head.

"Scott, what is it? What…" Her voice caught in her throat when the same type of dark, jet-black, viscous liquid that drew them to the area wrapped around Scott's neck. The thick fluid began to vibrate, warp, and slither its way over his jaw and lips. It seeped into his mouth, nose, and the edges of his eyes and ears, as his body jerked with a force that knocked him backward. Jessi screamed, as he fell down the rest of the hill, convulsing violently, he was immersed in a pool of mysterious liquid. He felt as if he were suffocating as the liquid consumed him, and his last vision was of her frightened face. With his last breath, he let out a gargled command.

"Run," he managed, as she tried to reach him. The desperation and strain in his words made her stop in her tracks and watch in horror, as the liquid seeped into his body. Out of the corner of her eye, she saw another pool of onyx liquid slithering her way. She screamed, as she stumbled up the slope. She clawed and scraped at the snow and ice, pulling herself along as she edged closer to the light. The hole they crashed into was jagged and sharp, but she managed to grasp onto it with her gloved hands. The cold, artic air filled her lungs and stung her throat, as she pulled herself out the opening of the cavern. She cried out for Scott and looked back down into the dark cavern to see if she could spot him. She stumbled to her feet, dazed and confused, about what exactly had just happened. Her eyes remained trained on the icy opening, but she took a step away from it as her thoughts finally caught up with the rest of her body. Suddenly, her back pressed into something as solid as rock and she let out a blood-curdling shriek when she turned to see Scott standing behind her. His eyes were as onyx as the liquid trickling from his mouth and nose. Before she could register what was happening, he forcefully pushed her back into the cavern and frowned when she reached out for him as she fell. The sound of her scream echoed off the walls of the cavern as she dropped. He tilted his head in fascination. She crashed to the icy floor and her lifeless body slid down the slope into the darkness. The man looked himself over, flexing his fingers, and stretching his neck before looking around at the artic terrain. He didn't speak a word as he turned to walk away from the cavern, leaving a trail of sable ooze in its wake.

CHAPTER 1

A Nightmare

Her heart was pounding. Her throat constricted and muscles burned from the pain of trying to push her body to fight back. Rage pulsed through her, and a hatred she had never felt before simmered inside her, urging her to move, but she couldn't. All she saw was pitch black. Joanie's eyes snapped open as she tried to catch her breath. She was disoriented as she sat up in bed. Chris's arms immediately wrapped around her, and his soothing voice calmed her.

"You okay?" he asked, concern evident in his eyes as he searched hers. She sighed in relief, and wrapped her arms around him as she regained her composure.

"Yeah, sorry. It was just a nightmare."

"A nightmare or a vision?" She gave a reassuring smile.

"Just a nightmare. I used to get them all the time. It's a very human thing too, not just because I'm the Seer. Besides, all of that is behind us now. I think I'm just wired. Maybe all that sugar before bed wasn't a good idea."

"Ice cream is always a good idea, especially with whipped cream. I really like whipped cream," he said, with a cheeky smile that made her giggle. She gave him a wink in return.

"We've definitely made it a favorite of mine," she agreed, and cuddled back into his arms. He rested his cheek on top of her head as he thought about what woke her up.

"What's it like?" he questioned. She began to stroke his hair as she gazed up at him.

"What do you mean?"

"Dreaming, nightmares. What are they like?"

"You still don't have dreams?"

"No. Is that weird? I mean, even for us? I don't think John or Randy do either, but I haven't asked them lately."

"Some humans don't dream either. Well, they do, they just don't remember them. Maybe it's like that for you."

"I read once that dreams can have meanings, especially nightmares. Are you sure everything is okay, and this isn't your abilities as Seer…"

"I'm fine, handsome. It was *one* bad dream. Nothing to write home about." He frowned in confusion.

"Why would I write home about…"

"It's just a saying. Didn't you read that book I gave you about phrases and sayings?"

"Yes, and it was the most confusing book I think I've ever read. There are too many idioms and colloquialisms to keep up with, and they constantly change. It's all very unrealistic."

"Says the immortal who read it in seconds." He shook with mirth, and kissed her forehead, before closing his eyes again. Joanie replayed the nightmare in her head as she rested in his arms. The nagging in the back of her mind warned her that it felt too real, that it was more than just a nightmare, but she refused to believe it. Absolution had been created and humanity had risen to the occasion quicker than any of them could have ever imagined. Their job was done, and the thought made her sigh in relief as her eyes drooped. She was safe in the arms of the man she loved. Her sisters, and all the people they loved, were safe as well. She could rest assured that any nightmares she had were due to the usual stressors of life and nothing more. At least that's what she told herself, as she pushed down the anxiety and embraced the peace that sleep brought.

○ ○ ○ ○ ○ ○

Meanwhile, downstairs in another part of the McNamara House, Victoria was not as lucky. Sleep had not come easy for her all night. Her mind raced and wandered, her nerves were on edge, and nothing could ease them. She found herself pacing around the kitchen as she waited for her tea on the stove. The house was frigid from the cold snap that had moved into the region overnight. It was early September, and the seasons were transitioning in Anderson. Victoria scrolled through her phone to keep her mind occupied. She had a few text messages from Alex, updating her with a daily recap about the department like he always did.

After returning to Anderson and coming up with an explanation for the explosion at the McCoy House and their abrupt departure after the wedding, Victoria decided to take a leave of absence. Alex became the interim sheriff but made a point to keep her informed about anything and everything. It didn't matter how often she reminded her deputy that she trusted him and didn't need the play-by-plays, he continued calling and texting as often as possible. They both knew it was more to stay in touch than focus on the cases in Anderson, or lack thereof. She scrolled through her usual social media apps and various news outlets next, looking for any signs or red flags about current events that should worry her, but nothing stood out. While the skeptic in her didn't want to admit it, it seemed they truly had created Absolution.

The War on Destruction had ended in days and people all over the world were rejoicing. The close call and near end of the world had brought leaders together to discuss issues that suddenly seemed frivolous. Protests turned into celebrations. Declarations of war gave way to treaties and proclamations. Crime rates slowly but surely began to drop and social issues became world issues. For the first time in her life, Victoria watched governments, nations, and factions all over the world see one another as human beings instead of institutions, ideologies, and entities. People were viewing one another as part of a species of humans, all trying not to simply coexist, but thrive together. If she asked John or his brothers, or even Alex, all would say a version of the same thing. The world was becoming a better place. It didn't stop her from being wary, though. She grabbed her mug of tea and headed for the porch. The crisp night air made her shiver, and she grabbed a blanket from the ottoman by the front door as well. By the time she sat down and settled into her rocking chair on the porch, her body started to relax again. The scents of the lake and forest swirled around her and brought her a peace that only home could. Her eyes slid shut and she brought the mug to her lips to take her first sip.

"Someone's off their game." She sputtered the hot liquid from her lips and had to put down the mug in order to not drop it as a giggle rang out around her. She glared at her younger sister, who was sitting comfortably on the rail on the other side of the porch. Stacie playfully glared back at her, which only made Victoria want to berate her even more as she loudly whispered.

"Damn it, Stace, you scared the hell out of me!"

"Well excuse me for living a little, but between being Sheriff McNamara and having super hearing now, I figured you knew I was out here."

"Does it look like I knew you were out here? Look at my mug. You almost made me drop it. I could've burned myself!" Stacie giggled at her theatrics.

"Burned yourself, huh? Yeah, no, not how that works anymore. It's the whole…" Stacie wiggled her fingers as red and white light glowed from her fingertips. Victoria rolled her eyes.

"Right, immortality, blah, blah, blah," she grumbled. Stacie frowned at the words and eyed her sister suspiciously as she approached her.

"Who 'blah, blah, blahs' at immortality? What's been up with you lately?"

"Nothing, I'm fine," assured Victoria. Stacie crossed her arms and arched an eyebrow at her sister, as she leaned against the railing.

"Come on, Vic, talk to me. Why are you up?" Victoria sighed, as she looked up at the moon and the clear night sky.

"Stace, our whole lives have been about overcoming adversity. When we were kids, it was the racists in town, or trying to find acceptance and a sense of belonging with dad's tribe. Then, mom and dad not being around, me trying to become sheriff and change this place. There's always been something, but suddenly these three guys come into our lives…"

"Wonderful guys," reminded Stacie.

"Absolutely wonderful guys. Trust me, I've never been happier with John, you know that. But they just show up one day and bring all these people into our lives. Joanie's the Seer, we're apparently Naturas, we touch a sorcerer's stone, and boom, peace on earth and goodwill for all mankind. It's a bit of a stretch." Stacie stared blankly at her for a moment.

"That settles it. You don't get to tell the story to our descendants. You'd blah, blah, blah and leave out all the cool parts. No memoirs for you."

"Stace, I'm serious."

"So am I. By the way, you glossed over a few parts there. Like the fact I almost *died* and we thought Joanie *was dying* while a freaking tornado tried to kill us, and I had to heal Ethan after Dominic went crazy, and this is the same Dominic who murdered Randy's parents and tried to have him kill Joanie…"

"Yeah, Joanie almost died a lot. She needs to be immortal. That was too much…"

"…not to mention Maya got kidnapped and the Praevians were willing to sacrifice themselves for us. Oh, and the war! There was a War on Destruction that apparently had everything in existence mere minutes from no longer being a thing, so…"

"Okay, okay, I glossed over some stuff. Death, tragedy, the end of the world, noted."

"Then what's really going on in that head of yours?"

"It all just seems too good to be true."

"Ah, got it. This is about you and John."

"Wait, what? No, that's not it."

"It was bound to happen. You've never really had a serious relationship, a few dates here and there, but nothing like this. I was wondering when the cold feet would set in."

"I don't have cold feet."

"Then why haven't you set a date? What happened to a summer wedding?"

"Um, I don't know. Learning how to be this immortal who can control plants and trees and all things rooted in the earth, for one. Besides, we aren't in a rush. We have forever, remember? Maybe you're the one with the problem. Why are you trying to force everything to happen so fast? We're just getting settled in. Hell, we spent most of the summer helping Ethan and Gabby rebuild their house…"

"I wouldn't call three weeks most of the summer."

"…okay, yes, the new strength and speed helped. It was nice to figure out how to use our powers in different ways, but…hold up, you're stalling." Stacie's eyes widened.

"Am not." Victoria smiled slyly at her.

"And you answered too quickly. There's something up with you."

"With you too," accused Stacie.

"Why are you out here in the middle of the night, Stace? Where's Randy?"

"At home, sleeping. He wanted to go for a walk with me, but…"

"You wanted time to process on your own, like I did."

"Yeah, I guess so," she conceded.

"What's up?"

"That's just it. I have no clue. I'm so happy, Vic. I've never been this happy. I mean, sure, helping Randy deal with the grief of what really happened to his parents and him not dealing with losing Dominic hasn't always been easy, but everything else just seems perfect."

"Maybe too perfect. I know for a fact it isn't."

"What do you mean?" Victoria pulled her phone out of her pocket to show her sister the photo Alex had sent her days before. Stacie smiled sadly at the smiling face staring back at her. It was a young woman who looked to be in her early twenties.

"It's still happening," Victoria informed.

"She's missing? Why hasn't this been all over the news?" Victoria sighed and put her phone away.

"When has it ever? Another Indigenous woman disappears from the face of the earth, and no one blinks, even now. Well, no one but her family and People. Governments all over the world are patting themselves on the back and we're all acting like we've solved world hunger."

"Technically, we did. That new organization that's pulling funds in from every nation to contribute is working wonders. Who thought such a complicated problem could be so, well, not complicated."

"And yet, Indigenous women are still going missing. Her name is Tiva Hensley. She's from just a few counties over. I don't care about that new agency that's cracking down on trafficking. Tell me a time in history when the sole purpose of a move in this country was to help Indigenous Peoples or our lands?"

"We both know you're preaching to the choir."

"Exactly, that's my point, Stace. You and I both know how this works."

"We were also there that night and know Absolution will take time. It's already working quicker than the Praevians thought it would. A lot has happened this year."

"Maybe, but I'm done waiting around while it does though." Stacie smiled knowingly.

"Don't tell me Sheriff McNamara is making a comeback."

"I don't know. What I do know, is we have all these abilities; some we're still figuring out. Why would we have them if we weren't meant to help people? It's not like we needed them to actually create Absolution. There has to be a reason we can do all this stuff. I can't just wait around and hope for the best."

"Well, if you need me, I'm there. I've never really been into the superhero stuff, but with cool supernatural abilities comes stuff you have to do." Victoria rolled her eyes and shook her head at her sister.

"That's not the line…that was never the line. That's not what he says in the movie."

"What movie? Oh, right…"

"We literally watched it together."

"I watch a lot of things. Superhero films? Not my thing, you already know this." Victoria pinched the bridge of her nose in frustration as Stacie waved her off and went inside to make herself a snack. While her sister annoyed her by botching one of her favorite lines from one of her favorite films, it was also clear she agreed with her. They may have created Absolution, but there was still more they could do.

o o o o o o

As streaks of bright sunlight and golden rays washed over the region that morning, Joanie's eyes fluttered open. She had managed to fall back asleep, with no more nightmares. Chris was still asleep beside her in bed and she smiled at her husband. She nuzzled his neck and giggled when he leaned into her touch.

"Morning, *tesoro*," he whispered into her ear.

"Morning, handsome. I didn't mean to wake you up. I just couldn't help myself."

"I'm not complaining." She slowly rolled out of bed and yawned as she headed for her closet. She felt his eyes trained on her and glanced at him over her shoulder.

"Don't even think about it," she warned. His cheeky grin told her everything she needed to know as he propped himself up on his elbows.

"I didn't say anything."

"You thought it."

"Not even the Seer can hear thoughts."

"But your wife can," she assured as she grabbed a sweater from their closet.

"I'll keep that in mind. So, what time will you be home today?" She giggled at the question and the annoyance that was clear in his tone.

"Chris, it's a job. I have to work the same hours Monday through Friday." His eyes widened.

"Wait, *all* those days? For how many weeks?"

"Well, most people here work at least five days and about forty hours a week until they reach retirement age."

"What age is that?"

"Sixty-five."

"Years?!" he exclaimed. She shook her head in amusement as she started to get dressed.

"Sometimes I forget just how sheltered and privileged you are."

"That's a long time. You have to admit that's a long time. Oh, and last I checked, you didn't exactly need to work. This is the only job you've had since we've met. Doesn't that make you privileged?"

"Very, but I'm also aware of it. Most people need to work to survive." He shook his head in disbelief.

"Money is so weird. I hope Absolution fixes that next."

"I doubt it. Some things are too deeply ingrained in society to change…at least not without one hell of a fight. Besides, don't worry. This arrangement is only until Gabby and Ethan get settled back in. It's been a lot of fun, but I've missed having a routine."

"And you enjoy looking at all the old stuff in there."

"That part is definitely nice too. You know, you could come by again, like you did last week. Maybe bring in some lunch," she suggested as she crawled back onto the bed with a seductive smile. Her jaw dropped when he quickly kissed her cheek and rolled out of bed.

"Can't. I'm going on a hike with John and Randy."

"What? Since when?"

"Since I found out Randy's been spending his days in the square watching people and listening in on their conversations. I know he's bored while Stacie is teaching all day, but we can't just have him invading the privacy of the humans. I mean sure, Cindy Lopez refusing to invite Gina Hughes to her gender reveal party because she forgot her birthday last year is interesting, but boundaries are boundaries." Joanie shook with mirth and tossed him one of his favorite shirts from their closet.

"So, you're essentially going to babysit Randy while Stacie is working?" He shrugged, as he put the shirt on.

"What's that saying? 'It's a hard job but someone's got to do it.' Might as well be his brothers." She kissed his cheek.

"Good, it will give you three some time to talk. Have you thought any more about us moving out?" He sighed and nodded.

"Yes, I suppose it's practical."

"Right."

"And it isn't like we can't afford it, even by human standards."

"Sure."

"I still don't quite understand this human obsession with money, and I do think Absolution could help humans understand that over time…"

"Don't get your hopes up on that one."

"…but I suppose it would be suitable to move out if it pleases you." Joanie eyed him carefully as he continued to get dressed.

"Suitable?" she questioned. He gave another sigh and nod.

"Yes, I suppose."

"But not exactly what you want?" He frowned in confusion.

"It's what you want, and I have no viable reason to say no, so it's suitable. Isn't it what you want?" She was silent and gave him a look before heading toward their bathroom. The moment the door slammed, he groaned.

"I said something wrong, didn't I?" he called toward the bathroom. As soon as she answered through the door, he hung his head in defeat.

"Yep!"

Downstairs, John and Randy glanced at each other as they overheard the conversation from where they were sitting in the kitchen. The two of them were packing snacks for their journey into the forest and Victoria gave John a look before he could speak.

"Don't get in the middle of that," she warned as she headed for the refrigerator.

"But why not, it involves all of us?" asked Randy.

"Because they are married and need to make that decision for themselves. What we want is secondary."

"Why?" Randy and John asked in unison. Victoria threw her hands up in exasperation.

"Didn't you two read all those books about marriage?"

"Yeah, but that doesn't mean they all made sense. You and I live here too, and Randy and Stacie come over all the time, so shouldn't we discuss this as a family?" asked John.

"Of course, big guy, but only after the two of them decide what they want. They are married and need their privacy. We all do."

"Stacie and I aren't married, so what does marriage have to do with it?" asked Randy.

"Speaking of that, you do realize you are the only one who has not proposed to the love of your life, right? You going to fix that anytime soon, or just keep living in sin?" John and Randy looked at each other and frowned even more. Victoria rolled her eyes.

"Right, wrong audience for that particular phrase, so how about this? What are your intentions with my sister?" Randy crossed his arms defensively.

"You know my intentions. I intend to spend our eternity together, but since we are on the topic of the archaic societal pressures of marriage that you abide by, I noticed you haven't set a date. Are you, in your own words, going to fix that anytime soon?" challenged Randy. John watched the two of them like a tennis match, as they stared each other down. While the tension between the two had ceased over the past months, they had fallen into a rapport that resembled a sibling rivalry. Victoria gave him one last glare before grabbing a bagel and quickly heading for the front door.

"Well played!" she called, which made Randy smile victoriously. John jogged after her and onto the porch as she put on her leather jacket.

"Where are you going? I thought you were still on leave?"

"I am, I just want to check on things. You know, make sure Alex hasn't burned the place down in my absence. Besides, I thought you were going to get out some energy in the forest today."

"I am, but…"

"Have fun, big guy. I'll see you when you get back." She got into her Mustang before he could question her again and he groaned in frustration as she sped away. He wasn't sure what was going on with his fiancée, but knew he needed to figure it out soon.

○ ○ ○ ○ ○ ○

Victoria was surprised by how much she enjoyed being back at the station. She was given a warm welcome with rousing cheers and greetings. While she realized quite quickly during her time away that she had been burying herself in work for years, she missed her officers and the sense of community she had worked so hard to build amongst the group. Sitting back at her desk and settling into the familiar environment made her day go by faster than it had lately. She helped Alex with paperwork and managed to field a few calls before finally addressing the pressing matter that had brought her back to work. She walked into her deputy's office and leaned against his desk to skim over it in search of any files that looked interesting. Alex noticed and gave her a playful glare as he sat back in his chair.

"Checking to make sure I'm keeping things in order around here, or are you itching for an update on that case I mentioned?"

"What do you think?"

"I think you're needed back at work, but if you still want to be on leave after whatever happened and you plan on staying out a bit longer, maybe it's time for an actual explanation."

"What are you talking about? I gave you an explanation already."

"No, you gave me my orders. I'm in charge. You're on leave indefinitely."

"Is that what happened?" she questioned teasingly.

"Vic, it's me. You can tell me anything," he reminded as he leaned forward.

"I know, and it's like I said. The boys had a family emergency and we needed to head out right away to check on a family member in…"

"New York, right, and why exactly weren't they at the wedding?"

"Old age. Travel can be hard on the body."

"That doesn't explain how you said goodbye to me."

"The good or the bye part?"

"Don't be a smart-ass."

"Aw, but that's like 99.9 percent of my personality! Without my witty remarks and sarcasm, I'm just a Taurus."

"Victoria," he warned with a chuckle. She playfully rolled her eyes at him.

"Look, it was a stressful day. Weddings always are and that got compounded with an emergency. With that and everything else going on…"

"Like the explosion at the McCoy House that you assure me had no connection to your abrupt departure?"

"Sure, yeah, that too; it just made for high emotions and anxious times. I didn't mean to scare you. Thanks for holding things down here ever since, by the way."

"Of course, it's my pleasure. I mean I haven't exactly been completely successful at quelling the rumors about what really went down, but for the most part, everyone in town accepts that Sheriff McNamara is taking a break."

"Rumors? What rumors?"

"Oh, I don't know, the conspiracy theories around the McCoy House explosion are pretty comical, but the rumors about Joanie and Chris are pretty nasty. You know the town gossips love a good mystery."

"What are they saying?"

"A range of things, but the main theory is that all of you left during the reception because Chris found out that Joanie was pregnant with Nathan's baby and was trying to rush along the nuptials to hide it." Victoria pinched the bridge of her nose and shook her head in disbelief.

"What's wrong with people?"

"Small town and bored people, Vic. The lack of a baby bump on Joanie when all of you returned has put a hole in that story, but people still talk about why that might be."

"Well, I'm glad Nate isn't around to have to deal with it. I'm not sure his marriage could take much more of that. Rumors are rumors, though, and I'm here now, so why don't you tell me about that case you were looking into?"

"You mean the Hensley case?"

"Is there another case I need to know about?"

"No, but there's not much on our end. The boys down in Billman County aren't exactly warm and fuzzy."

"They never have been, but we always seemed to play nice enough together."

"They gave me some load of crap about jurisdiction."

"So that's it? They're just going to stop looking? I told you this was going to happen, and you needed to go above their heads."

"And I told *you* we had to at least try to play it by the book with this one. You know I'm just as pissed as you are about it, but I'm walking a fine line as interim sheriff and trying to pick my battles here."

"Then tell them…"

"I've tried, but I'm not you, Vic. If you want them to listen, then talk to them yourself. You're still the sheriff of this town and maybe you need a reminder of that."

"And you're still the acting sheriff. This is your case, Alex."

"No, it's not, and that's the problem. You know these guys don't give a damn and never have. How many women have to go missing? They're acting like it doesn't matter and we both know why."

"They don't see it as their problem," she agreed.

"But it is *ours* and what's the point if we can't even help? Look, I get why you don't want to get involved right now. I'm sure you've got a lot going on, but…"

"I wouldn't be here if I didn't plan on getting involved." He perked up and straightened in his chair.

"Really? You're finally coming back?"

"You're still in charge. I'm simply assisting with a complicated case."

"Hell, I'll take it. Maybe you can light a fire under them. As of now, it's their case and they aren't giving me any updates."

"Not even on her last known location?"

"Nothing." Victoria slowly nodded and remained silent. Alex noticed her change in demeanor as she began to pace in front of him.

"What is it?" he questioned.

"Could be nothing but could be something."

"What kind of something, you thinking?"

"I dealt with something like this before, in a different county, years ago. Keeping a case under wraps like this? Not wanting help, no info, no updates, usually means someone is worried about what could leak to the press or the public."

"Because they don't want to arouse suspicion for the suspect?"

"Or incite panic. It might be time I poke around, go see for myself while you keep things in order here."

"And in what exact capacity do you plan on doing that in? Sheriff? Concerned citizen?"

"You let me worry about that."

"I'm just wondering when Sheriff McNamara plans on setting a return date."

"What is it with the men in my life wanting me to set dates?" she grumbled. He grinned slyly at her, but she interrupted him before he could respond.

"Don't answer that. Moving on," she said, before heading for the door and getting out of dodge.

"Good to have you back, sheriff," he called in a teasing tone. She gave a wave, and he smiled even more, knowing she had her sights on the case.

○ ○ ○ ○ ○ ○

By the time Victoria left the police station, school was ending for the day and children and teenagers of all ages filled the square. She spotted Joanie's car parked in front of Gabriella's antique store and parked beside it. She needed to speak with her sister, but a conversation in the distance caught her attention. It had taken her a while to hone her abilities and enhanced hearing, but she managed to learn how to switch it on and off, after several training sessions with John. She went in search of the voices and turned the corner into the alleyway by a row of shops to see three boys whispering to one another. She recognized the group and smiled as she approached.

"Hey, Ezra, Ollie, Jordan. What's up?" The boys blushed and two of them snickered as the other shushed them.

"Hi, Sheriff McNamara," they practically sang in unison.

"Ma'am," added Ollie. He received a punch in the shoulder in response from Jordan, and Ezra chuckled as the two bickered.

"What? She's a lady," Ollie whispered loudly.

"She's the sheriff, idiot," whispered Jordan.

"You're an idiot," argued Ollie. Victoria interrupted them, before the conversation could be derailed even more.

"What's with all the whispering today? Everything okay? Anyone have anything they want to talk about?" Ollie and Jordan looked at Ezra, who began to fidget as he stared down at his feet. Ollie nudged him.

"Tell her," he whispered, but Ezra shook his head.

"She won't believe me," Ezra whispered back. Victoria smiled warmly at the boys.

"Ollie, Jordan, why don't you two head to the comic-book store. Ezra will be there in a minute," she suggested. The two boys grabbed their bikes and nodded as they continued to whisper back and forth about the trouble Ezra was in. She waited for them to be out of earshot before turning her attention to him. Ezra leaned his bike against the brick wall and gulped as he rubbed his neck nervously.

"I didn't do anything wrong," he assured.

"I never said you did. You know, Ezra, people don't just talk to me when they do something wrong. A lot of times they talk to me when they see something that could be wrong. You're not in any trouble. I promise. I just want you to know that if you did see something, I'll believe you."

"Adults always say that."

"I'm not most adults."

"I don't know. I don't even really know what I saw."

"But you saw something, right?" He hesitated, but finally nodded reluctantly.

"Okay, fine, but you can't tell my mom."

"I'll only tell her if I think you're in danger."

"I'm out." She stopped him before he could grab his bike handle and take off.

"Whoa, calm down. Hey, look at me. What did you see, Ezra?" He groaned and got back off his bike.

"Fine, I was riding my bike the other day and thought I saw some lady inside a house."

"A lady in a house?"

"She looked real scared. I couldn't see her that good, but…but…"

"But what?"

"There was a man. He grabbed her. He saw me too."

"Do you remember what they looked like?" He shook his head.

"Where were you when you saw them? Where's the house?" He bit his lip nervously and she knelt down to look him in the eyes.

"You're not in trouble, Ezra, but this could be really important. Where were you?"

"Old Mill Road," he confessed. Her eyes widened.

"What were you doing all the way out there? You biked that?"

"It was a dare."

"By yourself?"

"Please don't tell my mom. You promised! Man, I knew I shouldn't have said…"

"Hey, hey, hey, focus. I promise not to tell your mom if you promise not to do it again, okay? Deal?" She held her hand out and he shook it.

"Deal."

"Alright, go inside, and no more long treks out of town. Go buy an anime or something." He rolled his eyes at her.

"I don't watch anime. I'm into manga."

"Is there a difference?"

"Anime are shows and movies. Manga are comics. I prefer graphic novels because they're way better," he stated, as if it were the most obvious fact in the world. She giggled and gave him a wink.

"Right, I totally knew that. Have fun with that." She turned to leave but noticed his hesitation and sensed his uneasiness once again.

"Unless there's something else I should know," she added. He began to fidget again, and her tone turned serious when she saw the fear in his eyes. She remembered what originally caught her attention, the words that stood out the most.

"Ezra, you saw something else out there, didn't you?" He nodded.

"Something that scared you, too?" He nodded again.

"I promise I'll believe you and I won't tell your mom. What did you see?" He had a faraway look in his eyes as he replayed the moment in his mind.

"When the man grabbed that lady, I got scared. I just wanted to go home, so I turned around, but when I did…I think…well, there was something across the street. Something in the forest."

"What did it look like? A big animal? A deer?"

"A demon."

"A demon?" she questioned. He nodded and let out a shiver at the memory. A sense of dread filled Victoria, as she searched the boy's eyes for any signs he was not telling the truth. She found none and swallowed hard.

"What exactly did this demon look like?" His shoulders slumped in defeat.

"You don't believe me."

"That's not true. I do believe you. I believe you saw something out there, something that scared you. So, what was it? What did the demon look like?" He rubbed his neck nervously as he spoke.

"He had white skin and black eyes. His face was really dirty."

"Good, what was he wearing?"

"A big jacket, like he was cold."

"Thank you, Ezra. You should go inside with your friends now. I'll be sure to check things out." She turned to leave, but he called to her.

"Sheriff McNamara, if you do see that…that demon…be careful."

"I will," she assured. He gave her a small smile before grabbing his bike and heading toward the comic-book store. She ran a hand through her hair as she tried to process what the boy had said. She believed him and the dread in her stomach urged her to follow her instincts. She rounded the corner and headed into the antique store where Joanie was sifting through an old book behind the counter.

"Hey, I only have an hour left and Chris said the guys won't be back in time for dinner. I figured you, me, and Stace could head to Ray's like old times," suggested Joanie, with a smile. Her smile faded when she recognized the look on her sister's face.

"Or we could have a girl's night in and talk. What's wrong? What happened?"

"I need to tell you something and you're probably going to think I'm crazy or just being paranoid or pessimistic, but I'm not. I…"

"You want to search for that missing girl." Victoria frowned in confusion.

"Wait, what? How did you…"

"I heard you and Stace talking on the porch."

"And the debate about if super hearing is a curse or blessing continues," grumbled Victoria, as she began to pace.

"I'm with you, Vic. I think it worked and we created Absolution, but it will take time. Doesn't mean we have to sit around when we know we can do something about it, though. If you want to go search for her, I'll go with you. We should have the guys help…"

"There's more."

"More?" asked Joanie. She closed her book and walked around the counter to her sister.

"Yep, and you're probably not going to like it."

"Why am I not going to like it?"

"Because it means I'm not a pessimist, I'm a realist, and maybe you were just a teensy bit wrong about creating Absolution."

"Okay, you're right. I don't like it. Vic, I get being upset about these missing women, but…"

"Ezra saw a demon in the forest on the outskirts of town," she blurted out. Joanie eyed her cautiously.

"Ezra as in Erica's ten-year-old, Ezra?"

"He's older now. Into manga, not anime. Apparently, there's a difference. Listen, I've been feeling off for a bit about this and I know you want to believe it's all over, but Joanie, what if it isn't? What if we have these powers and can do all these things, not so we could stop a human like Dominic, but something else…something that could have powers too?"

"Vic, I know with the wedding and being in limbo with work, you're under a lot of pressure…"

"Oh, don't patronize me. Seer or not, I'm still your big sister and *will* kick your ass."

"…under a lot of pressure and obviously stressed enough to threaten violence."

"Wait, why you were up so late…well, early, I guess?" Joanie gulped and tried to shrug nonchalantly.

"I wasn't."

"Wow, now we're just straight up *lying* to each other? Being the Seer has changed you." Joanie rolled her eyes.

"Okay, yes, fine, I was up because I had a teensy, not so big of a deal, nothing major, dream…that was more like a nightmare…but not really…just sort of with some moments of unease at times…and by at times, I mean most of it."

"That was a really weird way to say you had a nightmare."

"It wasn't a big deal."

"Uh huh."

"Really, it wasn't." Victoria crossed her arms and arched an eyebrow at her.

"Who are you trying to reassure right now, me or you?" Joanie ran a hand through her hair as she sighed.

"Okay, fair enough, um, remember when Caleb Delaney showed up?"

"Not exactly a fond memory, but certainly one seared into my brain, yes."

"I sensed that he was coming and had dreams about it. Well, visions, I guess."

"Right, and you think that's happening again? Why didn't you say something sooner?"

"Because I don't want it to be true, because life has actually been nice for us, again, and I can't see anything anyways. Since we created Absolution…"

"Or didn't…"

"We did, and since we did, my abilities as a Natura have grown in ways I never expected. Being the Seer should work the same way and I haven't seen anything substantial enough to create that type of panic for everyone."

"But you are seeing something, aren't you?"

"I couldn't make out anything really, but it's more of what I felt. It was pitch black and all I remember is feeling cold, and like I was suffocating. That's it." She let out a shiver as she remembered the nightmare. Victoria slowly nodded.

"Okay, so that sounds ominous as hell, not loving that at all for us."

"Not necessarily and it doesn't have to mean something."

"Joans, since when would that not mean something? What has been up with you lately anyways? I wasn't going to say anything, but you haven't exactly been embracing all things Natura lately and now you're ignoring visions? What's up with that? Stace and I finally embraced training and testing out what we can do, but you seem to want no part of it anymore. Why?"

"Because I need it to be over and it's been nice to not have to think about mortal peril for, oh, I don't know, a few months? Ever since I moved back to Anderson, life has been nothing but danger. Randy almost killed me…"

"Yeah, I need to give him his weekly punch in the arm for that…"

"Caleb almost killed Stacie. My wedding reception was ruined by Dominic, followed once again by mortal peril, and all I want to do is be in honeymoon bliss with my amazing husband and find a place of our own, which apparently isn't what he wants, but can't seem to come up with a viable reason to say no to!" Victoria winced.

"Yeah, I overheard that this morning. We should probably circle back around to that later."

"There's nothing to circle back to. My husband doesn't want to live alone with me. I'm perfectly fine with that."

"Probably less about you and more about the three of them, but not really the time with the world probably being in danger again and all that. We need to get Stacie and head out to Old Mill Road."

"Ew, why? That place gives me the creeps. Remember when everyone would throw Halloween parties and bonfires out there in high school?"

"Because they thought it was haunted," reminded Victoria. Joanie groaned.

"You're really going to make me go out there, aren't you?" Victoria patted her shoulder and nodded.

"Yep, uh huh, it'll be fun." Victoria watched in slight amusement as her sister stomped back around the counter to log out for the evening.

"Stupid prophecy…only making half sense…she better not be right, or Kaya and I are going to have a very serious talk…can never have nice things…" Joanie slammed the register closed and walked back around the counter.

"Say something?" asked Victoria, as she tried not to smile. Joanie glared at her with a syrupy sweet smile.

"Nope, just that I'm so happy to be spending the evening with you…out in the middle of nowhere…in a place we were told was haunted as kids…so fun."

"But at least we're immortal, right? If we created Absolution like you said, then I'm sure ghosts won't be an issue."

"Shut up," grumbled Joanie, as she followed Victoria out of the antique store.

○ ○ ○ ○ ○ ○

Joanie, Stacie, and Victoria had been told ominous stories about Old Mill Road since they were children. As adults, they assumed the stories were a way for parents in the town to keep their children from venturing too far outside the town. Ironically, the stories became urban legends and myths that were some of the most interesting aspects about life in Anderson, especially for tweens and teens. In their youth, Old Mill Road became a staple for Halloween, and the dilapidated slab of dead-end road in the middle of the forest was a hotspot for anyone from Anderson who embraced the paranormal, or teens looking to escape for a few hours. Joanie groaned as she got out of Victoria's Mustang and her sisters giggled at her. The youngest McNamara had never been a fan of the road or the stories that accompanied it.

"Good to see some things never change, Joans," teased Stacie. Joanie let out a shiver, as she looked at the old house.

"Why are we even out here? It's getting dark and I'm cold…" Stacie interrupted her.

"Naturas don't actually get cold beyond a certain point so…"

"You know what I mean," she whispered harshly. Victoria shook with mirth.

"This is where Ezra said he saw her," said Victoria.

"And the demon, right? Great," grumbled Joanie.

"Looks like no one's home. I still need to check it out. You two can stay here." Stacie scoffed.

"Um, excuse me, sheriff, but I didn't get dragged all the way out here just to stay in the car. We aren't teenagers anymore and Joanie doesn't need a babysitter just because she's scared," said Stacie. Joanie's jaw dropped.

"Hey! It was dark and raining. None of us had any business being out here that night," defended Joanie.

"And yet look at you now, an immortal. It's not even raining and you're still scared," taunted Stacie.

"First off, I'm not scared, I'm concerned. There's a difference. Second, we've been immortal for like a few months and I've almost been killed more times than I'd like to think about, so excuse me if my fight or flight still kicks in exponentially in places like this." Victoria nodded in agreement as she surveyed the house and surrounding area.

"She's right about that. This place is definitely creepy," agreed Victoria.

"Which is even more reason for me to go in as your backup," said Stacie. Victoria smirked.

"My backup?"

"What? I can be your backup. I'm a Natura and before you tease me about such things, we both know you wanted the two of us to come with you for a reason, so I'll go with you, and Joanie, you can stay out here by yourself…in the dark…and the cold. You'll be fine. I'm sure that Seer ability of yours will come to save the day if you get attacked by a ghost, or whatever is in the haunted forest. No worries, just stay in the car, be our lookout, and shout if you see anything. Actually, don't shout. We have super hearing now," said Stacie. Victoria tried to stifle her laughter, as Joanie glared at her sister.

"I hate you sometimes," grumbled Joanie, as she closed the car door and followed them up the driveway of the rustic house. Stacie giggled and looped her arm with Joanie's.

"I love you too. Don't worry, we'll protect you," teased Stacie. Victoria gave a nod, as she pulled her gun from her holster.

"Always do," added Victoria. She rolled her eyes when both of her sisters began to protest.

"Hey, whoa, what's that for?" asked Stacie.

"Is that really necessary, Vic?" asked Joanie.

"Um, yeah, this is still an open investigation and I'm not taking any chances."

"You have super strength, can harness energy in your hands, and manipulate the entire forest that surrounds us," reminded Stacie.

"Doesn't change that this is a very human problem and if we do run into an issue or someone rolls up on the house while we're here, I'd prefer not to reveal that the sheriff of this town also is an immortal with powers."

"Fine, but at least put it away until you need it," said Stacie.

"It's an open investigation and we are out in the middle of nowhere. I need it," assured Victoria.

"Okay, you're at a twenty out of ten with the gun culture vibes. Can you take it down a notch or two? No one is here. I've already listened out and so have you. Breathe, sheriff," said Joanie. Victoria rolled her eyes, as Stacie nodded in agreement.

"You do know other countries have found ways to investigate crimes and enforce laws without always needing a Glock, right? There's a whole global summit being held next month on it. I read it about online," added Stacie.

"You two are such babies and I already regret bringing you," said Victoria.

"Didn't even ask to come so…" said Joanie, as she looked around the surrounding forest again and a shiver went down her spine.

"She really didn't and spent the entire ride making sure we knew that…loudly," added Stacie.

"You know what Stace…" Before Joanie could sarcastically reply to her sister, Victoria interrupted their bickering.

"Okay fine, fine, you win. The gun is being put away. For now," conceded Victoria. She rolled her eyes as both of her sisters gave her condescending cheers.

"Yay, world peace does exist," said Stacie.

"Another sign of Absolution," said Joanie. The two of them giggled when Victoria put the gun back in its holster and showed them her middle finger.

"Alright, focus you two, we're just here to check out the house, and see if there are any clues. Seems whoever may have been here is long gone, but they might have left something behind that could help in the case. Stay on high alert and remember a woman's life is at stake. Time is running out," instructed Victoria. Joanie and Stacie nodded in agreement, as they followed Victoria into the house. The uninhabited dwelling was dark, stuffy, and held a stench in the air. The nineteenth-century home was battered and poorly maintained. The floors creaked as the sisters crept through the house.

"Okay, yeah, this place definitely is creepy, immortal or not," whispered Victoria, as they looked around.

"Thank you! That's all I'm saying," whispered Joanie. Victoria poked her head into the first door they came across, as they made their way through the house. The room was a fully furnished bedroom. The dresser drawers were haphazardly open, clothes were strewn all over the bed and floor, and a floor safe was open, but empty.

"Looks like someone was here, but left in a hurry," said Joanie, as she poked her head into the room as well. Victoria knelt down by the safe and searched under the bed. She found a small plastic bag with traces of powder at the bottom.

"Ezra was definitely onto something. I'll have Alex put in a request for a lab test but looks like there were drugs here. The type might lead to something. Let's keep looking," said Victoria, as she placed the small baggie in her jacket pocket. They nodded in agreement and followed her to the back of the house where a tiny kitchen was situated. Victoria sifted through the cabinets and drawers while Stacie perused the refrigerator. Joanie reached for the knob of the door in the corner of the small room but shivered as a sense of dread simmered in the pit of her stomach. The hairs on the back of her neck prickled and she glanced out the window beside her. It felt like someone was watching her and she pulled the sheer curtain back to scan the trees on the side of the house. Nothing stood out, but the feeling in the pit of her stomach remained. Before she could point it out to her sisters, Stacie spoke up.

"Someone's been here recently. The milk isn't even bad yet," said Stacie, as she closed the refrigerator door.

"Ezra might've scared them off. I doubt they wanted anyone to know they were here. Joanie, find anything over there?" asked

Victoria. Joanie cleared her throat and shook off the feeling she'd been experiencing since they arrived.

"Uh, yeah, I think this leads to a basement. May be worth checking out," suggested Joanie. Stacie rolled her eyes, as Victoria pulled out her gun.

"Vic, there's no one down there. We would hear…"

"Actually, I'm with her on this one, Stace. Just in case," said Joanie. Stacie eyed her sister carefully and nodded.

"Lead the way, sheriff," agreed Stacie. Victoria opened the door and noticed the stairs leading down to the basement.

"Good call, Joans," said Victoria, as she headed down the stairs. Joanie groaned.

"Yay, a basement. This is like that haunted house all over again," grumbled Joanie, as they followed their big sister down the stairs.

"You mean the one with the rule that no one can touch you…and yet you thought someone touched you?" teased Stacie.

"Someone did touch me."

"It was your ponytail," added Stacie, but Victoria shushed them.

"Looks like it's time to call Alex," said Victoria. Before either of them could ask why, they stopped dead in their tracks on the stairs. Bolted to the adjacent wall were chains and handcuffs. Victoria walked over and knelt by an empty plate and plastic bottle of water. She pulled out her phone to take a few pictures and make the call, but before she could, Joanie's senses were heightened once again.

"Does anyone else feel like we're being watched?" asked Joanie. Victoria stood back up as Stacie scanned the room.

"Uh, Vic?" whispered Stacie. Victoria and Joanie followed her gaze to a small camera protruding from the corner of the ceiling. Suddenly, they heard a click and the sound of beeping from a cabinet on the other side of the room. Victoria rushed over to it and her eyes widened when she saw the device inside.

"Go, go, go!" shouted Victoria. Stacie and Joanie ran back up the stairs, but Victoria rushed over to grab the plastic bottle of water before she followed them. The sound of one last beep filled her ears before the device detonated. The explosion erupted through the house and the three had to use their enhanced speed to make it out before the flames engulfed them. The blast from a second detonation in the already-dilapidated structure knocked them backward and they crashed into the ground as debris and splinters of the home rained over them.

"Everyone okay?" asked Victoria, as she sat up and dusted off her jacket.

"Yeah, I think so. Joans, you good?" asked Stacie. Joanie slowly sat up and let out a shiver as a chill went down her spine. It was stronger than before, and she frantically scanned the area, as debris and plumes of smoke cascaded around them. The moment she spotted the figure, she knew. It stood in the forest motionlessly as it watched her.

"Joanie?" Stacie asked again, but Joanie didn't answer. Instead, she stumbled to her feet and took a step toward the forest. The figure immediately darted away, seeming to disappear before her eyes, and she blinked several times before running after it. She was unable to get far though as she sped across the road. Her focus was solely on the eerie figure in the forest and did not immediately sense the car barreling her way. It swerved and skidded to a halt as she jumped out of the way. She let out a grunt as she rolled into a ditch. Her sisters were immediately by her side and helped her up.

"Joans, what the hell? You okay?" asked Victoria. Joanie's eyes remained trained on the forest in search of the figure. Before either of her sisters could ask what was wrong, two familiar voices echoed from behind them. Ethan and Gabriella got out of their car to jog over to them.

"Joanie, are you okay?" asked Ethan. Joanie didn't respond as she tried to regain her composure.

"What are you two doing here?" asked Stacie.

"The boys called us and said they sensed you were in danger. You didn't answer your phone, so we had Carlos track the Mustang. What's going on? Joanie, are you okay? We almost hit you," said Ethan. Victoria shook Joanie's shoulder when she didn't respond yet again.

"Joanie!" she shouted. Joanie snapped out of her daze and gulped as she noticed the four sets of eyes staring at her.

"Sorry; yeah, I'm good."

"The hell you are, you could've been killed! Well, you know what I mean," said Victoria. Ethan and Gabriella looked over the three of them in their disheveled clothes and soot-covered faces.

"Were you three in there? What's going on?" asked Gabriella. Stacie and Victoria glanced at each other before looking back at their sister. Joanie remained silent, as she tried to understand what she saw in the forest.

"I have no clue anymore," admitted Victoria. Ethan looked around at the destruction of the house and fire burning in the field.

He wasn't sure what was happening, but he had a feeling Chris, John, and Randy were right to be concerned.

○ ○ ○ ○ ○ ○

Gabriella paced back and forth at the McNamara House, as she listened to Joanie, Stacie, and Victoria explain why they were in the house that exploded on Old Mill Road. Ethan was on the phone in the other room, and she could hear a car speeding into the driveway. Randy, John, and Chris darted into the house before she could blink. She smiled at the way they immediately went over to embrace the women they loved. Chris looked Joanie over.

"Are you okay, *tesoro*?"

"I'm fine. Everything just happened so fast," admitted Joanie.

"And what exactly is everything? What were you three even doing out there in the first place? You shouldn't have been out there alone," scolded Randy. Victoria rolled her eyes at him.

"Cool it with the dramatics. We were just checking out a lead I got about something going on in town," said Victoria. Randy scoffed.

"So, this was your idea then? You almost got your sisters blown up, and *I'm* being dramatic?" challenged Randy.

"We can't blow up! Naturas, remember, or does that only apply when you keep reminding us of what we are?" defended Victoria.

"I'm with Randy on this one, Vic. Why didn't you tell me before you went? I would've gone with you," said John.

"I don't need your permission to do my job."

"Oh, don't give me that. You went out of your way to not tell us and had no problem getting Joanie and Stacie involved, but not me. Why?" asked John.

"Yeah, why?" asked Chris, as he crossed his arms.

"Because, unlike the three of you, I knew they would understand. I get it, okay? We created Absolution. That's supposed to mean peace on earth and all that crap, but that's not exactly working out fast enough for all of us. There are still people who are dying and being preyed upon and who tend to be forgotten and left behind. Even when the world is patting itself on the back for all the good it's doing. I made a judgment call and I'm not apologizing for that."

"A judgment call? About what? Not telling us? Someone being in danger? What the hell is going on?" yelled John. The ground beneath them shook and the pictures on the mantel rattled as the earth briefly quaked. He took in a deep breath to calm his nerves and scrubbed his face with his hands before kneeling in front of Victoria.

"I'm sorry. I know I have to keep my emotions in check, but that scared the hell out of me. I just…Vic, we thought you were going to die," he admitted, as tears filled his eyes. She frowned in confusion but cupped his face to comfort him, nonetheless.

"What are you talking about? We were checking out a lead about a missing persons case. Why would you think we were going to die?" asked Victoria. Chris let out a shaky breath as he scooted closer to Joanie.

"We were all training and actually having a lot of fun. We took John's car up to Turtle Mountain. Something told me we shouldn't be that far away, but I didn't have a good reason for why not. Everything was fine, but then we all got this sense of dread," explained Chris.

"It was similar to the feeling we had the night Caleb Delaney showed up in town," added Randy.

"But again, why? This case has nothing to do with us being Naturas. Even with the explosion, we weren't in any actual danger. I don't even have a bruise on me," said Victoria. Chris noticed the way Joanie looked away.

"Joanie, what happened?" he questioned.

"Actually, I'm wondering the same thing. What happened after the explosion, Joans?" asked Stacie. Joanie sighed and ran a hand through her hair in frustration.

"I don't know." Chris shook his head.

"No, you've done this before, and we agreed it would stop. You can't hide things from us, from me," reminded Chris.

"I'm not hiding something from you, Chris."

"Now you're lying to me too?"

"I don't know what I saw!" They all looked out the window, as the howling of the wind picked up. She groaned and shook her head in disbelief as she stood up to pace.

"Nothing makes sense. None of this makes sense!" she added. Chris stood up and laced their fingers together.

"Then talk to us and let us figure it out together," he suggested. Tears filled her eyes as she shook her head.

"You don't know what it's like," she whispered.

"What what's like?"

"To always have to be the messenger and have no clue what the actual message is. I don't know what's happening."

"But you know *something*, so let us help you. Joanie, you don't have to do any of this alone," he reminded.

"But I do. I'm the Seer. I'm the one who gets the visions, and has to decipher the coded messages and be the bearer of bad news, even when all I want to do is embrace all the good around us." Victoria walked over to her sister.

"Hey, he's right. You're not in this alone. You never have been, and you never will be. Joans, we've faced so much together. Never doubt that we can face this too, whatever it is," assured Victoria. Joanie took in a shaky breath and sat back down.

"I'm not sure what it is, but I did have a nightmare last night. I couldn't see anything, though. It was just pitch black. It was nothing but darkness."

"Okay, but what happened back at that house? It's like you saw something," said Stacie.

"Yeah, that's because I did, or at least I think I did. As soon as we got there, I felt like I was being watched but I didn't see anyone until after the explosion. Someone was in the forest. It was a man, but his eyes were pitch black. He was extremely pale and had on a parka. He was human…but not. It's hard to explain. He almost looked like…"

"A demon?" asked Victoria. Joanie gulped but nodded.

"Yeah, like a demon."

"That's how Ezra described it," added Victoria.

"Ezra? One of the kids from town? He saw it too?" asked Gabriella.

"He isn't sure what he saw but said it was out by Old Mill Road. He also saw someone I think may be the young Indigenous woman who went missing, Tiva Hensley. It was a long shot, but it was all I had to go on. It was at least a place to start searching. Alex told me about the case," said Victoria.

"And why isn't Alex doing his job then?" asked John.

"Because it doesn't fall in our jurisdiction. I wasn't technically there in my capacity as sheriff, but now that we have this evidence, we can start looking into the case as a department. I found a small baggie that might have traces of drugs and managed to grab an open water bottle. I can get it tested for prints and DNA. I need to get this to Alex." Stacie immediately shook her head.

"Vic, did you just hear what Joanie said? Whatever is out there might not be human. Do you really think Alex should handle this one?" asked Stacie.

"And back to more pressing matters, what exactly do you mean by a demon, Joanie? What are we dealing with here?" asked Gabriella. All eyes were back on Joanie as she sighed and wrapped her arms around herself.

"I don't know, but I felt this fear, and something else, when I saw it. It's the same feeling I had in my nightmare, but I don't understand. It's impossible. We created Absolution. None of this should be…"

"What's not possible, Joanie?" asked Chris, as he wrapped a protective arm around her.

"I don't know how and I sure as hell don't know why at this point, but when I saw that thing, only one thought raced through my mind and every instinct I have believes it's true. I think I saw the Ultimate Evil." Randy quickly shook his head.

"That's impossible. Dominic was the Ultimate Evil. He's gone. We created Absolution. All that's over now," assured Randy.

"I'm not sure it is," said Joanie.

"No. No! We didn't go through all of this just for…it's not true…Dominic betrayed us. He was the Ultimate Evil and now that evil is gone," argued Randy. Victoria sighed.

"Not to mention none of this changes that someone is missing and someone else just tried to blow us up. If the Ultimate Evil is out there, we'll deal with it, but this girl's life is on the line *now* and whatever is happening to her is very real. I'm going back out there. All of you can stay here arguing over the prophecy or whatever, but I have a job to do," said Victoria. Randy shook his head in disbelief.

"You never did get that part, Vic," said Randy.

"What?"

"Look, we get it, okay? You think the three of us are naïve because we didn't get to grow up in the world like you did, so we must not care about it the same way," said Randy.

"That's not…"

"That's exactly what you think of us," said John. She was surprised by her fiancé's words, but even more so by the hurt in his eyes. She shook her head as she pulled him into her arms.

"Hey, that's not true. I know you care. That doesn't mean you understand how the world works, or what it can be like," defended Victoria. Randy continued as he paced back and forth.

"Right. Because we didn't get to have parents to raise us and teach us about the world, right? That doesn't mean we don't grieve the ones we lost or understand evil," added Randy. Chris nodded in agreement.

"It also doesn't mean you three get to hide things from us," added Chris. Joanie sighed, but nodded.

"You're right. I'm sorry," said Joanie, before resting her forehead against his. Randy walked over to Victoria.

"I know you understand the world in ways that we don't, but that doesn't mean we don't understand it at all," added Randy. Ethan walked into the room and shoved his phone into his pocket.

"Or that you understand the world from the perspective of an immortal, Vic, especially when it comes to discretion. I just got off the phone with Zayneb. She had Carlos intercept the feed that was coming from that house. With the fire department on the scene now, we're lucky we got you out of there in time to not have to answer any questions. Most humans can't handle knowing about you. Carlos was able to find the remote devices that were used to cause the explosions and tracked down the owner. The house belongs to a man born a town over and Carlos is doing some digging as we speak. The feed is linked to another device connected to a location twenty miles up the road. If the person responsible for detonating the device is also connected to your missing woman's case, Carlos will find them," informed Ethan. Tears filled Victoria's eyes.

"Wait, you're going to help, even after everything Joanie just said about the Ultimate Evil maybe being on the loose?" asked Victoria.

"If that's true, then I have all the faith in the world you'll be able to handle that threat in time. However, time is of the essence with cases like this. The Praevians have the resources and we plan to use them to the best of our ability," informed Ethan. Gabriella smiled warmly at her.

"You don't always have to go it alone, sheriff. Besides, this is our town too. If there is someone sinister on the loose, we want to know about it. Plus, our job is to protect you, and if someone saw you on that video feed, we need to know about it. Let's go track down this guy," said Gabriella.

"Zayneb and the others are already on the way. The jet should land soon," added Ethan. Stacie frowned in confusion.

"The jet? Since when do you have a jet and why weren't we using it when Dominic was chasing us all over the place?" asked Stacie.

"It's a new perk, ever since the Brotherhood dispersed and Phillip filled our bank accounts. We figured having a jet in case of an emergency couldn't hurt," explained Ethan. Randy clapped him on the back.

"Great, let's find the missing woman and those responsible. Then, we can get back to our lives, and let Absolution play out," said Randy, before exiting the house. Joanie sighed and shook her head in disbelief.

"This is why I didn't want to say anything. I knew he wouldn't believe me." Stacie smiled sympathetically at her.

"I believe you and deep down so does he. I'll go talk to him," assured Stacie. Chris nodded in agreement.

"You know it always takes Randy time to accept things like this," said Chris.

"Why are you taking it so well? I figured you would be in more denial about the possibility of the Ultimate Evil still being out there," said Joanie.

"Honestly, after everything with Dominic, all I really know is that we don't know much about the prophecy or how it plays out. We were wrong once. We could be wrong again. It doesn't mean I want it to be true. In fact, I quite like the idea of Absolution being complete and just focusing on spending my life with you, but the world is a complicated place. All I know is, if the Ultimate Evil *is* out there, we were born to stop it. Stopping evil is what we do, so let's help Victoria solve this case and find this missing human." He was surprised when Joanie kissed him tenderly.

"You never cease to amaze me," she whispered. He smiled adoringly at her.

"The same goes for you, *tesoro*." Victoria rolled her eyes at the couple.

"Okay, you two; time is of the essence, remember? Stop drooling over each other. We have to go," announced Victoria. John chuckled at his fiancée, as he followed her out of the house, along with the rest of the group.

○ ○ ○ ○ ○ ○

Victoria frowned in confusion when Ethan and Gabriella's car stopped in front of a cul-de-sac in a small suburb north of Minot. She parked her Mustang behind their car and got out, along with John, Joanie, and Chris. Randy parked his SUV behind theirs, as well, and approached the group with Stacie.

"What is this place?" asked Randy.

"I have to admit, I didn't expect this case to bring us to the suburbs," said Victoria.

"You'd be surprised how often it does," called a voice behind them. They all turned and smiled when they saw Zayneb and Maya approaching from the van they had parked down the street. They each embraced the women who had helped them take down Dominic months before.

"You know, a human trafficking case wasn't exactly on my radar for the next time we met," said Zayneb.

"You know how to keep us on our toes, and trust me, that's saying something for us," added Maya.

"Thank you for coming on such short notice," said Victoria.

"We're always happy to help. Cases like this make my stomach turn, though. They rarely end with just one victim," said Maya. Ethan smiled sympathetically at her.

"Maya was a behavioral analyst for some agencies overseas before she joined us. She truly has seen the worst of the worst kind of humans. I'm guessing Carlos found something else," said Ethan. Maya nodded.

"It's an online ring. Less conspicuous than flying them overseas through New York. Same type of players, just a different method. Carlos already hacked the site and is sending information to Interpol and other agencies. There are some wealthy clients on the list. This woman is certainly not the first to be targeted," explained Maya.

"We think he goes in search of certain types, based on his client list, and was keeping them in that house until moving them was viable. His family is out of town, so he's home alone, which bodes well for us. I can intercept him, and Maya will interrogate him about Tiva," informed Zayneb. John frowned.

"We should be the ones intercepting him and did you say his family?" questioned John.

"It happens more than you think. Predators of this nature hide in plain sight. No one notices them because they're middle class, live perfectly normal lives, and keep up the perfect image. Carlos pulled every record available on the unsub. Two kids, a wife who's involved in the community. He flies right under the radar. I've seen it before," said Maya.

"I read about cases like this before, when we lived in New York. Not all monsters are supernatural," said Randy.

"*Most* are not, unfortunately," agreed Maya.

"My brothers and I will..." The objections started before Randy could finish his sentence.

"You aren't the Elements anymore, Randy. We're the Naturas. The six of us will handle this, not just the three of you," reminded Stacie. Gabriella interjected.

"Actually, it might be best to let Zayneb and Maya take the lead on this one. They both have the proper training to deal with suspects of this nature," advised Gabriella.

"While that may be true, it doesn't justify allowing them to put themselves at risk when we can apprehend the human," said Chris. Maya giggled at the sly smile that crept onto Zayneb's lips.

"Oh, I think we can handle ourselves. We appreciate your concern, but how about this? You give us ten minutes. If we don't get the information we need, you can take over. Also, don't worry, Vic. If we find out where Tiva is, we will let you take the reins in retrieving her," said Zayneb. Ethan chuckled at the perplexed looks on Chris, Randy, and John's faces.

"There's no need for you six to risk further exposure," reminded Ethan. Joanie giggled at the pout Chris gave and patted his chest.

"Don't worry, Ethan. We'll soothe their hurt egos while Maya and Zayneb take the lead on this one," said Joanie.

"But…" Before Randy could protest further, Maya and Zayneb headed for the house. Carlos chuckled, as he strolled over to them with his laptop in hand and Reo by his side.

"I see they got their way. I would love to say I'm surprised, but I'm not. Alright, I've already tapped in and shut down the feeds. Now, all I need to do is…boom," said Carlos, as he tapped a button on his laptop. Suddenly, all the electricity was disconnected from the house. Reo pressed the small device in his ear and trained his eyes on the house.

"Zayneb, Maya, you're good to go. Let us know if you need us to move in," said Reo into the earpiece.

"So, what now? We just stand here and wait?" asked John. Victoria tried to hide her laughter at his obvious displeasure at such a notion.

"Yes, but the six of you could help with something. How many people do you hear in there?" asked Reo. The six of them tapped into their enhanced hearing to sift through the noises inside the house.

"One heartbeat, downstairs, sounds close to the kitchen," said Randy. Carlos gave a nod.

"That's confirmed on the feed as well. Alright, Zayneb, do your worst…well, not your worst," said Carlos. Chris glanced over at Gabriella and Ethan, who were casually leaning against the hood of their car.

"And you two are okay with this? They could be in danger and…"

"Chris, listen," whispered Joanie. The six of them tapped into their abilities once again to listen to the commotion inside the house.

The sound of a man's grunt of pain, followed by a yell, made their eyes widen. They spent the next several minutes listening to Maya rattle questions off at the man as Carlos typed furiously on his laptop to use the information against the suspect.

"I think I've triangulated a location for Tiva, based on what Maya got out of him. You six should head to Rainey Bluff. I'll continue exposing his network of traffickers and law enforcement will be on their way soon to arrest him. Sending the list to some other agencies as well," informed Carlos. The six were back in their cars and headed to the bluff in no time.

"Why can't we just run again?" asked Victoria. Her patience was wearing thin as she raced down the street.

"If we need to call an ambulance, how would we explain being out there with no car, especially at this time of night?" asked John.

"I don't know, and frankly, I don't care. The chances of finding her alive are already slim. The more time we waste, the slimmer that chance gets," said Victoria.

"We're going to find her," assured John.

"I wish I had your optimism, but I've seen this all before. I know exactly why he would head out to that bluff. He was dumping her body, John."

"But he said she was still alive when…"

"He thinks he can outsmart them. The explosion destroyed all the evidence from the house where he kept her. He isn't going to just confess to her murder, but that doesn't mean she's alive. Unfortunately, that's the reality of these situations."

"Then, why are we going?"

"Because everyone deserves to be found, and no one deserves for people who are meant to protect them to just give up on them." John nodded his understanding but glanced at his brother in the backseat. Chris gave him a comforting pat on the shoulder. He sensed how disturbed his brother was by the situation. Dominic had always done his best to shield them from the evils of the world, even when they knew they existed. Realizing the types of evil humans unleashed on each other was something neither of them could fully comprehend. By the time they reached Rainey Bluff, the six of them were on high alert. Victoria looked out at the bluff and the expansive landscape and water around it. She pulled her phone out of her pocket and showed the picture of Tiva that Alex had sent her days earlier.

"Spread out. Let's do everything we can to find her," instructed Victoria. Randy gave a nod and glanced over the edge of the rounded cliff at the deep waters below.

"I hate to be the cynic, but do you really think this human survived?" questioned Randy.

"Doesn't matter. We'll bring her home either way. Right, Vic?" asked John. Victoria smiled appreciatively at him and gave his hand a comforting squeeze.

"Exactly. Everyone, fan out. I'll circle around to head north and check the rest stop up there," informed Victoria. Joanie and Stacie headed in the other direction, while John, Randy, and Chris peeked over the edge of the cliff again.

"Okay, this is the plan…" John interrupted Randy.

"Wait, who put you in charge? Vic already said to fan out," said John.

"And the three of them have already covered those sides, so I think we should check below. Like I was saying, here's the plan. Divide and conquer…"

"Isn't that the same thing as fanning out and…"

"John!" exclaimed Randy. John rolled his eyes and shrugged.

"Fine, what's the plan?" asked John.

"John, you're going to scale the cliff and see if you can spot anyone. Chris, you should jump into the water."

"Why me? It's your plan and not exactly warm out here. You jump." Randy smiled smugly.

"Because, dear brother, you're better in the water, of course."

"Just because I can't freeze, doesn't mean I want to test that theory out in this weather. A snowstorm is going to roll in tomorrow and it's already cold tonight. Besides, you'll have an easier time heating yourself up. You should go."

"Stop being…" John whistled loudly to stop their bickering.

"A life is on the line here, so can you two please focus?" Randy clapped him and Chris on their backs.

"You're right, sure thing. I need to focus…as soon as Chris checks the water." Before Chris could react, Randy pushed him off the cliff. John's jaw dropped as Chris plummeted into the water and Randy peeked over the edge.

"Oh, he's going to kill you," said John, as he peeked over the edge as well. Randy shrugged.

"He's tried before, and I deserved it much more back then. Don't see it happening now." Randy smiled and waved when Chris broke the surface and shook the water from his hair. John shook with mirth.

"I'm going to kill you, Randy!" yelled Chris.

"Now, dear brother, focus. We're on a mission. Can you sense the human?" called Randy. Chris glared at him before focusing his attention on the water. He closed his eyes and slipped back underneath to immerse himself. He sensed nothing out of the norm and re-emerged.

"She's not down here," called Chris.

"I'll head down the east side of the cliff," said John. He climbed over the edge and began to scale down as Randy looked around the expansive, lush land. He wasn't sure where to start and began to wander around the area. The frigid air and terrain reminded him of a familiar place, but he was still surprised when a memory rushed back.

○ ○ ○ ○ ○ ○

As a teenager, Randy struggled with change and hated every time the four of them had to move. It wasn't simply because of the different locations, but because of the disruption in his routine. Colorado was the most difficult move of all. While there, Dominic made him train even more in the mountains due to how much he hated the climate and altitude. He hated the cold, frigid weather, and always struggled not to be distracted by it, even though he knew it would not impact his body temperature. The more he complained, the more Dominic made him train. The Guardian saw it as a distraction that Dominic explained he needed to overcome, but it was difficult for the teenager.

"There is no guarantee the Ultimate Evil will fight you in a desert, Randall," teased Dominic. Randy groaned.

"But also no guarantee it will fight me on a snow-covered mountain." Dominic chuckled. He placed his hands on Randy's shoulders.

"There are going to be times in your life when you feel overwhelmed or even helpless." Randy scoffed.

"I am an immortal being. I should never feel helpless."

"But you may someday and if it comes, you must be prepared. In that moment, when time is not on your side, and you need to be quicker on your feet, stop, take a deep breath, close your eyes, and listen. Follow your instincts. I believe in you. You have instincts for a reason," advised Dominic.

∘ ∘ ∘ ∘ ∘ ∘

Randy gulped as he thought about his old mentor. He immediately shook the thought out of his head but decided to heed the advice, anyway. He sat down on the edge of the cliff and took in a deep breath to relax. The sounds around him filled his ears and overpowered his other senses. He could hear his brothers' hearts racing, and the water sloshing around Chris, as he swam to shore beneath the cliff. The pitter-patter of Stacie's feet racing around the trails caught his attention next. He pushed his mind farther and sifted through the noise again. The wind whistled around the tree Joanie scaled to get a better view of the bluff. Victoria's breathing, as she checked the stalls of the rest stop bathrooms. His senses were so overwhelmed with the noises that he almost missed it: the faintest heartbeat to the west of him. His eyes darted open as he jumped to his feet.

"Over here, on the other side of the bluff," he called, as he sprinted toward the noise. The sound of the heartbeat soon gave way to a faint whimper. He could hear the others drawing near as he raced ahead. Randy climbed a pile of boulders and peeked over them to see a woman haphazardly crumpled alongside another row of rocks. It did not take him long to reach her and her eyes barely focused on him, as he checked her for injuries.

"She has a head injury, but she's alive. Her pulse is faint, but she's alive," he informed in disbelief, as the others arrived. Tiva managed to let out another whimper, as he carefully scooped her into his arms.

"I got you. You're safe now," he assured before she fell unconscious in his arms. John and Chris watched as Stacie ran over to help. Victoria's eyes filled with tears and Joanie wrapped an arm around her big sister as they watched Stacie's hands glow with red and white light. Stacie ran a hand over the deep cut on Tiva's head and sighed in relief as the wound slowly began to close.

"She's okay. She's going to be okay," said Stacie. Joanie kissed Victoria's cheek and smiled at her.

"You did it, Vic. You didn't give up and you found her," said Joanie.

"*We* found her," said Victoria, before resting her head on Joanie's shoulder. It had been a stressful case, but they found Tiva Hensley alive.

o o o o o o

By the time the sheriff's department in Billman County arrived on the scene, everyone but Victoria had departed. They headed back to Anderson to fill in the Praevians about the good news and help make sure the human trafficking ring Carlos found was shut down. The authorities were already swarming the house of the main suspect and were confused, but grateful, for the sheer amount of evidence that was anonymously emailed to their agency to assist with the arrests. Carlos used one of the camera feeds from the house to show the others the faces of the agents who had arrived to find their suspect bound by zip ties, gagged, and with a hard drive in his pocket, loaded with his client list. While the others made sure everything went smoothly from afar, Victoria was all business at the bluff. She was a bit out of practice, but Sheriff McNamara was on the scene. It took everything in Victoria's power not to unleash her full wrath on the sheriff of Billman County, as he rubbed the back of his neck nervously and attempted to explain his handling of the case.

"Now listen, McNamara, we followed the leads we had, and none of them led us to human trafficking."

"Did you even bother to look?"

"For all we knew, this was the work of a serial killer. It would've been irresponsible to assume…"

"*Irresponsible*? You really want to go there with me right now?" challenged Victoria, as she stood toe to toe with the man. He cleared his throat and stood up straighter.

"The victim went missing…"

"*Her name* is Tiva Hensley. She went missing six days ago, after her night shift. Her family reported her three hours later. There was no body. In fact, no other bodies connected to her case, and yet your *best lead* was a serial killer?" He rolled his eyes and smiled condescendingly at her.

"How about we just agree that we lucked out on this one and all ended well?" Victoria smirked.

"If your department had done your job and actually looked for her when her family asked you to, she wouldn't have needed luck."

"Now hold on, we followed protocol and…"

"Well, your protocols suck, but I think we both already knew that." With that, she turned to leave and rolled her eyes when the man called after her.

"Always nice working with you, sheriff," he called. She shook her head in disbelief but got into her Mustang before she could make a flippant comment in return. She smiled when her phone rang, and she saw it was Alex. He yawned into the phone, and she giggled.

"Long day, sheriff?" she teased.

"Apparently not as long as yours, sheriff. I just got a call from a buddy of mine in Billman, says Tiva Hensley has been found alive."

"I was just about to call you, but first I had to deal with Osbourne."

"Oh yeah? How was that?"

"A sheriff from another county, who is technically on leave, busted his case wide open and exposed the department's refusal to address one of the biggest issues plaguing the region. How do you think it went?"

"How much of a smartass were you?"

"Just the right amount, as usual."

"Of course."

"So, listen, I know it's late, but I have something to give you that may assist with that explosion on Old Mill Road."

"You mean the mysterious fire that just broke out in an abandoned house?"

"Yep. Can I come by?"

"Always. I'll leave the light on for you." With that, they both hung up and Victoria sighed in relief. For the first time in months, she felt like she was on the right path. When Alex sent her the information about the Hensley case, she wasn't sure if she should step in, but it felt right to help. Something she couldn't quite figure out kept holding her back from returning to work and taking the helm as sheriff full-time again, but she felt a sense of relief knowing she could help when needed. It didn't take her long to arrive at Alex's house. The deputy lived on the outskirts of Anderson, in a small home on a spacious patch of land, north of Lake Cameron. She smiled when she saw the light was indeed on for her, as she got out of her Mustang. He stepped out on the porch fully dressed in his uniform and she shook her head in amusement.

"No need to dress to the nines on my account," she teased, as she made her way to the porch.

"I'm heading over to the hospital. I already called Tiva's sister and the family is headed that way. Hopefully, she can get checked out and start the healing process. I'm sure it was quite the ordeal. I can't imagine." She held out a sealed evidence bag with an empty plastic bottle and a small plastic bag with traces of white remnants at the bottom.

"I have something for you. I know Osbourne iced you out, but this should help. Don't ask me how I got it, but I may have found some evidence that Tiva was in fact moved from that house on Old Mill Road. I have a sneaking suspicion at this point that her DNA will be a match on this water bottle and this old baggie will have traces of whatever was used to drug her when she was moved."

"How did you…"

"I know her testimony should be enough, but whatever can tie her to Peters without a doubt is always nice. Plus, it'll be a good reminder to the Billman Boys that refusing to play nice and calling jurisdiction all the time means missing out on places that could hold evidence."

"You just happen to have evidence bags at your place?" he asked teasingly, as he took the bag.

"Of course not, that would be ridiculous. I keep them in the trunk." He chuckled and shook his head.

"You never cease to amaze me, Vic."

"Thanks. Now, I should head home and get some sleep. I can't pull all-nighters like I used to. You should do the same, you know? It's two in the morning. Take the win. The job can wait until a reasonable hour. I'm sure Nikole would appreciate it." He smiled sadly as he looked down and stuffed his hands into his pockets.

"Uh, yeah well, that didn't really work out."

"Wait, you and Nikole broke up? Why didn't you tell me? What happened?"

"We just wanted different things. I didn't tell you, because you've been busy and there wasn't really a time to bring it up that wouldn't make it awkward."

"Why would it be awkward?"

"I don't know. I just didn't want it to be awkward just in case it did get awkward."

"You said that awkwardly." He shook his head in amusement at her teasing.

"This is why I didn't tell you." She giggled.

"Hey, but seriously, you can always talk to me, no matter what. I never want you to feel like you can't."

"I know, I just…well, I guess it's just…it was my fault. I'll leave it at that. It was nice to put myself out there again and know I'm not that out of practice, though."

"You're going to find the one, Alex. My statement still stands, though. Go back to sleep. You need your rest."

"I will, but only once I know you've gotten home safe." She playfully rolled her eyes at him.

"Always worrying about me," she teased.

"I always will."

"Well, you can stop, because I'll be fine. I can promise you that."

"Because of John, right?"

"He's a great guy. You two just got off on the wrong foot."

"I misjudged him, but guys that are that squeaky clean either tend to be sociopaths or saints. Guess he has sainthood down, though, after everything that's happened since he first showed up in town." She eyed him carefully.

"What do you mean?" He eyed her right back.

"It took me a while to put it together, longer than it probably should have really. The way he just appears out of nowhere, the amount of incidents at your place since the three of them got here. Ever since they showed up, all these strange things have happened."

"Alex, John is a good…"

"I know. I also know there's something about him; well, the three of them, really."

"Alex…"

"Don't worry, Vic. I'm not here to stir anything up. Just know that I know he's a good guy. Even before, when I was jealous of him, I could feel it. Deep down, I knew he wasn't a threat to you, just to me, because…well...I was in love with you, and it sucked seeing someone who could be good for you. I was also pissed, because he kept bringing trouble around you and your sisters. I know you can handle yourselves, but I can admit, I don't like how ever since they arrived, you and your sisters have been in danger. I will never be okay with that."

"That's not completely accurate. We haven't been…"

"I know the way you said goodbye to me, Vic, like you weren't sure if we would ever see each other again. You were scared. You all were. You were acting like something was after you. Then, there's all that stuff that went down at the McCoy House."

"But, we did come back, and it's like I told you…"

"The sick family member in New York. Yeah, I remember. Listen, I don't need to know what's going on. Whatever it is, I'm sure you've got it covered, but you have to admit that whatever it is keeps interfering in your life. You're an amazing sheriff. John may be a good dude, but not even you can ignore how your life has been upended since he got here. Whatever threats are following him seem to be following you too, so I hope whatever demons the three of them have are settled and done with." Victoria gulped at the words.

"Demons? What do you mean by demons?" He waved her off.

"It's just a saying, Vic. Demons, dark pasts, criminals, whatever. I know John is a good guy. I've seen him do too much good to think otherwise anymore, but just know that if whatever he's doing starts to be too much or too dangerous, for whatever reason, you can always come stay with me. There's plenty of room for you, Joanie, and Stacie. I'll always make sure you're safe." He was surprised when tears filled her eyes, and she pulled him in for a hug. He hugged her back and grinned from ear to ear.

"What's this for?"

"For always being here for me." He kissed the top of her head.

"I'll always be here for you, Vic. I'll always care," he promised. She quickly wiped a tear from her cheek and nodded.

"Me too. Now, go get some sleep, and no waiting up for my text. I can take care of myself. Trust me on that."

"I know you can. Head on a swivel out there, though, sheriff," he called, as he watched her walk away.

"You too," she called back. She headed to her Mustang but stopped dead in her tracks when a sense of dread filled her. She let out a shiver and a chill ran down her spine. Her senses were suddenly on high alert. She felt it well before she heard the footsteps in the distance, drawing closer faster than humanly possible. She spun around just in time to see the figure Ezra and Joanie had both described appear from the shadows, right behind Alex on the porch. The rest happened in slow motion.

She was in a dead sprint as she sped over to her best friend, as fast as her legs and newfound abilities could push her. Alex let out a gasp and grunt of excruciating pain, as a blade pierced his back and sliced through his chest. Victoria made it just in time to catch him as he crumpled to the ground. The figure removed the blade as quickly as it had impaled him from behind. Alex tried to speak, as Victoria pulled him into her arms. She applied pressure to the wound, but it didn't stop the blood from gushing. Tears filled both of their eyes and she shook her head.

"No, no, no, this isn't happening. Stay with me!" she cried. His hand managed to reach up for her cheek and he grazed it with his bloodied thumb. He tried to form words, but nothing would come out. Instead, his hand fell limply to his side, as the life left his eyes. Victoria's body went numb as shock took hold. Her mind refused to register what happened and she stared blankly at her best friend's lifeless body in her arms. Only the sound of the enigmatic figure stalking forward, made her snap back to reality and scramble to her feet. She didn't recognize the man but knew exactly what it was. It may have taken human form, but everything about its essence was void of humanity. The entity's eyes were onyx, and its jet-black hair was slicked back. The heavy parka it wore covered most of its limbs, but its veins were gray and coursed with a dark substance that appeared unearthly in nature. Its voice was deep and gravelly as it spoke.

"Humans are so feeble. To think, they destroy this earth so easily, and yet face mortality in an instant. It will be a great kindness to eradicate this world of such filth. I'm sure you disagree though. Am I right, Sheriff McNamara?"

"How do you…"

"How do I know who you are? I suppose I could ask you the same. Deep down, your instincts make it so. You know exactly who I am, don't you, Victoria?" Her body shook with rage, as she looked down at Alex's crumpled body. The figure took her lack of a response as an answer.

"No need for introductions, then. I did expect a bit more pomp and circumstance. The species you side with is all for that, so I assumed you picked up their bad habits along the way."

"Why?" she cried out. The figure cleaned Alex's blood from its hand by wiping it on its parka. Victoria's eyes widened when the black dagger it had used melted and morphed into an onyx liquid that shimmered before absorbing back into its fingertips.

"Such a predictable question. As a force of good, your question is why. I suppose, in your eyes, that's appropriate. In mine, the question can be answered with another. Why not?" She grabbed for her gun and unloaded the weapon center mass into the chest of the figure. It stumbled backwards as she continued to pull the trigger until there were no more bullets. She gulped, when the figure smirked, and began collecting the bullets from the parka to hold in its hand.

"There's that human pomp and circumstance," it taunted. Her eyes widened and she jumped out of the way as the figure suddenly lunged forward. Victoria managed to dodge it and her eyes widened once again when tendrils of onyx, viscous liquid, seeped from the figure's hands. She took several steps back as the enigma stalked forward with its tendrils slithering behind it on the ground, dripping with a black, goo-like substance.

"I must say, I expected more from you. Is this really the best that one of humanity's so-called saviors can do?" Victoria gritted her teeth, and her eyes began to glow with white and green light. The figure's head tilted in fascination, as a swath of vines wrapped around the tendrils and yanked them backward toward the brush of the forest. The figure jerked away from the tendrils and onyx liquid flowed from them as they snapped off its limbs. It marched forward and Victoria sprinted over to meet it with a punch to the jaw. She landed another blow to its midsection, followed by another, and another, as the realization of what happened to Alex began to sink in. She repeated the violent blows and let out a scream of fury as she unloaded her wrath. The figure grunted in pain and fell to one knee as she continued to strike it. It hissed when she summoned more vines forward and the vines, thick with thorns, ripped at its already tattered skin. They tightened around its neck, as Victoria used her abilities as a Natura to hoist the creature into the air. The forest glowed with green and white light as she harnessed her full power to squeeze the life out of the entity. Her hands glowed even brighter as she seethed.

"You're never going to hurt anyone again," she practically growled.

"Squeeze harder," the figure taunted. Victoria was more than happy to oblige. The figure winced and wheezed in pain.

"Pain is a fascinating sensation. The oxygen leaving this putrid form, the bones cracking. But you are misguided in your efforts, Victoria."

"Shut up!"

"You asked me why, before," it wheezed out.

"I don't care why anymore," she shouted, as tears streamed down her cheeks. Her grip tightened.

"You do, but the answer will bring you no peace. He was just a life force, energy, light. I snatched his essence away, and I take pleasure in doing just that, because humans do the same every day. You too are a force of energy, of light, and I am the void. I am necessary, in ways you still don't seem to understand, but that doesn't make me any less inescapable." She frowned in confusion when the tightness of the vice-grip she had on the figure seemed to not impact it further. It smiled and grabbed one of the vines from its neck, relinquishing her hold, as its hand melted into a black, onyx liquid that seeped into the vine, turning the once green, vibrant vine black. Victoria watched in utter disbelief, as the liquid spread to cover the other vines restraining the figure. The black vines dripped with a sable substance and sought out more vines in the brush to infect and merge with. The figure smiled even more, as Victoria winced and was suddenly hit with a wave of fatigue. The onyx liquid began to pool into the plants and trees. The vines, leaves, and grass slowly lost their vibrant colors and were zapped of nutrients. The vegetation was sucked dry until there was nothing but gray ash in its place and the patches of brush on the land withered away into smoke and dust, which dissipated before her eyes. Victoria collapsed to the ground, as the figure slowly made it back to its feet.

"This will be even easier than I assumed," taunted the figure, as it looked down at its hands. More of the black, viscous liquid accumulated in its hands, as it stalked forward once again to hover over her. It tilted its head in intrigue, as it observed the light dimming from her glowing hands.

"And yet, so much power," it whispered in awe. Victoria glanced over at Alex's lifeless body and gritted her teeth. She mustered up the last of her strength to focus on the power coursing inside of her, until she could feel it vibrating. The figure frowned in confusion, as her body began to glow again with white and green light. The light burst in all directions and boosted the figure from the ground. She let out a sigh of relief and did her best to catch her breath, as the figure crashed into the brush in the distance. Victoria tried to make it to her feet but felt as if her body had been depleted of energy. Her hands were shaking, and her muscles burned, as she tried to will her body to move. She cursed under her breath when the brush began to rustle in the distance. Soon, the figure emerged, wincing in pain and flexing its fingers, as it slowly limped forward. The onyx liquid dripped from its fingertips and slithered closer, as she tried to crawl away with the last of her remaining strength.

More of the black ooze seeped into the ground, soaking into it like oil, as it spilled forward in search of her as if it had a mind of its own. Before it could reach her, the sound of wheels pealing into the driveway and speeding in her direction made them both look up. She frowned in confusion when she didn't recognize the black sports car. Her head began to spin, and she fell onto her back to stare up at the sky, as exhaustion took over. All she heard was the sound of glass shattering, before bright, blinding white light radiated around her. She was in sensory overload and her eyes started to droop, but she could hear the sounds of wailing and monstrous shrieking. She managed to turn her head and saw the grotesque figure stumbling backward toward the forest behind the house, as streaks of white light pulsed in waves from a bright, glowing orb on the ground. The figure disappeared into the forest and her ears began to throb and ring. Victoria could feel her heart pounding, while her eyes threatened to close. She could hear footsteps rushing closer, but her vision was blurry. She began to lose consciousness as someone scooped her up into their arms. Before she lost consciousness, she caught a glimpse of the person who was carrying her. Her lips moved, but no words formed as she looked up. Dominic gave a reassuring smile.

"You're going to be okay." Those were the last words she heard, before she surrendered to the toll her depleted body had taken.

CHAPTER 2

The Enemy of My Enemy

Dominic gulped, as he watched the last of the onyx substance slither into the forest, where the figure had disappeared. He frantically looked around to make sure the figure was gone, before turning his full attention to Victoria. He checked her pulse and sighed in relief when he felt her heartbeat against his fingertips. The pulse was faint, however, so he inspected her for other injuries, pressing gently against her abdomen and neck.

"Come on, Victoria, wake up. You're okay now. Wake up!" he urged, as he shook her shoulders. When she didn't budge, he gritted his teeth in frustration. He had barely made it in time. The thought raced through his mind as he wracked his brain for a solution. He didn't know what he expected to find when he returned to Anderson to go in search of the Naturas, but finding one already under attack by the Ultimate Evil was not it. He jogged to his car to get a first aid kit and his phone, but stopped in his tracks and gulped, when the ground beneath him began to quake. The ground gave way, and he fell through the fissure before he could gather his thoughts. His stomach dropped, and a wave of pain shot through him, when he crashed into a hard slab of rock. The jolt knocked the air out of him. He held his side, as he wheezed and gasped for air. Suddenly, the slab of rock surged back to the surface, and he let out a grunt of pain as the piece of earth haphazardly tossed him aside. He coughed and rolled onto his back to fill his lungs with oxygen but was dragged to his feet by the collar of his black dress shirt before he could catch his breath. John grabbed Dominic by the throat and gave a squeeze, as his eyes filled with rage.

"What have you done!?"

"I…didn't…do it," Dominic managed to wheeze out. Chris placed a hand on John's shoulder to pull him back.

"He wouldn't be able to do this. He doesn't have the tablet anymore. Put him down, John. We'll figure this out, but Vic needs you right now," advised Chris. John glanced over at where the woman he loved lay unconscious in Joanie's arms. Stacie was hovering over them both, focusing on the glowing white and red light from her hands and trying to heal her sister. John glared at his former mentor once more, before tossing him aside. Dominic fell to the ground with a thud and John darted over to Victoria's side.

"Stacie, why isn't she waking up? Why can't you heal her?" asked John, as he began to panic again.

"I don't know. It should be working. Why isn't it working?" Dominic winced, as he made it back to his feet.

"It drained her of her energy. I was barely able to arrive in time to stop it from killing her. It was as if…it was as if it was sucking the life force out of her," said Dominic, as he held his ribs.

"What are you talking about?" asked Chris. Before Dominic could answer, Ethan and Gabriella's car raced into the driveway. They hurried out of the car and were stunned by the carnage in front of them. Victoria was unconscious in Joanie's arms and a deep crack covered most of the front lawn of Alex's home. Ethan gulped when he saw Dominic, and instinctively took a step forward to attack his former friend, but the sight of Alex's bloodied body lying in a heap on the porch redirected his attention. He ran over to check on Alex while Gabriella checked on Victoria. Ethan's shoulders slumped in defeat when he could not find a pulse on the deputy.

"How did this happen? Who did this?" questioned Ethan.

"You know exactly who. I have been trying to prepare the boys for this their whole lives, but now it is too late, and Victoria is paying the price for it. I was able to stun it with a Lucis, but it will return soon. We have to go," instructed Dominic. He rolled his eyes when everyone ignored him. John scooped Victoria into his arms, as Joanie and Stacie scrambled over to Alex.

"How…what is happening? Why is this…Stace, can you…" Joanie stammered over her words. Dominic interrupted her.

"We do not have time for this," warned Dominic as he looked around for any sign of the creature's return. Stacie's hands were shaking, and she closed her eyes to take a deep breath and calm her nerves.

"I can do this. I just have to focus. It's like with Ethan. I can save him just like I saved Ethan," she whispered to herself, as Joanie nodded. Chris and Randy glared at Dominic, as he limped over to Joanie and Stacie.

"Again, we do not have time for this. It will return, and you are not ready to face it. You have to be at full strength and Victoria needs to recover for that to happen. She is strong and will be just fine, but we have to get her to a safe house and away from this place before it returns," said Dominic. Joanie glared at him.

"What happened to Alex? What did you do?"

"He was dead before I arrived, but I assume he suffered the same fate the Ultimate Evil tried to bestow upon your sister," said Dominic. Randy scoffed.

"So, we're just supposed to believe that you had nothing to do with his death?" questioned Randy.

"What reason would I have to take his life?"

"You killed our parents for no reason, you tell me!" challenged Randy. Dominic gritted his teeth in frustration.

"That was…it was a mistake, but that is not what is happening here. We have to leave now. It will return and there is only a limited supply of Luci. I do not even know how long they work, or can keep it at bay. If it returns now, we will lose, and this will all be over for not only us, but the entire world. We have to go," warned Dominic.

"We will make the time! Alex is our friend, our family!" declared Stacie. Randy stepped in between his former mentor and Stacie before Dominic could object.

"How are you even still alive? Let me guess, the Guardians betrayed us once again? I knew they couldn't be trusted and were still at your disposal, just like always."

"Look, I know you are upset with me for the past, but…"

"It doesn't matter! None of this is your call anyway. We don't answer to you anymore," said Randy. He turned his back on the man and knelt beside Stacie to give her an encouraging smile as she focused on Alex's lifeless body. She sighed in relief when her fingertips began to glow with red and white light again. The light spread to her palms, and she closed her eyes as she placed her hands on his chest. The light poured into him and began to spread throughout his body, but Randy, Joanie, and Chris frowned when the light began to flicker. Stacie winced in pain. The wound in Alex's chest sealed, as she continued to concentrate on healing the man who had always been like a brother to her. She struggled but managed to concentrate harder. Dominic's eyes widened in fear when he spotted it. Remnants of the onyx ooze that he had seen dripping from the plants, trees, and vines before, slithered from beneath Alex's body, up his neck, and to where Stacie's hands were placed on his chest.

"Stacie, don't!" shouted Dominic. It was too late. A trickle of the onyx substance seeped from Alex's chest and into Stacie's palms. She began to cough as Alex's eyes jolted open and he gasped for air. Stacie's hands began to burn, and the searing pain quickly spread up her arms. She grabbed at her throat as she coughed and tried to gulp down oxygen to alleviate the excruciating pain. Suddenly, her arms felt like they were on fire and her body tensed as she tried to form words, but nothing coherent came out.

"Stacie?" questioned Joanie, as she reached out for her sister. Randy caught Stacie in his arms as she collapsed and began to convulse.

"Stacie!" shouted Randy, helplessly watching, as she struggled to breathe. Joanie pulled her into a seated position as Stacie's body suddenly gave out and went limp. She fell unconscious and Randy tried to wake her up, but to no avail.

"What's happening?" asked Chris. Joanie let out a sob.

"Stace!" cried Joanie.

"This can't be happening," Dominic mumbled to himself. He scrubbed his face to try to stop himself from going into shock.

"I can't wake her up!" said Randy.

"I can hear her heart beating. Why won't she wake up? Ethan, what's happening?" asked Joanie.

"I...I don't know," mumbled Ethan, as he tried to grasp everything that had transpired so rapidly. Dominic was stunned into silence. He looked around at the scene before him and tried to comprehend what had unfolded. When he arrived to see the sinister figure hovering over Victoria, he immediately jumped into action to help, but not even he was prepared for the chaos that had ensued since. Victoria lay limply in John's arms. Stacie was unconscious in Randy's. Alex was lucid, but barely conscious, as he groaned and remained in a heap on the porch. Gabriella tended to him, while everyone else tried to figure out how to help Victoria and Stacie.

"It took two of them out in one fell swoop. It knew they would try to save him. We...we have to go," Dominic mumbled to himself. Ethan pulled out his phone to call Zayneb, but Dominic firmly grabbed his arm to get his attention. Ethan jerked away from him, but Dominic was not deterred as they glowered at one another.

"I knew this was going to happen! If we would have just left when I said, none of this would have happened. She should not be wasting her abilities on one human when billions are at stake!" scolded Dominic.

"His life is not up for debate, Dominic!" yelled Ethan.

"Ethan, we have to get out of here!" The panic and fear evident in Dominic's outburst gave Ethan pause.

"Dominic..."

"Ethan, it is here. The Ultimate Evil is here, and if we do not leave now, everyone is dead! Do you understand that? It is *here*," warned Dominic. Ethan looked around at the chaos before them. Randy stood up with an unconscious Stacie in his arms. John was clinging to Victoria and pleading for her to wake up. Chris and Joanie were trying to regain composure while Gabriella pulled out her phone to call the Praevians.

"Okay, we need to get Alex to the hospital and regroup," suggested Ethan, but Dominic shook his head.

"There are not enough Luci to hold that thing off for long. Not to mention we are now down to only four Naturas at the moment. We have to go," repeated Dominic.

"We aren't going anywhere with you! This is your fault!" shouted Randy, as he approached with Stacie in his arms. Dominic sighed.

"Randall..."

"My name is Randy, and I don't take orders or advice from monsters like you. You betrayed us once, and for all we know, you're the reason Stacie and Vic got hurt!" Ethan stepped in between Randy and Dominic.

"He's right, though. We need to regroup. John, repair the lawn and take Stacie and Victoria back to our house with everyone else," instructed Ethan.

"I just talked to Reo. The Praevians are on their way. They'll meet you at our place. Ethan and I will make sure Alex gets to the hospital," added Gabriella.

"This place is pretty secluded, but I'm sure the neighbors down the way could hear all the commotion. Take the back roads and don't bring attention to yourselves. The last thing we need is people asking even more questions," said Ethan. Dominic scoffed.

"At this point, being discrete is the least of our concerns. The Ultimate Evil will kill anyone in its way," warned Dominic.

"Even more reason to get Alex out of here and steer clear of as many people as possible," said Ethan. Chris glanced at Dominic and crossed his arms.

"And what about him? What are you even doing here, Dominic?" asked Chris. They all looked at the former Guardian, who sighed.

"You can cast aspersions on me when everyone is at a safe house. Ethan, there is no time to get Alex…"

"This isn't up for debate. He's innocent in all of this and they consider him family. I'm not letting anyone else get hurt, because you don't give a damn about anything but a prophecy and I am sure as hell not listening to your advice about it. We're going to make sure he gets somewhere safe," said Ethan. Dominic shook his head in disbelief, as he watched Ethan and Gabriella slide Alex into their car. Randy and John sped away in the direction of the McCoy House with Stacie and Victoria in their arms. Chris eyed his old mentor cautiously, before glancing over at his wife.

"What do you think we should do about him?" he questioned. Joanie warily eyed the man as well.

"Bring him along. I'm pretty sure John bruised at least one of his ribs when we got here. Besides, if he's telling the truth, we'll need him to tell us how he fought off whatever caused this." Chris leaned in, to whisper in her ear.

"We can't trust him, *tesoro*." Even he was surprised when her hands glowed with white and blue light. The wind surged from behind her and jolted into Dominic, knocking him off of his feet. He crashed to the ground and was knocked unconscious in an instant. Joanie smirked.

"Trust? Who said anything about trust? We don't have time for any games he'll try to play on the way there. Besides, if he's dumb enough to betray us again, he can deal with John and Randy's wrath. Hell, at this point, I'll kill him myself."

"I see that," said Chris, with a nod. Joanie slung Dominic over her shoulder and headed for the former Guardian's car. The black sports car's engine was still running, as she tossed him in the trunk.

"Joanie," Chris chuckled as she slammed it shut. She shrugged.

"He'll be fine." Chris listened for his old mentor's heartbeat and nodded in agreement when he heard it. So much had happened in a matter of minutes and neither knew what to do, but as they drove away from Alex's house in Dominic's car, they had a feeling that what once felt like the end, was just the beginning.

∘ ∘ ∘ ∘ ∘ ∘

Minutes felt like hours, making the wait for a course of action unbearable. The Praevians arrived at the McCoy House and got right to work assisting the group. Reo set up equipment to monitor Stacie and Victoria from the two upstairs bedrooms. Both sisters were in a comatose state, but Reo assured Joanie, Randy, John, and Chris that he would do everything he could to help them. Carlos was in Ethan's study sifting through news reports and tracking information from intelligence agencies that he'd managed to intercept, in order to find any signs of the creature. Meanwhile, Zayneb and Maya headed to Alex's home to make sure all traces of the disarray and chaos that ensued were gone. The front lawn was back to normal, except for the dead plants and trees in one section of the forest beside the home. They locked up Alex's residence and headed back to the McCoy home just as Ethan and Gabriella were pulling into the driveway. Both women greeted the couple, who looked exhausted.

"How is Alex?" asked Maya. Gabriella let out a sigh.

"Stable and recovering, but pretty shaken up. He doesn't remember much. According to him, he had a good talk with Victoria about the case, said he was watching her leave, and someone stabbed him from behind. He remembers Victoria rendering aid and the next thing he knew, he was laying on the porch with all of us there. He kept asking to see Victoria, but we told him she wasn't able to come," explained Gabriella.

"How long do you think we have before he grows suspicious? This isn't the best time for someone to be out there sounding the alarm or going in search of Victoria," reminded Zayneb.

"Especially with the full force of the sheriff's department behind them. Alex has always been persistent," added Maya. Ethan and Gabriella nodded in agreement.

"Which is why we decided to tell him as much of the truth as we thought he could handle," confessed Ethan.

"Do you think that's wise?" asked Zayneb.

"It's not ideal, but he took it pretty well. You two are right, we couldn't have him putting himself or others in danger by coming to look for Vic while this thing is still out there. We didn't have a lot of time or options, especially with the looming threat, so we told him. He's stubborn and would have eventually started asking questions, just like he did after we returned from Wyoming, so we gave him an abridged version of what's going on and why he can't be involved," explained Ethan.

"How did he take it? Most humans can't even wrap their mind around it. I still remember when I first found out," said Maya.

"Surprisingly well…well, considering everything. Apparently, we've all been on his radar for a while. The incidents at the girls' house, the accident at the lake, the explosion at our house. I'm not sure Alex is the type to believe in that many coincidences," said Ethan.

"He said he knew something was going on, when Vic said goodbye to him. He actually seemed kind of relieved to know. Again, still not ideal, but at least now we have an acting sheriff on our side to make sure the rest of the town is none the wiser," added Gabriella.

"Besides, right now he's more focused on getting cleared to head home," said Ethan.

"What do you mean? Shouldn't he be fine after Stacie healed him?" asked Zayneb.

"The doctor says he'll make a full recovery, but still needs to be treated. It's strange, really. He was stabbed in the back, but that seems to have healed. They found signs of smoke inhalation in his lungs," said Gabriella.

"Smoke inhalation, how's that possible?" asked Maya.

"We have no clue. Maybe something else happened to him that he doesn't remember. We can't exactly ask Vic about it at the moment, either, and the Ultimate Evil has always been quite a mystery," said Ethan.

"You said when Stacie healed him, she started coughing and struggled to catch her breath, right? Maybe it acts as some sort of smoke or poisonous gas," suggested Maya.

"Your guess is as good as ours right now. How are they? Any updates since we last spoke?" asked Ethan, as they entered the house. Before Zayneb could give the report Reo gave her, the Praevian walked downstairs to greet them. Reo smiled sympathetically at them as he approached.

"I need to run some tests and don't have everything I need here, but Victoria is stable, and I was able to give Stacie medication to make her comfortable. Neither has woken up, but it's clear Stacie's system is trying to fight something off. It's hard to say what exactly, but my best guess is it's acting as some sort of virus. Her immune system has detected it, so she's running a fever. Out of the two of them, she's the one I'm more concerned about, but like I said, I would feel better about my assessments of both if I could run some tests in my lab," informed Reo.

"We'll figure out how to get you what you need. There's a lab in Minot that may be useful. We may need to have you and Carlos take the jet," said Gabriella.

"Let's put a pin in that, until we can figure out our next move. Staying here doesn't seem like a viable option for multiple reasons," advised Zayneb.

"And we have some pressing matters to consider, as well," added Maya.

"Speaking of, how is our unexpected houseguest? Where is he?" asked Gabriella, as she looked around.

"His presence angered the boys, so I suggested making him comfortable away from them. Carlos handled it. He's down in the basement," revealed Reo. Ethan was heading down the back stairs of the house to the basement before his wife could advise against it. Gabriella groaned.

"Okay, um, Reo, just keep doing what you're doing. We know they're in great hands. Zayneb, Maya, be ready. I have a feeling you'll both be needed. I'm going to check on the others," said Gabriella.

"What about Ethan and Dominic?" asked Zayneb.

"There's no point in trying to stop him and I can't say I blame him. We've spent the past few months focusing on rebuilding and getting back to our lives, but Ethan has been struggling with the fact that if Stacie wouldn't have been there, he would be dead and it's all because of Dominic. A part of Ethan never thought he was capable of that."

"But he already knew he was capable of murder," said Zayneb.

"Yeah, but that's different from being capable of murdering a man that was like a brother to him. Ethan and Dominic didn't always agree, but a part of Ethan always looked up to him. That's over now. He has a lot of questions, so I'm sure they have a lot to catch up on," said Gabriella. Maya smirked.

"Oh, I think that's an understatement," said Maya.

○ ○ ○ ○ ○ ○

Ethan's heart was racing and his throat was tight, as he walked down the stairs of the basement where his former friend was handcuffed to a chair. He never imagined he would come face to face with the man again. He was surprised by how much his blood boiled at the very sight of him. When the remaining Guardians assured him Dominic would no longer be an issue and had been eliminated as a threat, he assumed that meant Dominic was dead. He chastised himself for trusting the Brotherhood on such a matter. Dominic had run the Guardians and kept a close eye on every aspect of the Brotherhood for decades. After Ethan's last conversation with Phillip, Dominic's downfall seemed inevitable and yet, there he was, in Ethan's basement. While Ethan could admit, Dominic did not look like the same, tailored, curated man he once was, he also did not look as haggard as would be expected for someone who was handcuffed to a chair. His tailored slacks and black designer dress shirt were dirty from his run-in with John, but he still held himself with all his usual status and prominence. There were more grays in his slicked-back dark hair and his eyes looked tired, but he still reeked of prestige. Dominic sighed, as Ethan approached.

"While I find myself sounding like a broken record as of late, I will ask you what I asked Connell. Are the handcuffs really necessary?"

"Connell?"

"Yes, it turns out he is now Trenton's right hand, and yes, still quite dull."

"He was a kid when I saw him last."

"Well, a lot has changed since then. Now, can you please take these off? It is not as if I could possibly escape, or would have anywhere to go, with the Ultimate Evil on the loose. If the boys did not stop me, that thing surely would." Ethan began to pace, as he mulled over the predicament he found himself in.

"Was any of this real?" Dominic's brow furrowed at the question.

"*This,* meaning what, exactly?" Ethan threw his hands up in exasperation.

"Your capture! The Guardians assuring me you…" Ethan gritted his teeth in frustration, as he stopped himself from continuing. Dominic looked down at his hands in his lap, and nodded.

"You are wondering why I am still alive and why they have not killed me yet."

"I'm wondering if this is yet another one of your calculated moves, or some warped strategy by the Guardians. They vowed you would be taken care of and that we would have all of the resources necessary as Praevians, which I thought was weird with the Ultimate Evil defeated. Now, I guess I know why. They knew this whole time, didn't they? *You* were in control this whole time."

"No, I was not. They did believe you and your group had helped the Naturas accomplish their mission. I, however, knew the truth. I am not the Ultimate Evil, Ethan."

"Was Phillip lying, too? Does he even care about me, about my father…"

"If there is one truth you should always believe, it is that Phillip always loved your father. I am only here because of their bond and his promise to keep you safe no matter what. He took that vow quite seriously and still does. Especially since your father passed."

"He kept the man who tried to kill me alive, because he wanted to keep me safe? I've watched you do some impressive things over the years, but how the hell did you manage to pull that off?"

"I told him the truth. I showed contrition, but also assured him you were almost as misguided as I was on the matter."

"You pompous prick."

"I am a lot of things, Ethan, but I am not the Ultimate Evil. It does not mean the past few months have been easy for me, though. I was imprisoned, and trust me, you are not the only one irked by my existence. Connell made that clear. But, Phillip and I made an agreement. As long as the threat of the Ultimate Evil existed, so would I. So, he kept me detained and watched my every move, but continued to search for any signs. Once they were found, my circumstances changed."

"So, I'm supposed to believe you just appeared tonight out of nowhere, at the same time as whatever the hell attacked Victoria and Alex? This is all a big coincidence?"

"No, I knew it would be coming soon. I didn't realize just how soon, but I came to warn the boys and provide the resources they might need. Arriving in time to save Victoria was just fate playing out."

"Of course. After all you've done, you still believe that you're destined to guide them, that fate will have it no other way. I've always been more of a fan of free will."

"And I've always believed both coincide. Darkness around the world ensures that evil remains present, and humans choose to tap into that evil. You and I were placed on paths as Guardians, but I chose to take up the calling while you chose to go your own way. Fate creates a way forward. Free will allows us to choose whether to move forward or not." Ethan shook his head in disbelief.

"So, you just showed up at the right place, at the right time at Alex's home?"

"Of course not, I tracked Victoria there."

"There it is. How did you even do that?"

"I was getting close to town and wanted to find the Naturas as soon as possible. Time is of the essence and I went to see the one already in town. The boys, Joanie, and Stacie were on the outskirts, and I figured it would be easier to talk to one in person first, instead of all of them…even though, admittedly, Victoria was not my first choice. The sheriff certainly knows how to impose her will and has very little patience, but like I said, time was of the essence."

"You've been tracking them this whole time, haven't you?"

"No, only since Trenton loosened my leash and tightened Connell's."

"But how?"

"Come now, I may have fallen out of grace with the elders to a certain extent, but the resources of the Brotherhood are now available to me again for dire situations. I do not know if you fully comprehend what is happening, since we are still in Anderson even after witnessing what that monster can do, but this is most definitely considered a dire situation." Ethan shook his head as realization dawned on him.

"Of course, you control the satellites. You are surveilling them."

"No, the Guardians are surveilling them. Even as the Brotherhood dissolves, Trenton and Phillip still have stakes in satellites owned by governments and corporations all over the world. I was simply given access to some when needed. I am not sure why you are surprised by that."

"Note to self, give Carlos permission to infiltrate all satellites and apologize for calling him too paranoid when he wanted to in the past."

"Well, one can never be too careful these days."

"So, you tracked Victoria to Alex's house and managed to show up just in time to save the day?"

"No." Ethan frowned at the words. He was surprised by the tears welling up in Dominic's eyes.

"I was almost too late and quite frankly, I failed. Victoria and Stacie are incapacitated. If I had arrived earlier, I could have saved them both."

"If all of this is true…"

"It is."

"…then, how did you even manage to live to tell the tale? Alex practically died and Stacie is fighting off whatever happened to her, because she saved him. Victoria is in a coma, and yet here you are, unscathed." Dominic winced, as he stretched his neck and squirmed momentarily from the ache of his ribs.

"I would not call this unscathed. Jonathan made sure of that."

"You deserve much worse."

"Maybe, but this is the situation we find ourselves in. The Ultimate Evil has arrived. It will return for them soon, and we do not have time to rehash the past or…"

"How convenient."

"The fate of the world is on the line here, Ethan. This is not about convenience. It is about survival, so how about you get me out of these restraints so I can help figure out what to do about all of this?"

"You didn't answer my question. How did you of all people come face to face with the Ultimate Evil and survive?"

"Because I caught it off guard while it was focused on Victoria. Most of it was luck in the timing and the Lucis did all the work. I used one to cast it away. I had the element of surprise on my side, but that will not be the case next time. Now, it knows we have the Lucis and can fend it off."

"A Lucis? I can't believe it actually exists. How is that even possible? I thought they were myths, since such a thing had never been found before. There's a reason the tablet has always been the artifact to seek out. We knew it was real from past writings of Guardians, but Luci? Have you been hoarding them this whole time in the same way you secretly collected the tablet? How many do you have?"

"Not enough, but I will have you know Archie was the one to discover them." Ethan laughed bitterly.

"You managed to manipulate Archie into this too? Why should anything surprise me anymore?"

"There was no manipulation needed. Henrik is assisting with this as well."

"Hold on, Henrik too? You got Henrik Oladele of all people to help? I suppose if Archie is involved, it makes sense he would be, but that may just be the biggest miracle of them all. He vowed to never work with the Brotherhood."

"They are not helping the Guardians. They are helping me, because they understand what is happening. Besides, who else could find such a hidden treasure after so long? The opportunity presented itself after one of the Luci was freed from where it was stuck underwater in China."

"And how long have the Guardians been keeping this a secret?"

"Archie just recently found all of them."

"And now, much like the tablet, these artifacts just so happen to be in your possession?"

"Yes."

"Where are they?"

"I have them in my car. Don't worry, they are safe. Archie gave me a case to keep them contained. It can only be accessed with my biometrics and no, you cannot have the case." Ethan glared at him.

"In what world would you be in a position to negotiate with me right now?"

"I saved her life. Victoria was dying and I used a Lucis to save her life."

"What does that have to do with…"

"You need me…and…well…I need you. This is not the time for petty vendettas. I saw that monster. It was every bit the darkness the prophecy always said it would be. We do not have time for vengeance or distrust…"

"Again, how convenient, coming from you…"

"You can say what you want about me, but you cannot doubt that I have vowed my life to put an end to the Ultimate Evil."

"And yet somehow you became it."

"I can admit that I became corrupted and obsessed, but I have a chance now to make amends. The fates have assured it and I will not fail again. Take these restraints off and allow me to help save us all." Ethan sighed and cursed under his breath, as he approached Dominic. The man smiled appreciatively and rubbed his wrists when Ethan removed the handcuffs. Dominic stood from the chair and stretched his neck.

"Good, now let us…" Ethan's fist collided with Dominic's jaw before the man could finish his sentence. The move caught the former leader off guard, and he stumbled backward from the force. He rubbed his jaw, as Ethan shook out his hand.

"Do you feel better now?" challenged Dominic.

"Better? About the man who killed me being in my home? Not even close." Dominic sat back down and gave a curt nod.

"Okay, fine, you seem to need to rehash this in order to move forward and get to the actual world-saving task at hand, so let us rehash the painful past, shall we? I would love to blame the tablet for my actions. At first, I did. I told myself that, much like Caleb Delaney, the tablet took hold of me, and I became obsessed with its power. I wanted to believe it made me paranoid, and maybe a part of it did, but…but I set that course of action in motion decades ago. I take responsibility for that."

"You had part of the tablet that entire time and told no one."

"I was scared that it meant everything was a lost cause." Ethan smirked in disbelief.

"That's absurd."

"They were merely children. They were *toddlers* when I found the first piece. There was no way they would be able to defeat whatever was coming and I worried that finding the piece of the tablet meant it was coming too soon to do anything about it."

"Well, you were wrong, and in turn, you continued to betray those boys over and over for their entire lives."

"I know."

"Do you? Do you have any idea what you've actually done? The man you've become? You are everything you've spent decades assuring others *they* would be!" The outburst echoed off the walls of the basement. Dominic fell silent for a moment, as he watched his former friend seethe. Ethan's jaw clenched in anger, as he paced back and forth like a lion.

"This is not about the boys or even the tablet, is it? This is about the past. Our past."

"Two things can be true at once, you self-righteous..."

"I am self-righteous? Do not go having revisionist history at my expense, McCoy. You turned your back on them..."

"You left me no choice!"

"There was *always* a choice! That is all life is, Ethan! We make choices and we live with them! That is what you could never understand. The Golden Boy with his charm and charismatic presence, having everything handed to him, even when we were children. You never wanted it and you made sure everyone knew it. You were never willing to make the sacrifices necessary."

"You mean kill, like you?"

"That was a mistake."

"That was a choice! You chose to kill, and you want to talk about sacrifice? You took those boys after murdering their parents and you left me to clean up your mess."

"I never asked you to do such a thing."

"You never had to! I did it because a part of me, the brainwashed, warped part of me still believed in the cause. I still believed in you. I believed you were my brother, my best friend, who simply made a mistake. I believed you were just scared, because damn it, we were kids. I don't care that the Elders deemed us old enough to go it alone. We were kids playing as adults just as much as we were playing Gods. So, yes, Dominic, I believed in you, so I cleaned up your mess. I gave them proper burials and searched for their families and carried the weight of your burden, because I wanted to believe that there was still good in you."

"I believed in you too! Well after the rest of the Brotherhood cast you aside as quickly as you cast all of us. Do you not yet understand that? You and I were always destined to be two sides of the same coin. We want the same thing, Ethan. We just have different ways of going about it."

"And your way made sure our hands could never be clean in the process." Both men were silent, as the words hung in the stifling air between them.

"Do you remember the Fall Dance?" asked Dominic. Ethan frowned in confusion.

"What?"

"The dance my senior year of high school when…"

"I remember. Why are you bringing it up?"

"It was my last year before graduation. My father already had every detail about my future planned out and soon, I would be an official Guardian. I would undergo the final stages of training and take my rightful place amongst the Brotherhood. Everyone assured me it was a joyous time." A sad smile crept onto Ethan's lips, as he remembered who they had been decades earlier.

"It was," he conceded.

"But not for the reasons they told us."

"None of this matters."

"I was scared of becoming a Guardian, but would never admit it to anyone, let alone myself. How could I? So, instead, I did what my mother advised and embraced the small moments I had left, before being a Guardian would be all I was known for in this world. The Fall Dance, all of us there, laughing and dancing, like we were just regular kids with no burdens placed upon us. That is what made it joyous for me. It was not that I was celebrating what was to come. I was celebrating what was in that moment. You were my best friend, and yet I always envied you. Not for what you were entitled to, or your self-loathing about your burdens, but because you always had a strength that I did not. I needed rigidity and rules to know how to exist in our world, but you only ever needed instinct. Even as an adult, I spent years trying to do right by the boys. It never once came easily or naturally, and yet they turn to you now. They listen to you and regard you in ways they never did me. I saw it well before that night months ago...well, before they realized my deepest regret and betrayal."

"That's because they have instincts too, instincts they know now to follow. It was those instincts that kicked in the night you wanted Randy to kill Joanie, and he defied you. It was those instincts that made Chris go against your teachings and embrace love. And John? Well, maybe he has better instincts than all of us put together. But you don't get to come here, after all you've done, and flatter me with stories of our past or reflections of your ways."

"That is not what I am trying to..."

"You remember the boy I was with reverence. He was entitled and self-loathing, but also loyal to a fault. He only knew true happiness when following his friend wherever he led because that is all he ever knew. That boy is not here anymore, Dominic. You can't sway him to your side or make him see from your point of view. You killed him."

"The night they created Absolution is a night I regret for so many..."

"You didn't kill him that night, old friend. You killed him the night you murdered their parents and made him just as guilty as you." Dominic flinched at the words and Ethan wiped an angry tear from his eyes, as he stormed up the stairs and out of the basement.

o o o o o o

John didn't say a word, as he clung to Victoria's hand. In his eyes, everything about Victoria was vibrant and buzzed with life. It scared him to see her so still. The sounds around him were muddled in the background. He could hear the beeping of the machine next door and the faint sound of Stacie's heartbeat. He heard the whispered conversations between the Praevians about the next steps. He even heard the anger in Ethan's voice during his contentious conversation with Dominic. None of it mattered, though. All he cared about was the steady beating of Victoria's heart. Joanie and Chris were speaking to Reo as the former doctor finished setting up the monitors at Victoria's bedside.

"She's in stable condition and her vitals remain strong. That's a good sign. I have no reason to believe she won't make a full recovery," said Reo.

"What about Stacie?" asked Joanie. Reo sighed, as he considered his words carefully.

"Stacie's body is responding like it has been exposed to some sort of infection."

"What do you mean, an infection?" asked Chris.

"Gabriella recounted the details to me about what exactly happened before Stacie went into the coma. It differs, somewhat, from what Dominic says occurred with Victoria."

"You can't trust a word out of that man's mouth," reminded Chris.

"Maybe, but their symptoms differ as well. Victoria is in a comatose state, but her pulse is strong. She appears to be trying to recover and rejuvenate her body after her encounter with the being. She's stable. However, Stacie is exhibiting a fever and her lungs are congested. Whatever this monster is, it appears to be able to leave remnants of something behind. Based on what I've been able to piece together, it seems that when Stacie healed Alex, she absorbed something poisonous." Chris slowly nodded as he replayed the events.

"It was black, like a goo, or maybe an oil?" questioned Chris.

"If I didn't know any better, it was almost like it moved on its own," added Joanie.

"Well, whatever it is has infected her system like a virus," said Reo.

"She's going to be okay, though, right?" asked Joanie.

"While I am hopeful that her abilities as a Natura will help her recover, the onset of her symptoms and lack of information about what is happening to her body concerns me. Your systems are similar to ours but operate and heal differently. I have no doubt she could recover if treated properly, but I'm not sure what a treatment would look like or even if one is necessary, since, in the past, her abilities have been enough to help her recover. For all we know, she will heal on her own, but I have no timeframe for that and believe we should keep all our options on the table just in case her powers won't stop the infection from taking over her system. In the past, she healed herself quickly. That's not the case this time. I've already spoken to Randy about it, and he was adamant that I should try whatever I think is best. I've been able to start her on fluids and am flushing her system, but without an idea of what the substance is made of, or more equipment, or access to specific medications that may be able to help, there's not much I can do to treat her, except keep her comfortable."

"We should go check on Randy," suggested Chris. John remained seated in his place beside Victoria's bed. Joanie smiled sympathetically at him.

"Keep an eye on her for us," suggested Joanie. John nodded numbly, giving Victoria's hand a gentle squeeze. All he wanted was for her to wake up and he could not help but replay the events of the night over obsessively in his mind and think about how he let it happen in the first place.

Like his brother, Randy's expression remained stoic, as he watched Stacie's unconscious form. Her breathing was shallow, and her pulse was sporadic. She was still feverish and looked extremely frail. Joanie took in a shaky breath as she entered the room with Chris. A fresh wave of tears threatened to spill, while guilt filled her more than the dread she'd felt since first seeing the figure in the forest earlier that night. Chris slipped his hand into hers, and gave a comforting squeeze, as they approached the bed. Joanie gasped when she noticed the dark grey streaks in the veins of Stacie's wrists and forearms. The mysterious dark matter that had originally disappeared into Stacie's palms seemed to be spreading throughout her body. Joanie reached out to gently touch one of her sister's hands and shook her head in disbelief.

"I don't understand why she isn't waking up. She healed Alex and she's healed herself before." Randy nodded.

"Reo will do everything he can and she's going to get better. She's an immortal now. She'll get better. She has to get better," mumbled Randy. Chris placed a hand on his brother's shoulder.

"She will. She's strong and we know this isn't how it ends. The prophecy…"

"The prophecy was wrong, Chris. All of it was wrong. We studied it for years. Dedicated our entire lives to it, like fools," said Randy. Joanie placed her hand on Randy's.

"That isn't true. It wasn't all for nothing. As the Seer, I know it to be true. The events were destined to happen, I'm just not sure of the order anymore. I'm still trying to wrap my mind around what all happened tonight, but we know Stacie will pull through," assured Joanie. Randy gritted his teeth.

"I know she will. I don't need to know exactly what happened out there, but I know who's responsible for it, and maybe it's time we get some real answers from him." Randy jumped to his feet and stormed out of the room. Joanie pulled Chris back to her before he could stop his brother. He frowned in confusion when she shook her head.

"He needs somewhere to place his anger right now."

"And you think directing it at Dominic will help anything?"

"Maybe not, but if it makes him feel a little more in control, maybe it's worth it…or maybe he tries to kill Dominic. Either way, not my problem," said Joanie, as she focused back on Stacie. Chris listened for his brother but gave his wife a nod. He knew Randy well enough to know he needed to focus his rage somewhere, and with Dominic back in their lives after all he had done, it was a confrontation that had been inevitable.

○ ○ ○ ○ ○ ○

Dominic sat with his face in his hands as he waited in the basement for others once again to decide his fate. It had been an all-too-familiar circumstance for the former Guardian over the previous months, but he steadied his resolve when he heard the basement door open. Footsteps drew near and he was surprised to see Randy emerge from the stairs with a steaming mug of tea in his hands. The two of them stared at each other in silence for a moment. Dominic could practically see the wheels turning in Randy's head, as the

Natura tried to process the onslaught of emotions spiraling inside of him.

"I must admit I am surprised to see you. I was not sure if you would want to talk, or if we ever would again," admitted Dominic. Randy remained silent, as he began to pace. Dominic glanced down at the mug in Randy's hand.

"Is that for me?" Dominic shifted uncomfortably, as Randy continued to pace in silence.

"If I did not know any better, I would think you were going to throw it at me," said Dominic. He chuckled nervously, as he tried to break the tension boiling in Randy and threatening to erupt.

"Please say something." Randy looked down at the steaming mug in his hand and turned to face the man.

"You show up out of nowhere and now Stacie and Victoria are hurt. I don't know whether to interrogate you like the common criminal you are, or kick you out onto the streets…but yes, I brought you tea. It's apparently proper etiquette."

"Proper etiquette?" Dominic gulped when Randy glowered at him with fury burning in his eyes.

"What is it you said to me in Wyoming when you were playing all those mind games to try to sway me to your side? Ah, yes… 'you look stressed, Dominic. Have some tea.'" Dominic winced at the words.

"Fair enough. I deserve that. Although, I must say, tea sounds great right about…"

"You get no tea!" Randy quickly gulped down the hot liquid and placed the mug by the stairs before pacing once again.

"Randall…"

"My name is…"

"Right, Randy, sorry. I apologize. Randy, I am not your enemy."

"Lying once again."

"I was misguided and I… I have made a lot of mistakes, but you have to believe me when I say I am not the Ultimate Evil. You know I would never harm them in such a way. Even if you do not believe my intentions, you know I am human and do not have the abilities. We need to stop the real Ultimate Evil before it comes back. The world will be at its mercy if you boys cannot…"

"I don't believe a word that comes out of your mouth. Luckily for me, I don't have to. I'm not the one asking the questions. They are. I just wanted to see the look on your face before they do. I heard them in action earlier. They can bring humans to their knees. I wonder what they will do to you." Before Dominic could question him, the door opened and footsteps drew near. Zayneb and Maya emerged, and he swallowed hard, as the women approached. Randy smirked.

"That was actually pretty satisfying. Now, I have more pressing matters to attend to. Have fun trying to feed them lies about whatever you're planning," said Randy, before storming out. Dominic sighed, as Zayneb began to circle him and Maya pulled a chair over. She sat in front of him with a sly smile and another mug of tea.

"Forgive him. He's a bit upset right now. I'm sure you can understand," said Maya. Dominic looked over his shoulder to see Zayneb leaning against the wall behind him with her arms crossed. Her stance was unnerving and quite intimidating. He looked back at Maya when she placed the mug of tea in his hand.

"This is not necessary," assured Dominic. Maya waved him off.

"What? The tea? I know, but I'm trying to be polite. It wasn't my first thought. In fact, I had half a mind to allow my beautiful wife here to go first, especially after you had your men hold me hostage before. But, you seem like a man who responds well to gestures."

"I was not in my right state of mind when I allowed that to happen to you, but I did make sure no harm came to you. I made them promise. I hope now you are willing to do the same. I am not here to harm anyone. I willingly came to help. I know it does not change what I have done, but I hope it does at least mean something." Maya crossed her legs, as she sat back in her chair.

"It does, which is why I am going first and not her. I love the woman, but we have philosophical differences about if torture actually works or not. You're a smart man, so I'm sure you can guess where she lands on the issue. Full disclosure, I'm not completely against such things, but I told her, your actions will decide if you want this the easy or hard way." He gritted his teeth in frustration.

"I understand your anger and distrust. However, we do not have time for this. The Ultimate Evil will be back, and if it was able to track down Victoria, I have no doubt it can track down all of the Naturas here, which means we are all in grave danger. We will need to work together to stop it. I know who you both are and what you are capable of. You truly are quite impressive. However, this is not some covert mission, and I am not a terrorist who needs to be interrogated. I am here to help, just like you, and, just like you, will be needed for the world to survive. You will just have to accept that you all need me, too. So, I do not need the easy way with you, Maya, or what I am sure is quite the hard way with you, Zayneb. I choose to opt out of both." He gulped, when Zayneb approached him from behind and firmly placed her hands on his shoulders. She leaned down to whisper into his ear as he squirmed.

"While I'm flattered, it's always interesting how people assume that being tortured by me would be considered the hard way." His eyes widened when Maya winked, and Zayneb walked away from him. She kissed her wife's forehead before heading for the stairs of the basement. She called over her shoulder to Maya with a smile, as she did.

"Have fun, but please at least try to leave the man some semblance of dignity by the time you're done." Maya's scrutinizing stare made him sit up straighter.

"Shall we begin?" she challenged.

"Zayneb, wait," called Dominic. She ignored him, as she climbed the stairs.

"I can get everyone to safety and help Stacie," he called again. He sighed in relief, when Zayneb stopped halfway up the stairs. Maya arched an eyebrow at him, as he continued.

"I can help Stacie *and* make sure Maya is safe this time. You want that more than anything, right? You want to be a good Praevian and protect the Naturas, but also protect your wife and ensure what happened before does not happen again." Zayneb leaned against the railing of the stairs.

"Oh, believe me, it will never happen again," assured Zayneb.

"Right, I know, but my offer could be appealing to you both. Just let me explain. Call her off." Maya sighed, as Zayneb walked back down the stairs. She placed her hands on Maya's shoulders and gave him an impressed nod.

"Well played. You're smarter than even I originally gave you credit for. Most people assume I'm bluffing," admitted Maya.

"Like I said, I know all about you. I made a point to after last time," confessed Dominic. Zayneb pulled a chair up beside Maya and arched an eyebrow at the older man.

"That sounds like a threat," said Zayneb. Dominic quickly shook his head.

"It is not. I just mean I knew if the Ultimate Evil arrived, we would need as many resources as possible. I learned about all the Praevians. You are all extremely impressive."

"And what resources do you bring to the table? I see you're still wearing your Guardian ring, which means they have not disbanded like we previously assumed," said Maya.

"The Guardians are no more, but my oath to them remains. Phillip and Trenton are the last remaining members. The others are cowards and in hiding, as we speak."

"Hiding?" asked Maya.

"Look, you did not see that monster. I did. You know it to be true, because Victoria and Stacie are upstairs fighting for their lives. They cannot do that here. We are sitting ducks and you know it. This place does not have the security measures needed to defend against the Ultimate Evil, even though I am sure plenty of measures are in place thanks to Carlos."

"You really did study us," said Maya. He nodded.

"I know Carlos is brilliant, and the Praevians have many resources, but you do not have the only one that can protect us all from the Ultimate Evil until the Naturas return to full strength. Zayneb, you are a woman of strategy. You know, as well as I do, that we must move them soon or it will be too late." Zayneb crossed her arms, as she sat back in her chair. She glanced over at her wife and Maya gave a nod.

"We're listening," said Zayneb.

"This is the part where you give us an offer we can't refuse, and then we find a way to persuade the others it is in our best interest, so what rare resource do you have at your disposal and how do you plan to use it to help Stacie and keep everyone safe? If I were you, I wouldn't try to bluff either," warned Maya.

"I would not bluff about such a thing. It is not my style," assured Dominic.

"Oh, I'm aware. You aren't the only one who caught up on some intel about people. You are here because you think you have some sort of leverage, so let's hear it. I assure you, you have our full attention," said Maya. Dominic gave a bow of his head and took a sip of his tea, as the two women stared at him. He knew he had one chance to persuade them that his plan would work, and he planned to take it, but also knew that he only had one chance to do so.

○ ○ ○ ○ ○ ○

Gabriella smiled sympathetically at her husband, as she joined him on the back porch of their home. She handed him a mug of tea and sat down beside him on the steps. He kissed her cheek in thanks and took a sip from the mug before gazing back up at the night sky.

"Chamomile and lavender; nice choice," he mumbled.

"I figured you could use something to help you relax."

"Probably going to need something stronger than this for that. Are Maya and Zayneb talking to him?"

"Yes."

"And you are sure Zayneb is just talking?" Gabriella giggled.

"I've been assured that she plans on letting Maya do the heavy-lifting on this one."

"*Maya* is taking the lead? If I didn't hate the bastard, I would actually feel bad for him."

"I'm sure she'll have him weeping over his deeply-rooted insecurities in no time."

"I'll toast to that," he said. He took another sip of his tea before sighing. She kissed his cheek and soothingly rubbed his back.

"You okay?"

"Honestly, I don't know how to feel right now. I thought that chapter of my life was closed, the chapter that had been gnawing at me for years, with all the secrets and heaviness of even just knowing about the Brotherhood. You know, when I first decided to get the Guardians involved about Dominic, I felt guilty. I knew he'd lost his way, but we were friends a lifetime ago. Making that call was hard, but surrendering him to them, and walking away, was even harder. I told myself that night that doing so sealed his fate, and I felt guilty about it, like blood was on my hands yet again. I grieved for my old friend that night and for what? For him to remind me that he will always find a way to come out of it? No matter who he hurts or what he does?"

"Maybe that's a good thing this time," she suggested. She put her hand up to halt his rebuttal.

"Gabby, what...?"

"Dominic is a lot of things. Hell, I've called him most of them and every name in the book, but he's a survivor. And, since there's something out there that could bring the world to an end, we should at least consider that he may know something that could help, not because he is the good Guardian he believes himself to be, in that warped head of his, but because he'll always find a way to survive."

"He's a distraction, especially to the boys."

"I know, and I still have my reservations. You know I do, but Stacie and Victoria are hurt, we have no clue what this thing is capable of, and he seems to have at least something to hold it off until we get all the Naturas back. It's like my mom used to say, when she had to do something she wasn't looking forward to: it is what it is, and ain't what it ain't."

"With Dominic, that's a whole lot of 'is and ain't.'"

"I know, but he isn't all we have. We have each other and the Praevians and four Naturas looking to put a stop to this as soon as possible. We've got this," she assured. She rested her head on his shoulder and closed her eyes. He slipped his hand into hers and kissed the top of it, as they took a moment to collect themselves, before heading back into the house. Both were surprised to hear an argument underway when they entered and made their way toward the sounds of Chris, Maya, and Zayneb in a tense conversation in the living room. Chris was pacing back and forth, and Joanie was sitting on the couch with her eyes closed, as she tried to sift through her thoughts. Ethan noticed the way Maya and Zayneb were silently communicating and immediately knew it had something to do with the man sitting in his basement.

"What did we miss? What did Dominic do now?" asked Ethan. Chris shook his head in disbelief.

"They believe him," said Chris. Zayneb sighed.

"No, I believe Maya, and if she says he isn't lying, then that's good enough for me. It always has been," informed Zayneb. Gabriella eyed Maya cautiously, as she walked over to her.

"Wait, you actually think Dominic, of all people, is telling the truth without an ulterior motive? There isn't a bone in that man's body that doesn't have an ulterior motive," reminded Gabriella.

"Oh, I'm aware, and I'm sure he has his reasons, but that doesn't change that I think he's telling the truth about what he knows," said Maya.

"And that's not all," grumbled Chris.

"Okay, what else are we missing?" asked Ethan.

"They want us to follow him blindly, into whatever trap he probably has waiting for us," said Chris. Maya smirked, and Zayneb tried to hide her smile, knowing her wife had plenty to say to the Natura.

"First off, totally not what I said, and I don't appreciate the misrepresentation. Second, I don't see you or anyone else with a better idea and we are kind of in need of one. Zayneb and I are two of the only people in this house right now who can be at least somewhat objective, and that's saying something, since the man held me hostage and leveraged my life to get to all of you, but hey, the enemy of my enemy and all that. Let's recap, shall we? There's something out there that managed to take out two of the most powerful beings in the world without even needing to be present to harm one of them. We have a guy who dedicated his whole life to obsessing over the damn thing, downstairs in the basement, screaming that the thing will be back to kill us all, and we have no clue how to stop it. So, yes, I'm open to any idea that doesn't have us sitting around waiting for the Ultimate Evil to arrive and essentially wipe everyone off the face of the earth. Excuse me for thinking outside the box a little here."

"Is that really what you call believing Dominic and suggesting we move everyone to his safe house?" challenged Chris.

"Wait, what? What safe house? He shouldn't even be alive at this point, let alone have Guardian resources at his disposal," said Gabriella.

"Well, apparently he does," said Maya.

"I have no doubt he has all their resources again. Whatever he said or did to persuade them seems to have won Phillip back over, somehow," informed Ethan.

"It's a compound. He says he has a way to keep that thing away from everyone, while Victoria and Stacie recover," explained Zayneb.

"And you *believe* him?" asked Chris. Maya rolled her eyes.

"I hate to be the one to break it to you, but if what you admitted is true, he was able to save Victoria from the Ultimate Evil, so why would I not believe in his resources now? He was a Guardian, Chris, remember? Richest, most resourceful people in the world all accumulating their wealth as the point one percent of point one percent of people and assuring themselves they're doing it for the cause," said Maya.

"Where's the compound?" asked Ethan.

"He wouldn't say, just that it's north of here. He said he'll give us the coordinates when we are in the air and on the way. He wants to make sure we don't ditch him and leave him to fend for himself," said Maya.

"Which may have been an idea I was considering," admitted Zayneb. Ethan sighed.

"We can't just let the Ultimate Evil come back and kill him," conceded Ethan. Zayneb shrugged.

"Why not? He tried to kill Maya, the Naturas, and you. We all thought he was the Ultimate Evil until tonight, so maybe we'll get lucky and kill two birds with one stone. Let the two face off and cancel each other out or something," said Zayneb.

"Deep down, everyone in this room knows he isn't the Ultimate Evil," reminded Maya.

"But that doesn't mean we should trust him," said Randy, as he entered the living room. Maya smiled sympathetically at him.

"Randy, I'm not asking any of us to trust him," assured Maya.

"You want us to blindly follow him to…"

"No, I want us to get Stacie and Victoria someplace safe, and I am confident that if Dominic steps out of line, or tries *anything*, we still have four Naturas and a very vengeful, petty Praevian, who probably has several options playing around in her head as we speakon how to kill him if he tries anything," said Maya. She glanced at her wife and Zayneb scoffed.

"I'm not petty…I only have one method in mind to kill the man…after eliminating the others due to how time-consuming they would be," conceded Zayneb. Maya playfully crinkled her nose at her wife.

"That's what I mean by 'a bit petty,'" said Maya.

"Well, I'm not going anywhere with him," said Randy. Maya sighed and clapped him on the back, which made him eye her carefully.

"Yeah, you kind of are, and before you say anything, sure, we could do this the hard way and talk about it even longer than necessary, but, Randy, do you know what I do, and why I was the one interrogating him in the first place?"

"I figured you were there to stop Zayneb from killing him," said Randy. Maya was about to object but then thought for a moment.

"Okay, fair, but no. I analyze people and trust me when I say I'm *very* good at what I do. I don't like Dominic. I don't trust Dominic. But, I know desperation when I see it, and there's something in his eyes that wasn't there the last time we saw him."

"What?" asked Randy.

"Fear. Not disbelief or denial, but actual *fear*. For better or worse, Dominic dedicated his life to stopping what's here and he's terrified that he won't be able to. I know the man has done evil things. Hell, I've seen them up close, but he isn't the Ultimate Evil, and if he isn't, that means whatever that thing is just so happens to be the thing we've all been warned about. So, no, I don't have to like him, or even believe he's a force of good, but in times of crisis, the enemy of my enemy is good enough for me," explained Maya.

"We don't actually know what happened to Victoria. Alex didn't see anything, and we all showed up after the fact. For all we know, Dominic orchestrated this whole thing," argued Randy.

"It's not Dominic," said Joanie. All eyes were suddenly on the Seer as she spoke.

"The nightmare I had before was a warning. It was like I was being consumed by darkness. I was suffocating, and the more I tried to fight against it, the more it overwhelmed me. At the time, I didn't understand what was happening, because…well, I don't think it was actually happening to *me*. I got nightmares before Caleb showed up and right before I realized that Dominic was evil. It wasn't a nightmare. That feeling of being consumed, of having the life force sucked out of me, it wasn't me, it was Vic. I was feeling what was going to happen to her tonight. I could have stopped it and I didn't," she said, as tears filled her eyes. Chris was immediately by her side.

"You don't know that."

"Yeah, I do, Chris. I knew something was up, but I didn't want it to be true and now my sisters are in comas, and we have no clue what to do to help them. It's here. I saw it on Old Mill Road, and I felt it in that nightmare. Dominic's right. This isn't on him. He isn't here to threaten us. This one is on me. It's the Ultimate Evil and I let it hurt my sisters."

"You aren't the only one responsible for stopping it, Joanie. We all are," reminded Randy. They all heard heavy footsteps coming down the stairs and looked up to see John walk in.

"Which is why we need to get Vic and Stacie somewhere safe, so they can recover. Randy, Chris, you know I get it. I don't trust him either, but Dominic isn't capable of this, not even when he had the tablet. I still don't fully understand what's happening. We created Absolution. I felt it, but the Ultimate Evil did this and if Dominic can help them, we're going to let him help them."

"John's right. We need to get them out of Anderson and away from the constant threat of an attack. As for creating Absolution, I need to talk to Kaya about that. Maybe she can give us some actual answers," said Joanie. Chris shook his head profusely.

"*Tesoro*, the last time you spoke to her, you were knocked out the entire time and couldn't defend yourself," said Chris. Gabriella nodded in agreement.

"It's too dangerous for you to go under right now, Joanie. Doing so would essentially take out half of the Naturas. If Dominic is even remotely right, the Ultimate Evil won't stop until it accomplishes its mission and we're going to need all of you for that," advised Gabriella.

"And what mission is that, exactly? It seems none of us actually know, anymore," said Chris.

"Either way, we're going to need as many resources as possible, like the ones Dominic has," added Maya.

"I hate to agree, but Dominic has the Lucis now and they may be our only hope until Stacie and Victoria wake up," admitted Ethan.

"What's a Lucis?" asked Chris.

"I thought they were either a myth or long gone by this point. Luci are orbs of light that can cast out darkness, like the kind the Ultimate Evil is made of. A Lucis can temporarily weaken it. There's a limited supply though. They are quite rare," said Ethan.

"Okay, then let's take them from Dominic, and get him as far away from us as possible," suggested Randy. Maya shook her head.

"He's too smart for that. He says the Luci are in a case, that only he has the ability to open," informed Maya. Randy shook his head in disbelief.

"It's like the tablet all over again. Dominic can't be trusted!" shouted Randy.

"I agree with Randy. I can't believe we're even entertaining such a thing after everything he's done," said Chris.

"This isn't about trust," assured Zayneb.

"Look, we appreciate everything you have done for us, but we can take it from here. You can go. It may be time for us as Naturas to start making our own decisions, since we're the ones who can end all of this," said Chris. Maya was about to intervene, but Zayneb took a step toward Chris before she could. Joanie was surprised by the woman's lack of hesitation, as she stood toe to toe with an immortal. Even Joanie found herself intimidated by Zayneb's challenging stare.

"You don't dismiss us like we're servants. Contrary to what you seem to believe, this isn't just about you. The fate of the world relies on the decisions made here tonight and I assure you that while I see you as forces of good, that doesn't make you always right, which has already been proven by the fact that Dominic is here offering us solutions to stop the evil you believed you already vanquished. The compound is our best and only option at the moment. However, that doesn't mean I trust Dominic. I'll tell you what I told him down in that basement. If I think at any point it is a trap, I'll put him down myself, and I assure you, I won't hesitate in the way all of you would. His survival is *only* contingent on how helpful he remains to us. The moment that ends, so will he, no questions asked, or permission given, because quite frankly, I am not asking for it. It appears the Naturas have a bigger issue to deal with than an old mentor. We need *everyone* healthy enough to fight. Reo needs a medical facility where he can run tests to speed up Stacie and Victoria's recoveries. Especially Stacie, who seems to be fighting for her life. I'm not telling you anything you don't already know, but I will tell you this. The Ultimate Evil appears to be a weapon that can kill you and every single person on this planet. We all know that, so Reo needs to be able to run tests and we need to be able to do our jobs to keep *everyone* safe so Absolution can remain in place. Dominic assures us he has the resources we need. He has no leverage here *but* those resources. It's time to call his bluff," declared Zayneb. John nodded in agreement.

"She's right. Besides, we have no clue what the Ultimate Evil plans to do or what it even wants at this point," admitted John.

"That's obvious. It wants us," assured Randy. Maya sighed.

"Is that why it didn't show itself until tonight? Is that why it was lurking around town instead of coming right for you? I have no doubt it's drawn to you somehow and looking for a fight, but we have no clue what's going on, and making assumptions when the world is at stake isn't smart, it's arrogant. For all we know, Dominic is right and something else may be going on," said Maya.

"Like what?" asked Randy. Carlos ran into the room out of breath.

"Like natural disasters all over the world and here. You should see this," he announced, as he turned on the television to the local news station. He turned up the volume on the television and began typing on his device to search for more information, while the others watched the news report.

"An emergency summit has been requested by the Global Climate Change Initiative, formed just last month. While many countries have increased resources and funds to address natural disasters and relief efforts to combat climate change, the initiative faces its first major test during the early phases of its tenure. Multiple reports confirm a record number of natural disasters over the past twenty-four hours around the globe. This is in addition to the record number of natural disasters and events that have occurred already this year. Three of the world's biggest oil pipelines have erupted and contaminated a catastrophic amount of land and waterways. The investigation is ongoing, but no connections have been found between those events and the wildfires spreading throughout Europe and Asia. Scientists and public safety officials are working diligently for answers to what appears to be a domino effect on a global scale. Previous reports of earthquakes and mudslides in…wait, we have more breaking news coming in from local authorities and have just received word that residents of Anderson are reporting water and sewage outages. Public safety officials are recommending the evacuation of any residents who live close to the area spanning from the local water plant to Old Mill Road."

"Evacuations are happening throughout the state and the governor already declared a state of emergency. Anderson needs to be evacuated as soon as possible," said Carlos, as he tracked public safety announcements on his phone.

"The town isn't equipped for that kind of emergency, at least not with the speed necessary," warned Zayneb. Ethan nodded his understanding.

"I'll call Phillip. He has some contacts in the military and can make sure everyone in the region gets the resources needed," informed Ethan before rushing out of the room.

"We have a problem up here!" called Reo from upstairs. Chris, Joanie, Randy, and John sped up the stairs, where the doctor was standing in the entryway of a bathroom. Reo's eyes were wide, as he pointed at the sink. A black, viscous liquid began sputtering from the faucet and drain, and onyx ooze splattered into the sink. Chris ran over and was about to grab the faucet, but Reo pulled him back.

"Don't touch it!" Chris nodded his understanding and closed his eyes to focus his attention on any source of water surrounding the house. His hands glowed with blue light, and he winced, as he tried to summon the water from the nearby pipes and ground to flush the liquid out of the house.

"It's contaminated the main water line," he informed. The plumbing creaked and groaned, as he tried to force the ooze out of the house's lines and sewage system. It took him several attempts, but he managed to push the water forward to break through and clear the line. He sighed in relief, when clean water began to flow again.

"That's not going to last long. I need to find the source of the contamination," said Chris.

"We can't take the risk right now. I need clean water for Stacie and Victoria. We need to move them soon," warned Reo.

"They're in no condition for a fight if the Ultimate Evil shows up here," reminded Joanie, as she walked over to the sink with her palm out. Her eyes were trained on the remnants of the black liquid that were left behind.

"Joanie, what are you doing?" asked Chris.

"I may be able to get a read on it and actually help for once," she said, as her hand began to glow with blue and white light. Chris, Randy, and John immediately pulled her away from it.

"Or that stuff could infect you like it did Stacie," warned Chris.

"You literally just…" Chris interrupted his wife's protest.

"I never touched it, and it still took everything in me to summon enough water just to do that. It's not going to hold long." Joanie's eyes locked back in on the sink.

"I might be able to get a vision if I can just…"

"It's too dangerous and we can't afford to lose you, especially right now. You need to seek out Kaya, not whatever this poison is," said Chris. Gabriella ran into the bathroom and her eyes widened when she saw the remnants of the onyx substance in the sink.

"Okay, I agree with Chris. New rule, no touching the black goo, please," announced Gabriella. Suddenly, the plumbing in the house began to creak louder in the walls and the foundation rumbled. Chris looked back at the faucet and gulped as the flowing water sputtered.

"We need to go!" he shouted. Chris pulled Joanie away from the sink, and Randy and John darted from the bathroom to get Stacie and Victoria while the others grabbed as many resources and belongings as possible. Carlos ran into the study and scrambled to gather his equipment. He shoved them into his backpack and checked to make sure he had everything he needed. The lights began to flicker in the house, and he frowned in confusion when a sense of dread filled the pit of his stomach. He let out a shiver and a chill went down his spine. Suddenly, a loud pop echoed throughout the house, followed by flickering lights, before they completely shut off. He checked his phone to see if other power outages had been detected in the region. When he realized there were no other reports of outages, he cursed under his breath, slung his backpack over his shoulder, and ran out of the study. The hallway was dark and eerie. He could hear the others on the other side of the house preparing to leave and he swallowed hard, as another chill ran down his spine.

"Randy, can you get the lights please?" called Carlos.

"We have to go, Carlos. Hurry up!" called Randy. An eerie sensation washed over him, and Carlos searched the hallway for any signs that he was not alone. His heart began to race, and shadows crept into the corners of the hallway where moonlight peered through the windows. His heart pounded louder in his ears. He tried to move but was paralyzed with fear, when shadows around him began to dance along the walls.

"Uh, guys? Can...can someone...uh...not afraid of the dark or anything but uh..."

"You should be," whispered a voice in his ear. Carlos screamed, as he spun around to see a ghastly figure with pale skin and black eyes. It reached out to grab him, but Chris intercepted the figure before it could. Chris's hands glowed with blue light, and he let out a yell, as he used both fists to punch the enigmatic figure in the chest. The move boosted it off its feet and forced it through the wall of the study. Carlos sighed in relief and Chris inspected him for injuries.

"You okay?" asked Chris.

"Yeah, thanks. Where the hell is everyone?"

"Getting Stacie and Vic in the car. Come on, let's..." Both of their eyes widened as the shadows swirled around the hallway once again. Incoherent whispers and hissing echoed off the walls, as the house creaked and groaned.

"Uh, Chris," mumbled Carlos, as he pointed back toward the study. The ghastly figure had made it back to its feet and jerked its dislocated shoulder back in place before stretching out its neck. Chris protectively stepped in front of the hacker.

"Get out of here, Carlos."

"Copy that," said Carlos, as he sprinted down the hallway and out of dodge. Chris took in the appearance of the figure. It had onyx, soulless eyes and looked disheveled. The parka it wore was tattered and soaked with onyx liquid. That same sable substance flowed through the veins protruding from its sickly skin.

"It's actually you," Chris whispered, in disbelief. Joanie raced down the hallway and over to Chris. She gasped when she saw the figure as well.

"Stace and Vic are in the car. So are the others, we have to go," she whispered to him. The haunting voice of the figure made them both stop in their tracks. The voice was deep and gravelly as it spoke.

"We could end this now, you know. Dragging it out just seems so unnecessary."

"Joanie, let's go," urged Chris, as he grabbed her hand. She wouldn't budge and her eyes remained trained on the figure as it continued.

"Yes, Joanie, run. Just like you ran away to Seattle, away from your sisters, away from Nathan." It chuckled when her hands began to glow with white and blue light.

"Joanie, come on!" yelled Chris.

"We can stop it," she mumbled, as her eyes focused on the figure.

"Joanie, it's trying to trick you. Hey, look at me! Think about Stacie and Vic!"

"Yes, Joanie, think about Stacie and Vic. Think about what you did to them. It wasn't enough to lose your parents. You failed and now you'll lose them too," it taunted.

"No!" screamed Joanie before charging forward. Before she could lunge at the sinister immortal, Chris wrapped an arm around her midsection and picked her up. The demonic figure crouched, ready to attack, but let out a shriek when the sound of glass crashing on the ground was followed by a blinding white light. Chris managed to toss Joanie over his shoulder and darted from the house. The shrieks and screams of the force of evil echoed off the walls, as it slithered back into the darkness and away from the bright light. Once Joanie and Chris were outside, she angrily jumped out of his arms.

"What the hell was that caveman act back there?" His eyes widened in disbelief.

"Me? You're mad at me? Joanie, you could've been killed! That thing wanted you to attack it!"

"Good! Then maybe we could've put an end to this and gotten back to trying to have safe, normal lives where the people we love aren't constantly in danger!"

"That thing almost killed Vic and Stacie. You were acting like you wanted to be next in there!"

"I don't want to…"

"Enough!" The roar of Dominic's voice, as he emerged from the house, made them both stop to look at him. Ethan took a step forward to intervene, but Gabriella stopped him with a shake of her head. The rest of them had been watching the scene unfold between the couple as they finished packing up and filing into the cars.

"Seer, you of all people know how this works. It will take all of you to defeat the Ultimate Evil. I know you are tired, and scared, and worried about your family, but this is not the time for reckless abandon and emotion. We need you, Joanie. *They* need you. Now, we must go. That was the last Lucis I brought with me. The rest are at the compound," he explained. He headed for Joanie and Chris's vehicle and Joanie scrubbed her face with her hands in frustration. Her heartrate began to slow and the anger boiling inside of her lowered to a simmer in the pit of her stomach. The others began filing into the cars, as she tried to regain her composure. Chris pulled her into his arms and cupped her face with his hands.

"Hey, look at me," he urged.

"I'm sorry. I don't know what happened."

"It's okay. I get it. That thing was trying to get in our heads."

"Well, it worked. I guess I'm not as strong as you are."

"What are you talking about? Joanie, it knew exactly what to say to you. It knew things about you. It knew what buttons to push. How is that possible?"

"I don't know. I feel like I don't know anything anymore." Both of them looked up when Maya approached them.

"What do you mean it knew things about you?" asked Maya. Joanie shivered, as she thought about the haunting voice that taunted her.

"It knew about my past, that I went to Seattle, and even about Nathan. It's weird because I never talk about that stuff, about how I knew I was running from my problems…it was just creepy."

"Do you think it means something?" asked Chris.

"It could, but…and I can't believe I'm saying this again…Dominic is right. We need to get out of here," said Maya. Chris and Joanie nodded in agreement and headed for their car. Randy frowned, as he watched Dominic slide into the backseat of

Chris and Joanie's car as well. Zayneb intervened before Randy could comment on the situation.

"Your concerns are valid and noted, but you've been outvoted. We're heading to the compound," informed Zayneb. Before he could protest, she walked right by him and over to her vehicle where the rest of the Praevians were. By the time everyone was inside the cars, the ground began to quake, and a small sinkhole was forming on the front lawn. They hurried out of the driveway as it slowly grew in size. John immediately answered his phone as he turned on his car.

"Uh, John, please tell me this is you and there's just something you need to work out really quick," said Gabriella.

"Nope, definitely not," said John, as he watched the sinkhole grow bigger.

"That's not good, this is not good. Everyone needs to get out of here as fast as possible," she warned. John stepped on the accelerator and led the way. He focused his attention on the land rapidly crumbling around them and began patching it with rock and slabs of earth to provide safe passage. One by one, they sped away from the house, but Ethan and Gabriella watched in despair through the rearview mirror as their home crumbled behind them. Ethan's phone began to ring, and he answered it with the speaker enabled.

"Chris is on the line as well, Ethan. Everyone okay in your group?" asked Zayneb.

"We're good here," said Ethan.

"Joanie, are you okay?" asked Gabriella.

"I've been better, but yeah. I'm fine," mumbled Joanie. John looked back at the plot of land that once held the McCoy House. All that was left was a crater and a pile of rubble.

"How in the hell is this happening? I didn't even have time to try to…Ethan, Gabby, I'm so sorry," said John.

"It isn't your fault. Anyone got eyes on the Ultimate Evil? The last thing we need is for it to follow us. Dominic, any idea how long those Luci work? I don't see it, but it has to be behind all this damage," said Ethan.

"I have a few theories. That beast needs time to heal. It is gone, for now," said Dominic.

"Then why is the earth still quaking? I'm trying, but I can't stop all of it. It's not just coming from one place," said John.

"I don't know. There shouldn't be any sinkholes here. I checked topographic maps of the area, but if they keep popping up like that, Anderson could be one big crater soon," warned Carlos.

"Based on this, and what happened to Stacie, it appears its remnants can remain, even after it is pushed out of the light and back into the darkness," suggested Reo. Gabriella gripped the steering wheel tighter.

"Great, just great. You know, I'm starting to take this personally. Does it always have to be our house?" she asked. Ethan placed his hand in his wife's.

"We can rebuild anywhere. As long as I have you, we always can," he assured. The couple glanced back one last time at the gaping hole in the earth where their home once stood. With so much uncertainty and danger looming, only one thing was clear. The Ultimate Evil had arrived.

CHAPTER 3

Fallout

Joanie squeezed her eyes shut even tighter as she tried to concentrate on tapping into her abilities as a Seer. She knew if anyone had answers it would be Kaya, yet seeking out the original Seer was more difficult than she expected. She steadied her breathing, and tried to calm her racing mind, but to no avail. Each time she tried calling Kaya she was unsuccessful, no matter how bright her hands glowed or how hard she pushed herself. There were no white lights or whispers from a soothing voice in her head. Her head began to ache from the attempts, and she was startled when she felt Chris shake her shoulders. Her eyes snapped open, and she winced as she held her head. The room was spinning and dizzying for a moment, but she managed to refocus on the present. She rubbed her temples and blinked several times as she looked around. They were on the Praevians' jet, headed for the compound Dominic assured them they would be able to utilize as a safehouse. Carlos was flying the jet to the coordinates Dominic provided and John and Randy were sitting in the back with Victoria and Stacie. Both of her sisters had not stirred once during the events at the McCoy House and the mayhem that had transpired. Reo was still by their side, writing notes in his journal and checking on them periodically. Joanie smiled appreciatively at the man. She did not know him well, but was grateful he was there once again in their time of crisis. Zayneb and Maya were sitting across from Dominic, who seemed annoyed by their presence. Neither woman said a word to him. In fact, they acted as if he were not even there. However, it was clear that while Dominic was not handcuffed, he was most certainly not in control, or free to move around as he pleased. Unlike the two Praevians, who were casually conversing and whispering back and forth near the former Guardian, Ethan was well aware of Dominic's presence. Joanie noticed the way Gabriella kept her hand on Ethan's the entire trip, as if waiting for her husband to lunge at the man any moment. The couple was sitting toward the front of the jet and Ethan had not said a word. So much had happened and been derailed so quickly, after so many months of peace and bliss. Ethan's face wore all the stress and anger he felt, and Joanie could relate. After creating Absolution, she was sure her days as Seer were over, and she could focus on newlywed bliss with Chris. Instead, they were once again on the run and in danger, but it felt different. Nothing made sense to her anymore. Chris gave her hand a comforting squeeze, before placing a kiss on her ring finger.

"We're going to figure this out, *tesoro*."

"How could I have missed it, Chris? I should've known everything was too good to be true. It was too easy to create Absolution. After what Kaya told me, though, I thought that was it. She showed me everything about the tablet and what I needed to know about the prophecy."

"Are you sure we didn't need to bring the tablet?" asked Chris.

"No, it was simply a vessel to hold my powers and unlock my sisters' as well. It's nothing more than an artifact now. It was an impressive piece of ancient stone, but it doesn't hold any power or answers for how to defeat the Ultimate Evil because I thought we already did."

"Did Kaya actually say that?" Joanie frowned in confusion.

"What do you mean?"

"Did she say we defeated the Ultimate Evil?"

"No, because we hadn't yet. Why are you grilling me about this? I've done everything I can and didn't ask for any of this. I didn't ask to be a Natura, or a Seer, and I sure as hell didn't spend my whole life training to be one like you, but I'm doing the best I can and don't need you questioning me about my decisions, okay?" He pulled back from her and placed his hands in his lap.

"Sorry, I was just trying to help. I know how stressed you are, but this isn't all on you, Joanie. It's on all of us."

"How? I'm the one who's supposed to guide everyone and know what's going on. You're right, though, and I'm sorry. I'm stressed and I'm taking it out on you. That's not fair. I'm sorry." She reached back out for his hand. He smiled sympathetically at her as he slipped his hand back into hers.

"It's okay. I get it. I mean not the whole Seer part of it, but it's a lot. I never realized how much until recently, though."

"You grew up knowing you would someday have to save the world. I can't imagine what that was like for you."

"Honestly, not that bad. I mean, sure, we didn't have a real childhood and we missed out on a lot by not being exposed to the world, but we never doubted that we would defeat the Ultimate Evil, not once. I doubted a lot of things about humanity and if humans were even worthy of being saved by such a thing if they could allow it to consume everything so easily, but I never once doubted my abilities. Dominic wouldn't even allow such talk. We grew up knowing we were heroes. Dominic always regarded us as such. I didn't really know it back then, but there was a certain safety in that. It was clear-cut and simple. We were good, the world was bad, and we would change it by defeating someone even worse. There was an odd comfort in knowing that. There was no nuance, no second-guessing ourselves. It was black and white, right and wrong, good and evil. In that way, I guess Dominic did keep us safe from the uncertainty in the world."

"I had an amazing childhood. My parents were good people. You would've liked them. They would've loved you, but I learned very quickly in life that there's a lot of darkness in the world. Growing up in Anderson wasn't always easy."

"All the things you've told me about your experiences there, about the racism you faced, it at least makes me understand that part."

"What part?"

"Why he kept us hidden from humans. I always thought it was because he was worried about our powers and that someone would find out we were immortals, but that wasn't the only thing he worried about. I always knew humans wouldn't understand us, but not just because of the color of our skin. I still don't get it. I've read the books. I know the history of the world and yet I still don't get it."

"Trust me, I've experienced it firsthand, and I still don't understand it. Then, too, maybe that's the point. Evil is *supposed* to be unfathomable. We aren't *supposed* to understand that kind of hate."

"He's a flawed man, but at least he managed to protect us from that," said Chris.

"It doesn't matter, Chris." The words came in a whisper from Randy, who was still seated at the back of the plane. Joanie and Chris looked behind them and down the aisle to where Randy was sitting. John looked at his brother as well. Randy's eyes remained trained on Stacie, but his attention was on their conversation. Chris sighed, but nodded, as he turned back around and rested the back of his head against his seat.

"I know," he whispered back. Their enhanced hearing allowed them to communicate quietly without the prying of human ears. While it took Victoria some time to learn how to properly utilize the ability, even she found it useful, when she wanted to communicate with her sisters, or any of them throughout the house or when in public. John, Chris, and Randy had communicated that way for years. As triplets, their bond was strong, and their abilities made it even stronger. They taught Joanie, Victoria, and Stacie about the benefits of such a power as well. The loud sound of the jet engines added another level of privacy as they whispered back and forth to each other with the humans on the jet being none the wiser.

"He murdered our parents, so please spare us the stroll down memory lane and revisionist history," whispered Randy.

"I'm aware; I don't need to be reminded. It isn't revisionist history, though. Dominic's raising us doesn't change what he did. It also doesn't change that he raised us," defended Chris.

"Like I said, it doesn't matter. I don't even know why you're bringing it up," said Randy.

"We were having a private conversation. Just because you're eavesdropping, doesn't mean you are owed an explanation," said Chris.

"I wasn't eavesdropping."

"You were totally eavesdropping," informed John, which made Chris smile smugly.

"Thank you. At least someone is on my side today. Why is everyone biting my head off?" asked Chris.

"Ew, I would never bite your…"

"It's an idiom, Randy," whispered Chris. Joanie giggled and shook her head in amusement.

"You three really have to get used to human slang and sayings," whispered Joanie.

"Nope, they're weird," the three brothers said, in unison. Joanie rolled her eyes.

"Sometimes, I forget you three are triplets," said Joanie.

"Yep, we know you do," said Randy.

"Randy," warned Chris.

"Drop it," added John. Joanie frowned in confusion, as Chris shifted uncomfortably in his seat. She turned to look back down the aisle at Randy, who crossed his arms and arched an eyebrow at her.

"Okay, what am I missing?" asked Joanie.

"Nothing," Chris said quickly.

"Randy is just trying to pick a fight because he struggles to cope with his emotions in healthy, mature ways, and he's stressed about Stacie and Vic. Oh don't give me that look, Randy, you know I'm right. I even read a book about it. Psychology is a fascinating, but convoluted field," explained John.

"Don't let Maya hear you say that," teased Chris.

"Um, I'm not. That's why I'm whispering, obviously," said John.

"Okay, let's get back to Randy's comment," said Joanie.

"How about we not? *Tesoro*, we have enough going on. Plus, you're stressed. You both are. We can save this for later," suggested Chris.

"So, there's something to save?" challenged Joanie. Chris groaned.

"No, Randy is just being Randy. You know, grumpy, temperamental, petulant," listed Chris.

"Oh, bite me. Huh, I guess some sayings are effective for communication after all," said Randy. Chris turned in his seat to glare at his brother.

"Real mature, Randy," admonished Chris. John chuckled, as Chris and Randy began to bicker back and forth until Joanie interrupted them.

"Hey, I'm serious. What do you mean you know I forget you three are triplets?"

"It isn't a big deal, Joans," assured John.

"Yeah, you want to move out? Move out," said Randy.

"Damn it, Randy," whispered John.

"Expletives are still beneath you, brother," said Randy.

"And yet starting petty confrontations is not beneath you, I see," argued John. Joanie looked over at Chris, who was suddenly very keen to stare out the window.

"What does any of this have to do with us living together? We're married. Of course, we should move out. We can't all live together forever."

"Says who? The three of us have lived together our whole lives," reminded Randy.

"Randy, you live with Stacie and none of you seem to have a problem with that. Why, when it comes to me and Chris, the only couple out of all of us that's actually married, is that a problem?"

"Stace and I live mere miles from you. It's a quick run. That is very different from you taking Chris to live wherever. And I will say this, I love and care about you deeply, Joanie, but if you move my brother to Timbuktu, I will be very displeased, very displeased indeed." Joanie frowned in confusion.

"I'm sorry, what?" asked Joanie.

"I hate to agree with Randy. We all know I do…"

"Hey!"

"…but he's right. Timbuktu is too far away. I'm sure it's a great place and I respect the vast history of its region but…"

"John, what the hell are you two talking about?" asked Joanie.

"You want to move out and take Chris to Timbuktu. Stacie told us," said Randy. Joanie looked over at Chris for confirmation and he nodded. She pinched the bridge of her nose in frustration.

"Okay, wait, pause. What did Stacie say exactly? And I want to hear it from you, Chris, since you've apparently been talking about this to everyone but me." Chris sighed and turned in his seat to face her.

"When you first suggested moving out, I thought it was a great idea, but then I started to worry about being so far away from my brothers. I talked to them about it, and it just made the three of us more upset, so we asked Stacie for her opinion about it."

"We asked Vic too, but she said it was none of our business and that we should let you two figure it out as a couple. We vetoed that idea," added John.

"Vetoed?"

"Yes, it's a very effective way for us to deal with our disagreements as siblings. Dominic taught us it when we were kids. We used to argue a lot…which would lead to fights…which would inevitably lead to us using our powers and breaking things, so Dominic taught us the veto system. We each get one veto a month. The three of us split that one so we decided we each still get to keep our veto this month," said Chris.

"It's only fair," agreed Randy.

"Okay, this is beginning to feel like a fever dream. I have so many questions and there are so many rabbit holes to go down, but let's stay on track. You went to Stacie to talk about Chris and me moving out. What, *exactly*, did she say?"

"She said that she understood our concern and that it would take time to adapt, but no matter what, the three of us would always be brothers and remain close, even if you and I lived all the way in Timbuktu," explained Chris.

"There it is. I had a feeling. It's just an idiom," said Joanie.

"What?" the three brothers asked in unison. She shook her head in amusement.

"She wasn't being literal."

"But Timbuktu is a real place. I looked it up. I even mapped it out and looked at the houses there. It is a very dry, hot place," said John.

"Yeah, not looking forward to it, but I'll add a few rain showers from time to time to cool down," said Chris.

"It sounds quite nice to me. Just far," said Randy.

"Idiom!" shouted Joanie. Everyone else on the jet was startled by the outburst and she waved them off.

"As you were," she announced. Chris frowned even more in confusion.

"So, when she said Timbuktu, it was just a turn of phrase?" questioned Chris.

"Of course, it was, I'm not trying to take you all the way to Timbuktu, and I would never take you away from your brothers. I know how important they are to you."

"But you want to move out."

"Yes, to another house in *Anderson*." Chris's eyes widened, when realization dawned on him.

"Oh," the triplets said in unison. Joanie nodded.

"Yeah, moving out just means out of the house, just like Randy and Stacie. I didn't mean we had to leave the country. That's what you were worried about?"

"Well, yeah, all the books on marriage said as your husband, I am expected to provide for you. You want to move out, we move out."

"Wait, what books on marriage have you been reading?"

"The ones I found in the library. I go sometimes when you go to work."

"I really have to check in with you about your reading materials. Chris, those books are outdated, and most are based on ideals from the 1950s, not to mention they are heteronormative as hell."

"So, you don't want me to be the breadwinner of the family and bring you home bacon every day?"

"Hold on, is that why you made me a BLT the other day?"

"Well, that, and they're delicious," said Chris.

"I ate two of them," added John.

"Okay you three, listen up. You each are in committed relationships and if we survive this hellscape of a scenario with the Ultimate Evil, you're going to need to know this information. There's no one way to have a successful marriage. It isn't about gender roles, or being the sole provider. It's about loving the person you want to spend the rest of your life with and growing as people together. That's it. Chris, I love you and I want to spend our lives together. I would never come between you and your brothers. I just want privacy, so I don't have to hear my big sister having sex and vice versa." Chris sighed in relief.

"So, no Timbuktu?"

"No."

"But yes to maybe a nice house on the other side of the lake?"

"Yes, preferably." He tenderly kissed her and leaned his forehead against hers.

"I love you so much, *tesoro*."

"I love you too, and I can't wait to find a place of our own…that is, if there's a world to actually live in after everything is said and done." Chris frowned at the words.

"Joanie, we are going to figure this out. I know it's scary right now. I hate that Vic and Stacie are hurt. I hate that we need Dominic's help and I hate that we didn't see this coming, but I know we are destined to stop the Ultimate Evil."

"But what if we aren't? What if it's a bad sign that I can't connect with Kaya anymore? I thought we already defeated the Ultimate Evil, but she lied to me. Why would she give me all this hope and act like everything had been figured out if this thing was on the loose?"

"Wait, you didn't answer me before. What did Kaya actually say?"

"What do you mean?"

"You're really good at clarifying things for me, so how about you let me try? All of this is still new for you, but Randy, John, and I have been dealing with it since we were kids. Maybe you're the one misinterpreting something for once, so let us help," suggested Chris.

"Chris is right, Joanie. Let us help," said John.

"I don't even know where to start. I feel like my life has been a whirlwind since I moved back, but those journals Nathan gave me back also mean I was having visions of all this well before the night we created Absolution."

"Start from that night then. What did Kaya tell you?" asked Randy.

"She said she'd been waiting for me since the day I was born. She said the prophecy had been warped by humans over the years and then she told me to touch her hands. When I did, I saw everything about the tablet and how it would help us create Absolution."

"Did she call Dominic the Ultimate Evil?" asked Chris.

"No, but she said we would have everything we needed to defeat it. Then, I woke up and we defeated Dominic."

"No, you woke up and we created Absolution," corrected Randy.

"What's the difference?" asked Joanie. John sifted through his memory of that night and the explanations that were given after.

"It was all about the tablet," he mumbled. Chris nodded in agreement.

"Yep, and unlocking the powers of all the Naturas," agreed Chris.

"Wait, so that could mean Absolution was…does that mean what I think it means?" asked Randy.

"You three are doing that thing you do every once in a while, you know…the thing that reminds me you're triplets," warned Joanie. Chris smiled sheepishly at her.

"Right, sorry, *tesoro*. We may have figured something out. It doesn't exactly explain why you can't reach Kaya now, but it may explain where the misunderstanding in the prophecy occurred.

Everything leads to us battling and defeating the Ultimate Evil, but the tablet never revealed who that evil was, or how it would be defeated," explained Chris.

"The inscription says 'beware of the one who splits six into three.' That's what he tried to do," said Joanie.

"So did Caleb Delaney, but he wasn't the Ultimate Evil either. The inscription on the tablet was a warning, to make sure all of us became the Naturas. I think maybe everything about the tablet was connected to the origin of our powers," said John. Joanie gulped, as realization dawned on her.

"She never said Dominic was the Ultimate Evil. She said I'd be stronger than him. She said we were born for this and that…" She swallowed hard as she remembered that fateful encounter again.

"I would say fare thee well, but I already know how this part ends," whispered Joanie. John and Randy walked over and sat down beside her and Chris.

"What is it, Joans?" asked Randy.

"She doesn't know. Kaya's job as the original Seer was to make sure I received the tablet, and we became the Naturas so we could create Absolution."

"Right, which defeats the Ultimate Evil and saves the world," said John.

"She never said that. The tablet, everything she showed me, even most of the prophecy focuses on us gaining our powers and uniting as the Naturas. We know we have to defeat the Ultimate Evil to save the world and that if we do, good will prevail over evil in the human world as well."

"Right, we created Absolution, which defeats the Ultimate Evil," said Randy.

"Nothing Kaya saw says that. We got the order wrong. It was an assumption, one that would make sense, but that doesn't make it true. We now know Dominic isn't the Ultimate Evil, but we also know we created Absolution that night. We've seen the good deeds being done all over the world," said Joanie. John cursed under his breath, as he caught on as well.

"But it's a process, it takes time," said John. Joanie nodded and he groaned as he placed his face in his hands. Randy and Chris glanced at each other and frowned in confusion.

"Okay, what are we missing?" asked Chris.

"Everything Kaya told me that night was about becoming the Naturas, not about actually defeating the Ultimate Evil. We needed to become the Naturas to eventually get to the point where we could defeat it, but that isn't what the tablet was for. The tablet held everything we needed to know to become the Naturas and create Absolution, but what if we just assumed creating Absolution meant it would be the end of it? What if creating Absolution was actually just the beginning and we started the process, but there's no guarantee it will be completed? That night, we started Absolution and set everything in motion. We unleashed a force of good into the world and pushed the odds back in our favor," said Joanie.

"But you triggered another process as well and that's why the Ultimate Evil is here now," said Dominic, as he approached. Joanie gave a nod of approval to Zayneb, who had her eyes trained on Dominic. The Praevian nodded her understanding and allowed Dominic to stay put. Randy glared at him.

"No one asked for your input," said Randy.

"Well, I am giving it, anyway. The night you created Absolution also triggered seismic activity that allowed the Luci to break free and be discovered in that lake in Asia. That was the first night in a wave of natural events that have been occurring for the past six months. I think the night you created Absolution just set everything in motion. You unleased a force of good into the world and the Ultimate Evil is now trying to unleash a force of great evil to counteract what you did," added Dominic. Randy ignored him, but John mulled over the words.

"So, you think all those events have been leading up to something?" asked John.

"I am not completely sure what it is leading up to, but I think the only way to stop it, is to stop the Ultimate Evil," said Dominic. Ethan walked over to the group.

"We're about to land at the coordinates you gave Carlos for the compound. He sees the hangar. If this is a trap of any kind, I highly suggest you call it off now," warned Ethan.

"I am well aware of what will happen to me, if I step out of line. I read up on Zayneb's impressive prowess and am sure she would be able to take me down with ease. I am not the man I was that night, Ethan. I hold no tablet and harness no powers. All I want to do is help put an end to this."

"Good, then you can start, by showing us where the other Luci are. I have a feeling we're going to need them," said Ethan. Dominic gave a curt nod and turned to make his way back to his seat. Joanie eyed him carefully and Chris did as well.

"His heartrate just sped up. He's nervous," whispered Joanie.

"Which means he's hiding something," whispered Chris. Randy smirked.

"Well color me surprised. I'm going to check on Stacie. He better have the resources Reo needs, or Zayneb won't get a chance at him," warned Randy. John followed him and Joanie looked out the window as the jet descended. A large cluster of buildings, enclosed by a sleek, metal security wall came into view. Strobes of white light pulsed in waves around the perimeter of the formidable wall and Joanie felt her senses heighten as a surge of energy filled her. She wasn't sure what to expect when they landed but prepared herself for a vast range of possibilities.

o o o o o o

By the time they arrived at their destination, slivers of sunlight were peeking over the horizon. Streaks of light, mixed with smatterings of clouds, as night gave way to dawn. The hangar where Carlos landed the plane was located inside the west end of the compound. The group grabbed the belongings they managed to salvage before the McCoy House imploded and followed Dominic toward the main building of the compound. The others were on high alert and kept an eye on their surroundings, but Dominic was more disturbed about the flight.

"That was a horrible landing. If I had known you lacked a pilot, I would have enlisted one from the long list of expertly trained pilots the Guardians have employed over the years. None of this matters, if we end up dying in a plane crash along the way," scolded Dominic. Carlos rolled his eyes.

"Well, I think I did a great job," said Carlos.

"You ran over a crate," reminded Dominic.

"No, I lightly tapped a crate, because it was in the way," corrected Carlos.

"Ethan, you may hate me right now, but take my advice. Get an actual pilot. You have plenty of money and resources to do so," advised Dominic. Ethan ignored him, but Carlos did not.

"I am an actual pilot!" Dominic scoffed.

"And where and when did you learn to fly?"

"Online. The day after Maya told me we were getting a jet from the Guardians." Dominic stopped in his tracks.

"You all just fly on a plane with an amateur at the helm?" he questioned in utter disbelief. Maya rolled her eyes at him.

"Carlos is a literal genius, Dominic. He spent a week learning everything possible about being a pilot and has all of his certifications."

"So, you're telling me he went through all the proper training and went to flight training school that quickly?" challenged Dominic. Carlos shook his head and waved him off.

"Of course not, I taught myself, hacked into some databases, forged some certifications, and boom, pilot," said Carlos. It was Dominic's turn to roll his eyes, as Carlos high-fived himself.

"I am never flying on that thing again," grumbled Dominic. Ethan smirked.

"Who said you'd ever get the chance? That was a one-way trip for you. Once this is over, we'll go back to our lives and you'll go back to whatever agreement you weaseled your way into with the Guardians," called Ethan over his shoulder. Dominic used his thumb to trace the Guardian ring on his finger. It was a sign of the good-faith agreement between him and Phillip; one he planned on keeping but was not enthused about.

"That is what I am worried about," he mumbled to himself. Chris, Joanie, Randy, and John heard the comment, and glanced at him over their shoulder, but ignored it as two towering doors opened to the entrance of the main building. Two men emerged from the building and Zayneb casually placed her hands behind her back, tracing a finger over the pistol tucked into her jeans and under her leather jacket. Maya eyed the men curiously but immediately relaxed. Their stances and body language were not aggressive or on the offensive. If anything, they seemed welcoming. She was surprised by how their eyes lit up and the bright smiles that appeared when they drew near.

"You must be the Naturas. I'm…are they okay? What happened? How is this even possible?" asked one of the men when he spotted Victoria and Stacie in John and Randy's arms.

"We need to find a place for them to rest. The flight didn't help with their recovery," said Reo. The other man quickly nodded.

"Of course, right this…" Zayneb stepped in between the men and Reo.

"Reo, wait. We need to make sure the area is secure first. We've taken enough chances by coming here," whispered Zayneb. He nodded his understanding, but Randy frowned.

"You're the one who wanted us here in the first place. Now, you have doubts?" asked Randy.

"I don't doubt it was necessary. We were right to leave. We had no choice. Doesn't mean we shouldn't check the place out first," said Zayneb. Chris nodded in agreement.

"She's right. Let's take a beat," said Chris, as he used his enhanced vision to survey the place. One of the men smiled even more.

"The Naturas! I can't believe it's actually you. I...wow," chuckled one of them. Joanie had to stifle her laugh, as the man pulled Chris in for a warm embrace. Chris stiffened at the action and frowned. Before Chris could, the other man pulled them apart.

"Forgive him, it isn't every day we get to meet the saviors of the world."

"And who are you, exactly?" questioned Gabriella, as Zayneb and Maya scanned the perimeter. Ethan smiled fondly at the men.

"This is Archie and Henrik. I can't believe you two are here. I never would've imagined in a million years we would be the group standing before the Naturas today. What are you doing here?" asked Ethan. He chuckled when the men ran over to hug him. Ethan glanced over at Zayneb and Maya. The women gave him a nod and Carlos gave them all a thumbs up as he scrolled through his device.

"The place is clean, and they aren't decoys," informed Carlos. Ethan clapped both of the men on the back.

"Of course, they aren't. I'm just surprised they got wrapped up in all of this. We all went to school together. It's been decades. How have you been and since when do you work for the Guardians? Dominic told me as such, but I wouldn't have believed it, if I didn't see you standing here now," asked Ethan.

"Well, technically, we don't work for them, but you know how it is. They tend to make offers that are hard to refuse," said Henrik.

"And pay more than can be denied," added Archie. Ethan pulled his phone out of his pocket as it buzzed and smiled politely.

"I need to take this. I'll be right back," said Ethan. Dominic rolled his eyes.

"Tell Phillip I said hello," said Dominic.

"Phillip? Why would he be calling again?" asked Gabriella, as Ethan walked away to answer the call.

"He always did play favorites," grumbled Dominic. Gabriella wanted to press the issue, but Henrik and Archie's chuckles caught her attention.

"Still jealous of the Golden Boy. Good to see some things never change," teased Henrik.

"I am not jealous, and we are not children anymore. This is not high school. We need to focus on the task at hand," reminded Dominic. Maya nodded in agreement.

"Yeah, speaking of which, where are we?" asked Maya. Carlos pulled up a map on his device and showed her their location.

"Manitoba, east of Winnipeg, and right where that patch of forest is supposed to be. This place is off the grid, but nothing is off the grid for me. I already sent our location to the safehouse overseas as well," informed Carlos. Zayneb smiled proudly at him.

"You took the proper precautions. I'm impressed," said Zayneb, as she clapped him on the back.

"Of course I did! I'm not an amateur," he assured.

"Except when it comes to flying," mumbled Dominic. Carlos waved off the comment.

"I know the protocols, Zay. We've been over them plenty. I even passed your quiz, remember?"

"Did you lock down the safehouses?" she asked.

"Obviously."

"Re-route the servers?"

"Naturally."

"Turn off all the lights at the house before you left?" Maya cleared her throat to hide her laughter, as Zayneb smiled smugly at Carlos and his eyes went wide. He quickly pulled out his phone, typed furiously, and pressed several buttons. Once his device notified him the lights had been turned off remotely, he smiled and straightened back up.

"Of course, I did." He chuckled, as Zayneb scowled playfully at him. Reo leaned over to Zayneb to whisper in her ear.

"Hate to break up the party, but I still have two patients who need medical attention."

"I'm aware. They will receive it once the place is deemed secure," assured Zayneb.

"I thought you already did that?" She winked at him.

"Almost done," she whispered back, before locking back in on Henrik and Archie.

"So, just outside of Winnipeg. This is a pretty impressive compound. I'm guessing the Guardians had it built?" said Zayneb. Archie nodded.

"Yes, and I assure you this is a secure location. The perimeter, including a mile radius of the surrounding forest, is equipped with security measures to ensure there are no breaches and everything here is state-of-the-art," informed Archie. He gulped when Zayneb began to circle him and inspect his stance.

"Not military, definitely not a fighter. Your partner is trained, though. Ethan knows him and so does Dominic. Former Guardian, maybe?" assessed Zayneb. Archie's eyes widened in surprise and Henrik bowed his head in acknowledgment.

"How did you know that?" asked Archie. Maya smiled adoringly at her wife.

"She's very good at what she does," informed Maya. Henrik pulled Archie over to him and gave Zayneb a warm smile.

"I assure you neither of us are Guardians. We aren't here to cause trouble, only to help," assured Henrik.

"I hope for your sake that's true," said Zayneb. Ethan walked back over to the group and gave Zayneb a nod of confirmation.

"All is well. Phillip was checking up on us and had a few updates of his own. We'll get to that in a bit but don't worry, Zayneb. This is a safe place," said Ethan.

"Let me guess, Phillip told you? You're putting a lot of faith in that Elder Guardian," warned Zayneb. Dominic smirked.

"Like I said, always highly favored," said Dominic. The others glanced back and forth between the two men as the tension returned, and they tensely stared at one another. Ethan gave Dominic a curt nod.

"In the grand scheme, Phillip is a good man. I don't completely trust him, but he has no reason to lie at this point, unlike you. He assured me the Luci are in your custody."

"That they are," said Dominic, as he crossed his arms. Ethan crossed his arms as well.

"Show them to us."

"You have already seen one," he informed. Ethan shook his head in disbelief.

"I knew it. I knew you were lying about having them here. There's always a technicality with you!" The two men began to argue, and Gabriella did her best to intervene, but both were more than happy to unload on the other with angry words. Joanie paid them no mind, though. Instead, she nudged Chris and John. Randy noticed her eyes were trained on the massive tower positioned at the center of the compound. She held her hand out and closed her eyes as she took in a deep breath.

"What is it?" asked Chris.

"Don't you feel that?" she asked. Chris closed his eyes as well and slowly nodded as a smile crept onto his lips.

"What is that?" asked Chris. John and Randy closed their eyes and focused on the low hum coming from the tower. Pulses of waves emitted from the elongated building and washed over the compound. They all sensed the energy from the tower.

"What's in that tower?" asked Joanie. Dominic smiled smugly.

"That is what I was trying to explain before Ethan lost his temper. You have already seen Luci on the premises. It is what makes this location so secure. That tower is being powered by a Lucis that is sending out energy waves to protect the perimeter. As long as everyone remains here, you are safe. I did not lie, Ethan. I meant every word. This is a safe place for everyone here, but especially the Naturas. Everyone can hunker down and our focus should turn to helping Victoria and Stacie recover as quickly as possible. The world is vulnerable and up for the taking as long as the Ultimate Evil is out there. We need every Natura at full strength for it to be defeated," informed Dominic. Reo nodded in agreement.

"Good, finally! So, can I have some help getting these two inside? I was told you may have a place to run tests and assess the next steps of their treatment," said Reo. Henrik nodded and approached John and Randy, but stopped in his tracks when both men took steps back. They held Victoria and Stacie protectively in their arms and made it clear by their expressions that they still did not trust the stranger. Henrik put his hands up and smiled sympathetically at them.

"I come in peace. I just was going to get the stretchers for you. The compound is equipped with whatever medical supplies they may need," he explained.

"Stretchers aren't necessary. We'll be taking them wherever Reo needs to treat them and will be by their sides the entire time, so if Dominic has put you up to something, I highly recommend standing down," warned Randy. Henrik nodded his understanding.

"Trust me, I get it. You don't trust him or the Guardians. You have no reason to, but I'm not a Guardian. Neither is Archie," said Henrik.

"But you have ties to them. It's the only way you would even know about us," said John.

"Yes, but let's just say we severed those ties long ago. I'm here because I want to help *you*, not them," assured Henrik. Reo cleared his throat to interject.

"And you believe you have the equipment to do so? What about imaging tests?" asked Reo.

"We have an entire medical bay and testing center. X-rays, ultrasounds, MRIs…"

"Ideally, I would run PET scans on both, but I suppose I could work with that."

"We have a PET scan in my lab that you can use."

"Wait, you have all of that on-site?" asked Reo.

"And much more, this compound was built to be self-sufficient and provide us with all the resources necessary in such a time of crisis. That includes a fully equipped medical facility and two laboratories. Right this way," said Henrik. John and Randy scanned the area one more time for any signs of danger, before following Reo and Henrik into the main building of the compound. Ethan smiled appreciatively at Archie as he looked around.

"This place is quite impressive. Why do I have a feeling it was your doing?" asked Ethan.

"The bunkers underneath were built decades ago, but when Phillip reached out with his concern that the Ultimate Evil would arrive soon, Henrik and I got to work designing a structure formidable enough to withstand whatever forces may arrive. I based it on various architecture from different civilizations, but of course with the technological advancements only the Guardians could provide," explained Archie. Carlos let out a low whistle when he spotted the drones hovering above the compound.

"Those are military-grade. Whoa, what does that building over there house? The way it's outfitted must be for peripheral subsystems. There are servers in there, right?" asked Carlos.

"Good eye! The compound has its own server room on a secure, fortified network with access to anything you may need. Dominic informed us that the Praevians have a cyber intelligence specialist. I assume that's you?"

"I've hacked into some of the most secure bases in the world. Most don't even come close to this level of tech. You're seriously telling me you found a way to incorporate the power of a Lucis into your security system? Ethan says a Lucis is like nothing of this world. How did you manage to reverse-engineer it and figure out how to do that?" asked Carlos.

"When Phillip contacted me, I went in search of the Lucis while Henrik drew up plans for the compound. We have drones, satellites, and cameras to keep the place under constant surveillance. There are weapons to confront any type of intruder and we have artificial intelligence tracking the perimeter to alert us to any threats. After I found the first Lucis, I gave it to Henrik to study. It took time and we may have accidentally destroyed one in the process, but he figured out how to utilize the Luci and implement their energy into the security system," said Archie.

"Wait, you destroyed one? Are you out of your minds? Those things are too rare to just waste and you *accidentally destroyed* one?" asked Ethan.

"Thank you, my thoughts exactly," said Dominic. Archie rolled his eyes.

"Henrik needed to test it. He's a scientist, after all, and we did figure out how to house its energy in the process," defended Archie.

"That's really impressive," said Carlos. Gabriella still was not as enthused as the youngest Praevian.

"Definitely impressive, so you and the Guardians have been secretly working on this for a while? Just in the middle of nowhere in case it was needed? How convenient," mumbled Gabriella, as she continued to look around.

"Not convenient, but necessary, Phillip grew wary of…well…Dominic. This was his backup plan; a compound that could hold off the Ultimate Evil if something went wrong," informed Archie. Ethan smirked, as he glanced over at Dominic.

"Grew wary? That's one way of putting it. Phillip just told me he suspected for a while that Dominic had lost his way and was plotting something. I guess you weren't as good at keeping your betrayal of the Brotherhood as hidden as you thought you were. He originally planned for it to be a bunker for the Guardians and their families, but based on how everything has played out, he believes it can be of more use to us. He assured me we can stay here for as long as we want. Gabby, I know you don't trust Phillip, but he's rooting for us to find a way to help the Naturas end this," explained Ethan.

"Well, I would hope so. If we fail, everyone in the world dies, including him," said Gabriella.

"No pressure there," mumbled Joanie. Gabriella smiled sympathetically at Joanie.

"Sorry," said Gabriella. Joanie shrugged.

"You aren't wrong," she assured.

"Okay, so under this place there are bunkers that were built for Guardians and let me guess, only Guardians, no one else allowed?" asked Maya. Dominic gave a curt nod.

"And their families, yes," he answered. She smiled slyly as she began to circle him and he sighed, knowing she was analyzing him. Ethan smiled as well when Maya made a show of looking Dominic up and down.

"So, the Guardians built a bunker for their families in case the so-called Elements failed, and the Ultimate Evil destroyed the rest of the world? You were all just going to hide like cowards in here and watch it happen, weren't you?" questioned Maya.

"For the record, I never planned to hide anywhere. I always knew my place was beside the boys, but yes, that was…an option. I will be the first to admit that the Guardians are…well…*were* imperfect and it was an imperfect system," conceded Dominic.

"Well, I'm not so sure the Guardians are no longer in play. Look at this place, it's built like a base. We all know who the soldiers would be," said Zayneb.

"I will have you know the only ones left to focus on the cause are Phillip and Trenton. The Brotherhood has disbanded and even Ethan knows it to be true. It is over. Centuries worth of a Brotherhood is over. All we have left is now in the hands of you Praevians," said Dominic.

"We're really supposed to believe these are the last resources and shows of wealth of a Brotherhood who was in existence for centuries? That ring on your finger suggests otherwise," challenged Zayneb. Dominic swallowed hard, as he looked down at the ring on his finger.

"This ring was given to me by the Elder Guardians in charge at the time of my vesting ceremony. I keep it for sentimental purposes. Anyway, where are my manners? It has been a long night, and I do not know about the others, but I am starving and could use some breakfast. Come, let us head inside," suggested Dominic. He sighed when Ethan grabbed his arm.

"This isn't a house call, and you still haven't shown us the rest of the Luci. I know you're up to something. You always are, so show us the rest of them," said Ethan. Dominic jerked away from him.

"Well excuse me for focusing on everyone's well-being. You know the Luci are here, and that I used two already to defend against that monster. Much has happened, it has been a long night, and no matter how long we have prepared for it or how stubborn you may be, I know a moment for us to collect ourselves would be helpful. Victoria and Stacie are getting the attention they need. The facility here is the best money can buy. All we can do now, is wait until they recover. Are you really going to starve yourself to prove a point?" challenged Dominic. Gabriella stepped between the two and looped arms with her husband.

"I hate to admit it and you know that I do, but he's right. We're exhausted and while I know I won't be able to get any sleep knowing that monster is out there, breakfast would be a good way to regroup. There's not much we can do until we figure out how to help Stacie and Vic," said Gabriella. Ethan glanced over at Zayneb and Maya, who both nodded.

"I agree with Gabby. What better way to get to know more about the compound and those in it than breaking bread with them?" encouraged Maya. Ethan gave a curt nod at Dominic and followed him into the compound with Archie and the rest of the Praevians. Chris pulled his wife into his arms as she looked out at the sun peeking over the horizon. He rested his chin against her shoulder.

"Breakfast does sound nice. Ethan's right though. Dominic is always up to something," said Chris.

"That's why we'll keep an eye on him. John and Randy aren't going to leave Vic's or Stacie's sides, so we need to be the ones making sure Dominic isn't trying to betray us, again. I still can't believe this is happening. Chris, if Stace and Vic don't wake up..."

"They will."

"How can you be so confident?"

"Well, one, they're immortals. Two, I trust Reo and his ability to help them. And three, while I wasn't initially on board with all of this, if Dominic thinks we should be here, we probably should. Dominic is only out to serve himself and now that the Ultimate Evil is here, that means we are his only hope for survival." She turned in his arms and cupped his face with an adoring smile as she gazed into his eyes.

"You know, it's okay to not hate him. It's like you said before, he raised you. Even after all he's done, there's a part of you that still thinks he has good in him, deep down, don't you?" He sighed and nodded.

"I know it's ridiculous, but yeah, I do. I want to just pretend like he never existed, but now that I know he's alive and has been working on all of this with the Guardians and whoever these men are that complicates things in my head. Knowing he's not the Ultimate Evil changes things a bit for me too. I know he's extremely flawed and misguided, probably in more ways than I could ever imagine, but he still raised us to defeat the Ultimate Evil. So, it's starting to look like we may have to work with him to do it. It may give us our best shot and with Vic and Stacie hurt, we could use as many people helping us as possible right now. A part of me hates him, but another part…it just…doesn't. Sorry, I know I'm not making sense."

"No, hey, that makes more sense than thinking you can just flip a switch and hate someone who has been the only person you could trust since you and your brothers were kids. I get it."

"You do?"

"Of course."

"Well, I guess that makes one of us. Emotions are annoying," he grumbled. She nodded in agreement and hugged him. While she had no trust in the man, her instincts were telling her what Chris's instincts were telling him. If they wanted to defeat the Ultimate Evil, working with Dominic may be a necessity.

○ ○ ○ ○ ○ ○

Joanie watched from the window in the hallway as Reo and Henrik rolled equipment over to the gurneys where Stacie and Victoria rested. She felt a bit aimless without her sisters by her side, and watching them lay so still left a heavy pit in her stomach that made her nauseous. She managed to keep it at bay when they were at the McCoy House, but hours had passed and neither Stacie nor Victoria had shown signs of improvement. She felt her heart race and thunder in her chest. Memories from years ago that were buried deep in her psyche of the emergency room waiting area in Anderson filled her mind. She remembered waiting with Stacie and clutching her hand while Victoria spoke with the doctors. Anderson County Hospital was small, compared to other medical facilities, but it felt massive as it held her whole world in that moment. Joanie jumped when someone tapped her shoulder, pulling her from the dark memories of the past. She spun around to see Carlos standing there with a sheepish smile.

"Sorry, I didn't mean to scare you. I figured you would hear me."

"My mind was wandering a bit." He glanced over her shoulder and through the glass window where John and Randy were sitting with Victoria and Stacie.

"They're going to be okay."

"You say that as if you know. Are you sure you're not the Seer?"

"They're fighters and also immortals, which I'm sure works in their favor."

"Maybe just a bit."

"Yeah," he said, with a chuckle. He noticed the way her hands fidgeted, as she averted her eyes from the room.

"Why aren't you in there with them? Sorry, that was a stupid question. It's none of my business. I don't know why I…"

"No, it's okay. It's a question I keep asking myself. Even though I know the answer, my feet won't move. I know it sounds ridiculous but machines like that, all this medical stuff, it just gives me the creeps. It's sterile and too bright from the fluorescents. It reminds me of hospitals, and I hate hospitals."

"Because of your parents, right?"

"Wait, how did you know…"

"Ethan told us." She slowly nodded.

"Yeah, because of my parents."

"Well, you're in good company, because I hate hospitals too."

"Because of your parents, or something else?"

"No, uh, I don't have any of those. I grew up in the foster system, but before you give me pity eyes or apologize, which people tend to do for some strange reason, like they're the ones that abandoned me and my sister or something, based on what I found out about my birth parents later, I'm pretty sure we dodged a bullet. They left me and my sister at a hospital when we were kids. I was barely a year old, and my sister was three. The system definitely sucks, though."

"Yeah, I've heard. So, is that why you hate hospitals?"

"I hate them for a lot of reasons, but no, not just because we were left at one. My sister Carla and I were in the system for a while. We bounced around a lot. The older we got, the harder it was to stay together, but we managed for the most part. Carla is the one who got me my first video game and my first laptop, so I owe her a lot. There's no way I would've embraced who I really am without her."

"So, she's responsible for you hacking into a government agency's database at nineteen?"

"How did you…Ethan?" She nodded.

"Ethan. He didn't tell me which agency though."

"That's classified," he said, with a wink. She giggled.

"Fair enough."

"I have the best big sister in the world, well three big sisters, technically, if you count Zayneb and Maya. I got really lucky to have so many people in my life looking out for me, but there have been some dark times along the way. Carla protected me, even ran interference, and made sure she took the blows so I wouldn't sometimes. We ended up in a really bad foster situation when we were teenagers. They were emotionally abusive, but our foster dad, if you could even call him that, well, he would drink and fly off the handle. I guess his wife figured better us than her. One night, it got really bad. I tried to stand up to him, but he was a lot bigger than me. I was only fourteen. Me and Carla ended up locking ourselves in her room. He smashed all the phones in the house, but I snuck his laptop and sent an SOS. The cops came and we ended up at the hospital. I got banged up, but Carla was pretty bad off. She had to stay a few days and I never left her side. Everyone tried to make me leave, but I always found ways to sneak back in. I stayed there and ate gross hospital food and wandered around for three days, just trying not to think about what I was supposed to do if she didn't make it. She was the only one to ever take care of me. I didn't know what my life would be like if she wasn't there to do that anymore."

"I'm sorry, Carlos."

"There's that apology and the pity eyes," he teased.

"No one should have to go through that. You were just kids."

"Yeah. So, that's why I hate hospitals. Luckily, she got better. We were removed from Mr. and Mrs. Douchebags' home and ended up moving in with a really nice older lady until we were both old enough to go it alone. I'm really glad that new organization is looking into foster care reform. That's when I knew Absolution really was working. No one ever thinks about foster kids or just how messed up the whole process is; not enough to do anything about it, anyway. Before I joined the Praevians, I used to try to patch the system up from time to time, flag a bad foster home for the authorities, swap assignments in databases to keep siblings together, erase a juvie record here or there, but I knew it was too big of a problem to solve alone. That's why I joined. Gabby recruited me. They all became my chosen family and gave me the stability I didn't even know I needed."

"What about your sister? Do you get to see her still?"

"I've always had to stay under the radar, but I fly her out to an island sometimes for a holiday so we can meet up. We don't get to hang as much as either of us would like, but we see each other when we can."

"If you grew up to be a hacker, what does she do for a living?"

"Grand larceny. There's honor amongst thieves, right?" Her eyes widened.

"Yeah…sure, I'm sure there is. Sorry, I wasn't trying to judge…" He chuckled.

"I'm just messing with you, Joanie. She works for Doctors Without Borders. Her job keeps her pretty busy. That started to change a few months ago, though; yet another good thing about you creating Absolution. You know, I didn't really believe in all of it at first. I was definitely skeptical about the whole voodoo of it all, good versus evil, a Big Bad ready to destroy the world, but you start seeing people do stuff right out of comic books and colorful flakes floating in the sky, and a guy starts to believe that maybe Ethan and Gabby weren't on shrooms when they came up with that origin story after all." Joanie shook with mirth. They heard footsteps behind them and turned to see Chris approaching.

"Food's ready," he informed. She smiled appreciatively at Carlos.

"Thanks for the talk. You coming?"

"No, they set me up in a pretty sweet lab, so I'm going to get to work on some things I'm looking into. We have some contacts that I want to check on and make sure they made it to a safe house. Maya and Zayneb will save me something. They always do."

"Don't work too hard," she called over her shoulder, as he headed down the hall. Chris wrapped an arm around her.

"You okay? I know it's hard seeing Vic and Stacie like that."

"Yeah, it is, but sometimes you just need a pep talk from a Praevian to get through the day," she informed.

∘ ∘ ∘ ∘ ∘ ∘

To say breakfast was awkward would be an understatement. Dominic and Archie cooked the early morning meal, and everyone gathered in the main dining hall of the compound to eat. Henrick joined them, but Reo stayed behind to monitor Victoria and Stacie. Chris and Joanie brought the Praevian a plate of food as a thank you and made sure John and Randy ate as well, before heading to the dining hall to eat with the others. Joanie admonished herself for not getting out of dodge like Carlos did and made a note to follow the genius's lead in the future about such things. Gabriella glanced at Ethan, who was sitting back in his chair with his arms crossed. His eyes were fixed on Dominic, who was more than happy to eat his meal leisurely. Maya and Zayneb shared a look, but remained quiet, as the awkward tension sucked the air out of the room. Gabriella kicked Maya under the table and the Praevian jumped, causing her wife to giggle. Everyone looked over at the couple and Maya playfully glared at Gabriella as Zayneb spoke up, knowing Maya was too exhausted to play mediator.

"So, Henrik, Archie, care to fill in the gaps a bit? You say you aren't Guardians and we figured we killed everyone crazy enough to work with Dominic, so what does that make you?" asked Zayneb. Joanie choked on her orange juice and Chris's eyes widened at the comment, but he kept quiet. Henrik and Archie weren't quite sure how to respond. Gabriella shook her head in amusement.

"See, this is why Maya usually does the talking," said Gabriella. Dominic glared at Zayneb.

"That is not funny," said Dominic. Zayneb shrugged.

"I'm not laughing. They still didn't answer my question. You said you knew each other when you were younger, but that doesn't really explain what you do now." Archie took a sip of his water to clear his throat before speaking.

"I'm a paleontologist and Henrik is a mechanical engineer. Phillip hired us to help with the Luci and this compound. He knew he could trust us because of our ties to Dominic and Ethan," explained Archie.

"Archie was one of our classmates and Henrik was in the Brotherhood with us until the bigotry of the Guardians reared its ugly head," added Ethan. Dominic dropped his fork and glared at Ethan.

"I thought you were not up for trips down memory lane," challenged Dominic.

"That was last night, before my house got sucked into a sinkhole. Today's a new day," said Ethan.

"Bigotry?" asked Chris. Archie smiled sadly at Henrik as the engineer spoke up.

"I was disavowed from the Guardians. My father chose to remove me and while I was torn apart by that at first, it was the best thing that could've ever happened to me," said Henrik. Archie reached out for his hand and gave it a comforting squeeze before returning to his meal. Chris frowned in confusion.

"Your own father betrayed you in such a way? Why?" asked Chris. Henrik sighed, as Dominic averted his eyes.

"Because people like me aren't allowed to be Guardians."

"People like you?" asked Chris. Maya laced her fingers with Zayneb's.

"People like us, Chris," she added.

"What do you mean? Why would anyone not…" He looked down at the rings on Maya and Zayneb's fingers and the rings on Henrik and Archie's fingers as well. Realization dawned on him, and he shook his head in disbelief.

"That's absurd!" declared Chris. Ethan kept his eyes trained on Dominic.

"Yep, it really is," agreed Ethan. Dominic rolled his eyes at Ethan's glare.

"Of course, you act as if I am at fault for it. I did not make that archaic rule," reminded Dominic.

"No, you just followed it. You could've changed it when you took over, when those narrow-minded enough to believe in such hate were no longer in power, but you didn't, because you believed it too," accused Ethan.

"I believe nothing of the sort, and I am offended by such an allegation. I am not homophobic and disagree with those who are. Henrik and Archie are good men. I am glad they found each other. But the rules were clear and I warned them that if Henrik's father found out…"

"That's not what I'm asking, Dominic. Why didn't you change the rules when *you* were in power?" challenged Ethan.

"They were already gone by then and Henrik had made his choice, which I respected then and still do."

"You still aren't answering my question. So, I will ask it again," said Ethan in a menacing tone. Henrik and Archie glanced over at Dominic, as the others watched the two men's tension boil to the surface.

"They were your friends. They stood by you. They stand by you now, after all of your betrayals and corruption. We know of the old ways, but you were in charge, so why didn't you change it?"

"Because I took an oath and even once the Elder Guardians were gone, the main rule, the rule that applied to not only Henrik but you as well, was still one I still believed in. Love, no matter with whom, was forbidden. It was seen as a complication at best, no matter the sexual orientation. I see the error in that logic now, but at the time…"

"Just admit that you were a coward!" Dominic slammed his fist onto the table.

"I was a child!" he shouted. Everyone fell silent, as he tossed his napkin onto the table and stood to leave.

"It appears I have lost my appetite," he mumbled, before marching out of the dining hall. Gabriella looked at Ethan, as he pushed his chair back from the table.

"I never had one in the first place," said Ethan, before storming out as well. Gabriella sighed. It surprised everyone when Archie let out a low whistle.

"Those two haven't changed one bit, I see," said Archie. Henrik chuckled.

"Well, at least they aren't going to blows in the cafeteria this time," teased Henrik.

"Or making us choose sides," added Archie.

"Ethan and Dominic used to fight a lot?" asked Chris. Henrik and Archie guffawed.

"Are you kidding me? Sometimes, it felt like that's all they did," said Henrik.

"I've only been told the abridged version about his time at the school for Guardians, but I'm curious. What was Ethan like back then?" asked Gabriella. Archie smiled at the memories.

"It wasn't just for Guardians, but yes. We went to a very exclusive private school for the elites. It was extremely difficult to get into. You had to be in certain circles to even know about it. My parents were both well-known researchers and I was considered gifted from a young age. No one ever believed me, but I really was more interested in the academics than the social networking the school provided. I never wanted to be a Guardian. I just happened to be friends with them. I wasn't even supposed to know about the Brotherhood, but Henrik told me. Back then, that was a huge deal. Outsiders weren't supposed to know, no matter what. I had my suspicions pretty early on and figured they were ditching me after school because of some secret group or something. Secret societies weren't exactly a secret for us, but I had no clue just how exclusive their group really was. I had known Dominic for two years before he introduced me to Ethan and Henrik. In that time, he never said a word about it, but I could tell he was worried about something. He always put so much pressure on himself. When Henrik told me, I realized just how much pressure Dominic was really under," explained Archie.

"So, Henrik, you were born into the Brotherhood?" asked Maya.

"Yes, just like the others. I moved from London and transferred to the school, while I started my training as a Guardian. Dominic and I were in the same program and grade, so my father asked his father to show me the ropes for the first year. I became friends with him, Ethan, and Archie, but Archie was always different. It was hard coming from another country and culture. Everything operated differently, even the racism. I was the only Black kid in my class, so you can imagine what it was like also being gay back then. I wasn't ready to come out of the closet, but Archie was there for me every step of the way as a friend. I always had a crush on him, but I never thought he had one on me. I knew that telling my father meant there was a chance I would no longer be able to become a Guardian, but I needed to live my truth. I refused to hide anymore, so after we all graduated, I told him."

"And he refused to accept you? I don't understand that," said Chris.

"My father was one of the most powerful men in the UK. Status meant everything to him, even more than family. In his mind, I was the one who had betrayed him. He would've preferred if I had kept it a secret, married a woman, and had a family with a lover on the side, but I never wanted to live that way," explained Henrik.

"And you shouldn't have had to. How could the Guardians call themselves a Brotherhood if they couldn't even be loyal to their own?" asked Chris.

"I asked myself that a few times after everything went down and the answer always seemed to be true for the Guardians and most other institutions like them. People like us have always been seen as a threat to the ideals of institutions like that and our refusal to lie, to conform or obey based on their values. That makes us rebels in their eyes. All I have ever been is me, and I don't regret the life I have because of it," said Henrik. Archie kissed Henrik's cheek and Joanie smiled at their interaction.

"If the Guardians don't accept you, then why are you helping them now?" asked Joanie.

"We aren't. We're helping you, and ourselves in the process. This world has a lot of changing to do, but we don't want anything to happen to it, before it has the chance to continue changing. Our loyalty is not to the Guardians, or even Dominic. It is to you, the Naturas, because you're the force of good we can believe in, when the world makes us question why we should even care," explained Henrik. Maya frowned in confusion.

"Something I still don't understand is how the Guardians could forbid love. I mean, sure, from an emotional standpoint, the whole rule is a mess, but even more so biologically. The Brotherhood was all about lineage, right? They carried on the lineage by having kids, so how could they be upset with Ethan for loving Gabby, or any of you for wanting to find love? Ethan and Dominic both had mothers, so how did they reconcile that so-called forbidden emotion?" asked Maya.

"All marriages to Guardians were arranged. Each young woman chosen was through a program administered by the school," informed Henrik.

"Oh, so they went full-on Stepford Wives? That tracks," said Maya.

"And the red flags for the Brotherhood just keep piling up," added Zayneb. Gabriella smirked.

"Talk about an understatement. Ethan told me about it and it's even more warped than it already sounds. My parents shielded me from all of that stuff when they told me about our lineage as a kid. I couldn't imagine going through any of it," said Gabriella. Henrik shook his head at the very thought.

"Outdated doesn't even begin to cover it. Becoming a Guardian ensured our lives would be loveless if we stayed on that path, but wives of Guardians had it even worse, in my opinion. At least Guardians get recognition and are honored in the Brotherhood. All women, except for Kaya as the Original Seer in the prophecy, are essentially erased. The assistant of the headmaster ran the program for the girls. Our school wasn't just for boys. Plenty of generations of wealthy, powerful families went there, and most weren't Guardians or part of our programs. Much like with the Guardians, lineage played a huge role in who was allowed to join and be selected by the parents of a newly appointed Guardian to become their wife," explained Henrik.

"That's a cult if I've ever heard of one," said Maya.

"Tell me about it," mumbled Gabriella.

"But, Gabby, you're still a descendant of Gabriel. Wouldn't that have made you a prospect? Why would they even have an issue with you being with Ethan?" asked Joanie.

"Because my parents refused to place me in that world and play nice in it. Long before that was even their choice, my family left the

Brotherhood. My parents fell in love the old-fashioned way. They met at Woodstock," said Gabriella.

"I read about that! Joanie played me some music from the era. It is quite fascinating," said Chris.

"They met watching Santana and were in love by the time Jefferson Airplane took the stage the next morning. I didn't grow up in the world of the Guardians and I'm really glad I didn't. That's how I knew Ethan and I were soulmates. Even though our paths weren't meant to cross, they still did. I don't know if I would have been chosen by his parents if I went to that school, or if I would have even joined the program, but I know we were meant to be no matter what. Our love proves that."

"So, most of the Guardians were married, but they weren't allowed to love their wives?" asked Chris.

"Exactly. It was a business transaction more than anything. I always believed it was one of the reasons most of our fathers were so cold. Everything about their lives was molded by the Brotherhood. The way the Brotherhood viewed marriage and parenthood proved that. If nominated, girls from the school could join a program like we were in to become Guardians. It was treated like some prestigious honor, but even back then I knew it was disturbing. When they graduated, they were added to a list that a newly appointed Guardian's parents would choose from, and the two would get married. If they had a kid together, the mother would raise them until the age of ten, and after that, the children would be isolated from their mothers to focus on training to become a Guardian," explained Henrik. Archie smiled sympathetically, as he thought about his friends and husband.

"He doesn't really talk about it, but I think that's why Dominic refused to ever get married. There was a lot of pressure on him to have a wife chosen for him and continue his bloodline, but he refused. It's the only thing I can ever remember him standing up to his father over, and I think it's because he didn't want to be like him. He never admits it, but I think Dominic never wanted to raise a child in a loveless marriage. Dalton pressured him for years about it, but once the boys were found, it didn't matter as much. Carrying on the lineage became secondary to raising them. He never wanted kids, but he ended up with them anyway," explained Archie.

"So, there was an entire program dedicated just to making wives for Guardians and forcing young adults into loveless marriages? Yep, that's a cult," said Maya. Henrik winked at her.

"Trust me, there's a reason why most of us have daddy issues," said Henrik.

"The amount of therapy that Brotherhood needs would bankrupt even their deep pockets," added Maya.

"I guess that explains some things about Dominic. What was he like back then?" asked Chris. A small smile crept onto Henrik's lips, as he thought about the young man Dominic used to be.

"Serious, studious, and very moody. He could brood with the best of them, but I don't know. I kind of got it. Dominic had to try hard at everything all the time. He wasn't the social butterfly Ethan was. He had to study every day to keep up his grades, while living up to the standards and training schedule his father obsessed over. He was socially awkward but driven. It always felt like he was pushing himself just to stay afloat and trust us, that school was full of sharks, but none of them compared to his father. He was a ruthless man. He was quite callous really and cut from the same cloth as my father. I guess that's what made them so close. Dominic's father and mine had an alliance for years as Guardians and always managed to get their way, except about one thing, Ethan," explained Henrik.

"Ethan said some of the older Guardians didn't want him to be the one to guide the boys," said Gabriella.

"His lineage made him the chosen one, but my father and Dominic's tried everything they could to make sure Ethan wouldn't be seen as that. They weren't the only ones with an alliance though. Ethan's father and Phillip were best friends, and their word was bond in the Brotherhood. At the end of the day, Ethan was the descendant of Eamon. His lineage was tied to the founder of the Guardians and the first Seer. My father and Dalton hated it, but that's all that mattered."

"Did Ethan brood as much as Dominic did as a teenager?" asked Gabriella. Henrik rolled his eyes and Archie sighed dreamily.

"Go ahead, I know how much you want to," teased Henrik. Archie smiled even more as he remembered the first time he saw Ethan McCoy.

"Ethan was the Golden Boy. He was handsome and charismatic. He had a way of making people gravitate toward him and knew how to put us at ease. I remember the first time I saw him at school. I swear he walked on air, and everyone immediately noticed him. He strolled right in, and it was like he owned the place, which was really saying something. Everyone at that school was someone, but Ethan was even bigger than that. Back then, I may have had a small crush on him," admitted Archie. Henrik smirked.

"A small one?" asked Henrik.

"Fine. I thought he was perfect, but I wasn't the only one. Everyone there either wanted to be in his circle or on his arm. He was funny and charming..."

"Everything Dominic wasn't," suggested Maya. Henrik gave an impressed nod.

"Oh, you're good. That was precisely it. That was always the point of contention, whether they realized it or not. Dominic was determined, studious, and obedient. He aspired to be the best Guardian ever. Ethan was boisterous and rarely studied, but he still managed to ace exams that the rest of us had to pull all-nighters to study for. He excelled in the training program, school, socially, you name it. He handled it all with ease. Ethan was always a natural at everything," explained Henrik.

"Yeah, he was annoying that way," added Archie.

"Sounds like they couldn't have been more different. Were they even really friends or more like frenemies?" asked Joanie.

"Don't get me or Archie wrong. They were friends; best friends, just complicated at times. They understood the gravity of the situation they were in and related to each other over it. They both had the same goal, to be Guardians, and Dominic vowed to always be by Ethan's side. When Ethan realized the time had come and what we thought were the Elements were born, he almost crumbled under the pressure. To be honest, none of us thought it would happen in our generation. It hadn't happened for centuries, so we didn't have much reason to believe it would be different for us. Each generation had an Ethan who would be ready to step in to guide the Elements when the time came. It just never did," explained Henrik.

"Dominic was there for Ethan. He was like an older brother to him, and they agreed that Ethan would guide the boys and Dominic would guide him," added Archie. They all jumped when they heard Dominic's voice.

"I hope you two are not gossiping too much," said Dominic. He sat back down at the table and Archie smirked.

"No more than you do," teased Archie.

"I will have you know, I do not gossip," assured Dominic. Archie took a sip of his water.

"Sure, right, never. I just know everything there is to know about the Naturas from Henrik, right?" teased Archie. Dominic playfully rolled his eyes.

"I suppose I have sent a correspondence or two, but only to catch you up," conceded Dominic.

"Filling in an outsider? That's forbidden, remember?" asked Ethan, as he approached the table. Everyone was silent as he and Dominic glanced at one another. The silence hung between them a moment longer, before Ethan decided to break it.

"I'm sorry for bringing up the past. It doesn't matter. It is what it is at this point, and we have bigger fish to fry," said Ethan. Chris perked up.

"I know that one," he whispered to Joanie, who shushed him. Everyone looked at the couple and Joanie blushed.

"We're still working through idioms. Anyways, you were saying? I believe this is the part where Dominic apologizes for being…well…him," said Joanie. Dominic scoffed at the notion, but sighed when they all gave him a look.

"Fine, as I have already said, I am not proud of my past, or the past of the Brotherhood. I cannot change that, but I am here to help now…which is why I have to confess that I have not been completely honest with you," said Dominic. Ethan threw his hands up in exasperation.

"I knew it," said Ethan. Randy and John darted into the room. They had been listening to the conversation from their perches by Stacie and Victoria's side. Randy glared at Dominic and Chris had to hold his brother back as he yelled at the man.

"What did you do now, Dominic?" shouted Randy.

"Nothing to earn such rage from you, so calm down. I just may have embellished a bit about the number of Luci at our disposal," he confessed.

"How much of an embellishment?" asked Ethan.

"We may only have one left to use," revealed Dominic. Ethan frowned in confusion.

"What? How? Phillip said there were six. Where are the rest of them?" questioned Ethan. Maya noticed the way Archie and Henrik glanced at one another, as Dominic continued.

"Yes, but we are talking about ancient artifacts. Things happen. However, I promise you are all safe here. The Ultimate Evil will not dare try to penetrate these walls and the protective barrier around the compound ensures that," said Dominic.

"You mean the barrier made up of Luci? What exactly are these Luci made of anyways? I felt the energy as soon as we landed. It's quite powerful. I know you said earlier that a Lucis was being used for the tower as part of a security system, but how?" asked Joanie.

"Essentially, the machine sends the Lucis particles through the air. The Luci are made of some sort of nanoparticles that I've never seen before on earth," explained Henrik.

"Since we're running low on Luci, how long will the machine work and what happens when it runs out?" asked Zayneb.

"That's the fascinating part. It won't run out. It has an unlimited source of power," said Henrik.

"I thought the Lucis Dominic used lasted only a few seconds against the creature?" asked Ethan.

"Yes, but that's because the creature absorbs the energy. That's what injures it. The machine we are using stabilizes the Lucis and only needs to emit a few nanoparticles at a time. Without a power source sucking all the energy at once, Luci particles have restorative components that can cycle through and create more particles," explained Henrik.

"Which means it can work on a continuous loop. Are you sure?" asked Zayneb.

"It has been tested multiple times for several days at a time. It never runs low on energy," assured Henrik. Gabriella sighed, as realization dawned on her.

"Okay, so that means the good news is, the compound truly does act like a fortress to protect everyone inside. The bad news is, if we leave the compound, there is only one Lucis left in case of an emergency, which means we have to be careful not to come in contact with the Ultimate Evil again," said Gabriella. Before Archie could speak, Dominic interrupted him.

"Precisely, which is why we should stay put and rest. Nothing good could come from leaving the compound until Stacie and Victoria have recovered," advised Dominic. John gave a curt nod.

"Speaking of which, I need to go check on Vic," said John.

"I'll go with you," said Joanie. Randy followed them from the dining hall so he could check on Stacie, hoping for good news about her condition.

o o o o o o

Joanie felt the pit in her stomach grow once again, as she stood in the doorway of the room where Reo monitored Stacie and Victoria. Randy and John watched closely as Reo studied the scans he had conducted on both of them. Randy was doing his best to be patient as they waited, and John paced back and forth, as he focused on the sound of Victoria's steady heartbeat.

"Well?" asked Randy. Reo turned the screens so they could see the results of the scans.

"I conducted PET scans on each of them. In regular humans, the scans can give me a better idea of how a patient's organs and tissues are functioning. I'm able to see even more with Stacie and Victoria. I believe these flares of white running throughout their bodies show the energy you tap into as Naturas. You see how it flows in all directions and into every part of the body but is more concentrated in their hearts? I think this scan is showing how your powers operate inside you," informed Reo.

"Why do the scans look different from each other? Why is one darker than the other?" asked John. Reo sighed, as he pointed to one of the scans.

"This scan represents Victoria's body. The white flares are consistent throughout her body, but more concentrated in her chest. That confirms what I suspected. Whatever happened during her encounter with the Ultimate Evil drained her energy, but she's recovering. The energy that fuels you as immortals is healing her body, but it will take time." Randy swallowed hard, as he looked over Stacie's scan. The white flares on the scan were not as concentrated or bright in her chest, while blots of gray covered her hands and arms.

"What do these images mean? What about Stacie?" asked Randy.

"Whatever that matter was that managed to infiltrate her system is spreading and attacking the energy that helps her cells rapidly regenerate and heal. Unfortunately, I was correct in my previous assessment. It's spreading like a virus and while her system appears to be trying to fight it off, it is continuing to spread," informed Reo.

"Then stop it. Treat her," demanded Randy.

"I've tried different treatments and antidotes that they have stored here. This compound has an impressive amount of medications and chemical elements, even some experimental ones I didn't know were available. Her body has not responded to any of them."

"Then try others. You just aren't looking hard enough," said Randy.

"I have tried everything that could treat the human body or even act as some sort of catalyst, including radiotherapy, but she isn't technically human, Randy. What infected her isn't of this world."

"What are you saying?" asked Randy, as the lump in his throat grew. Reo's shoulder slumped in defeat.

"I don't know how to stop it from spreading and I'm not sure how long her body can fight it off," he confessed. They looked up as they heard Joanie's gasp. The tears in her eyes made Randy shake his head.

"No, this isn't...you don't have to cry, Joanie. She's going to wake up. He doesn't know what he's talking about!" assured Randy. John tried to place a hand on his brother's shoulder, but Randy shrugged it off.

"She's a Natura. She can bring people back to life. She'll find a way to heal herself..."

"Randy," said John, as he tried to comfort his brother. Randy profusely shook his head.

"If she can't, then I'll find a way myself," he declared, before marching out of the medical bay. Reo looked down in shame.

"I'm sorry," he whispered. John put on a brave smile.

"We know you've tried everything you can. We appreciate it," said John.

"I'll continue to monitor her and do whatever I can to keep her comfortable. It's spreading slowly, so there's still time to find an alternative treatment. I just...I can't find one at the moment. I promise I'm..."

"We know you're doing your best. Randy's just upset. You should take a break. Take a moment for yourself," suggested John. Reo slowly nodded and exited the room, while Joanie shook with sobs. She wrapped her arms tightly around her body as John walked over to hug her. She crumbled in his arms, and he kissed the top of her head.

"This isn't over. Maybe defeating the Ultimate Evil can heal her," suggested John.

"We don't know that and Kaya won't even answer me. Everything we've been told says all of us will be needed to defeat the Ultimate Evil and there are only four of us to even try to fight."

"We'll find a way," he vowed. She nodded, as she wiped her tears from her cheeks.

"Yeah, you're right. We will. You should go take a moment too. You haven't left Vic's side and should take your own advice."

"I'll be fine. Where's Chris?" asked John, as he peered out into the hallway.

"I'm not sure. He said he wanted to look into something, but I mean it. Go regroup. I'll stay here with them."

"Alright fine, I guess I should go check on Randy, anyway. Are you sure you'll be okay?"

"Yeah. Thanks, John." He kissed her cheek.

"Always," he assured before heading in search of his brother. Joanie took a shaky breath and closed her eyes, as she tried to muster up the courage to enter the room. The pit in her stomach and anxiety made her hesitate, but she took a step inside and grabbed one of the empty chairs. She put it between the gurneys her sisters laid on and sat down. She stared at her hands in her lap for a moment as she collected her thoughts.

"I don't know how to do this without you two," she whispered. She let the words hang in the air, before continuing.

"I never wanted this. All I wanted was to come home and be with the two of you. Falling in love with Chris is the best thing that has ever happened to me, but how dare that come at this cost? What kind of universe would even allow it? We get to find our soulmates, but only because we've all been placed on this earth to endanger our lives? That's just cruel. I found this amazing love, but have to sacrifice the other people I love in the process? I can't do that. I'm not strong enough for this. After we lost Mom and Dad, I couldn't deal. You both know that, so how in the hell am I supposed to be okay now, especially since this is my fault? I knew that damn nightmare meant something, but I didn't want to, so I ignored it and now you both are..." She gritted her teeth in anger and let out a shaky breath.

"I can't do any of this without you. I just can't," confessed Joanie.

"You can, but you don't have to." Joanie jumped to her feet when she heard Victoria's voice. The oldest McNamara winced, and let out a groan, as her eyes slowly opened. Joanie let out a cry of happiness as she rushed to her sister's side.

"Vic?" Victoria gave a tired smile as Joanie hugged her tightly.

"In the flesh...well...sort of. Easy, Joans, I'm a bit sore." Joanie pulled back from the hug and immediately began checking her over.

"But, you're okay? What hurts?" asked Joanie. John darted back into the room and Joanie smiled as he pulled Victoria into his arms. Randy was not far behind him.

"Easy," whispered Victoria. John pulled back and let her go.

"Sorry," he said. She smiled adoringly at him.

"Hi, big guy." Relief washed over him and, for the first time since he had found her unconscious, he allowed himself to feel the full weight of almost losing her. Victoria cupped his cheek, as tears slid down his face. She wiped them away and tenderly kissed him.

"I'm okay," she assured. Reo jogged back into the room and sighed in relief, as he held up his phone.

"I was hoping it wasn't a false alarm. I synced the monitors to my phone to alert me of any changes. How are you feeling, Victoria?" asked Reo, as he scanned over the monitors to check her vitals.

"Tired, but also like I slept for a year. What happ…where's Alex? Wait, something killed…"

"He's okay, Vic. Stacie was able to heal him," assured Joanie. Victoria sighed in relief, but it was short-lived when she saw Stacie from the corner of her eye.

"What the hell happened? Stace?" asked Victoria. Reo tried to stop her, as she yanked the wires off and leapt off of the gurney. She winced and held her midsection as she doubled over from exhaustion and fatigue. John wrapped his arms securely around her to keep her upright.

"Easy, you're still weak," warned John, but she ignored him.

"What happened to Stacie?" she asked again.

"She was able to save Alex, but got infected by something in the process," said Joanie.

"It's some black substance that latched onto her when she was healing him. It's some sort of poison," added John.

"From the Ultimate Evil, right? Looks like oil, but moves like something out of a horror film?" mumbled Victoria as she slipped her hand into Stacie's. Randy's eyes widened.

"How did you know that?" asked Randy.

"I saw it. Hell, I felt it." Reo grabbed a stethoscope to examine Victoria, as she sat down beside Stacie's gurney. She kept her hand in her sister's but allowed the doctor to assess her.

"Vitals are good, but I would like to run some more tests. In the meantime, anything you can tell us about what happened when you encountered the Ultimate Evil may be helpful. It could help us better understand what's happening to Stacie," informed Reo.

"I'll fill you in if you fill me in. Where are we? Where's Chris? Did he get hurt too?" Randy sat down on the other side of Stacie and John pulled a chair over to sit beside his fiancée.

"No, he's fine, just roaming somewhere around here. Did you guys find him?" asked Joanie.

"No, but he's probably just clearing his head. The compound is fortified with a Lucis, remember? I'm sure he's just taking a walk or something," said Randy. Victoria frowned in confusion.

"The what is fortified with a what now? Where are we? This definitely isn't Anderson County Hospital." Joanie sighed.

"Yeah, you've missed a lot," said Joanie.

"Understatement of the century," mumbled Victoria, as she looked around. She wasn't sure where she was, but she had a feeling much had happened since her encounter with the Ultimate Evil.

○ ○ ○ ○ ○ ○

Chris watched Dominic head into a smaller building, adjacent to the main structure of the compound. While he knew they needed

Dominic's help, he still did not trust the man and decided to follow him. He needed to make sure their former mentor was not plotting anything nefarious. He slipped into the double doors before they could slide shut and followed Dominic down a corridor. His former mentor entered a dark room and flipped on a switch to illuminate the space. The circular room was a library with a litany of books adorning two stories. He climbed the stairs and headed over to a small bar on the upper level of the room to pour two glasses of liquor before walking back down the stairs and over to the fireplace. Chris heard the double doors behind him open again and hid at the other end of the corridor as Archie made his way into the library. Dominic handed Archie a glass and Chris peeked around the corner as the two men conversed.

"Still a whiskey man I see," said Archie. He took a sip of the drink as he sat down on the sofa. Dominic chuckled and grabbed a remote to turn on the fireplace.

"Some things never change," said Dominic. He sat down in a chair by the fireplace and sighed.

"Thank you for helping me with all of this," added Dominic.

"I'm not doing it for you."

"Well, I will say thank you anyway."

"Why are you lying to them, Dominic?"

"This does not concern you, Archie."

"The hell it doesn't! This isn't your decision to make. We're talking about the fate of the world."

"Yes, we are, and I am the one who spent the past months trying to explain to everyone that I am not the Ultimate Evil, but no one listened. I was the one who knew none of us would be prepared for when it arrived, so I do not need a lecture about it or what it can do. I am the one who sat in that makeshift prison where Trenton locked me away. I am the one who remains steadfast in this mission while the rest of the Guardians washed their hands of everything. No one wanted to believe that I was not the Ultimate Evil and now we are all in danger, so yes, I am calling the shots, and how I do that is none of your concern." Archie shook his head in disbelief.

"Why do you always need to be in control? You can't control everything, Dominic. You aren't the one meant to save us, but you're right. Some things never change." Archie finished his drink and placed the glass on the coffee table before standing up to leave.

"You have told a lie or two yourself," called Dominic. Archie crossed his arms as he turned to face him again.

"What are you talking about?"

"You may have your hard feelings toward the Brotherhood now, but we both know there was a time when you would have done anything to join it."

"Not anything. I would've never given up Henrik for it. I will always choose him, just like he always chose me."

"That does not mean you are not relishing the fact that you are here, essentially in the capacity of a Guardian, while the others are not."

"I'm not relishing any of this, but I am happy for Henrik. He deserves to be here. He's more of a Guardian than the others ever could've been."

"Maybe, but do you know why you were never chosen to be one?"

"You mean besides the archaic rules about bloodlines and heteronormativity?"

"I can admit that the Brotherhood's selection process was flawed and misguided, but no, that was not the reason. To be a Guardian, one must be willing to put all other distractions aside and accept a very hard truth. The world is a harsh, dark place, and control is how we survive in it. You were always too passive, too docile; while that made you a kind friend, it was also your weakness. I appreciate all you have done, but your services are no longer needed, and neither is your input. I highly suggest you remember who pays you and the agreement you signed. So, like I said, this is none of your concern." Archie smirked.

"You know, I never believed the rumors, or even what Connell said about you, that you lost your way, that you let the power corrupt you. I told myself that wasn't the boy I used to know. You were my first real friend at that school. Henrik may have been the one to tell me about the Brotherhood, but you trusted me enough to bring me into your world. That's the boy I remember, so I figured he had to have his reasons and now I know. You may think you're some savior, some Guardian with a noble cause willing to do whatever for it, but all I see is that same, scared little boy hoping no one sees just how broken his daddy made him. You aren't the hero here, Dominic, so stop trying to justify your obsession with trying to be one." Dominic took a long pull of his drink as Archie walked out. He waited until he heard the closing of the double doors again before throwing the glass into the fireplace. The flames roared and flickered from the splash of the alcohol, and he scrubbed his face in anger. He took a deep breath to regain his composure. Chris gulped as he watched his old mentor plop down on the sofa in silence. Chris darted out of the building and went in search of his brothers and Joanie. He sensed his wife first and headed into the medical bay.

"We need to talk about...Vic, you're awake!" She giggled when he ran over to hug her.

"Yeah. I hear I missed a lot."

"You could say that," he agreed. Carlos jogged into the room with a device in his hand and Henrik on his heels. Ethan, Gabriella, Zayneb, and Maya filed in as well. Reo alerted them that Victoria was awake, and each embraced the oldest McNamara.

"I have news," announced Carlos.

"As do I, but Vic, we're glad you're awake. Reo says you'll make a full recovery, but how are you really feeling?" asked Ethan.

"Worried about Stacie and the fact that thing is still out there," said Victoria. Ethan smiled sympathetically at her.

"Same here, which is why we all need to talk about a couple of things. I got another call from Phillip with an update. He's keeping tabs on the evacuation efforts being carried out in Anderson and the surrounding areas. The military's resources are running thin," informed Ethan.

"Wait, they had to call in the military? What about law enforcement?" asked Victoria.

"I requested military assistance from Phillip and apparently it was the right call to make. All hands are on deck, but this isn't the only evacuation happening. There are several disasters happening around the country and not enough people to help get everyone to safety. Phillip knows how important the people in Anderson are to you, so he wanted us to know just in case there's a way to help. I told him the Praevians would head there to assist with the efforts," informed Ethan.

"I'll go too," said Joanie.

"I will too. John, Randy, I understand if you need to stay with Vic and Stacie. We'll make sure Anderson is evacuated safely," said Chris. Victoria scoffed.

"I'm not staying put. I'm going too," said Victoria.

"No way, Vic. You just woke up and are still too weak," said John.

"We can't just do nothing, as Anderson continues to be attacked. That monster is behind this and it's there because of us, John. We brought danger to my hometown. I grew up there and I'm still the sheriff. I can't just watch it be torn apart."

"I know, which is why we'll go, and you'll stay here to recover," said John.

"John…"

"Vic, I can't lose you again. I'm not strong enough for that. We're going to stop this thing and keep Anderson safe, but I can't do that unless I know you're safe too." She sighed, but slowly nodded as she rubbed her chest.

"Fine, okay, I guess I am still a bit sore and tired," she conceded. His eyes widened.

"Wait, really? That's it? No big argument or pouty lips about it?"

"Would you prefer if I made it into a big argument?" she challenged.

"No please," he said quickly. She smiled and gave another nod.

"Then I won't. I'll stay here with Stace while you go help. Besides, I can admit I still need a bit more energy before going back out there." Randy turned to Reo.

"Have there been any changes in Stacie's condition?" asked Randy. Reo shook his head.

"There's been no progress, but the infection has not spread either since the last scan."

"Then I'll go too. I know how much Anderson means to Stacie. She would want me to help if I can," said Randy. Carlos walked over to Ethan and Gabriella as he typed furiously on his laptop.

"Good, because we're going to need all the help we can get. I've been tracking every anomaly and weather pattern around the globe. This is what I've mapped out so far," said Carlos. He showed them the screen, which had a map of the globe with several red dots.

"So, all of those red marks are what exactly?" asked Maya.

"Natural disasters; all severe, all with casualties, and all considered ongoing threats," said Carlos.

"Phillip did mention that it's gotten pretty bad out there," admitted Ethan.

"Why didn't you tell us about this sooner?" asked Joanie. Chris glared at Dominic as the man entered the room and spoke before Ethan could answer the question.

"Because he knows what we all do. None of this matters, unless the Ultimate Evil is defeated. You cannot worry about such things. If you defeat the creature, you will save the world. That must be your sole focus," explained Dominic. Ethan rolled his eyes.

"I didn't say anything, because I wanted to make sure Vic and Stacie were safe. With Vic finally awake and Stacie being monitored here, we can come up with a plan," said Ethan.

"The plan is simple. The Naturas must stay here where they are protected from the Ultimate Evil, until Stacie returns to full strength," said Dominic.

"That isn't an option if people are dying. How bad is it out there?" asked Randy. Chris noticed Archie slip into the room as Carlos explained what he had been keeping an eye on.

"I think we're dealing with a global catastrophic event," confessed Carlos.

"But how? We created Absolution. The world should be getting better," reminded Victoria.

"Actually, Vic, we're starting to think that's not how it works. You may have been right that night. It was too easy. We were talking on the way here and we think we *started* Absolution that night. All the changes and acts of good around the world show that, but we also think it was only ever supposed to be a start. I'm not sure, and I can't seem to connect with Kaya to ask, but I think we have to defeat the Ultimate Evil to *complete* Absolution," explained Joanie.

"Okay, I guess I really did miss a lot," grumbled Victoria.

"That's my working theory as well, which is why you need to stay here and focus on Stacie, not put yourselves in harm's way," argued Dominic.

"How bad is it, Carlos?" asked Zayneb.

"Well, if I'm right, it's not a coincidence that the areas being impacted the most are also known for fracking, drilling, and heavy pollution. The arrival of the creature seems to have sped up what corporations and people around the world have already started. The sheer number of natural disasters is destabilizing the earth's core to the point of creating an even bigger event and reaction in the core that could lead to the mass extinction of every species on the planet. It could wipe out everything," explained Carlos.

"So, truly a global catastrophic event," said Ethan.

"Public safety alerts have been blowing up my phone, and several are coming from near Anderson," said Carlos.

"But why is the Ultimate Evil still targeting Anderson? We're not even there anymore, so what's drawing it to the area?" asked Joanie.

"I think it has its sights on the water supply. Wildfires, earthquakes, tornadoes, there have been natural disasters happening all over the world for months in very strange patterns, but no attacks on water supplies until last night. I did some digging about the water reserves mentioned in that news report we saw at Ethan and Gabby's house. The reservoir is connected to the Missouri River. If the Ultimate Evil finds a way to contaminate that water, it could do far more damage than just in Anderson. That's the largest river in the U.S. If it contaminates that river, it could spread to other waterways and eventually the oceans. It could poison our drinking water and every main water supply in one fell swoop," said Carlos.

"We have to intercept it," said Chris.

"No, you do not! Without Stacie, you are not capable of putting an end to all of this. I am all for the Praevians going to help with the evacuation and I will go as well. I still have some contacts in FEMA, but it is too dangerous for any Natura to leave this compound. There is too much at risk. I cannot allow you to leave," said Dominic.

"You don't *allow* us to do anything, and it would be in your best interest to remember that," warned Randy.

"You are not thinking rationally. I understand your connections to Anderson, but that is the problem. This is all bigger than one town. The entire world is relying on you to make decisions for the greater good," argued Dominic.

"Don't lecture us about the greater good!" yelled Randy.

"Then start acting like you understand what that actually means! This is simple! The six of you are needed in order to defeat the Ultimate Evil. At this point, that is not my guess, or opinion, or even advice. It is a fact! You cannot defeat it alone and are not going to be able to until Victoria is stronger, and Stacie is healed. You cannot afford to encounter the Ultimate Evil now, Randy. It will kill you and if so, the world will be lost. So, yes, the smart option is for you to stay here where you are protected by the Lucis barrier." Randy glared at him.

"Anderson can't afford to be left defenseless. You want us all to hide here, but what about the fact that the Ultimate Evil is out there destroying the world as we speak? If we all stay hidden behind this shield, it will deter it from attacking us, but not from attacking everyone else. All that does is shift its attention to the vulnerable. With Anderson evacuating, every human there would be essentially led to slaughter if it goes after them. It has killed before. We have no reason to believe it wouldn't kill again. There may not be an earth or people left to save if it continues this path of destruction," argued Randy.

"I understand that but…" Victoria interrupted Dominic.

"No, you don't. I watched it kill Alex in cold blood. There was no reason. It said itself it didn't need one. It kills because it can. It hunts and preys on people. It doesn't care about your morals or ethics or these philosophical debates about who should be sacrificed for the greater good or not. It will kill everyone in Anderson," said Victoria.

"Which is why the Praevians and I should go. There is one Lucis left, and I will use it, if necessary, but you are our last line of defense. If one of you is harmed, that is it. Forget just Anderson. The world is slaughtered. This is not a philosophical debate, Victoria. I understand what is at stake. This is about real life-and-death situations. Call it cold-hearted if you want, but we cannot risk billions of lives and the fate of the world for thousands," defended Dominic. Randy crossed his arms and gave Dominic a challenging look.

"And who is going to stop us from leaving here? You? You tried that once. It didn't bode well then and we won't hold back this time," warned Randy. Dominic sighed.

"Randy, I am not going to stop you, but…"

"Good, then we're in agreement. The Praevians will head to Anderson to assist with the evacuation. Vic will stay behind, with Stacie. John, Chris, Joanie, and I will head to the reservoir to intercept the Ultimate Evil and keep it away from town. You can do whatever you like," announced Randy.

"Do not be stubborn about…"

"This isn't a discussion and again, we aren't asking for your permission! Besides, you should like our odds. Four Naturas are much better than the three Elements you assured us would be needed to save the world. If you had it your way, I would've killed Joanie and we wouldn't have stood a chance in the first place. Four Naturas? Well, that's more than you could've ever imagined," said Randy, before storming off. Dominic shook his head in disbelief.

"This is a mistake. Ethan, you must talk some sense into them before it is too late," warned Dominic.

"You can't expect them to sit back and do nothing. It isn't who they are," reminded Ethan.

"Let us hope for the world's sake who they are is enough right now. I will go prepare and be ready to depart soon." Chris stepped in front of him to stop Dominic from leaving.

"You should stay here. Your help is not needed," said Chris.

"Well, I am giving it anyway. Move aside, Christopher," said Dominic. He was surprised when Chris grabbed his arm. Joanie, John, and Victoria glanced at each other, as Chris stared his former mentor down.

"I know you are up to something. I heard you and Archie in the library, and I promise you that whatever it is, I'm going to put a stop to it," warned Chris.

"I do not know what you think you heard, but I assure you I am not the enemy here. I may not agree with your plan to put yourself in danger, but I do not want anything to happen to Anderson. You heard Ethan, all hands on deck. I am going to help." Chris glared at Dominic as he stepped around him and exited the room.

"I could always detain him. There are plenty of rooms to hold him in. Just say the word," offered Zayneb. Chris sighed and shook his head.

"If he's up to something, I would rather have him close by to keep an eye on him, than here with Stacie and Vic. He can come," grumbled Chris. Zayneb gave a curt nod, knowing the Naturas were still not enthused about the presence of the man.

○ ○ ○ ○ ○ ○

Dominic closed the door to the room where he had been residing since Phillip released him from Connell's custody. He grabbed the titanium briefcase specifically made for him and placed his thumb over the biometric security screen. The case beeped and unlocked. He sighed when he opened it. The briefcase that had once held five Luci was empty. He shook his head at the predicament he was in. He never expected to have to use two of the most valuable artifacts in existence when he headed for Anderson, but the Ultimate Evil was even more powerful than he had anticipated. He closed the case and locked it again, before staring down at his Guardian ring. The moment it was jerked from his finger by Trenton and he was tossed into an empty room, would be forever etched in his mind, just like the moment Phillip returned it to him. He played with it on his finger and thought about the first time the ring was placed on it. He had never seen his father so proud of him.

"You should be careful about that logic of yours." The voice startled Dominic, causing him to clutch his chest as he spun around to see Zayneb casually leaning in the doorway.

"You will not have to worry about killing me, if you keep sneaking up like that. My heart is in good health, but I am not as young as I used to be." Zayneb smiled slyly.

"Don't worry, I'm not here to kill you…at least not yet."

"Well, I appreciate that. What are you doing here? What logic do you mean?"

"Callously sacrificing the few, for what you think will be the many is a flawed way of thinking. The people of Anderson are not pawns in a game. They are people and if you want the Naturas to trust you, you should remember that."

"It is not callous to think about the grand scheme. Sometimes, we must make pragmatic, but hard decisions to save the most people possible. It is a hard truth, but one we must accept."

"Oh, I'm aware. I used to think the same way. It made it easy to cut ties and not think about the things I'd done."

"Used to? What changed?"

"My sensibilities changed after a covert mission that went wrong. It was years ago, well before I joined the Praevians, but it left an impression."

"A covert mission, you say? For what agency? What government? I checked up on you, but it seems you had your hand in all types of…"

"I can neither confirm nor deny such a mission ever existed." He chuckled and sat down on his bed.

"I am sure you cannot. What about the mission changed your mind?"

"There was a terrorist cell that threatened to spread to a new region."

"There always is."

"Exactly. The plan was simple enough. Plant the device under the leader of the extremist group's car, blame a rival group, and get out of dodge. We wanted to cut the head off of the snake and hope one didn't grow back. But, they always grow back, and that explosive took out a lot more than the snake. Something malfunctioned and there was a lag in the detonation time. By the time the car exploded, it was in the middle of a busy intersection in the city. Hundreds of people were killed, thousands more injured."

"I see how that would leave an impression."

"My superiors assured me it was a tragic part of the job, but I couldn't shake it. I tried to justify it just like the agency did. We hit our target and casualties happen all the time, but I couldn't stop thinking about the people killed, the families that grieved the loss, and the seed of hatred that was planted because of it. Violence raged on in the region for months after that. The leader we killed was treated like a martyr. More people joined the terrorist cell, and a new leader took the place of the old and on and on it went. Hatred grew and so did everyone's justification for that hatred. I told myself I was trying to stop violence by being violent, that sometimes fire needs fire, and I still believe sometimes it does. But at the end of the day, I was in the business of killing people, actual people. Yes, many of those people earned their fate. Many of them deserved it and if I didn't stop them, they would go on to kill many more, but not all of them deserved to die."

"Sometimes hard decisions have to be made. You did not set out to kill those people."

"But they were still people and at the end of the day, we are a species of animals who are here to survive. People will do anything to survive. The family members and the community that was left in shambles after, all turned to survival. No one speaks long about casualties of war, or the cost of mass violence. We can't. If we do, it starts to ring hollow. It sounds more than callous, it sounds hateful, and before we know it, we sound like the people we want to stop, assuring ourselves that our self-importance is a worthy cause that is so much better and more moral than theirs. So, be careful with that logic of yours, Dominic. That logic tells you that you shouldn't worry about the few because the many are the goal, but war and violence are still acts of annihilation. The world is full of conflicts started by self-important men assuring others that their cause is better than someone else's, but in the grand scheme when we look back, we tend to find faults and half-truths in all sorts of places. War is annihilation. I have participated in all sorts of annihilation and annihilation is *never* an act of good."

"I think that oversimplifies the issue a bit. I know Anderson is important to them, but the world is full of Andersons. There are towns and cities and homes everywhere. By going out there, the four of them are putting the *entire world* at risk. If they risk *everyone's* version of Anderson just to protect their *own*, how is that okay? I am not saying it is easy. I am saying it is necessary." Zayneb arched an eyebrow at him.

"And who are you to decide what's necessary? Who made you the right person to make that call? You were wrong about Joanie. You were wrong about a lot of things. Let's say it is *just* Anderson and all the people they know and love there. What about all the damage the Ultimate Evil does while they hide? What about the damage *already* done? Stacie can't heal everyone, and I have yet to hear a version of the prophecy that says Absolution will bring back the dead. So, who must be sacrificed next, while you want them to hide? First Anderson, then what? The state? The entire country?"

"That's absurd."

"Oh really? What's your number, Dominic? A thousand? A hundred thousand? A million? A billion to save billions? How many people are you willing to sacrifice for your version of the greater good, and who made you the authority on that decision?"

"Sacrifice is a painful part of the process. I wish it was not and I most certainly do not wish for such things, but hard choices have to be made."

"Yeah, I've heard that before. It's why I walked away and did some soul-searching. When I first met Maya, I kept her at a distance because I didn't think I deserved her. I didn't think I deserved love after what I had done. She helped me come to terms with all of that, and being a Praevian helps me at least make some sort of amends, but it doesn't change my past, so forgive me for being wary of those who preach sacrifice. There's always someone out there, far from the violence and the inhumane acts, telling the people who are being used and exploited that their sacrifice is for a greater cause. It isn't your sacrifice to give, Dominic. That's the point. I have sacrificed my life plenty of times and I have no problem doing it again, because it is *my choice*. Those willing to sacrifice themselves for others? That's the noble act you seem to be confusing with the logic you hold. It can't be a sacrifice without free will. Telling others it is, because you deemed it to be? Well, many a war has been started and never ended that way."

"Look, I see your point. I may not fully agree with it in this context, but I see it. I have watched the world led astray by all types of institutions that assure humankind they are there for the betterment of society, while doing nothing but improving their bottom line, or only caring when it somehow benefits them. I fear the Guardians became such an institution. Maybe we have always been a way for a small few to stay in power under the guise of protecting the many, but we are dealing with otherworldly forces here, Zayneb. One person, group, or government's failing did not automatically mean the end of the entire world before. If the Naturas fail, we all die."

"I'm aware and so are they. They aren't children. They know what's at stake. They don't need you reminding them that the world is on their shoulders. You raised those boys with that fear every day of their lives and now that they finally have an ounce of happiness, it's time to fight and that happiness could potentially be snatched away. They have plenty to lose and tons of motivation to survive, so I assure you they don't need you to pressure them or to try to control their every move. You really want to help them be a force of good? Then, be what they need."

"And what is that? I am starting to wonder if I even know anymore."

"A resource, not a cynic doubting their abilities and focus. If you can't be that, then don't come." He gave a silent bow of his head in acknowledgement and Zayneb closed the door behind her as she left. He looked down at the empty briefcase beside him before focusing his attention on the ring on his finger. A small, fond smile crept onto his lips as he remembered what Phillip told him, once the Luci were found, and his ring was returned. Like the Elder Guardian said, he would see it through, even if the Brotherhood could not.

o o o o o o

Victoria tried her best to put on a brave smile and not show just how worried she was, as she watched Joanie, John, Chris, and Randy help load the jet with supplies the Praevians and Dominic planned on bringing to Anderson. The compound and hangar were stocked with first aid kits, non-perishable food items, clothing, and weapons. She knew they would have everything they needed to help safely evacuate Anderson, but the sheriff could not help but worry. John noticed the way she fidgeted, and he walked over to pull his fiancée into his arms. She was more than happy to nestle into them as he gazed lovingly into her eyes.

"I know you want to come and that this is hard for you, but I promise we'll be careful, and I'll look out for Joanie," assured John.

"Joans can take care of herself. I just…there's so much going on right now. Anderson's under attack, the world is melting down, and I don't even know if Alex is really okay. I know Stacie healed him and Ethan and Gabby visited him in the hospital. I even know it's not a good idea to call him right now. He probably has more questions than I can answer, but I just wish I knew he was really okay after everything that happened and what he knows now."

"Ethan and Gabby already checked on him again. He's been discharged from the hospital."

"Great, he's probably out there trying to lead the charge instead of heading out of town himself."

"I'll make sure to check on him while I'm there." Victoria sighed in relief.

"Really? Even though you hate him?"

"I don't hate the guy. I'm just not a big fan of his adoration for you, but I get it and can't blame him for seeing how amazing you are. I love you, Vic."

"I love you too. Make sure you come back to me, big guy."

"I will. We've been training to face the Ultimate Evil since…"

"Yeah, yeah, since you were kids. Don't get cocky. As the only one to actually face that thing, I'm telling you it's not going to be easy. I know the four of you have to go, but if you can find a way to evacuate the town and steer clear of it, do it, okay? Promise me."

"I promise," said John. She tenderly kissed him and leaned her forehead against his.

"Come home to me."

"I always will," he vowed. Dominic watched the couple from the bottom stairs of the jet and Gabriella noticed the way he observed them. Soon, his attention turned to Reo, who was saying his goodbyes to the other Praevians as well. It was clear that while Reo needed to stay behind to monitor Stacie, he was worried about not being there with his friends. Dominic was intrigued by the way the doctor ruffled Carlos's hair and Reo laughed as Carlos playfully punched his shoulder before embracing the man. Gabriella cleared her throat to make her presence known as she approached Dominic. He rolled his eyes when he noticed her.

"If you are here to threaten me, I assure you my sole purpose is to make sure Anderson gets evacuated as quickly as possible, so the Naturas can return to the compound safely."

"It's beautiful, isn't it?" He frowned in confusion at the question.

"What is?"

"How close the Praevians are. Ethan told me when all of you were younger, you had a version of that, but everything changed once you officially became Guardians."

"Well, this display of affection and the heartfelt goodbyes are cute, but they also distract from the task at hand. A force of evil is trying to end the world and we are wasting time with pleasantries."

"That, right there, is why I will never be able to hate you, even though I can't stand you."

"What?"

"The world is on the brink and yet all you can do is watch, as others find solace in the ones they love, because you're alone. You killed my husband. Stacie being able to save him doesn't change that, but no matter how hard I try, I can't bring myself to hate you because I feel bad for you." He smirked.

"I do not need you to feel bad for me."

"I never said you did, but it doesn't change anything. Dominic, I don't know if you are truly on our side or not, but what I know is that no matter how all this ends, I can say I lived an amazing life with the man I love and the amazing connections we've built along the way, while you have no one. No more Guardians, no one to love, and no one to be loved by, so no, Dominic, I don't hate you. I pity you." He gave a curt nod.

"Well, as fun as our little chats always are, we should all probably get going. I will be on the jet, whenever all of you are done with this nonsense." He turned to head up the steps of the jet, but she grabbed his arm to stop him.

"But, just so we're clear, if you ever try to kill my husband again, I will rip out your heart, just to see if it actually is as cold as you want everyone to believe it is." Dominic gulped at the words, as she clapped him on the back with a polite smile.

"Good talk as usual," she added, before jogging up the stairs to the jet. He rolled his eyes at her, before glancing at Victoria, who was hugging Joanie tightly as they all prepared to depart. He wanted to focus on the mission, but something continued to nag at the back of his mind, telling him Gabriella was not completely wrong.

o o o o o o

Anderson, and the surrounding regions of North Dakota, were in a state of chaos, much like the rest of the globe. As the jet headed for the landing strip outside the town square, Joanie took a shaky breath. Everyone was looking out the windows as the jet descended. Their bird's eye view of the region showed the devastation. Anderson looked nothing like the calm, quiet place it once was. Thousands of cars lined the narrow roads out of town, military and law enforcement vehicles peppered the area, and a hazy smog hovered in the air. As soon as they landed the aircraft at the same landing strip they used to escape from Anderson before, Joanie, Chris, John, and Randy got to work pulling supplies from the cargo bay of the jet and putting them in the trunk of Ethan and Gabriella's car. The last time they were there, they were deserting their cars and heading to the unknown location of the compound. The moment they returned, a sense of dread fell over the four Naturas, as they surveyed the area.

"Do you feel that?" asked Joanie. Chris nodded, as he kept his eyes trained on the forest in the distance.

"Yeah, I do. I felt it at Ethan and Gabby's house too," said Chris.

"I felt it on Old Mill Road. It must be close. We need to hurry up," said Joanie.

"I don't pretend to know at this point how any of this works, but if we can sense it, does that mean it can sense us too?" asked John, as he placed a crate of water into the trunk.

"Probably, which means it knows we're here," said Chris.

"Okay, but where is it? I feel like I need to be on guard, but I don't see anything. Joans, any of that Seer ability of yours picking up on anything?" asked John. Joanie clenched her jaw in frustration as she shook her head.

"No, nothing. I've been trying since we left the compound. I can't get a feel for anything, except dread, which just makes that thing even more terrifying." Chris watched Randy walk out into the field and peer into the forest in the distance. When he could not spot the figure or any signs of it, Randy sat down in the grass and closed his eyes to heighten his other senses.

"What's he doing?" asked Carlos. Dominic smiled knowingly at Randy, as he tossed his briefcase into the back of the car.

"He is allowing his surroundings to give him clues about where to start. The Naturas are at their strongest when they are immersed in nature. It is one of the reasons I thought Anderson would be good for them. Good to see at least some of my teachings rubbed off on them," said Dominic. Chris, John, and Joanie approached Randy and watched him curiously, as his hands began to glow with red light. In the distance, farther than even he imagined being able to use his senses, he detected incoherent whisperings. The sounds washed over the forest floor and lingered in hisses and whirs of noise.

"Do you hear that?" asked Randy. John frowned in confusion.

"You're going to need to be more specific. The cars honking, people arguing, military presence or…?"

"No, farther away, west of here," said Randy. Chris took a deep breath and closed his eyes, as he tapped into his heightened senses. The faint sounds of hissing and jumbled murmurs caught his attention.

"What is that?" asked Chris. Joanie and John closed their eyes to listen as well and Joanie gulped when she heard it.

"That's it. It has to be. I know that part of town too. It's already at the reservoir. We have to go," informed Joanie. Chris and John nodded and followed her, as they headed in the direction of the noise. Dominic grabbed Randy's arm before he could leave as well.

"This is not what we agreed on. Facing the Ultimate Evil now will only work in its favor. How can you not see how dangerous this is? I raised you better than…"

"You raised us to fight the Ultimate Evil and now you want us to cower?"

"I want you to be smart about this!"

"If we can sense it, I have no doubt it can sense us as well. It already tracked us here once. We aren't going to let it disrupt the evacuation efforts or follow us into town," argued Randy.

"If it wanted to disrupt the evacuation, it already would have. Randy, listen to me…"

"We're going. If you want to help, go help the others. If not, stay out of our way." Before Dominic could protest again, Randy darted away. He pushed his feet as fast as they could go and spotted Chris, Joanie, and John entering the forest. He managed to catch up when they suddenly stopped at a cliff, overlooking the vast bodies of water on the horizon. The reservoir dwarfed Lake Cameron to the west of it. The dam towered over the Missouri River Basin, and the water flowed into the manmade waterways.

"Where do we even start?" asked John.

"It's close, I can feel it," said Randy, as he searched the area. Joanie's gasp caught their attention, and she pointed toward the entrance of the dam.

"There! Wait…what's it doing?" she questioned, as she spotted the figure standing on the dam by the waterway. Chris's eyes widened when he spotted it as well. The ghastly figure was stoic as it stood with its arms splayed out and palms facing the water. Its eyes were closed, and tendrils of onyx liquid flowed from its chest. The thick tendrils of viscous liquid slithered from the chest of the sinister creature to the bodies of water.

"That's the service reservoir. It's the main source of clean water for the entire region. If that's contaminated, it'll taint all the water in Anderson and spread across the entire state," said Chris.

"If not farther," added John.

"Fan out. Let's try to come at it from different directions and surround it. We have to stop it before it does any more damage. We might not be able to eliminate it yet, but we can stop it from doing even more harm. If we get a chance to capture it, we should try and figure out a way to get it back to the compound. If we can't, though, at least try to slow it down. In other words, do your worst," said Randy. Before they could stop him, Randy sped off in the direction of the figure.

"I don't have a good feeling about this," said Joanie.

"I know, but Randy's right. We have to at least try to lure it away from here," said Chris. The three of them hesitated for a moment but followed Randy. The closer they got to the grotesque creature, the more their bodies responded and put them on high alert. As they reached the dam and surrounded the figure, they each felt a shiver and chills went down their spines. The tattered parka it wore was soaked with black ooze and dripped at the seams. The sable substance flowed in each direction in tendrils and seeped into the concrete of the dam. The tendrils of onyx fluid inched closer to penetrating the water. Chris's hands glowed with blue light as he focused on the water and pushed it away from the dam. The currents of water splashed onto the shores below as he harnessed all his ability to keep the water away from the dark matter.

"We're going to need a plan here. I can't exactly move all the water out of the way," warned Chris.

"Maybe we should go get a Lucis," suggested Randy.

"Dominic said there's only one left," reminded John.

"Even more reason to use it now. The Lucis can stun it and we can do the rest. Maybe with the Lucis, we can put an end to this now," urged Randy. Joanie shook her head.

"We know how this has to end. It will take all of us," said Joanie.

"We don't know anything anymore, except we have to stop it and that thing is going to kill everyone in its path. Chris, keep the water safe. John, Joanie, one of you go retrieve the Lucis from Dominic. I'll keep it distracted," instructed Randy. John shook his head.

"That isn't a good idea," said John. Chris gritted his teeth as he concentrated even more on the dam.

"Uh, maybe we should've had this discussion before intercepting the thing. Someone better do something because I can't hold this for long. It's too much water," said Chris. Randy took a step in the figure's direction.

"Randy, don't," warned Joanie.

"It hurt Stacie. I'm not giving it a chance to hurt anyone else, not if I have anything to say about it," said Randy. Joanie cursed under her breath, as Randy sped in the direction of the dark force. John and Joanie raced after him, as Randy summoned lightning from the sky. He hurled it at the being, causing it to jolt backward and crash to the ground. The impact of the collision made the dam crack in half, as fissures of the concrete fractured and splintered. The figure made it back to its feet. Randy seethed with rage, as he approached it with red light glowing from his hands.

"I've been waiting for you, Randy. The all-powerful Natura of lightning and fire. Your energy is quite remarkable," said the figure. Balls of fire formed in Randy's hands as he burned with anger.

"How do you know my name?"

"I know all of your names. Why wouldn't I?"

"What did you do to Stacie?" The figure tilted its head in fascination.

"The bringer of life? I suppose she *is* missing."

"Don't play games with me! Tell me how to help her and I'll make this painless." The figure looked around the dam and sighed.

"Only four Naturas. I suppose Victoria's absence was to be expected. Something else happened though, something that works in my favor? The balance must finally be swayed. The fates have chosen."

"What did you do to her?!" Randy roared. John and Joanie darted over to hold him back, as the Ultimate Evil sighed.

"Nothing that can be undone. It is fate. Not even the great Naturas can undo fate. Know that I take no real pleasure in her death. The power, the energy, it's truly magnificent, but she must've gotten in the way of what must be done. All of you are simply in my way, but I guess some things…well…they just are." Randy let out a scream of rage as he blasted the being with another bolt of lightning. The Ultimate Evil crashed to the ground with a grunt and let out a hiss of pain. The ghastly figure closed its eyes and let out a low rumble as it made it to a seated position. Joanie gulped, as the whispers they detected before grew louder and the tendrils thickened. Its hands glowed with black light and the onyx ooze dripping from its clothes slithered toward them.

"You care much about her. You care about them all. That is a mistake," it whispered, as its eyes began to glow with black light. Randy pushed Joanie and John away and surged forward, as lightning crackled in the sky. The storm clouds darkened the already cloudy sky as bolts of lightning rained down on the figure. Joanie and John raced forward, but Chris's yell stopped them in their tracks.

"I can't hold it off," called Chris, as he crumbled to his knees. His hands shook as he pushed the water onto the shores to try to circumnavigate the tendrils of onyx surging forward. Water flooded the forest as the dam began to give way. Joanie changed directions and raced back over to help Chris, while John rushed over to Randy. With each blast of lightning, the Ultimate Evil grunted in pain but did not falter, as it glowed with more dark energy and began to hover over the dam.

"Is that all the powerful Natura of lightning and fire has?" taunted the figure. Before Randy could reach out to grab the sinister being, John pulled his brother back.

"Let me go!" shouted Randy.

"You're making it worse!" shouted John.

"Go get the Lucis! We can stop it!" The Ultimate Evil's head jerked up and it let out a growl as it heard the words.

"The Luci are here. I thought I sensed more energy than possible from you. You don't play fair, so neither will I." The ground began to shake, and waves of black light began pulsing toward them, as the creature hovered above the dam. In a strong pulse of energy, waves of black light crashed into John and Randy, causing them to be boosted from the dam and hurled to the shore below. A ball of black light materialized in its hand, and it hurled an orb of energy in Chris's direction. Joanie summoned a gust of wind and managed to redirect the orb before it could reach Chris. She raced over to stand protectively in front of him while he focused all his energy on the water. She noticed the way he winced and grunted from the force.

"You okay?"

"I can't stop it from reaching the water like this. I have to be immersed in it."

"No, it's too dangerous! Maybe Randy's right. We need to get that Lucis."

"It's too late for that. I have to try and…"

"Chris," whispered Joanie. He noticed her eyes were no longer on him and turned to see the Ultimate Evil, floating in the air higher above the dam. Its chest began to glow as it shook with fury. A burst of dark light poured from its chest and penetrated the ground. The earth began to quake and rumble around them even more. Randy helped John to his feet on the shore. They both gulped when the earth began to crack. Patches of earth disintegrated into rubble as sinkholes appeared. They morphed and destroyed the forest. Another group of sinkholes formed and surged in the direction the four of them came from. John's eyes widened.

"They're heading for the town," said John.

"Go, I'll keep it busy," said Randy. John gave him a look.

"Randy…"

"Go!" bellowed Randy. John sighed, but nodded, knowing he had no choice. If the sinkholes reached the town of Anderson, there would be nothing left in their wake.

o o o o o o

The town of Anderson was in disarray as law enforcement, public safety officials, and military officers assisted in the evacuation of the county. All roads leading out of the area were full of cars moving at a snail's pace. Gabriella zoomed past the cars as she drove in the opposite direction toward town. She recognized most of the people from the community. As the owner of the only antique store in town, she had many regulars who perused the store. Her heart dropped as she thought about what would be left of the town where she had made a home with Ethan. They sped down the main road leading into Anderson and made it to the barricade the military had set up. A soldier approached the vehicle, and she rolled down the window.

"Ma'am, you need to turn around. This area is being evacuated."

"We know. We're just here to help," informed Gabriella.

"Well, while I appreciate that, you can help by steering clear of..."

"Let them through. They're with me." Gabriella sighed in relief, when Alex moved the barricade and waved them through. The soldier was surprised by the request, but stepped aside to let the vehicle pass. They parked in the town square and Alex jogged over to them as Zayneb, Maya, and Carlos grabbed their gear from the back of the SUV. Ethan smiled appreciatively at Alex.

"Thanks for the assist. I didn't want to have to make a call to get through unless I really had to."

"Connections in high places, huh? You two are just full of all sorts of surprises. What are you doing here? Where's Vic?" asked Alex. Ethan and Gabriella glanced at each other.

"She's safe. We're here to help. How's the evacuation going? How many more need to be moved out?" asked Ethan.

"Don't change the subject. I want to see Vic."

"She's busy right now. I don't know if you've noticed, but it's been a bit chaotic lately," said Gabriella.

"You mean with the world coming to an end? Yeah, I've noticed. Look, I just want to talk to her. I appreciate all that you've done for me, but I want to talk to her myself to make sure she's okay." Ethan nodded his understanding.

"We'll let her know to call you soon, okay? We need you to focus right now, though, sheriff. How's the evacuation going?" asked Ethan. Alex wanted to press the issue, but the helicopter flying overhead reminded him of the urgency of the situation.

"There've been power outages and the sewage system has gone to crap. Pun intended."

"Making jokes. Good to see you're back to normal," teased Gabriella.

"I wouldn't exactly call knowing I was killed by the source of all evil being back to normal, but yeah. Let's go with that. We've set a perimeter and have officers going from house to house. The hospital is clear, but it's been a slow process."

"Where's everyone heading?" asked Ethan.

"Well, that's complicated. The military bases are filling up quickly, but we're hoping to fit most of the town at the one west of here. Minot is a mess right now. People are trying to head in and out of the city. No one knows where to go or what to do. We aren't the only area in a state of emergency. The entire state is putting out fires, literally in some places, and we're better off than most. You seen the news about New York?"

"Yeah, we learned about it on the way here," said Gabriella.

"First a hurricane and then a blizzard? Our infrastructure is barely holding up. I can't imagine how theirs is doing. The entire city is practically frozen in place, and no one can leave. Their best shot is to hunker down, but ours is to get as many people out of the region as possible. This is all because of that thing that attacked me?"

"Unfortunately, yes," said Ethan.

"And the girls are supposed to stop it? How?"

"It's a long story, but know they are doing everything they can to…" Ethan stopped in his tracks as he felt a tremor. The ground began to quake under their feet and Carlos rushed over to them.

"My phone is blowing up with alerts of seismic activity throughout the area. We have to get everyone out of here. *Now*," warned Carlos. Alex looked at the main road heading out of town.

"We need more time. Traffic can't move much faster," said Alex. Zayneb and Maya ran over to them.

"Ethan, we have to move," warned Zayneb.

"Carlos, give me options," said Ethan. Carlos unzipped his backpack and pulled out two devices. He typed furiously on both screens before handing one to Alex and one to Ethan.

"Okay, uh, here are the routes that can be used to get out of town. That road is closed, but they can cut across the farmland to get to the interstate," informed Carlos.

"These alternate routes aren't heading toward the bases," said Alex, as he skimmed over the map.

"Most of the activity is coming from the west, so if we can get people to head east that should at least buy some time," assured Carlos.

"Alex, you should get your officers out of town. Lead the townspeople away. We'll stay behind," offered Zayneb. Alex wanted to object, but Maya stopped him before he could.

"She really isn't asking. Just saying it politely as a courtesy. Go," said Maya.

"Fine, but I expect to hear from Vic soon. Tell her I need to know she's okay."

"We will," assured Ethan.

"Oh, and thanks for…you know…trying to save the world. Good luck," added Alex. He jogged over to two of his deputies to give them their new orders. Gabriella's eyes were trained on the main road out of town.

"There are too many people. This is going to get ugly if that line of cars doesn't start moving," she warned. Ethan pulled his phone from his pocket.

"I'll call Phillip and tell him to contact whoever is in charge. They need to switch their routes. Carlos, will you send me the map? I'll let him know…"

"Ethan," mumbled Carlos, as he stared off into the distance. They all turned to see what he was staring at. Zayneb cursed under her breath. Dominic walked over to the group and eyed them cautiously.

"I called Henrik to fill him in on…what are all of you looking at?" asked Dominic. He followed their stares to the plains west of the town square. Several sinkholes were barreling toward Anderson and swallowing any structure or piece of land in their way.

"Ah, hell," he mumbled.

"Back in the car. Go, go, go!" shouted Ethan, as the ground began to quake even more. Everyone sprinted toward Ethan and Gabriella's SUV, as the sounds of glass breaking and structures collapsing filled their ears. Zayneb stopped, as she heard a cry behind her. She spun around and noticed a car stuck in a ditch on the other side of the town square. Smoke was coming from the hood and a tire was blown from where the car had slid off the road. Two teenagers were banging on the window and frantically motioning for someone to help them. She smoothed her face and kept a calm demeanor, as she waited for Carlos and Maya to file into the SUV. Ethan, Gabriella, and Dominic were already inside and ready to get out of dodge. Zayneb knew if she gave her plan away, they would all go after her, so she steadied her resolve. As soon as Maya was in the car, she slammed the door and banged on the hood.

"Go!" she shouted. She gave Gabriella a stern look when Gabriella shook her head.

"Zay..."

"You agreed," she reminded her. Tears filled Gabriella's eyes and she gave a curt nod. She locked the doors before Maya could get back out and slammed on the accelerator to speed away.

"No!" shouted Maya. Gabriella remembered the vow she made to Zayneb after the last close call they had with Maya. Even after she was safely back with the Praevians and the Naturas managed to stop Dominic to create Absolution, Zayneb was shaken to her core at the thought of losing the woman she loved. Planning for the worst while hoping for the best was one of her strong suits and she made Gabriella promise her if they were ever in a situation where Maya was in danger again, she would do everything to keep her safe, even if it meant risking Zayneb in the process. While she didn't agree, Gabriella promised and knew Zayneb would do the same for Ethan. At times, their duty as Praevians was in direct conflict with their duty to protect the people they loved. For Zayneb, Gabriella's promise was how she balanced both.

Zayneb spotted an empty vehicle parked in front of the grocery store and ran over to it. She used her elbow to shatter the driver's side window and unlocked the door. It was not the first time in her life she had hotwired a car and she was able to start it with ease. By the time she pealed out of the parking lot and over to the car the teenagers were trapped inside, two sinkholes had opened at the outskirts of the square. The sinkholes were completely swallowing patches of earth while causing other masses of land to crash and shift against themselves. Buildings caved in and crashed into one another as she hurried over to help the teenagers. The car was leaning precariously on one side of the ditch, but she managed to open the trunk of the SUV.

"Climb over, hurry," she called. The two teenage boys quickly followed her instructions. She pulled both out one by one, but swallowed hard when she saw the building collapse behind them. The ground felt as if it was rolling in waves as it began to rupture and collide haphazardly. The creaking and groaning of metal caught her attention and she turned just in time to see the vehicle shifting. She pushed the teenagers out of the way before the soil deteriorated beneath them and the vehicle sank farther into the ditch. Zayneb yelled out in pain, as the car twisted and pinned part of her leg underneath it. Most of the car's weight teetered on the side of the ditch, but she cursed again when she realized her leg was trapped.

"Give me your hand," called one of the teenagers. She spotted another sinkhole ripping through the ditch and shook her head.

"Take the other car and go!"

"But…"

"Go!" she called again. The two teenagers glanced at each other as tears filled their eyes.

"Thank you," they said. She put on a brave smile and gave a nod. They got into the other car and quickly drove away from the rubble to head out of town. She winced in pain and rested her head on the ground to look up at the sky as she heard the ground fracturing around her. She braced herself for impact as she felt the earth give way. The ditch disintegrated and the vehicle slid down the slope leading into a gaping hole of fractured earth. Zayneb tried to grab at the rubble behind her as she was freed from under the car, but it was too late. Her fingers slipped through it as she began to fall. She closed her eyes as she fell but was suddenly jolted to a halt with a force that dislocated her shoulder. The pain shot through her, and her eyes widened when she looked up to see Maya holding onto her wrist.

"Gotcha! Give me your other hand, Zay," called Maya. Carlos had a hold of Maya's leg with one hand and a piece of pipe from the exposed sewage lines with the other as Maya clung to Zayneb's hand. They hung precariously over the sloped, sinking edge of the gaping hole as sinkholes left paths of destruction around them. Zayneb felt herself slipping again, as Maya and Carlos tried to hold onto her.

"That pipe isn't going to hold us all. Let me go!" shouted Zayneb. Maya shook her head profusely.

"Nope, not doing this, not having this dumb discussion about sacrifice! Too busy trying to save you!"

"Maya, if you let me go, you can save yourself and him!"

"If you go, I go. Pretty simple, so you better not let go!" shouted Maya.

"Same!" added Carlos.

"Damn your stubbornness! Let go!"

"My stubbornness? Damn *your* stubbornness!" called Maya. Carlos felt the pipe begin to shift and slide down the slope as the soil beneath them gave away.

"Just so you know, I love you both. I have been and always shall be your…"

"Carlos, I swear if you finish that line!" screamed Maya.

"If I'm going out, I'm going out quoting Star Tre…" He yelled, as the pipe broke and they slid down the slope. They braced themselves for the impact but were surprised when the earth began to fuse underneath them and the soil rapidly gathered around them. They rolled back onto solid ground and into a heap of dirt, rocks, and debris. The billows of dust made them cough as they all sat up. The dust settled around them, and they saw John standing before them. The immortal usually looked formidable in stature with his broad chest and muscular build, but he looked Herculean as he stood there with green light glowing from his hands.

"You okay? Are any of you hurt?" Maya sighed in relief when he helped them to their feet. She pulled him in for a tight hug and he smiled at the warm embrace.

"Thank you," she whispered.

"Of course, I'm just sorry I couldn't get here sooner. Trying to control that many sinkholes at once was more difficult than I thought it would be."

"Well, you made it, and that's all that matters," said Maya. He smiled when she turned to Zayneb and cupped her face. She captured her wife's lips in a passionate kiss before pulling back to look her over.

"Are you okay?" she asked. Zayneb nodded, but winced in pain when Maya's hands ran over her shoulder.

"Yeah, fine."

"Liar. Your shoulder is dislocated," said Maya. Carlos nodded as he wrapped an arm around Zayneb's waist for support.

"That leg looks pretty beat up too," said Carlos.

"Get her to that car over there. I'll get you out of town. Just follow the path I pave for you," instructed John. Zayneb looked around the deserted square.

"Where are Ethan and Gabby? Are they okay?" asked Zayneb.

"I don't know. We jumped out of the car to go after you. Carlos overrode the locks," said Maya.

"You really thought we were going to let you leave us behind?" asked Carlos. Zayneb sighed.

"No, but I knew I had to try. Where are they?"

"They were trapped by a sinkhole, but I got them out of town in the other direction. You can go catch up to them. I have to go help the others. Hurry," instructed John. Maya and Carlos helped Zayneb to one of the abandoned cars and followed his instructions as he looked around at the damage. The town square had been razed and the surrounding area was not much better.

o o o o o o

The strong winds and water swirling around the reservoir left Chris and Joanie fatigued as they tried to use their abilities to keep the water away from the tendrils of onyx ooze threatening to take hold of the river. Randy was wearing down as well as he attempted to keep the Ultimate Evil at bay and distracted with lightning and balls of fire. Chris could see the exhaustion setting in for his brother and glanced over at Joanie to see her energy levels waning as well.

"I have to do it," he said through gritted teeth. Joanie shook her head.

"No, you don't!"

"Joans, Randy isn't going to last much longer. It's the only way." Before she could stop him, he jumped off the cliff and into the water. He closed his eyes and focused on being immersed in the ice-cold liquid. Being submerged in the river enhanced his control of his abilities and he pushed the water back into the river to try to flush the onyx ooze out of it like he did at the McCoy House. The tendrils dissipated in the water as he surged forward and used the current to wash over the dam. The water flowed freely, and he concentrated on each droplet doing its part to hold off the sable substance. His eyes shot open as a fresh round of the onyx liquid poured out of the dam. He quickly resurfaced and looked up at the top of the dam to see the Ultimate Evil slowly approaching Randy as the Natura hurled more fire and lightning at it.

"Something's wrong. Joanie, something's…" Chris was caught off guard when he was suddenly jerked back underneath the water. He looked down at his leg where a thick, onyx tendril was wrapped around his ankle in a vice grip. Another slithered around his waist and he watched in disbelief as the blue light flickered and dimmed from his hands. He fought with all of his might against the tendrils as they dragged him deeper under the surface. Joanie jumped into the water and Randy was about to as well from his position on the dam but had to lunge out of the way of the onyx tendril that shot out at him. He tried to hurl another ball of fire at it but found himself feeling drained of energy.

"You lasted longer than I thought you would. Still, not enough to stop what is coming, though. Tell me, did your bringer of life fail so easily?" The taunt made Randy shake with fury. His fists glowed bright with red light, and he felt his chest constrict as energy pooled into it. He let out a guttural yell and the Ultimate Evil stumbled back as red light collected into Randy's chest and surged forward. The ray pierced the Ultimate Evil in its arm, causing it to shriek in pain as it held it. Onyx liquid poured from the wound and Randy made it back to his feet as the red light continued to course into the Ultimate Evil, but his eyes widened when the sinister figure's chest began to glow with black light as well. The light surged forward toward Randy and collided with the ray of red. The two stood their ground, battling for dominance as the forces of energy surged and faltered back and forth to try to consume the other.

"You aren't going to hurt anyone else!" yelled Randy.

"So much rage. I feel how deep it runs in you; the distrust, the betrayal. How very human of you." Randy winced as the Ultimate Evil pushed forward. Smoke seeped from the figure and wafted over to swirl around Randy. He began to cough as the red ray of light pouring from his chest dimmed and flickered and the smoke began to suffocate him. He fell to his knees as the ray of light retreated back into his chest. He tried to push forward as the Ultimate Evil stood before him. He wanted to fight, to scream, anything, but his body hung limply in exhaustion as the light barely hung on and the black light surged dangerously closer.

"It seems the fates have chosen their side and chosen well," it taunted. Randy was surprised when a strong gust of wind barreled into the creature. The Ultimate Evil was boosted off the ground and landed with a thud on the edge of the dam. It looked around to see what impeded its path to Randy and let out a growl as the wind picked up in speed. Joanie harnessed the power of the wind to gracefully fly to the top of the dam with a haggard-looking Chris in her arms. They landed on the dam and Chris helped Randy to his feet as Joanie stood protectively in front of them. The Ultimate Evil made it back to its feet as well and glowered at her.

"There's no point in this, Seer. You've lost, one way or another. You just haven't realized it yet." The ground shook beneath them with a boom and the figure glanced over its shoulder to see John approaching from the opposite side of the dam.

"It's not over yet," called John. Joanie sighed in relief, as John's hands glowed with green light. She concentrated and the Ultimate Evil gritted its teeth as her hands glowed with blue and white light. Joanie and John raced forward to attack the figure but were surprised when it jumped from the dam and into the water.

"No!" shouted Chris. The four of them rushed over to the side of the dam and scanned the area, but the ghostly figure was nowhere to be found.

"Where did it go?" asked John.

"I don't know, but something's not right. We were still on the defensive. It had no reason to stop attacking. That was too easy," said Joanie. Randy rubbed his chest.

"Speak for yourself," grumbled Randy.

"Maybe it was too weak to take us on again," suggested John.

"Yeah, maybe," she conceded, as she continued to look around. Suddenly, the dam vibrated beneath their feet and their eyes widened, as the concrete cracked and fractured. Streams of onyx erupted from the fissures, causing the structure to crumble. Onyx ooze poured from the dam and flowed into the water. Slabs and blocks of concrete crumbled over the Naturas as they hit the water and the sable substance surged forward. By the time they resurfaced from the rubble, the oil-like substance was flowing in the current and heading down the river, effectively contaminating the water and all the waterways in its path.

○ ○ ○ ○ ○ ○

Ethan paced impatiently as he, Gabriella, and Dominic leaned against the hood of the SUV and waited for Maya, Zayneb, and Carlos on the side of the road. They had made it to the next county over, when Carlos called to assure them Zayneb was fine. He pinged a location, and told them to wait for them there so they could regroup. The town had been evacuated, but the entire state was under siege with natural disasters impacting every city.

"They're taking too long. I knew we should've just turned around," said Gabriella.

"I am sure your precious Praevians are fine. Zayneb is far more resourceful than you know," said Dominic.

"Oh, really, and what makes you think you know more about her resourcefulness than I do? We've known each other for well over a decade," argued Gabriella.

"Because I read her file, including all the redacted parts. Trust me, she can take care of herself. Any word from the boys?" Ethan shook his head, as he checked his phone again.

"No, not yet," admitted Ethan. Dominic gritted his teeth.

"I knew this was a bad idea. If anything happens to them, I will…" He stopped midsentence as a sense of dread filled the pit of his stomach. He noticed the way Gabriella shivered, and he gulped when a chill went down his spine. Before any of them could react, the Ultimate Evil appeared in front of Dominic. His eyes widened when it picked him up by the throat with one hand and knocked Ethan and Gabriella back with the other. The force of the blow sent the couple crashing into the brush on the other side of the road. The ghastly figure glared at Dominic and the former Guardian winced and clawed at its hand as its grip tightened.

"Where are they?"

"Where are who?"

"Not who, what. Where are the Luci? I know you have them. I can feel their energy. Lying will only prolong your suffering. Give them to me and I will spare your life. Refuse, and it'll be the last thing you do on this earth."

"There are no more," Dominic wheezed out.

"Liar! Do you really think I believe that? There are six. You've only used two on me. Where are the rest?"

"It is the truth." It dropped Dominic and he coughed and gasped for air.

"Fine, maybe they'll be more forthcoming." It stalked toward Ethan and Gabriella, and Dominic looked on in horror as the creature picked them up by their throats to lift them off the ground. It smiled sadistically at Dominic as it began choking them, squeezing tighter the more they tried to fight back. A tendril formed from its chest and slithered menacingly toward Ethan's mouth.

"Okay, stop! I'll tell you, just stop!" shouted Dominic. It released its hold on them and shook its head in disgust as it made its way back over to Dominic. Ethan and Gabriella sputtered and gulped down air as they tried to catch their breaths.

"You humans are so easy."

"I'll tell you where the Luci are if you promise to leave them alone."

"Dominic, don't," wheezed Ethan. The creature smirked.

"Your species is so pitiful. Is this your attempt at being noble? It doesn't suit you, but fine. I'll spare their pathetic souls. Now give me the Luci."

"I need your word they will be left alone."

"You know, a human has never encountered me and lived to tell about it. Yet, here you stand, and you bargain with me?"

"That's not true. You miscalculated," said Dominic. The Ultimate Evil tilted its head in fascination.

"In what way?"

"They are stronger than you think they are and so are humans." The enigmatic figure sifted through its encounters with the Naturas and smirked when realization dawned.

"The deputy. That's how the bringer of light was weakened. She was absurd enough to save him and absorbed the darkness for his life. You're all truly more foolish than I thought. No wonder the fates are done with you. No matter, she'll be dead soon. So will all of you. Give me the Luci so I can end this."

"I need your word you will leave them alone." The Ultimate Evil glanced over at Ethan and Gabriella.

"Why do you care so much about them? Why do you even bother to try? There is no need for this charade. I see the darkness in you, the one you try so hard to fight. I can sense it: the hatred, the rage. Do not fear it. Embrace it. You should be relieved I'm here. I will put this putrid earth out of its misery. It's dying already. Your species is nothing more than a disease that has long infected it. The Naturas you have so much faith in are just prolonging that reality."

"Then why do you even need the Luci? No need to answer. I already know. Absolution has already begun. You're running out of time, and you know it. The Naturas are going to defeat you. It is you that has much to fear, not me."

"You truly believe that, don't you? You believe your precious Naturas can save you, but they can't. They won't. The time is upon us, the event will arrive on this earth soon enough, and so will the end of your world. Now, give me the Luci or die," it warned. The Ultimate Evil grabbed Dominic with its tendrils to pull the man closer. Another tendril slithered toward Ethan and Gabriella. Dominic glanced over at Ethan before glaring back at the Ultimate Evil.

"You know, I had a lot of theories about you, but never proof. I even thought I had truly gone mad and that you never existed. For a time, even I thought I was the Ultimate Evil, but you're wrong about me."

"You will never be able to outrun the darkness in you. So much hatred. So much rage."

"You sense my hatred and rage, but don't know where it stems from. That's why they'll defeat you. That's why you are the one with much to fear. You have no clue what it means to be human or what fuels us. You can't conquer what you refuse to ever really understand. They're going to stop you. I'd hoped I'd be there to see it when they did, but it seems I'm out of time. I've stalled enough. Just so you know, I was told it may not kill you, but this one should sting a bit." Before it could question him, Dominic reached for the ring on his finger that had been bestowed upon him when he first vowed to be a Guardian. He had only taken it off twice in his life. Once when Trenton took it from him, and once when he gave it to Henrik to repurpose as an explosive in case of an emergency. He twisted the piece of jewelry, and the ring began to beep. He looked over at Ethan and gave a sad smile at his old friend.

"One left," he whispered.

"No!" shouted Ethan. The Ultimate Evil's eyes widened in shock as bright white light exploded from the ring. The sinister figure let out a blood-curdling shriek of pain as the detonation of light surged in every direction to pierce its form. The rapid release of energy violently erupted, boosting both of them into the air. Dominic crumbled to the ground. His ears were ringing and vision blurred, but he managed to see the figure. It was badly injured, with puddles of ooze dripping from its limbs. It managed to limp and stumble painfully into the brush with its tendrils of onyx slithering behind. Dominic tried to sigh in relief, but it came out in sputters of blood as the sharp pain in his chest registered. He rolled onto his back and stared up at the sky. The sound of his racing heart filled his ears. He could hear the moment it started slowing in pace.

Dominic never thought much about death. He spent his entire life obsessing over saving humanity. There was never time to consider actual death itself. Memories from his childhood flitted through his mind and played right before his eyes. He saw his mother's smile and laugh as they sat in the kitchen eating the homemade cookies they made together. He saw Ethan hugging him after he told him he would soon be a Guardian. He even saw the Fall Dance. Tears swelled in his eyes as he watched the boy he used to be on that carefree night, dancing with his friends and celebrating. He saw the early days of taking care of the boys. The late nights, the long days, but also the moments that made him proud of them. Memories of each of them in various stages of their lives flashed before his eyes. Soon, the memories faded, and he was left with the sight of a crying Ethan hovering over him. His old friend pressed his hands to Dominic's chest to try to stop the bleeding.

"Come on, stay with me. Stay with me, damn it! We have to finish this!" Ethan's sobs made Dominic reach up for him with a bloodied hand. He cupped his friend's cheek and let out a wheezing cough as he used the last of his energy to find his voice.

"I lied."

"None of that matters now."

"There's one more...but only one more, Ethan." Ethan shook his head.

"Save your breath, old man."

"You wound me in my last moments by mocking my age?"

"These aren't your last moments. You're fine." Dominic gave a weak smile.

"You were right about love...to find it, to have it," whispered Dominic. Gabriella knelt beside them and grabbed his other hand to give it a comforting squeeze.

"Dominic, I shouldn't have said what I said before about..."

"You were right, Gabby. I was so worried about failing to create Absolution, I failed to live, to love. I never showed the boys all the beauty of what they were saving."

"Stay with us," urged Gabriella. Dominic gazed up at the sky with a faraway look in his eyes.

"Dominic..." said Ethan, but Dominic spoke up again.

"I'm not afraid. I thought I would be...but...just tell them...tell them I love them. Tell them I get it now. I broke the rule too. I broke it because I've always loved them." Dominic's eyes lost focus and his hands went limp in theirs, as his heart took its last beat. Ethan's body was wracked with sobs as he buried his face into Dominic's shoulder. Gabriella closed Dominic's eyes and kissed his forehead. They sat there with the former Guardian in Ethan's arms and the grief crept in over the loss of one of Ethan's most complicated, but oldest friends.

CHAPTER 4

Survival

The flight back to the compound was spent in silence as everyone processed Dominic's death in their own ways. For all their complicated feelings about the man, some more complicated than others, it was sobering to have the former mentor not returning with them. Chris, John, and Joanie kept a close eye on Randy the entire trip, sensing the strong emotions he was battling with. He remained stoic, however, as they exited the hangar and headed for the main entrance of the compound. Gabriella gave Ethan's hand a comforting squeeze as Archie approached the couple with tear-stained eyes. Henrik was at a loss for words but did his best to stay composed. Ethan had called ahead to tell the couple the news of Dominic's death. Archie pulled Ethan in for a hug.

"Are you okay?" asked Archie.

"I'm fine. Just want to kill this thing so we can give him a proper burial. Phillip assured me that he would make sure his body is handled with care. Connell is retrieving it from the base as we speak."

"And sending him where? Back to New York? The place is an ice rink right now," reminded Archie.

"No, Singapore."

"I thought there was a volcano eruption there?"

"There was, but the bunker they are sheltering in can withstand it if it reaches them. Phillip says it doesn't appear it will anyway. They can keep his body safe there."

"Wait, bunker?" asked Henrik.

"I guess the compound was only one option for the end of the world," said Ethan. Henrik shook his head in disbelief.

"Of course it was," said Henrik.

"Enough about all of that. Are you okay? Are you injured?" asked Archie.

"No, just a bit banged up. It all happened so fast. We didn't even know it was following us. I checked several times, so did Dominic. The area was clear when we arrived, but it just came out of nowhere. Gabby and I didn't even have a chance to try to stop it. It felt like it was there just as quickly as it was gone. Dominic saved us," explained Ethan, as a fresh set of tears filled his eyes. Gabriella wrapped a comforting arm around her husband.

"Not that I'm not grateful, but how did he get a ring that could do that? It worked like a Lucis, looked like one too, so how did he manage to get one in his Guardian ring?" asked Gabriella.

"Yeah, how did that happen, Henrik?" challenged Ethan. Archie glanced over at Henrik who looked down guiltily as he spoke up.

"Dominic asked me if there was a way to construct a Lucis that he could keep close in case of an emergency. The energy of a Lucis needs to be contained in order to preserve it and Dominic worried he wouldn't always have access to the case I manufactured for him."

"He shouldn't have even needed it," called a voice behind them. They turned to see Randy approaching. It was the first time he had spoken since they left Anderson. His jaw was clenched in anger.

"We should've listened to him. He would still be alive if we would've just listened to him," said Randy. Before Ethan could defend their choice, Zayneb walked over.

"And Anderson would've perished, along with everyone in it. John saved us and all those people. He stopped those sinkholes from taking out the evacuation routes. It wasn't all for nothing," assured Zayneb.

"This doesn't make sense. None of this makes sense. We're supposed to defeat the Ultimate Evil. We've trained our entire lives to do it and we can't even save…Stacie…Stacie can save him. We just have to wait for her to wake up and then she can heal him," said Randy. Ethan smiled sympathetically at him.

"It doesn't work that way, Randy," said Ethan.

"She saved you and Alex! Of course, she can save him," assured Randy.

"Both of us were still holding on. Our hearts were still able to be restarted, we…we weren't completely gone yet. Dominic is gone, Randy," said Ethan.

"And Stacie is in no condition to save anyone. She's getting worse," added Reo. Randy searched Victoria's eyes for confirmation, as the two came out to discuss what had happened. Randy shook his head when he saw her tears.

"No, this isn't going to happen. I won't lose her too!" Randy darted down the hall to the medical bay to be by Stacie's side and Chris ran a hand through his hair in frustration.

"He's right. We have to do something. We can't lose Stacie. It seems like all we're doing is losing and reacting after the fact," said Chris.

"Especially since the fate of the world depends on it," reminded Zayneb. Reo knelt beside her to examine her leg and the makeshift brace fastened to it.

"We need to get you off of this leg. You may be stubborn and very good at hiding it, but I know you're in pain. Who popped your shoulder back in place?" asked Reo.

"John did, on the way here. Maya and Carlos refused," said Zayneb.

"I'm not apologizing for not having the stomach to make you scream like that," said Maya. Carlos nodded in agreement and shuddered at the memory. Reo sighed, as he checked over her shoulder as well.

"I need to get a closer look and an x-ray of both, and no, Zay, I'm not asking," said Reo. Zayneb gave a curt nod and allowed Maya and Reo to help her to the medical bay. Gabriella watched them head down the hallway, with concern evident in her eyes.

"We're running out of options here. Zayneb can't go back out there. Anderson is in shambles and we're dropping like flies," said Gabriella. Henrik shoved his hands into his pockets.

"There is one option left. It's a bit risky, but could be worth a try," suggested Henrik. Archie shook his head in disbelief.

"You can't be serious right now," said Archie.

"I already ran it by Reo," reminded Henrik.

"And he said there's no way to know for sure it would work," argued Archie.

"He also said it could. Listen, I know this isn't ideal, but I've studied them. This could work, Archie," defended Henrik.

"What could work?" asked Ethan.

"Whatever is infecting Stacie came from the Ultimate Evil. What is the one thing we know can weaken it?" asked Henrik. Victoria sighed.

"The Lucis, but we're out of those. Dominic used the last one to save Ethan and Gabby," reminded Victoria. Ethan's eyes widened as realization dawned on him.

"There's one more. Dominic lied. He told me before he died that there was one more. He was keeping it for who knows what reason, just like he had one in his ring," said Ethan.

"Wait, that's what they were talking about. Archie, I heard you two talking in the library. What was Dominic up to? And don't you dare lie!" warned Chris. Archie put his hands up in surrender.

"For the record, it wasn't my plan, and I didn't agree with it, but the man is…well, was… a control freak. I guess he had his reasons, though, and he wasn't completely wrong," said Archie.

"Wrong about what?" asked Joanie.

"When we found the Lucis, Dominic knew they would be needed to stop the Ultimate Evil, so we came up with a way to make sure they were used wisely after Henrik and I accidentally destroyed one…"

"How were you able to destroy a Lucis anyway?" asked Ethan.

"Henrik was studying one and we were curious to see if it was truly indestructible, so we sort of…kind of…we used a laser on it," confessed Archie.

"Technically, three, but the first two didn't leave a scratch. We needed to find a way to break down the particles and it turns out lasers are pretty powerful, even against supernatural nanoparticles," said Henrik.

"We were able to use that knowledge to create the machine that's keeping this place safe. I was arguing with Dominic about not telling you about the Lucis so you could decide for yourselves as Naturas, Chris. He essentially appointed himself as the Guardian of the Lucis and made us agree to keep one in the vault as a last resort. He didn't trust anyone else with the Luci and that's what I was angry about. It wasn't his job to keep them safe or sacrifice himself to do it. I knew the moment he asked Henrik to place one in his ring, he planned on sacrificing himself," explained Archie. Chris took in a shaky breath.

"Because he didn't think we could protect everyone. He wanted a backup plan in case we failed," said Chris.

"No, Dominic believed in you. The way he talked about the three of you, about the mistakes he feared he made with you, if you believe nothing else about the man, believe that. He knew exactly who you were, and he believed in you," assured Archie. Ethan nodded in agreement.

"His last words were that he wanted to make sure you knew he loved you. He was never good at showing you three, but he loved you," added Ethan. Chris and John nodded as they processed the words and the emotions they brought. Victoria pinched the bridge of her nose.

"So, there were six Luci. Archie and Henrik destroyed one while they were trying to be mad scientists…"

"Sorry, again, about that," said Henrik.

"I told him that last laser was powerful," added Archie.

"…right, which left us with five. Dominic used one to save me, and another at Ethan and Gabby's house. How many did you use to keep the compound safe?" asked Victoria.

"We only needed one," said Henrik.

"Okay, then there was one in his ring, and he made sure there would be one left in a vault somewhere for a rainy day?" asked Victoria. Archie nodded.

"It's in Henrik's lab," said Archie.

"Well, it's raining like hell, so the day has arrived. If we can use the Lucis to help Stacie, we should," said Victoria.

"Yeah, but how?" asked Joanie.

"Do you really have the tech to do that?" asked Carlos. Henrik nodded.

"When I was creating the security system for the compound, I figured out how to separate the Lucis nanoparticles from their containers and inject them into a sealed compartment within the machine. I could do the same so we could inject the Lucis particles into Stacie," explained Henrik.

"Wait, inject them directly into her body?" asked Joanie.

"Yes, her heart, to be exact," said Henrik.

"Wouldn't that kill her?" asked Joanie.

"Not if my research is correct."

"But we have no clue if it is. Plus, we would be destroying the last Lucis we have just making the attempt. It's insane, right? Ethan, tell him it's insane," said Archie. Ethan rubbed his neck nervously, as he began to pace and mull over their choices.

"Dominic and I didn't agree on much when it came to the Naturas, but we always agreed on one thing. Without them, we can't defeat the Ultimate Evil, and the world will end. It really is that simple," said Ethan.

"The risk of being wrong is too great. We don't even know what injecting that would do to her. The whole idea is based on one of Henrik's theories. I love you, but you can't know for sure that you're right, Henrik," defended Archie.

"The energy in the Lucis may be like nothing we've ever seen but so are the Naturas. Reo and I both believe they could be made of the same energy. If so, injecting the Lucis into her heart would jumpstart her body and essentially give her immune system a boost against what's attacking it," explained Henrik.

"So, you think it could heal her, like her energy heals others?" asked Gabriella.

"Exactly," said Henrik.

"What do the rest of you think?" asked Archie.

"I think it was always meant to come down to them, Lucis or not. Stacie has to wake up. If we have some tech that could help with that, I'm down," said Carlos. Ethan looked over at his wife, who gave him a nod of confirmation.

"I think it should be up to the ones who it will all come down to in the end anyway. Naturas, what do you think?" asked Ethan. Victoria nodded without hesitation.

"We have to try," said Victoria. Joanie, Chris, and John nodded in agreement.

"I think we all know what Randy's answer will be," added Joanie. Henrik sighed in relief and smiled brightly at Carlos when he clapped him on the back.

"Hey Carlos, want to see the most powerful laser in the world?" asked Henrik. Gabriella shook her head in amusement when Carlos pumped his fists in joy.

"Oh, I love this plan!" exclaimed Carlos. Archie sighed, but nodded, knowing they were officially at their last resort.

○ ○ ○ ○ ○ ○

Maya watched Randy from the doorway of the room in the medical bay. He had his face in his hands and looked emotionally drained. She gave a knock on the open door. He cleared his throat as he sat back up in his chair.

"Is everything alright? I thought they already decided to use the Lucis and help Stacie," said Randy. Maya frowned in confusion as she walked into the room.

"Uh, I missed that part, but I'm sure the tech nerds are on it. I was making sure Zayneb was okay. I think I heard Carlos rejoicing down the hall though, so I guess that explains that." Randy gave a small smile.

"I can hear them in Henrik's lab. What is *Star Trek* and what exactly is an omega directive?" asked Randy.

"It's a fictional show that Carlos loves and has made me watch a few times. The omega directive was mentioned in one of his favorite episodes, which he made me watch twice. Once when I was getting to know him and once because I lost a stupid bet. He counts cards and is banned from Vegas, but I had to learn that the hard way. Anyway, there are like a million episodes of the show and different versions that he assures me I should appreciate, but whatever. Long story short, in his favorite episode, the captain of the ship is looking for a molecule that is considered the most powerful to exist. It's called an omega particle. I hate myself for knowing that," said Maya. He slowly nodded.

"Okay, that makes more sense. I'm pretty sure this place isn't called Starfleet, so I was confused."

"You never know. Henrik and Archie seem like Trekkies, so who knows what they call it."

"Trekkies?" She waved him off as she sat down across from him.

"Never mind, how are you holding up?" He shrugged and looked down at his hands in his lap.

"I don't know. I'm relieved they're going to try to help Stacie, but...I don't know. How is Zayneb?"

"She'll be okay."

"It was brave of her to risk her life for those two strangers."

"You do the same, you know? Going out there to face the Ultimate Evil, even though you knew you needed all six of you to take it down, was brave."

"Or stupid. Dominic is dead because of us…because of me. I was just so angry at him for everything he's done. I didn't want to listen to him, but I should have. If I had listened to him before, Stacie wouldn't be fighting for her life right now, he wouldn't be dead, and the world wouldn't be on the brink of not existing. I did everything he taught me not to do. I let my emotions get the best of me and now people I care about are dealing with the consequences."

"Randy, Dominic wasn't right. Hard decisions had to be made, but that doesn't mean good didn't come from them. Alex is alive because of Stacie and a lot of people in Anderson are alive right now because of all of you." He angrily wiped a tear from his cheek.

"What does it matter, if the Ultimate Evil wins in the end?"

"It won't, but I understand feeling hopeless right now. What you're feeling is grief and you're allowed to be angry. It's a natural emotion, but it doesn't mean all this is for nothing."

"Emotions are horrible. I hate them."

"They can be, yeah."

"And yet, you specialize in them. You study humans based on their emotions. Why?"

"I did for a while, in a lot of different capacities. I'd like to think it's because I'm good at analyzing people, but I guess it started out as a way to cope."

"Cope with what?"

"My parents kicked me out of the house when I was fifteen because my father found out I was gay. He found my diary and while

I wasn't ready to admit it to anyone else, I admitted to myself in it that I liked girls how a lot of girls liked boys. Finding out at such a young age that the unconditional love of parents actually can be quite conditional is a lot for a kid. I struggled with that for years. My father was never very affectionate or loving, but I expected more from my mother because we were so close. Having her turn her back on me hurt the most. Looking back, I realize she was trapped in an emotionally abusive marriage and couldn't be what I needed her to be. I don't think either of them was capable of truly loving me the way I deserved. I hated the world for it for a really long time, but it made me driven. I studied psychology in college so I could figure out what makes people tick. I thought people couldn't hurt me if I could figure out their patterns of behaviors and I became very good at reading people, so good that I became a behavioral analyst and worked to track down very human, but very real monsters."

"Is that why you were recruited by the Praevians?"

"Yes, and no. I met Zayneb while I was working on a case. She was still doing some work for a few agencies at the time and requested my help tracking someone down. My reputation preceded me back then. It wasn't easy at first because we were both very guarded and Zayneb was all about professionalism and rules, but we fell in love and that's when she told me about the Praevians."

"Sounds like it was fate."

"I'm not sure if I believe in such a thing, but maybe."

"But you're a Praevian. You believe in prophecies and good versus evil and…"

"I believe in *you*, but I didn't always. Before that, I believed in Ethan and Gabby, and before that, just Zayneb. I've never been in the business of fate, Randy. I believe in people."

"Even after what your parents did?"

"Even after that. That's what makes the emotions, even the hard ones, worth it."

"I don't have a lot of practice dealing with the hard ones and if I'm being honest, I don't know how to deal with them now. That thing is still out there. It's killing the woman I love and killed my...well, whatever Dominic was."

"Your father." Randy clenched his jaw in frustration as a tear escaped and rolled down his cheek.

"Dominic killed my real parents. He lied to us for years. He almost made me a killer, too, and we had to stop him to create Absolution. How am I supposed to call him my father? How am I supposed to know how to feel about him?" Maya placed a comforting hand on his.

"You don't have to know that right now. All you need to know is that you aren't alone. That's what makes all of the emotions and hurt worth it. You have a woman who loves you and a pretty great family who supports you. I can't imagine what you're going through right now, but don't push down your emotions. And when it hurts so much you can barely take it, remember one thing that's pretty important."

"What's that?" he asked, as he wiped away his tears.

"Your father loved you. He was a complicated and flawed man. He did things I know he wasn't proud of, maybe even unforgivable things, but when it came down to it, he loved you, and sacrificed himself because he believed in you. It doesn't change what he's done. It can't bring back your parents, but deep down I know you loved him, too. Take it from someone who spent a lot of time trying to search for the love I didn't get from my parents. He may have been horrible at times, but at least he wanted redeem himself, to show he cared. Whether he is or not, is up to you, but he loved you." He let the tears fall as he let the words sink in. She smiled sympathetically at him and gave his shoulder a comforting squeeze. They both turned around when Carlos jogged into the room.

"We're ready and think it's going to work," said Carlos. Randy wiped his cheeks and jumped to his feet as Reo entered the room. The doctor slid the sides of Stacie's gurney up and rolled it out of the room with Randy, Maya, and Carlos behind him.

"Where are you taking her?" asked Randy.

"To Henrik's lab, we'll need to do the procedure in there," informed Reo.

"What kind of procedure?" asked Randy. Carlos shrugged.

"It'll take five minutes tops," assured Carlos.

"How's Zayneb?" asked Maya.

"Being a horrible patient as usual," said Reo.

"That tracks," said Maya. Randy eyed the man when he detected his racing heart.

"You didn't answer my question. What kind of procedure?" repeated Randy. Carlos glanced over at Reo, who sighed.

"It isn't ideal, but we're going to use a laser as the method of injection," said Reo. Maya responded before Randy had the chance to.

"I'm sorry, you're going to do what now?" asked Maya.

"I know it sounds risky…"

"It doesn't sound risky. It *is* risky. You want to shoot her with a laser," reminded Maya.

"A regular syringe won't work. It can't contain the Lucis particles," said Reo.

"So, you thought a laser was a better alternative?" questioned Maya.

"Not just any laser, the most powerful laser in the world," corrected Carlos, with a smile. Reo rolled his eyes.

"You aren't helping, Carlos. Look, I know how it sounds, but we've each done the research," said Reo.

"Really? You did the research on the best way to inject otherworldly matter into an immortal?" challenged Maya.

"You know I wouldn't take such a thing lightly. I've tried every other option. This is our best chance at saving her," assured Reo. Randy nodded.

"I know it is. Thank you for trying to help her," said Randy. Carlos opened the double doors of Henrik's laboratory and Reo rolled Stacie in. The rest of the group were waiting for them. Victoria looked less than enthused.

"If you three are just trying to experiment on my sister, I swear I'll…"

"We're aware of what's at stake, Victoria," assured Henrik.

"Says the man who destroyed a Lucis with the same laser he's about to use on my baby sister," grumbled Victoria.

"So, how exactly is this going to work?" asked Joanie. Randy placed Stacie on the table under the laser and Reo attached electrodes to her chest and temples.

"I'll continue to monitor Stacie, while they perform the procedure. Henrik has already loaded the Lucis particles in the laser. It should only take one short injection for the particles to pierce her chest cavity and reach her heart," explained Reo. Victoria started pacing nervously.

"I'm not sure about this. Ethan, you've known these guys the longest, what do you think? Should we really be trusting them right now? My baby sister's life is on the line and the fate of the world," said Victoria. Whatever hesitation Ethan felt dissipated when Henrik looked him in the eye.

"It will work," assured Henrik. Ethan slowly nodded.

"I've never questioned Henrik's brilliance before, so I'm not going to start now. He knows what's at stake. He's known about all of you...well...the three of you, before you were even born. I trust him," said Ethan. Henrik smiled appreciatively at him.

"Fine, let's get this over with," said Victoria.

"And let's hope it works," added Joanie. Henrik positioned the laser over Stacie's chest and Carlos typed in the code to start it up. The low hum of the laser buzzed and a light on the machine turned green. Randy slipped his hand into Stacie's. He noticed it was colder than before and the gray streaks of the substance spreading through her body were mere inches from her heart. Her pulse was faint, and she was barely breathing.

"Do it," said Randy. Henrik gave a nod to Carlos, who pressed the button. Bright, white light shot out of the laser and into Stacie's chest. She remained motionless, as the laser powered back down and the light dissipated. Reo surveyed the monitors as Randy frowned in confusion.

"Did you do it right? Nothing happened. Did you push the right button?" questioned Randy.

"Yeah, I'm a tech genius. I assure you, I can push a button," said Carlos. Henrik let out a groan of frustration.

"It should've worked. We went over the numbers together twice," said Henrik.

"I don't understand," agreed Reo. Carlos threw his hands up in exasperation.

"Are you telling me we shot her in the heart with the most powerful laser in the world and nothing happened? Not even a little something? How does one get shot with a laser and…"

"Carlos," said Reo, as he noticed something on the monitors. Victoria nudged Joanie and the two sisters eyed their sister carefully.

"Do you hear that?" asked Joanie. Victoria nodded as she, Chris, John, and Randy heard the subtle uptick in Stacie's heartrate. A dim, white light glowed from her chest and began to brighten as it spread over Stacie's body. The streaks of dark matter rescinded, and the substance slowly dissipated from her chest, arms, and down to her fingertips. Her body glowed with a blinding, bright light that caused them to shield their eyes. Her fingertips began to glow with white and red light as her body hummed with energy. Stacie's eyes shot open, and she gasped as her body jolted awake. Randy helped her into a seated position as she coughed and sputtered.

"Stace?" he asked. Reo's eyes remained trained on the monitors that were keeping tabs on her vitals as Stacie gasped for air. She took in some deep breaths and rubbed her chest as she collected her faculties.

"Ow," she managed to whisper. For the first time since she saved Alex, Randy let out an exuberant laugh. He hugged her tightly and her sisters joined in to embrace her. She looked around the room and glanced up at the heavy-duty machinery above her.

"Hi, so…what did I miss?" asked Stacie. John and Chris walked over to hug her as well and Reo, Carlos, and Henrik all high-fived. Gabriella hugged her husband and Maya sighed in relief as they watched the group embrace and welcome Stacie back. It had been a long couple of days, and they were more than happy to celebrate a win, even if just for a moment.

○ ○ ○ ○ ○ ○

Stacie was speechless. She stared blankly at the group as they finished explaining the events that led them to that moment. Each piece of information was one she felt she needed an eternity to process. Randy never left her side, as they all recounted the past twenty-four hours. Archie and Henrik had brought everyone food, while they regrouped and reflected on the situation. Carlos was scrolling through the news on a device and sifting through reports. Maya was sitting beside Zayneb and making sure she kept the compression machine on her leg. Reo agreed that she could leave the medical bay, but only if she kept the machine on. Ethan and Gabriella were trying to think of their next move, while John and Chris paced back and forth. Henrik handed them sandwiches and they thanked him with appreciative smiles. Victoria and Joanie accepted sandwiches as well, but kept their eyes trained on their sister as they tried to gauge her response.

"So, let me get this straight. I almost died. Alex almost died too, but I saved him. Ethan and Gabby's house is gone…again. The

Ultimate Evil destroyed most of Anderson. The world is in chaos and natural disasters are happening everywhere. Dominic is dead and you saved me by shooting me in the heart with a laser full of nanoparticles?" Joanie nodded.

"Lucis, yes, I know, it's a lot," said Joanie. Stacie flailed her arms into the air.

"A lot is having a classroom full of kids hopped up on sugar after an ice cream party. This is a bunch of a lot's, wrapped up in a lot of other a lot's, and shoved into a laser that shoots me with a lot's in the chest!" Victoria cleared her throat to stifle her laughter.

"I see you're taking this well," said Victoria. Stacie rolled her eyes at her sister's sarcasm.

"What are we going to do? All this is…oh, Randy, I'm so sorry. I know this must be hard. Dominic was a complex man, but he was your father. I can't imagine how you're feeling," said Stacie, as she pulled Randy in for a hug.

"We aren't going to let it all be for nothing. The Ultimate Evil has taken enough from us. We aren't going to let it take any more," said John. Chris gave a nod.

"We have to fight it. Stace, do you think you can help? Vic is just now feeling back to normal," asked Chris. Stacie rubbed her hand over her chest.

"Actually, I feel better than ever. It's like that laser gave me a boost or something."

"Well, technically, it did. You have billions of particles of Lucis flowing through you right now," said Henrik.

"Henrik, right?" asked Stacie. The man gave a bow of his head.

"Yes, and it's nice to finally meet you."

"Thanks for saving my life."

"It was a group effort, but you're welcome," said Henrik. Carlos nodded happily.

"I finally got to use a laser," added Carlos. Zayneb pinched the bridge of her nose, as Maya slapped Carlos upside the back of his head. He rubbed the spot and pushed his bottom lip out in a pout.

"What? I did, and you can't take that away from me," whispered Carlos. Stacie shook her head in amusement.

"Uh, then congrats, I guess. So, what now?" asked Stacie.

"Now, we figure out how to stop the Ultimate Evil," said Randy. Chris noticed Henrik nudge Carlos, who shook his head.

"What is it?" asked Chris. Carlos stood up straighter.

"Nothing!" said Carlos.

"You're lying," said John.

"No, I'm not."

"Carlos, we can hear your heart racing right now," reminded Joanie.

"Yeah, take a breath and slow it down, before you pass out," added Victoria. Carlos's shoulders slumped in defeat.

"Okay, yeah, I'm totally lying." Ethan arched an eyebrow at him and crossed his arms.

"Since when do you lie?" asked Ethan.

"Um, since I've had to be the bearer of bad news over and over," said Carlos.

"Oh, I get it. Trust me," said Joanie.

"Great, more bad news, now what happened?" asked Maya. Carlos pointed dramatically at Maya.

"See? This is why I lie," said Carlos. She playfully rolled her eyes at him and nudged him.

"You know I love you and no matter what it is, we'll deal with it," assured Maya. Carlos took in a shaky breath as he tapped the ceiling-to-floor screen on one of the walls in Henrik's laboratory. Satellite images of the sun and Earth appeared on the screen.

"Okay, so you know how we've been wondering what exactly the Ultimate Evil is doing and why it's doing it and how it just shows up like the Big Bad in every creepy horror film with one jump scare after another?" asked Carlos. They all nodded.

"Precisely the reason I hate scary movies, but continue," said Victoria.

"Well, we know it's trying to destroy the earth and already doing a pretty good job with all these natural disasters, but now I think I know how it's doing it and why. It's tapping into the solar maximum." Victoria raised her hand.

"I'm sorry, solar what?" asked Victoria.

"A solar maximum occurs once every eleven years when the sun reaches peak activity. When that happens, particles of energy are released through solar flares. Scientists have studied them for centuries, but every solar maximum is different. They can build up, and once the energy reaches its peak, it can impact the planet. This one is going to be the biggest solar maximum we've ever seen, which could be catastrophic, due to the instability of the earth's core and the disruption to the magnetosphere." Victoria raised her hand again.

"The Magneto what?" He loaded reports onto the screen and videos of first responders arriving on city blocks as people ran through the streets.

"Not Magneto, the magnetosphere. Stuff like this can essentially mess with our magnetic field and cause disruptions here on Earth. There have been blackouts and radio outages before. Years ago, one in New Delhi took out an entire neighborhood for a week. This one could potentially be the largest ever recorded, which means the Ultimate Evil could essentially use the power of the sun to harness its energy and destroy the Earth. I think it's already tapping into it to do all this damage around the world. Solar maximums have peaks, but that doesn't mean there haven't been surges already. Between that, and the impact of humans on the planet, it wouldn't take much. Exacerbate an earthquake caused by fracking here, a flood where sea levels are rising there." Victoria pinched the bridge of her nose in frustration.

"So, you're telling us an ultimate force of evil that has already been handing our asses to us has essentially been prepping the earth for a world-ending event and creating all these natural disasters so it can use the power of the sun to destroy everything?" Carlos thought for a moment.

"I prefer to call it a global catastrophic event, but yes, essentially," said Carlos.

"I guess that does roll off of the tongue better," grumbled Victoria.

"So, how do we stop it? How much time before the solar maximum is complete?" asked John.

"If my calculations are correct…"

"And we know they are, when it comes to bad news," mumbled Maya.

"...I will take that backhanded compliment. We have a few hours...give or take a few hours," said Carlos.

"So, it could already have happened?" asked Randy.

"Based on the solar flares I've recorded, yes."

"Then, we have to go now. We have to find that thing, but I'm not sure how to stop it or if it's already too powerful to even stop. I felt its power when I was in the water. I couldn't hold it off. If it somehow gets stronger, we aren't going to be able to stop it," said Chris.

"This thing always feels like it's a step ahead of us. Carlos is right. It just pops up out of nowhere, how are we supposed to even know where to start?" asked Joanie. Zayneb smiled adoringly at her wife as Maya stood up.

"I might be able to help with that," offered Maya.

"How?" asked Stacie.

"Maya used to hunt down the worst of the worst before she joined the Praevians. Tracking down evil is kind of her thing," informed Gabriella as Carlos handed Maya a device. She cleared the screen that was projected on the wall and typed onto it.

"When there was an unsub I struggled to find leads on, I would make a profile to see if there were any patterns of behavior. Sometimes there were, sometimes there weren't, but doing it helped me gain a better understanding of them," explained Maya.

"I don't want to understand anything about that thing," said Randy.

"You don't want to sympathize with it, but you most certainly want to understand it. If you don't know what it's doing or why it's doing it, you can't be prepared for when it makes a move. We have to figure out how it keeps getting the jump on you. I think the first step is to come up with a name for the thing. I can't keep calling it the Ultimate Evil. It makes it too creepy and supernatural," said Maya.

"Uh, it is creepy and supernatural," reminded Carlos.

"Building a profile is about giving the suspect a face, a pattern of behaviors, so it is easier to track and understand, but also to not fear it. The Ultimate Evil gives the thing way too much power over us. Humor me here."

"Fine, um, what about just calling it…well…It?" suggested Ethan. Joanie, Victoria, and Stacie all let out a shiver and shook their heads.

"Like the clown from that movie?" questioned Carlos.

"Veto," said Victoria. Reo nodded in agreement.

"I don't do clowns," said Reo.

"Alright, no It. What else you got?" asked Maya. Randy shrugged.

"I've been calling it the Ultimate Evil my whole life. It's pretty much stuck in my head now," said Randy.

"Always the helpful one, Randy. Others? Anything that doesn't make you want to crawl out of your skin?" asked Maya. They were all quiet for a moment as they searched their brains for a name. Joanie perked up as one came to mind.

"What about Gedeon?" suggested Joanie.

"Actually, that's not bad," said Maya.

"In ancient texts, it means destroyer," said Joanie.

"Then, Gedeon it is. So, what do we know about Gedeon? Vic, let's start with you. You encountered it first. What stood out?" asked Maya.

"You mean besides it killing my best friend in front of me?"

"Yes, besides that. You said you tried to fight it off. What was Gedeon like? What did it do? How did it move? What did it say?" John wrapped an arm securely around Victoria as she relived her memories from that night.

"It was cold, calculated. It knew who I was. I wasn't expecting that. It knew my name."

"It knew ours too. How is that possible? Dominic always kept us hidden," said Randy.

"He's right. Not even the Guardians could find the boys," said Ethan.

"So, either it's all-knowing, or it's connected to you somehow. I'm leaning more toward that explanation since it being all-knowing would mean it would already know how to stop you and the thought of an omnipotent ultimate force of evil is terrifying to me. For our sanity, let's consider that it is somehow connected to the Naturas," said Maya. Chris frowned at the very notion.

"It's the epitome of evil and we're not. How could it be connected to us?" asked Chris.

"For exactly that reason, everything about the prophecies and the different versions of the stories talks about the universe and fate. This is all about the battle of good versus evil, which makes you six the opposing force of Gedeon. It disrupts your very existence and you can disrupt it. If I'm right…"

"And she usually is," said Carlos, as Zayneb nodded. Maya winked at them.

"...if I'm right, it may be able to track you, but if so, you would be able to track it too. That's what happened, wasn't it? When we went to help with the evacuation, you didn't hear it. You sensed it. You tracked it."

"Yeah, that's why we were trying to steer clear of the evacuation routes. We didn't want it following us there, but it didn't matter. We still failed," said Randy.

"Okay, but even if that is true, that doesn't explain why it went after Dominic, Ethan, and Gabby, or how it found them," said Zayneb.

"When we were fighting Gedeon at the dam, it was worried about the Lucis. Henrik and Reo think the Luci are made of the same particles as us, which is why that Lucis could heal Stacie. If that's true, wouldn't it be able to sense the energy of the Luci too?" asked Joanie.

"And sensed it in Dominic's ring. It kept asking Dominic about the Lucis," said Ethan. Maya added the information to the profile.

"Good, so we know Gedeon can find you and the Lucis and you can find it. What else?" asked Maya.

"That black goo it spews is poisonous to the touch. When I healed Alex, it felt like my hands were on fire," said Stacie. She let out a shiver as she thought about it. Randy kissed the top of her head.

"We also know the goo can move on its own based on what we saw at Ethan and Gabby's house," said Reo.

"It can drain us without even touching us too," added Victoria.

"How?" asked John.

"When I was trying to save the water at the reservoir, it took everything in me to hold on and that stuff still managed to overtake the water. It has these tentacles that can expand as well. If Joanie hadn't jumped in to get me, it would've dragged me under. I couldn't get it off me."

"I felt something similar. I was using the trees and vines to try to restrain it, but that goo soaked into them. It's like it sucked the life out of them," said Victoria.

"When we got there, Vic, there was an entire section of the forest rotted and dead from where it took off," said John.

"Not only can it create that oil-like substance, but also smoke. It was able to create this smoke that almost suffocated me. I was throwing everything I had at it, lightning, fire; it didn't matter. It would only stun it for a moment and then it just kept pushing forward. I was so tired. I just remember being exhausted. I've never felt like that before, not to that extent. If Joanie hadn't intervened, it would have killed me," added Randy.

"So, if we use our abilities against it, or it touches us, we're screwed. Nothing can beat it? Awesome," grumbled Victoria.

"The Luci can," reminded Henrik.

"Yeah, and they're all gone," said Victoria.

"But their power isn't. Henrik's right, the Luci could be the key. I think they are just concentrated amounts of the same nanoparticles that reside in you. One was able to eliminate the poison from Stacie's system and the scans I performed earlier show that a white light similar to the one in the Luci flows through Stacie and Victoria. I bet it flows through all of you as well. What if you tapped into it?" suggested Reo.

"We've been training our whole lives and haven't been able to tap into such a power," said Randy.

"That's not completely true," said Chris. Before Randy could question him, Chris focused on his hands and smiled when they glowed with blue light.

"We know this energy comes from within," said Chris.

"And Gedeon has it too, but its light is black. When I was rushing back to help after I saved Zayneb, Maya, and Carlos, I saw it. Gedeon was practically glowing with it and the light was the most concentrated in its chest," said John.

"Like the light in the scan I saw; that's why we injected the Lucis into Stacie's chest. We knew we needed the energy to start inside of her heart first and spread throughout her body," explained Reo.

"Then that's how you can defeat Gedeon. The six of you share some sort of connection with it. Using most of your abilities will not drain it, just drain you, but that light is the key," said Maya.

"But how are they supposed to figure out how to tap into such a thing in the next few hours?" asked Ethan.

"Give or take, the solar maximum could start any second, unless it already has," reminded Carlos.

"Right, so less than a few hours. How are they supposed to know how to tap into it?" asked Ethan. Maya sighed as she looked over the profile.

"I don't know, but according to everything we're saying here, Gedeon is a force of darkness that can only be stopped by the light of the Lucis, which could be made of the same particles as them. I have a feeling it's going to take all of you tapping into that light to defeat it," said Maya.

"Then we'll figure it out. I was able to figure out how to heal myself without even knowing it when Caleb shot me and then how to tap into it to save Ethan. If this energy really is inside of us, then we'll figure it out, but we have to go soon," said Stacie. All eyes were on the Naturas. They glanced at one another, knowing there was nothing left to do but face the evil force that they had been waiting on for years.

o o o o o o

While the rest of the Naturas showered and dressed to get ready to head out in search of Gedeon, Randy found himself drawn to the room his old mentor resided in at the compound. He still had so many questions and emotions that he wasn't sure how to unpack. A part of him hoped learning more about Dominic would help. He wandered around the room where Dominic's belongings remained. The space was organized, tidy, and pristine. The bed was impeccably made, and Randy straightened the corner of one of the pillows before turning his attention to the dresser beside it. He hesitated for a moment, fearing what he might find inside as he invaded the man's privacy. However, his curiosity got the best of him, and he opened the top drawer. He smiled at the black dress shirts that were folded and placed neatly inside. He went through each drawer, finding the same clothes with similar designs as the last, until he reached the bottom. Randy swallowed hard when he saw a black binder inside and a leather-bound journal. With a shaky breath, he sat down on the floor and opened the journal, immediately recognizing Dominic's handwriting scrolled across the pages with notes and journal entries about his accounts of the days. His fingers traced over the pages and opened to one toward the middle of the journal. Randy rarely read books in the way humans did, instead usually opting to soak up the knowledge with a simple touch, but he found himself curious to know the inner workings of Dominic's complicated mind, even if the very thought terrified him. He noticed the date of the entry and took in another shaky breath as he read a passage of Dominic's thoughts after finding out about Chris and Joanie's relationship.

o o o o o o

Disappointment does not even begin to describe the emotions I feel at this very moment. How could they do this? If I am being honest, I would suspect such a thing from Jonathan. He has always been curious about humans, but Christopher? The level of absurdity knows no bounds. I know it is my fault for letting them be around Ethan. Of course he would poison them with such ideas, but I thought my teachings and values were instilled enough to overcome such temptation. The more I sit with such a thing, the more I cannot help but wonder where I went wrong. Maybe I failed them. Maybe Joanna McNamara is the Ultimate Evil. I shall fight either way, but I know no matter how much I try, it does not change what this means. They have failed and so have I.

o o o o o o

Randy slammed the journal shut and shook his head as tears filled his eyes. He admonished himself for looking in the first place. It was his fault that the words angered him. After all, they were never meant to be seen by anyone but Dominic. He tossed the journal back into the drawer, but frowned when six envelopes slipped out and scattered onto the floor. Randy's heart thundered in his chest when he saw the names scrolled on the front in black ink. Each envelope was addressed to a Natura, and he stared blankly at the one addressed to him. His name was written in Dominic's handwriting. He swallowed hard when he thought of all the possibilities of what Dominic could have written. The two of them were not on good terms before his death. Randy didn't know how to feel about the fact that the letters even existed. He wasn't sure how long he stayed like that, refusing to move, as he tried to decide if he should put the letters back or not, and cursed under his breath as he grabbed the one addressed to him. Before he could talk himself out of it or second-guess his decision, he neatly opened the sealed envelope and unfolded the letter inside. Tears filled his eyes as he read over the words.

o o o o o o

Dear Randall,

I have started and discarded this letter multiple times at this point, too many to count if I am being honest. It is the last one I am writing and has taken me the longest. Sitting with that is almost as challenging as writing this. Phillip suggested that if I want to make amends, I cannot simply show it through my actions. I must be willing to be a gentleman and carry out the same practices I preached to you for years. Doing so in the other letters was oddly cathartic. I apologized sincerely to each of the McNamara's. They did not deserve to be put through such an ordeal and my bitterness was unwarranted. It was more difficult to apologize to Christopher and Jonathan. How can one ever truly apologize for such an act? I justified killing those innocent people, your real parents, by placing my past burdens and fears on all of you. I became a version of the very man I resented my entire life. Because of that, I am not sure if you will ever accept this letter or read it, but I hope that if you do, you will at least understand how I came to such mistakes.

My father was a hardened man. As a child, my mother assured me that he was not always that way. She used to say the honor and responsibility of the Brotherhood came at a price. She was a kind woman, but she was not prepared for the world of the Brotherhood, or the structure and rigidity forced upon them. Mothers of future Guardians were only allowed to raise their children until the age of ten. That is when the boys would start a program at a gilt-edged school that molded us into the men we would become, and prepare us for the Brotherhood. Guardians did not focus on their children except when it came to training and business. My father was not around much when I was a child, so from birth to the age of ten, I was hers and only hers. I find myself missing those times. My childhood was wonderful because of my mother, but it was fleeting. Once I turned ten, I became my father's only child, his only son, and my life was dedicated to the Guardians, well before I could choose it to be. I told myself that your parents were not prepared for the sacrifices and dedication that would be forced upon you by this cruel world, so I would be the one to make the hard choice. I was wrong. It was not my choice to make. While I do believe that you needed to be prepared, that we never knew when the Ultimate Evil would arrive to try to eliminate the three of you, it was not fair to take you from them or take them from this earth the way I did. So, with this letter, I deeply apologize, and yet know it will never be enough. However, that is not all I wish you to know.

I never wanted a child. I knew from a young age it was not in the cards for me, but if that young boy who had tea with his mother and talked of a future quite different from the one I grew up to have would have thought of a child, he would have thought of you. Contrary to what you and your brothers believe, your sense of duty and structure are not your strengths. Your strengths are your loyalty and fierce protectiveness. You protect the ones you love, with a fire I could only hope to have a fraction of in this life. I was taught that love was forbidden, but I know now that was a falsehood; you and your brothers are proof of that. I became obsessed and blinded by the fear that love had somehow made you weak, that it was a temptation or spell the McNamara Sisters put you under, but love is not just for paramours. Love comes in all forms. While it took time for me to show it in my own way, I grew to love you and your brothers. No matter what happens with the Ultimate Evil, know that you have served a great purpose. Whether that means this earth continues to spin or we perish, know this world is better with you in it. You are truly the force of good we need, even if an old man who has made plenty of mistakes like me does not deserve it.

Godspeed.

○ ○ ○ ○ ○ ○

Randy closed the letter with shaky hands and wiped the tears from his eyes with his sleeve. He heard heavy footsteps approaching and quickly jumped to his feet. He neatly folded the letter and placed it in his pocket before scrambling to gather the others.

"Look at the jacket Dominic…are you okay?" asked John, as he noticed the tears in his brother's eyes.

"Yes, fine, I just…"

"What are those? What are you doing in here?"

"Nothing."

"Liar."

"Am not."

"Are too."

"Not."

"Too, what are those?"

"Where did you get the jacket?" John smiled as he fixed the sleeves of the leather jacket.

"Dominic left us clothes. He even picked out rooms for us. Archie just showed us. You should change. But before you do, what are those?"

"Nothing, I..." John used his enhanced speed to dart over and swiftly grab the letters before Randy could put them away. Randy sighed and John frowned in confusion as he looked them over.

"Is this Dominic's handwriting?"

"Yes, he wrote us letters," he conceded.

"All of us? Vic, Stacie, and Joanie too?"

"Yes."

"That's weird. Why didn't he tell us?"

"I don't know. I think he was worried we would not accept them, but I read mine."

"So, that's why you're crying? Was it that bad?" A sad smile crept onto Randy's lips.

"No, it was that good," he assured. John sat with the words for a moment before giving a nod.

"Okay, good." He handed the letters back to Randy, which made his brother frown.

"You don't want to read it?" John shrugged.

"I'll read it after we face Gedeon."

"What if you never get to read it, then?"

"Jeez, Randy, that's dark. Of course, I'll get to read it."

"John, you know as well as I do that the Ultimate Ev..."

"Gedeon," corrected John. Randy stomped his foot.

"Whatever! It could kill us! You don't want to know what Dominic said to you before we go out there and risk our lives?"

"No."

"How can you be so cold? I know he did horrible things, but…"

"He loved us…well…the best he could, anyway." Randy was taken aback by the words.

"What?" John placed his hands on Randy's shoulders and smiled warmly at him.

"Dominic loved us, Randy. The anger I have for him over what he did to our parents comes and goes. I don't know if it'll ever fully go away, but I know he loved us in his own way. And based on the fact that you're crying, I know that letter was him showing that." Randy nodded as he looked down.

"Yeah, it was."

"Good, I know you needed to hear it."

"Why don't you?"

"Because Vic is right. He was a bastard, but he was *our* bastard."

"John, watch your language, especially when speaking about the dead."

"What? That's what she said." John chuckled, as Randy pinched the bridge of his nose in frustration.

"What am I going to do with you?" John stood tall and puffed out his chest with a cheeky grin.

"Save the world, of course." Randy shook his head in amusement, as his brother strolled back out of the room. He wanted to scold him for his cavalier attitude in such dire times, but he didn't. Instead, he glanced back at the room one more time and turned off the light before heading for the room Dominic made sure he had there.

○ ○ ○ ○ ○ ○

By the time the six of them changed their clothes and said their goodbyes to the Praevians, Archie, and Henrik, the sun had set, and the moon hung high. It was the only light illuminating the forest, as they set out on foot away from the compound.

"So...we're just walking out into the darkness?" questioned Victoria.

"I'm with Vic. Just waiting for Gedeon to sneak attack us while we hope for the best, seems a bit bold," said Joanie.

"No, Zayneb's right. We should be the ones to decide where this takes place, not Gedeon. It can track us wherever we are and will steer clear of the compound, so we're in control. We've always trained in the forest. It's where we're most comfortable, so we're going to make sure we get to choose where we confront it," reminded Chris.

"So, where to? Any ideas, Joans...or visions of where we should head to be victorious?" asked Stacie with a hopeful smile. Joanie rolled her eyes.

"I already told you. The visions are on the fritz right now. I tried to connect to Kaya when I was in the shower..."

"Too much information," teased Victoria. John shook with mirth, but it was Randy's turn to roll his eyes.

"Can you be serious? This isn't the time for jokes," scolded Randy.

"Um, excuse me, we're venturing out into the middle of the forest, in hopes of luring a force of evil to us, which has already almost killed me, my best friend, and one of my sisters, all so we can try to stop it from reaching some sunny peak…"

"Solar maximum," corrected Stacie.

"…whatever, all so we don't die, along with every living thing in the world. If I'm too serious, Randy, I'm going to pee myself from freaking out!" Randy smiled sheepishly.

"Yeah, okay. Fair enough. As you were," said Randy.

"Nope, now you took all of the fun out of it. To the battle we go. I do admit though, at least these boots are comfy. It's kind of nice, in a creepy way, that Dominic had clothes there for us. Is it also weird that he planned for us to need clothes at his compound in the middle of nowhere? Sure, but nice threads, all the same," conceded Victoria.

"It's not creepy. He used to always make sure we had clothes," defended Randy.

"Fine, maybe not creepy, but definitely anal-retentive and a bit controlling," said Joanie. Stacie nodded in agreement, as she dusted off her white, long-sleeved shirt and zipped up her black leather jacket.

"At least he didn't put me in red to match Randy," said Stacie.

"What's wrong with matching?" asked Randy.

"Nothing, I just don't need to be color-coded with the man I love, for everyone to know I love him. Besides, I like simple black and white," said Stacie. Victoria looked over their outfits. After all the chaos that had ensued, each was more than happy to take Archie up on his offer for showers and fresh clothes. The man made sure to let them know Dominic stocked clothes for them based on what he hoped would be comfortable for each of them. They each wore jeans, boots, and leather jackets to protect against the elements, but had different styles and colored tops. Randy, Chris, and John were in their usual red, blue, and green attire. Stacie's long-sleeved thermal shirt was white, Joanie's turtleneck was gray, and Victoria's hooded sweater was mahogany.

"Not exactly my style, but I appreciate the effort…I think. Wait, should I be worried that Dominic knew my size in everything?" questioned Victoria.

"And we're back to creepy," said Joanie. Randy shushed them as he searched the forest.

"Okay, focus, if Gedeon can track us, it probably already has been. We should decide where to intercept it," advised Randy. John pulled out his phone and scrolled over the map of the area.

"If we head southwest, we'll run into the national park. Heading east will put us too close to the city. The park is closed, at least. Everyone has already been evacuated," informed John.

"Why was it evacuated?" asked Chris.

"Wildfire. It was put out last week, but they are keeping it closed with everything else going on," said John.

"That's it then, that's the place. Anyone disagree?" asked Randy. They shook their heads, and he took a deep breath to calm his nerves. They darted off in the direction of the national park and kept a steady pace with one another as the forest sped by. The acrid stench of smoke and burnt wood filled their noses as the moon slipped behind the haze in the air. They jumped over the large creek that separated the lush greenery of the forest from the fire-stricken ruins and slowed to a halt when they were deep inside the national park. Each of them looked around at the frail, burnt trees and the ashes covering the soil. The acrid scent grew stifling as it thickened. The deeper they went into the forest, the heavier the scent wafted over them. The stench hung in the air.

"Are we sure this is a good idea? Everything is dead here. No nature, water, or fresh air to tap into. That seems kind of counterintuitive," said Stacie.

"That's the point. Nothing for him to kill. It's already been done. Besides, none of that helped us last time," said Randy.

"Are we even sure it'll show up?" asked Victoria. Before any of them could answer her, a sense of dread filled their stomachs, each let out a shiver, and chills went down their spines.

"I'm going to say that's a yes," whispered Joanie, as they scanned the area for any signs of the creature. Chris frowned when he heard a faint beeping sound in the distance.

"Do you hear that?" he asked. The sound grew closer, and an object whizzed past them before rolling onto the ground. Randy's eyes widened when he saw it.

"Bomb!" he yelled. He lunged forward to jump on the explosive and managed to land on it as it detonated. The chemical reaction and high-pressured gas brewed beneath him as Randy focused on extinguishing the blast. He was able to limit the radius of impact but was momentarily dazed by the explosion. Victoria grabbed the back of Joanie and Stacie's jackets and used two trees' branches to grab Chris and John when another device exploded. She whipped the five of them backward with the branches to avoid the blast and rolled down a small hill in the process. Randy flipped to his feet as Gedeon darted into the opening.

"I guess humans are good for something. I was surprised when I sensed your essence all the way up here, but even more so, when some of the humans tried to confront me on the way. To think, they really thought their mighty military could stop me. They sure do know how to make amazing weapons of destruction, though. I got those off a tank. How very strange of their species to think weapons of destruction can help save the world in such a state." Before Randy could react, Gedeon grabbed him by the arm and flung him backward. Randy crashed into a tree with a snap and thud before falling to the forest floor. He was momentarily dazed, but made it back to his feet as an eerie fog crept toward him. He squinted to try to see through the dense mist and search for the others, but to no avail. The sound of hisses and incoherent whispering filled his senses as the fog surrounded him.

"Stace? John? Chris? Can any of you hear me?" he called. In the distance, Victoria heard him as the fog impeded the visibility in the forest.

"I'm over here. Everyone okay?" called Victoria.

"I'm good," called Joanie.

"Same," said John.

"Me too," called Stacie.

"Anyone have eyes on it?" asked Chris. Victoria rubbed her eyes as the fog inched closer. A shadowy figure caught her periphery, and she spun around.

"I think I see some…thing…" she managed to get out as the figure drew closer. A lump formed in her throat when Alex emerged from the fog, bloody and trying to apply pressure to the gaping wound in his own chest.

"No, no, not again," she cried, as she darted over to tend to him. He fell to the ground and gazed up at her.

"Vic," he whispered. She shook her head and applied pressure to the wound. Viscous, onyx liquid slithered from under Alex to surround her, but she was too distracted by his pulse slowing to notice.

"Hey, stay with me."

"Why didn't you save me?" he asked, with hurt and betrayal in his tone. She shook her head.

"I did. We did. Stacie saved you once and she can do it…"

"They lied to you. That thing killed me. It's holding me hostage, Vic. My soul, it…it won't let me go unless it can have you."

"No, that's not true. They saved you. They told me."

"They didn't want you distracted. John didn't want you thinking about me. You know he's always been jealous of what we have." Stacie heard the false words in the distance. She couldn't see her sister, but could hear her sobs and the way her heart raced. She wanted to assure her that Alex was safe, that she had indeed saved him, but two shadowy figures in the fog halted her train of thought. The two were holding hands as they emerged from the fog wearing identical smiles.

"Mom? Dad?" she questioned, as tears filled her eyes. The woman nodded.

"It's us, sweetie."

"No, you're…you're not real. Neither is Alex, this isn't…none of this is…" The woman smiled warmly at her.

"If we weren't real, would I know that meeting your father at that conference was the best day of my life?" asked the woman.

Stacie gulped as the man took a step toward her. His hazel eyes and black, wavy hair were identical to her father's, but she shook her head again.

"You aren't them. You can't be. You're Gedeon. You're just messing with my head." The man frowned in concern.

"Who's Gedeon? Your mother's right, you know? Who would've known that meeting at that conference would've started all of this? I figured I would learn some tips about land contracts and the business, but I got so much more."

"How did you know that? No...he did this to Joanie. She warned us about this. You know things about us. This...you aren't really my parents," she recited to herself, trying to believe it as the two people she yearned to see again for years stood before her.

"We're so proud of your sisters and the women they've become. Joanie is a Seer? That's amazing. Victoria has always made her own path, no matter what," said the woman. Stacie tried her best to not let out a sob, as the woman stepped closer to her.

"We all miss you so much," confessed Stacie. The man tilted his head in fascination at her.

"Then why haven't you tried to save us?" he questioned. She gulped.

"What?"

"Your father is asking you a simple question, Stacie. You are the bringer of life. You have the power, but you won't use it for us. Why?" asked the woman. Stacie shook her head.

"That's not how it works. I can't bring back someone who has been gone for so..."

"Ethan lied to you about that. He doesn't want you to bring us back, because then you wouldn't need him to guide you. We can't believe you would fall for such a blatant manipulation, but you always have been naïve. You were always the weak one," said the woman.

"What? How could you say that?" The man smirked.

"Come on, deep down you know it's true. Victoria is strong. She would be strong enough to do it, but you? What have you done? Victoria was strong enough to take care of the family after that drunk human snatched us away from you. Joanie was strong enough to venture out on her own to try to find her own path, but you? You hid in Anderson and clung to your big sister because you're weak," taunted the man.

"I'm not weak!" shouted Stacie. Randy spun around in the direction of the outburst. He couldn't see more than a few inches in front of him but took a step in Stacie's direction.

"Stace? Stacie, where are you?" he called.

"Randy," whispered a voice that made him perk up.

"Chris, what's…" Chris interrupted him with a shush.

"It's Gedeon. He's messing with their heads. I can't get to Joanie either. I can't see. John, can you hear us?" asked Chris.

"I need to get to Vic. She's panicking," whispered John.

"I know, but don't worry. Focus on my voice. Both of you come to me and we'll go find them together. We've trained for this. Remember when Dominic blindfolded us in that cave? Rely on your other senses. Follow my voice," whispered Chris. He could hear John and Randy's footsteps drawing near. After all their years together as triplets, they knew each other's gaits and the sounds of their walks. Chris grabbed John's shoulder when he saw him, and John jumped.

"Don't do that! You scared the hell out of me!" whispered John.

"You've got to stop cursing like a sailor. Vic is a bad influence on you…in fact, how do we even know it's actually you?" questioned Randy, as he found them as well. John huffed.

"Because I don't curse like a sailor…I curse like a sheriff," said John.

"Okay, yep, that's definitely John," whispered Chris.

"What's happening to them?" asked Randy.

"Gedeon is…" Chris stopped midsentence, as he spotted a shadowy figure behind Randy. John and Randy sensed it too and both gulped when they spun around to see the figure emerge from the fog. There stood Dominic, wearing his usual black, designer dress shirt and black slacks. He fixed the cuffs of his shirt as he smiled wickedly.

"Hello, boys," said the man. Randy took a step forward, but Chris and John pulled him back.

"That's not Dominic," warned Chris. The man scoffed.

"Always such a tough crowd; been that way since you were a kid, Christopher. You know, your cynicism was just your way of hiding the truth, you weren't strong enough for this."

"That's not true. Dominic never believed that," said Chris.

"You didn't even believe in the cause. You hated humans. Not that I blame you, but the arrogance and superiority complex were a bit much. Well, until you met one you actually liked, right?"

"Don't listen to him, Chris," whispered John.

"If it weren't for Joanie, would any of this even matter to you? You didn't care about them before, so what's the big deal now? Is that why you left me back there to die? You just discarded me like any other human," said the man. Chris swallowed hard at the words. John could sense his resolve faltering.

"That's not true," said John, as he glared at the man.

"You're right, Jonathan. It's *your* fault. You know, I would expect such rage from Christopher, but you? I thought you were better than that. Who knew you would be my downfall? The rage you had when you found out about your real parents? How can such hate ever leave room for love? Let alone the ability to defeat the Ultimate Evil. The only one who ever cared about me was Randall and even he was too angry to give me just one chance to explain and say how sorry I was."

"Dominic," whispered Randy, as he took a step forward again. Chris grabbed him by the arm to pull him back.

"That isn't him, Randy," warned Chris. Dominic smirked.

"Surprise, surprise, Chris is cynical. Randall, take my hand. I can help you through this. I know how scared you are, but I'm not gone." Randy took another step forward, but John grabbed his other arm.

"Chris is right. Randy, Dominic is gone," reminded John. Randy frantically shook his head.

"He's right there! I knew he'd find a way back to us. He always does. Just let him help!"

"He's right, boys. Just let me help. You can't do this alone, Randall. You don't have to. Just give me your hand," urged the man.

It took all of Chris and John's strength to hold Randy back as he tried to jerk away from them to get to the figure.

"Let me go! He's right there!" yelled Randy.

"I'll forgive you for letting me die, Randall. All you have to do is take my hand now. Don't fail me again. It's coming back for me. Hurry!" Randy let out a sob as his brothers continued to pull him away from the figure.

"It isn't him!" assured John, but even his resolve began to falter when the Ultimate Evil appeared behind Dominic. Chris's eyes widened as well.

"Don't let him take me again! Please, I'll do anything. I'm sorry. Please," begged Dominic, as he reached out to Randy again. Chris winced and looked away as Dominic's scream filled their ears. Randy cried as his brothers dragged him in one direction and the Ultimate Evil dragged their mentor into the other.

"Let me go! We can't just let him die again!" shouted Randy, through angry tears.

"It isn't him! Gedeon is messing with our heads," assured John. He sighed when Randy pushed him away from him.

"You don't know that!"

"Yeah, we do, Randy, and so do you. Deep down," reminded John. Randy's shoulders slumped in defeat. Suddenly, the three of them jumped when Dominic's voice echoed behind them.

"So weak," bellowed the voice. They spun around just in time to see a black light glow from the figure's hands and surge toward them. A blast of energy crashed into the three of them and boosted them off the ground. They violently collided with the charred forest floor and let out grunts of pain as smoke engulfed them. Joanie heard the crash in the distance, but the thick smoke engulfing her surroundings was too dense and disorienting to push through. The edges of the vapors receded as she spotted a shadowy figure approaching in the distance. She sighed in relief when she saw the familiar gray cloak of the woman she'd been trying to reach for days.

"Kaya?" The woman removed the hood of her cloak as Joanie looked around.

"This is different from last time. Where are we? Why are we here?"

"I really thought you would be able to do it. I waited all these years, but I was wrong. I was so wrong."

"Wrong about what? Do you know now how we can end this? Why didn't we stop it when we created Absolution? Were we wrong about all of it? Kaya, why are you just standing there? What were you wrong about?" asked Joanie, as she took a step toward the woman. She stopped in her tracks as the pit in her stomach grew and a sense of dread filled her.

"You," said the woman. Joanie gulped.

"Wh…what do you mean?"

"You aren't the Seer. How could you be? Your job was to protect them, to guide them through all this, and yet what happened? Dominic is dead. Anderson is gone. You are lucky Stacie was there to save Alex, but at what cost? She's too weak now, Joanie. She can't possibly help in her condition."

"What are you talking about? Stacie is fine. Better than fine, the Lucis…"

"Oh, please. You were there. You saw the way the Ultimate Evil depleted her of energy."

"She just needed to rest."

"You should've seen it coming. Even Dominic tried to warn you, but did you listen? No. You never do."

"That's not true."

"You aren't strong enough to be the Seer, Joanie. The prophecy was wrong. All this is wrong."

"This doesn't make any sense. None of this makes sense."

"I tried to warn you in your dreams. I've done all I could for you, but now? Look around you. The earth is dying, and soon, everyone you love will be dead, too."

"We won't let that happen."

"It's too late. It's inescapable at this point. It always was. The fates have chosen their side." Joanie frowned in confusion at the words.

"What did you just say?"

"It's too late."

"No, about fate. That's not what she thinks. Kaya doesn't believe any of that. She showed me the way. I felt her hope, her joy." The woman shook her head in disappointment.

"Things change, Joanna, but let me help you. You can't do this alone, but I can guide you once again. Just give me your hand." The woman took a step toward her, but Joanie took a step back. She looked around again at the smoke billowing and surrounding them.

"This isn't where I saw her. This isn't her home."

"I'm right here, sweet girl. Where else would I possibly be, in such a time?"

"I don't know, but I think it's time to ask her myself." Joanie closed her eyes, and her hands began to glow with white and blue light. The figure's eyes widened.

"No!" Before it could reach her, pulses of light surged forward from Joanie's hands. The figure shrieked and retreated into the distance as the wind swirled around Joanie, dispersing the fog. She began to float in the air and her eyes glowed with white light, as she used all her might to summon Kaya to her. The fog cleared, her breathing steadied, and bright, white light replaced the darkness that surrounded her. She sighed in relief as she looked around at the familiar safe haven.

"Kaya?" she called out. A small smile crept onto her lips when Kaya approached from the distance. The older woman removed the hood of her cloak to reveal her gray hair, heart-shaped face, and wise, gray eyes. Her beautiful umber skin contrasted against the white of her hair and the warmth of her smile immediately put Joanie at ease.

"I'm glad you didn't fall for such a trick." Kaya giggled when Joanie hugged her tightly.

"It's really you, isn't it?"

"You're safe here," assured Kaya.

"I'm less worried about my subconscious and more worried about my actual body out there. Are you sure this is safe? Last time, my sisters were able to watch my back."

"Your light banished Gedeon." Joanie's eyes widened.

"Is that really its name?"

"No, but it fits. You were able to daze it, but it will return, once it regains its power."

"How is that possible? I don't even know what I did. I just called you."

"You called me, but also upon the light within."

"Okay, enough with the riddles. What does that even mean?"

"Your light. You each have it, you always have, but you have to tap into it now, more than ever."

"But I thought we already created Absolution."

"You put the process into motion, but it's just that, a process."

"Why didn't you tell me that before?"

"I told you everything I knew at the time. Like I said then, I knew how that part ended. I'm not sure about this one. You created Absolution and gave humanity a chance, but by doing so, Gedeon was unleashed as well. You see, the universe always gets what it needs and finds the balance. The question becomes, is a great good like the Naturas the balance needed to ensure that humans will be what is needed moving forward, or is a great evil needed as a reset for this part of the universe?"

"How can the fates and universe accept mass extinction as a solution?"

"Not a solution, a consequence, and nothing has been accepted. The events unfold when they need to, not when we want them to, Joanie, but you have a say in those events. The Naturas were created to be a great force of good. I hope with all my heart that you will be enough to win. I believe you are. Hope is the message, after all, but understand that nothing is given that cannot be taken away. The Ultimate Evil has arrived to feed off of humankind and finish what the humans started. If you believe it is a flawed path forward, then you must stop it."

"Okay, but how?"

"I cannot show you that. The future is uncertain."

"Is that why I haven't been able to see anything?"

"You haven't been able to see anything because there is nothing to see."

"So...not that I'm complaining...but why are you here then?" Kaya smiled mischievously.

"Because the fates do indeed always have their way. I can't show you the future, but I can show you what has transpired. Your friend, the Praevian, is right. Sometimes knowing why and how can reveal patterns," explained Kaya. She held out her hands and Joanie immediately placed her palms on them. Their eyes glowed with white light as the events from the moment the Ultimate Evil arrived replayed in her mind. Every move, every spoken word was retraced. She saw the scientists it murdered, the night it arrived in Anderson, and all of their encounters. She gasped as the visions returned back to that moment in time. Realization dawned on her and Kaya gave her a wink.

"I can't say anything else. Doing so could do more harm than actual good, but I believe in you, Joanie. Follow your instincts. You have everything you need. Fare thee well," whispered Kaya. Suddenly, Joanie was jolted back into the darkness. She blinked several times and wiped her eyes as she took in her surroundings. She was back in the forest. Chris, John, and Randy were crumpled on the ground. The sound of Victoria coughing and gasping for air caused Joanie to jump into action. Smoke swirled and suffocated Victoria, as she fell to her knees. Joanie caught her sister before Victoria could collapse. She closed her eyes and harnessed the wind around her to clear out the smoke in strong gusts. Joanie sighed in relief when Stacie ran over to kneel down beside Victoria to heal her.

"You okay, Stace?" asked Joanie.

"Yeah, but that thing has officially pissed me off." Victoria coughed and rubbed her chest as Stacie finished healing her. She was able to make it back to her feet and dusted herself off.

"Really, *now* you're pissed off?" grumbled Victoria.

"It tried to use mom and dad against me," said Stacie.

"I thought it was Alex. It used him to play on my fears. What the hell is this thing?"

"I don't know, but I knew that wasn't mom and dad. They always thought I hung the moon. That thing may have wanted to play off my insecurities about being the only sister who hasn't exactly branched out, but using mom and dad was the wrong move," said Stacie. The sound of John, Randy, and Chris's coughs had the three of them racing over to be by their sides. Stacie's hands glowed with white light and each of the brothers slowly began to breathe easier as she healed them.

"Thanks, Stacie," said John, as Victoria pulled him into her arms to look him over.

"You okay?" asked Victoria. John gave a nod.

"Yeah, I think so, but I really hate this thing," said John.

"Stace, are you okay? You're using a lot of your power and just woke up. Do you have the energy for this?" asked Randy, as he checked for any signs she was injured.

"Actually, I'm great. It's like those Luci gave me a jolt or something. I've never felt better," said Stacie. Joanie frowned when Chris could barely make it into a seated position on the forest floor.

"Chris, what's wrong? Stace, I thought you healed him," said Joanie.

"I did," assured Stacie. Chris rubbed his chest as he gave a nod.

"She did. I'm just tired. Gedeon was draining us, but I'll be fine. I just need a minute," he explained. Chris was surprised when Randy and John hugged him tightly. The force of the hug sent them backward and he let out a grunt as they continued to hug him.

"Little tight," wheezed Chris. They immediately let go.

"Sorry," chuckled John.

"Did we miss something?" asked Victoria. John smiled warmly at his brother as he helped him to his feet.

"Chris took the brunt of it to save us. Gedeon was using his power to drain us of ours. We were huddled on the ground and Chris shielded us."

"He sacrificed himself for us," added Randy.

"You're my brothers. Of course I did." Joanie pulled Chris into her arms and noticed how he was barely able to stay on his feet. She cupped his cheek and he leaned into her touch.

"Don't worry about me, *tesoro*. I'm okay," he assured. He tried to put on a brave smile but sighed when he let out a small cough. She smiled as realization dawned on her.

"Stacie healed you, but you still have smoke inhalation, just like with Alex. Victoria was exhausted from fighting it off. It touched the vines, but never her. That's how it was draining her, through the nature she was connected with, but never directly touching her. Alex, Stacie, and Chris all came into direct contact, so Gedeon managed to do more damage. Its remnants infected Stacie, so it worked even though it wasn't there," said Joanie.

"Wait, how do you know that?" asked Victoria.

"Kaya showed me the events leading up to now. I know how Gedeon's powers work and how to do this." She cupped her husband's cheek again and smiled adoringly at him. Her hand began to glow with white light.

"I got you," she assured before tenderly pressing her lips to his. White light pulsed through his body as their lips meshed together. Chris could feel his body buzzing with energy. She pulled back with a smile at his stunned expression. John and Randy's eyes widened as Chris's hands began to glow with white light.

"What the hell?" asked John. He smiled sheepishly when Randy slapped his shoulder to scold him for his language.

"Okay, maybe Vic has rubbed off on me a bit," he conceded.

"Whoa," whispered Chris. He flexed his fingers as white light surged again through his body.

"How is he doing that?" asked Randy.

"Because we can all do that," revealed Joanie. She scanned the area for Gedeon to make sure there were no signs of the creature before pulling them all over to her.

"Gedeon will be here soon. When we were in that fog, I was able to connect with Kaya. The light I used to get to her dazed him, but he'll be back soon." Victoria pinched the bridge of her nose.

"I know I say it often…but, what?" exclaimed Victoria.

"I know it's a lot, but trust me. We got this," assured Joanie.

"Got what? Chris, do you know what she's talking about? How are you doing that? What power are you tapping into?" asked John. Chris smiled adoringly at his wife and shrugged as he looked down at his glowing hands.

"I don't know, but this feels a lot like déjà vu, doesn't it? The night we created Absolution, we knew it meant something when we felt that power surge through us," said Chris.

"Stace, try it. It should be pretty easy for you now," suggested Joanie. Stacie frowned in confusion.

"Try what?" asked Stacie. Joanie's hands continued to glow with white light as she reached out for her sister's hand. The moment their hands touched, Stacie's began to glow with the same white light. Stacie beamed with happiness.

"Are the Luci doing this?" asked Stacie.

"No, it's you. You just finally believed that you were powerful enough to do it because you have a boost from the Lucis in your system. I know how to beat Gedeon. Kaya helped me see it. We just have to tap into the light."

"The light?" questioned John.

"Yeah. I know you feel it. Think of how you feel every time you are with Vic. How it felt to see her that first time at the carnival, how you just knew she was special," instructed Joanie. John closed his eyes and felt a surge of energy pump through his heart when he thought about Victoria. He focused on that feeling and embraced it as it flowed through his body. He grinned from ear to ear when he opened his eyes and saw his fists glowing with the white light.

"Okay, that's pretty cool," he admitted. Joanie winked at him, but Victoria flailed her arms to get their attention.

"And yet again, with a freaking demon on the loose, I ask a simple question. How?" asked Victoria.

"Love," said Joanie. Victoria rolled her eyes.

"Joanie, I swear if you start singing a Beatles song right now…"

"Vic, I'm serious. John, Stacie, and Chris have already tapped into it. All you have to do is let go of the fear and the hate. Gedeon feeds off it. I saw what happened when you fought Gedeon before. You were so enraged that it fed off your hate. You were beating it, Vic. You have way more power than you realize, but Gedeon fed off that hate."

"Of course I was full of hate. Gedeon had just killed my best friend."

"I know, but this time is different. You know now that won't work. The same happened with you, Randy. You were so angry about what Gedeon did to Stacie. It used that anger against you. We can't beat Gedeon with hate. That's what fuels it," explained Joanie.

"How am I not supposed to hate the very thing that killed Dominic and wants to harm everyone I love?" asked Randy.

"Don't focus on what you've lost. Focus on what you gain from stopping it. You gain a future with Stacie, and us. You can give the world a chance to do better, to be better. You can't change what's been taken from us, Randy, but you can stop it from doing even more harm. This isn't about duty or revenge or honor anymore. It's about casting out the darkness with the light," said Joanie. She closed her eyes and began to glow with the white light even more, as she focused on the people and home she wanted to save. Chris's senses perked up as the sounds of hissing and whispering returned behind them. They turned to see Gedeon stalking forward with two onyx tendrils trailing behind him. It shook with rage as its body glowed with black light and the tendrils thickened. Their phones buzzed in their pockets and they each read the text message from Carlos but didn't need to as they felt the surge in energy as well. The sky was black, haze smothered the moon, and fog had crept back in. They could feel the energy crackling in the air as the solar maximum began. Gedeon stretched its neck and sighed.

"Let's finish this," said Gedeon.

"Pretty sure that solar maximum is now a problem. It's now or never, so what's the plan?" asked Victoria.

"Chris, John, Stacie, and I will fan out to surround it. Remember, focus on the good, not the bad," instructed Joanie. Randy frowned.

"What about me and Vic?" asked Randy. Joanie smiled slyly.

"We need you to keep it busy. Do your worst," urged Joanie.

"My worst? Joans, my worst is not full of love and rainbows and butterflies. You're sending me mixed signals about not using hate here," said Victoria. Joanie winked at her sister.

"If the four of us can get in position, we can stop it, but only if you two can hold it off while we do. We'll need your help finishing it off though," said Joanie.

"And how are we supposed to know when that is?" asked Randy.

"We'll have a code word. When you hear it, try your best to tap into everything you love, and all the energy should flow through you. Let's make the code word Lennon," she instructed. Victoria rolled her eyes and Randy frowned in confusion.

"What is…" Victoria cut him off.

"We'll explain later. Focus," said Victoria. Gedeon smiled, as it looked up at the sky and rain began to fall. Chris held his palm out and glared at Gedeon.

"It's acid rain," informed Chris. Gedeon closed its eyes and exhaled slowly as the earth began to quake and gales of wind morphed into tornadoes.

"You're too late. The blackouts have started as we speak. The magnetic field is too powerful and the geo-storms are beginning. The world will be shrouded in darkness and there's nothing you can do. The humans don't deserve your kindness. They polluted the earth. They eliminate entire species in order to dominate the food chain, but conquer each other, to wipe out their own. Leave them to me and I will spare you. I'll be sure to leave you some scraps to rebuild with," taunted Gedeon.

"Can I go punch it in the face now?" asked Victoria. Joanie nodded and John smiled adoringly at his fiancée.

"I would love to see that," said John. Victoria gave Randy a nod. He summoned lightning from the sky and Gedeon laughed as a bolt struck its chest. It stumbled backward for a moment before stalking forward again.

"Is that really the best you've got? Did you not learn from last time? There's nothing you can do to me that I can't take!" Victoria's hands glowed with green and white light as she and Randy circled Gedeon. Another bolt of lightning struck it just as Victoria lunged forward to punch Gedeon across the face. John, Chris, Joanie, and Stacie began to circle the Ultimate Evil as it focused its attention on trying to block Victoria's blows and Randy's lightning bolts. Gedeon stumbled backward as Victoria kneed it in the stomach with all her might and Randy followed the move with a ball of fire. Gedeon noticed the others surrounding and chuckled darkly as it cracked the earth beneath them. The ground began to slowly sink away. Joanie gave a nod to Chris, John, and Stacie.

"Now!" she called. She used the wind from the tornado to boost them off of the ground as they focused on the white light surging through them. They hovered over the gaping holes and the light gathered in their chests. The white light surged forward from each of them, but a barrier of black light materialized to form a shield around the creature. Gedeon smirked as it fought off Victoria, dodged Randy's advances, and deflected the white light. Victoria punched it repeatedly as she raged on, but Gedeon fed off the strong waves of hatred radiating from the Natura. Gedeon sprung forward and grabbed her by the neck. It hoisted her in the air as it tightened its grip on her.

"So much rage for a Natura," it taunted.

"Vic!" yelled John. His light began to flicker as he watched his fiancée struggle against Gedeon's hold.

"I got her!" assured Randy. He charged forward to attack Gedeon, but one of Gedeon's tendrils reached out to snatch Randy from the quaking earth. Randy fought against the tendril, but to no avail. Its hold tightened like a vice grip around Randy's neck. Randy let out a wheeze of pain.

"Randy!" shouted Stacie. Gedeon sighed as he smiled sadly at them.

"Such a waste of power. It doesn't have to end like this. I'll make the same offer to the two of you as I did before. Your rage shows me that you understand. This earth, these humans, they cause nothing but pain. Let me finish this and you can do with the remains what you like." Randy and Victoria glanced at each other and

Gedeon's head tilted in fascination as their hands began to glow with white light. The light flowed through their bodies, flooded into their chests, and surged forward to pierce Gedeon in the chest. The sinister figure was caught off guard and immediately relinquished its hold on them. The light began to overpower it, as Victoria and Randy closed their eyes to focus. Instead of rage surging through her, Victoria thought about her parents, her sisters, the people in her life she loved, and the thought of seeing Alex again. Randy thought about his brothers, the way Stacie made him feel, and the letter Dominic wrote. Gedeon's onyx tendrils drooped, and the sable substance began melting into pools. The black light shielding Gedeon from the others flickered and dimmed until it disappeared altogether.

When the light from Joanie, Chris, Stacie, and John pierced it from different directions, Gedeon fell to its knees. White light began to pulse in waves through Gedeon and the creature looked up at the rays of light that began filling the night sky. With one final surge of energy, the sky erupted, blasting them all backward. They each crashed to the earth as billows of smoke and dust swirled around. They coughed and sputtered. The earth stopped eroding, the tornadoes dissolved, and the acid rain ceased. The Naturas slowly sat up as the smoke cleared and streaks of blue, red, green, and white fluttered across the sky. Flakes of color seeped into the soil as the six of them looked around at the desolation. There were sinkholes surrounding the clearing, the burnt forest floor was flooded with acid rain, and trees were toppled over from the strong winds. The flakes of color began shimmering in the soil as the earth shifted and slowly closed the sinkholes. The acidic rain turned to clean water that nourished the earth and grass sprouted from the charred destruction. The trunks of the trees were restored, and branches straightened, as the forest began to heal. They each scanned the area for any signs of the Ultimate Evil. Victoria sighed in relief when they found none. She giggled as John helped her to her feet and scooped her up into his arms for a warm embrace.

"We did it!" he chuckled.

"Yeah, I think we actually did," agreed Victoria. Joanie smiled teasingly at her sister.

"What? No smartass comments this time about that being it? Was that enough for you?" asked Joanie.

"I mean last time it did seem underwhelming and I was right. The battle, the boom, much more like it. I thought you were going to say Lennon," said Victoria.

"There was no need. You and Randy work well together and I knew you would figure it out. After all, all you need is love," said Joanie with a cheeky grin. Victoria playfully glared at her and shook her head.

"You just had to ruin it. It's ruined," grumbled Victoria, as she continued to look around the clearing. Stacie smirked.

"Well, I, for one, could've done without having my body infected by that monster and people I love almost dying, but hey, beggars, choosers, and all that," said Stacie. Joanie shook her head in amusement and Randy chuckled as Stacie jumped into his arms. Chris laced his fingers with Joanie's and sighed happily.

"We did it, *tesoro*." Joanie looked up at the sky as the streaks of red, green, and blue bowed out gracefully and dissipated to make way for the aurora borealis dancing in waves above them.

"Yeah, we did," she said, as relief washed over her. She smiled when he pulled her in for a kiss as waves of euphoric energy swirled around them. Every instinct inside the Naturas buzzed blissfully as they knew it to be true. The Ultimate Evil had been defeated and the process for Absolution was able to continue.

EPILOGUE

The Fates Will Always Have Their Way

Victoria rolled down her window as she cruised into Anderson in her Mustang. The cool breeze kept the air crisp on that sunny Spring morning, and she couldn't help but have butterflies in her stomach as the nerves threatened to get the best of her. It was her wedding day and her sisters suggested meeting in town for breakfast before focusing on all the things they needed to do before the ceremony. Almost six months had passed since the prophecy was fulfilled and the Naturas defeated the Ultimate Evil. Victoria found herself finally able to focus on the future. The months after were a whirlwind of rebuilding and restoration for Anderson, just like for the rest of the world. Part of the process of Absolution was healing the earth after the destruction caused by Gedeon. The energy the Naturas created reversed much, but not all of the damage. The sinkholes closed and the contaminated water cleansed itself of the toxins. The tumultuous string of natural disasters around the world came to an end and the earth was able to stabilize. While not everything could be undone, the process ensured that humans all over the world could come together to focus on repairing the damage, but also mend the relationships between countries and people as a whole. For the first time in a long time, the world focused on hope and peace more than spreading hate and hysteria. Victoria returned to work as sheriff to help Anderson rebuild with the funds anonymously donated to the town by the Guardians. The last act of the Brotherhood was to officially dissolve and disperse the remaining funds of the group to global initiatives and organizations focused on recovery and disaster relief. The entire world was upended when the Ultimate Evil arrived, and the months of restoration were only the beginning of the healing process.

Victoria parked her Mustang in front of the antique shop and looked around the square. There was still much work to do, but construction had been completed on the main road in town and most of the buildings of the square were in various states of renovation. She entered the antique store and saw Joanie thanking two customers. The regulars waved at Victoria as they left, and Joanie made her way around the counter with a sheepish smile.

"Last one, I promise."

"Shouldn't you be wrangling me on my wedding day, not the other way around?"

"No wrangling needed. I just had to drop in to get your gift and they wanted to pick up a few things before I closed back up."

"My gift, huh? So, this is where you've been hiding it."

"Yet another benefit of moving out will be not having to find creative places to hide presents from you."

"It's going to be weird returning from the honeymoon to an empty house."

"I know, but let's not get too dramatic about it. We're just down the road and you can come over whenever you want. We both know Stacie already plans to make herself at home the moment me and Chris move in." They both giggled when the bell over the door cued them to someone entering the store and Stacie walked in with a playful glare.

"I heard that," said Stacie.

"I was counting on it," teased Joanie.

"Why are you parked over here? I thought we were meeting at Ray's for breakfast. Is Joanie being a workaholic again?" asked Stacie. Victoria nodded as Joanie rolled her eyes.

"I just had to grab something," said Joanie.

"And make sure Mr. and Mrs. Ross got that set of vinyl they've been eyeing for weeks," said Victoria.

"Are you going to take your gift or keep teasing me?" asked Joanie.

"I can do both. I'm versatile like that. Now, give it to me," said Victoria. Joanie handed her the wrapped present and Stacie peeked over Victoria's shoulder as she opened it. Victoria gasped when she saw the framed picture of their parents.

"Joans, where did you find this?" asked Victoria. Tears filled her eyes as she traced over the smiling faces of her parents in the picture. The couple looked very much in love as they gazed adoringly at one another in their white dress and black tuxedo.

"I found it while I was going through some of the stuff in the attic and knew it would be perfect for today. I know how much we all wish they were here, so I figured at least we can have a picture of them from their wedding day on your wedding day." Victoria pulled her sister in for a hug and Joanie giggled when Stacie hugged them both as well.

"Thank you," said Victoria.

"Okay, me next," said Stacie. She handed Victoria an envelope.

"What's this?" asked Victoria as she opened it.

"Two tickets to Costa Rica. I figured you could add it to your trip. John mentioned wanting to zipline there and I figured it would be perfect for the two of you."

"And the dates fit into our itinerary; I'm impressed. Thank you both. I can't believe we leave in a couple of days. Time is just flying by."

"Yep, and by the end of the day, you'll be married. How do you feel about that? Full disclosure, I've been waiting on a meltdown over it and am a bit surprised you haven't had one yet," admitted Joanie.

"I don't have meltdowns…anymore," said Victoria.

"Our big sis with all the commitment issues has finally grown up. About time," said Stacie. Victoria playfully nudged Stacie with her hip.

"I will have you know, I'm great and there will be no meltdowns. Is it a little nerve-racking that the entire town is giving me googly eyes and congratulating me? Sure. Is it strange to have people asking about my honeymoon and older women teasing me about being a lucky woman? Obviously. Am I worried about everything going off without a hitch or that our wedding day will get derailed, like Joanie's? Maybe…"

"And here she goes," whispered Stacie as Joanie eyed their sister carefully.

"Vic," warned Joanie.

"I mean sure, I'm getting married and you're moving out and Stacie moved out without actually telling anyone she moved out months ago…"

"I like to keep it light, so sue me," said Stacie, with a shrug.

"And everything is changing, now and even though I'm sheriff again, I don't know how much longer I can be sheriff as an immortal or even if I should. When will people start noticing that I'm not aging? When should I walk away and just retire? I'm about to spend months on leave yet again, so I can travel and have an extended honeymoon with John, so should I just hang it up now and let Alex take over for good? I mean, how am I even supposed to decide that after everything has happened? And on top of that, how much longer can we even live in Anderson? Are we going to have to leave our homes soon, to keep a low profile? Where would we even live next? Would we move to the same place or go our separate ways?"

"And just like that, she's spiraling. Vic, breathe," said Joanie. Victoria started to pace as she fanned herself.

"Is it hot in here? It feels hot in here." Stacie placed her hands on her sister's shoulders and steered her over to the chair Joanie pulled out for her. Victoria sat down and took some deep breaths as Stacie gave her a comforting smile.

"Vic, you're about to marry the man you love and spend the rest of your lives together," said Stacie.

"Yep, our whole lives, our entire immortal, eternal, forever-living lives," said Victoria. She tried to get up to pace again, but Joanie stepped in and placed her hands on her shoulders as well.

"Vic..." Victoria interrupted her sister.

"I can't be sheriff anymore. Why did I agree to take back over? But if I did force myself into retirement, who even am I if I'm not Sheriff McNamara anymore? Just someone's wife? Only known to the world as John's wife? No longer Victoria McNamara..." Joanie frowned in confusion.

"He's taking our last name," reminded Joanie. Stacie shook her head in amusement.

"Oh, she's losing it," whispered Stacie.

"Who am I? Who are we? What is our purpose as immortals now that we've created Absolution? Is John having doubts since he's no longer trying to save the world every day? He proposed when we were on the run from Dominic. Now that all of that is over, does he still feel the same...is it actually over?"

"And, she's gone," said Joanie.

"We've been wrong before. What if we're wrong now? What if...?" Joanie interrupted her.

"No, no more what if's or what about's. Vic, you deserve to be happy. You have spent most of your life watching out for others and for us. You've sacrificed and put everyone else first. Yes, things are changing, and they'll continue to change, but that's a good thing. You love John and he loves you. You're worrying about nothing. So, today, we're going to eat breakfast at Ray's and then go back to the house to get ready and you're going to have a beautiful wedding. Life is good. I know how easy it is to look for the bad when things are so good, because we aren't used to having this much good for so long, but it's all real, Vic. You get to be happy, and no one is going to take that away from you, no matter if that is today or centuries from now," said Joanie.

"Centuries! Who said anything about centuries?" asked Victoria. Joanie threw her hands up in exasperation.

"Just breathe, Vic," added Stacie. Victoria took a shaky breath and regained composure.

"Okay, I'm breathing now," said Victoria.

"Feel better, now that you got that out of your system? You done?" asked Joanie. Victoria took another deep breath and slowly exhaled.

"Yeah, I'm fine now. Thanks."

"You sure? We've been waiting for this," asked Stacie.

"Yes, I'm good. I'm sure. I just needed a minute to…"

"Freak out?" asked Joanie.

"Create an imaginary abyss to stare into?" asked Stacie.

"I was going to say vent my concerns, but sure, yeah," said Victoria.

"Look, why don't we head to Ray's and get some breakfast?" suggested Joanie.

"Actually, I'm going to go for a walk," said Victoria. Stacie and Joanie glanced at each other nervously.

"You sure?" asked Joanie. Victoria nodded as she headed for the door.

"I'm sure. I'll meet you there in ten," Victoria called, before exiting the antique store. Joanie grumbled under her breath, as she pulled out her phone and Stacie smiled smugly.

"Sending fifty bucks to you now," grumbled Joanie.

"Always a pleasure predicting the predictable for you, Seer," teased Stacie.

"I really thought she would forego the meltdown. She loves John and was doing so well."

"Of course, she loves John and that's just it. None of this is about him. It's about her. Victoria hasn't allowed herself to just focus on herself since we were teenagers. She thinks it's selfish to go for what she wants and to have it all. A lot of amazing changes have happened, and she just needs a beat to wrap her mind around them," assured Stacie. Joanie nodded her understanding as they watched their sister walk down the street of the square.

Victoria found herself wandering aimlessly, as she walked around the renovated square. She sat down on a bench in front of the grocery store and took a deep breath of fresh air to calm her nerves. Her shoulders began to relax as she closed her eyes and allowed the spring breeze to wash over her. The smell of the trees and flowers in bloom brought her peace, while she sat there processing all of her emotions and thought about the changes in her life. She was still the sheriff, but had delegated more responsibilities to Alex as her deputy, so she could have more time away from work. That included stepping away to embark on a new adventure with the man she loved and traveling for a couple of months. Her life wasn't the only one changing, either. Stacie and Randy were settling into domestic life and quite enjoying the routine of living together. Randy had taken a liking to raku pottery. He was even in the process of building his own workshop space and kiln after Stacie's encouragement. Joanie and Chris were heading to Maui for a vacation, before she officially took over as owner of the antique shop. With Ethan and Gabriella deciding to move to Spain to be closer to the other Praevians, Joanie was offered the storefront. She was more than happy to take it. Their lives were changing and while Anderson would always be home, Victoria wasn't sure how to feel about everything happening at once. Boisterous laughter and teasing caught her attention, and she opened her eyes with a smile when Ezra, Ollie, and Jordan strolled out of the grocery store with candy in their hands. They waved when they spotted her.

"Hi, Sheriff McNamara," they said in unison.

"Where's John? Why isn't he with you?" asked Ollie. He received a punch in the shoulder in response from Jordan, and Ezra chuckled as the two bickered.

"What was that for?" asked Ollie.

"That's none of your business, idiot," argued Jordan.

"I'm not an idiot. You're an idiot, idiot," argued Ollie. Victoria giggled at their interaction.

"Hey boys, John is at home. I'll tell him you said hi, Ollie. What are you up to?"

"Nothing, just getting some candy and going to the comic-book store," said Jordan.

"So same old, same old, for you three. Nice."

"Aren't you getting married today?" asked Ollie. Victoria took a deep breath to calm her nerves and nodded.

"Yes, I am."

"At your house?" asked Ollie.

"Yes."

"My mom said it's weird that you're getting married there and not at the new church," said Ollie. He dodged Jordan's hand before his friend could hit him again.

"Stop hitting me!"

"Stop saying dumb stuff, idiot!" said Jordan.

"I'm not an idiot! I'm tired of you calling me an idiot and…" Victoria shook her head as she and Ezra watched the two boys bicker again.

"Are they always like this?" asked Victoria. Jordan and Ollie blushed at the question.

"Yep, always," said Ezra.

"Well, you three have fun at the comic-book store. I should get going. I have a wedding to get ready for, after all." She heard Ezra following her, as she walked away and turned back to face him.

"Everything okay, Ezra?" He smiled sheepishly and stuffed his hands into his pockets.

"Yeah, uh, I just…well I was just wondering about…uh…never mind…"

"You know, things have been so crazy around here that I never did get to thank you for the tip about Old Mill Road." His eyes widened.

"You went out there?"

"Yep, but you don't have to worry anymore. It's all been taken care of and that woman you saw is safe because of you."

"Really?"

"Really. You did a good thing, Ezra, so thank you." She turned to leave again, but he called to her.

"What about that other thing we talked about? You know…the demon?" he whispered, as he looked around suspiciously.

"You have nothing to worry about anymore," she assured.

"Are you sure? It looked really scary. When the military came and we had to leave, I thought it was because the demon was coming, but Ollie and Jordan didn't believe me." She knelt in front of him.

"This stays between you and me, but you were right. There was a demon, but it's gone now, and it won't be back, ever again. The town is safe and you're the reason why. Telling me what you saw that day helped a lot, so thank you. That was very brave." He smiled shyly.

"It was no big deal. It's cool to know I can tell you stuff, and you'll believe me."

"I'll always believe you," she promised.

"Cool. Well, have fun at your wedding," he said, before jogging back over to Ollie and Jordan, who were still bickering. She headed back down the block. She playfully rolled her eyes when she spotted Alex leaning against his patrol car in the parking lot.

"What are you doing out here? I'm not even on my honeymoon yet, and you're already slacking," she teased.

"Aren't you supposed to be getting ready to walk down the aisle? What are you doing?"

"I just needed some fresh air and decided to say hi to some of the kids. I'm cool like that."

"Oh, yeah, that's what kids think of the sheriff, that you're totally cool," he teased back.

"How long is your shift? You better not be late to my wedding."

"I'll be done by noon and promise to be on time. I wouldn't miss a chance to see you walking down the aisle."

"I'm glad you'll be there."

"Even if you're not walking down it to me," he added. He chuckled when she nudged him.

"See, you had to go and make it weird."

"Wouldn't be me if I didn't. So, why are you really out here?"

"I don't know. I guess I'm just thinking. A lot has happened over the past few months."

"That's one way of putting it. I still can't believe my best friend since childhood is actually an immortal who saved the world. I always knew you were bigger than this small town, but I had no clue just how big."

"You know, with everything that's been going on, we haven't really had time to talk about…you know…everything. Are you sure you're okay?"

"It's taken some time to process everything, and I still don't really understand it all, but you saved me and our home. That's all I really need to know. I still don't know how you managed to get the funds for all of this though. This place has needed a facelift for years. Leave it to you to take a disaster and turn it into a positive." She sighed as she looked around the town square. There were fewer signs of the attack on the town every day. The roads were repaved, and the debris was gone. The hospital and schools were the first to be rebuilt and each was given the upgrades in technology and design that the small town had needed for decades. The new park was in the process of being completed and construction trucks and groups of renovation teams were scattered throughout the square, as the small businesses, city hall, and police department underwent repairs.

"I just wish I could've done more."

"Vic, we've talked about this. You've done plenty. This place would've been wiped off the map if not for all of you."

"I had no hand in that, remember?"

"You and Stacie may have been down for the count after that thing attacked us, but you still did plenty."

"Then why do I feel so guilty?" He nodded his understanding.

"So *that's* why you're out here, instead of getting pampered and ready for your big day. You don't think you deserve it."

"A lot of people died that day, Alex. We might've saved the world, but we didn't save everyone in it. It feels weird knowing that and still feeling so…"

"Happy?" She nodded and he wrapped an arm around her with a sigh.

"Look, I get it. You wouldn't be you if you didn't obsess over doing more, and yeah, a lot of people died, but a lot more would've died if not for you. You did everything you could to save as many people as possible. You and Stace almost died in the process, so none of that, especially today of all days. Take it from someone who has watched you bury yourself in work for years; you get to be happy today, Vic. You get to go on your honeymoon and know that you did your part. Anderson is safe; hell, the world is safe because of you, and now you can actually enjoy it."

"You know, I never expected you, of all people, to give me a pep talk on my wedding day," she confessed.

"I can admit it sucked for a while knowing that you and John were getting married, but let's just say the world almost ending gave me some perspective. Life is too short to not be able to move on and enjoy it. I know you're going to worry, no matter what I say, but just remember that life is too short. Make sure you celebrate the happy moments."

"Yeah, not that short when you're an immortal." He rolled his eyes dramatically.

"Okay, okay, you're an immortal. You don't have to rub it in my face."

"What's the fun of being an immortal if I can't do that? Thanks again for the pep talk. I should head to Ray's." She kissed his cheek before heading in the direction of the diner. She felt much lighter than when she first arrived in the square. As soon as she walked into Ray's, she noticed John sitting in their usual booth and beamed with happiness. He was sitting there, casually perusing a menu, and sipping a mug of hot chocolate. He grinned from ear to ear when she slid into the booth beside him.

"Hi, big guy, what are you doing here? I thought you were going to be at Randy and Stacie's all day."

"A little birdie told me you could probably use a hug."

"A little birdie, huh?" She arched an eyebrow at him, and he smiled sheepishly.

"Stacie. It was Stacie," he confessed.

"It's always Stacie." He let out a chuckle and she sighed in relief as she nestled into his side. She played with the wisps of hair at the nape of his neck, and he kissed her forehead.

"Should I be worried that you're so stressed on a day that should be a happy time for us?" he questioned.

"Of course not; I'm not stressed about us. I'm just…I'm not used to having so many good things happen to me. I've told myself for a very long time that my job was to make others happy and that's all I needed to be happy. It's kind of scary suddenly focusing on my own happiness and putting myself first."

"I understand that." She frowned in confusion.

"You do?"

"Vic, I learned I was here to save the world when I was just a kid, well before human children even go through puberty. I've always accepted that, but it came with a lot of responsibility and pressure. I'm looking forward to spending time just being me, not an Element or a Natura, but just me, and I want to spend that time with you." She cupped his face and gazed adoringly into his gorgeous gray eyes.

"You really are perfect, you know that?"

"You're pretty perfect yourself. I love you."

"I love you too. I can't wait to marry you. Speaking of which, how much time do we have before we have to head back? Are Joans and Stace going to eat with us, or did they ditch me for being a bridezilla?"

"They said they would meet you back at the house when we're done. So, now that I have my beautiful fiancée to myself, I can ask the really hard questions. Are you ready? Brace yourself, it's a very complicated one." Victoria giggled and already knew what he would ask.

"Waffles, pancakes, or French toast?" she asked. He nodded happily.

"Exactly, how am I supposed to decide? It's a big day."

"It really is. Getting all three might just be in order," she suggested.

"Only if you split them with me."

"Deal," she agreed.

"See, compromise and communication; all staples of a good marriage. Trust me, I read about it," he said with a wink. She giggled and kissed him sweetly, before skimming the menu as well. While the neurotic part of her brain tried to convince her that there was no time to relax, and she had too much to do before the ceremony, she found herself relaxing into John's arms and letting herself be excited. He was right. So were her sisters and Alex. It was a good day and she deserved to embrace it.

o o o o o o

Randy stood nervously in front of the stone he'd been staring at for the past several minutes. He wasn't sure what compelled him to go there, especially on such a day. John and Victoria were getting married, and while he still did not fully understand the human ritual of marriage, the happiness radiating off of John let him know it was something to embrace once again. Chris and Joanie's wedding was beautiful, but the night ended so abruptly that he did not have much time to consider why such a thing was important. It was the reason he hesitated to engage in the tradition with Stacie. He had known for quite a while that eternity with her was what he wanted. Everything with her felt effortless, and yet he found himself confused and nervous, which is what brought him to the cemetery where Dominic was laid to rest months earlier. Randy took in a shaky breath as he found his voice and searched for the words to say.

"I'm sorry I haven't come sooner to see you again. It feels strange, knowing you're just here, buried in the ground. Stacie explained to me why such a thing happens and I understand it. I just don't really know what to do with it…I mean…with all of this. I have all these feelings lately about you, about the future now that we've created Absolution for good, but you were never someone to come to about feelings or emotions. I guess that's why I don't know how to feel about you now. Maya says relationships are complicated and vary depending on the people. I've actually become quite fond of her. She's nice. I think you would like her…well…after you got over her analyzing you so much. She's quite perceptive. She's the one who suggested I see you, but I've admittedly been putting it off. I told myself I didn't come when the others paid their respects before because I've been busy ever since Ethan put me in touch with some of his contacts. I've been talking to humans about how to prevent more wildfires in national parks. There were a lot when Gedeon arrived, but you know as well as I do that humans were doing plenty of damage well before it did. Carlos created some credentials for me and I've been working with Henrick to create a more efficient extinguishing agent. Who would've thought that I would be teaching the humans ways to put out fires? I wonder what you would think of all this?" He looked up at the sky and took another deep breath to steady his resolve.

"I forgive you," he finally whispered. The words brought tears to his eyes that surprised him and he quickly wiped one from his cheek. He cleared his throat before speaking up again.

"I forgive you for what you did to our parents. I still don't understand it, and I don't think I ever will, but I think Maya is right. You guided us to try to help us understand why we were here and how to help humans, but you are probably the most complicated human I know…well…knew. I hope it's okay that I requested for Phillip to move you here. I'm sure it's not the Guardian burial they assured they could give you, but I thought it would be nice. I don't have many plans to be in Singapore that often but we'll be here. This is our home and I guess a part of me wanted you here with us." He heard a car drawing near and smiled when he saw Ethan park the car alongside the trail. Ethan wore a sheepish smile as he approached with his hands stuffed in his pockets.

"I hope I'm not interrupting." Randy shook his head.

"No, I'm just trying to do what Stacie and Maya suggested. I'm not sure today is the best day for it, though. What are you doing here?"

"Maya suggested the same for me. We've been busy since we got back to town, so this has really been the only free moment I've had. I can come back if…"

"No, I'd like for you to stay." Ethan nodded his understanding and placed a comforting hand on Randy's shoulder.

"It's okay if you can't forgive him."

"I know, but I do. It's strange feeling so much all at once, but I think I really do forgive him. What about you? Are you having a hard time forgiving him for everything?" Ethan smirked.

"He killed me, Randy." It was Randy's turn to smile sheepishly.

"Right, sorry." Ethan shrugged.

"But he also saved me. Gedeon was going to kill me and I was prepared to die for all of you. You know that, but when I saw it grab Gabby, I faltered. The resolve I had about sacrifice faltered because I will die a thousand deaths for the six of you, but losing her in the process isn't something I could ever truly be okay with. So, while I still have…feelings…about the fact that he killed me, Dominic also saved me, but more importantly, he saved Gabby, and he sacrificed himself to do it. When I needed him in the end, he protected the woman I love, much like a good friend or brother would, so yes, I understand feeling quite complicated about him."

"That tracks," called a voice behind them. Randy spun around with a bright smile to see Stacie walking over to him. Ethan smiled when the young couple embraced.

"What are you doing here? I thought you were having lunch with Vic?" asked Randy.

"She had that meltdown I told you was coming."

"You won the bet?"

"Easy money, my love," she said with a giggle. He chuckled and kissed the top of her head.

"Good, now I just have to decide who to tease about it first, Vic or Joanie," said Randy. Stacie winked at him.

"Tease Joanie first. Call it a wedding present for Vic," suggested Stacie.

"So, no teasing Vic about it?" questioned Randy.

"Oh, you can totally tease her. Just wait until after they get back from the honeymoon." He chuckled again.

"That seems fair," said Randy. Stacie gave Ethan a sympathetic smile.

"You two okay?" she asked. Randy and Ethan glanced at each other before nodding.

"Yeah, I think I'm done. I'm still not sure how all of this works," admitted Randy.

"You say whatever you want for however long you want. Everyone grieves differently," she assured. Randy knelt to touch Dominic's gravestone. His fingers traced the name that was etched into the stone and sighed.

"Thanks for the letter, Dominic. I love you too." With that, Randy laced his fingers with Stacie's and the couple headed back down the trail together. Ethan watched them depart before kneeling in front of Dominic's gravestone. He pulled a small box from his pocket and smiled sadly at it.

"I'm sure your dad is rolling in his grave at the very thought of you not having a proper Guardian burial, but I think Randy is right. This is where you belong. I had another ring made for you, the last of its kind. I think it's fitting that you receive the last one. For all of your wrongs, you were right about one thing in the end. We couldn't have done it without you." Ethan dug a small hole at the edge of the gravestone and slipped the ring deep inside of it before covering the rare piece of jewelry with soil.

"Mission accomplished, old friend. Godspeed," he whispered. He dusted off his hands as he stood back up and took a deep breath. He felt the weight that had been heavy on his chest dissipate and knew Maya was right. The past was the past and moving on meant accepting everything about his old friend, the good, the bad, and the complicated in between. Dominic was all of those things, and yet so much more in the end.

○ ○ ○ ○ ○ ○

Joanie sat on a bench in the garden, taking in the beautiful early evening air. The sun hung low in the clear sky and cascaded golden light over the backyard where they celebrated John and Victoria's reception. From her perch, between two lush trees that served as an entrance to the garden in the distance, she could see all the guests and the happy couple joyously celebrating the nuptials. Chris, Randy, and Stacie were speaking with Maya and Zayneb about their trip to Finland. Carlos and Reo were conversing with Henrik and Archie about the latest research the couple was working on. Once the Ultimate Evil was no longer a threat and the compound had served its purpose for the Guardians, Phillip gifted it to Henrik and Archie as a show of gratitude and an acknowledgment of past wrongdoings. Ethan made sure everyone in their circle knew that in the end, it was a cast-aside former Guardian and the man he loved who took on the helm the Brotherhood failed to see out to the end. Henrik and Archie used the compound as a new home and facility where they each continued their respective research. Reo and Carlos were planning a trip to the compound soon to check out the new work the couple were branching out into. Ethan and Gabriella were mingling and catching up with old friends from town. While they missed Anderson, they were enjoying their time in Spain and their new home on the outskirts of Barcelona. Joanie smiled even more when she saw Victoria throw her head back in laughter as she danced with John.

"It appears the second time was the charm." Joanie's eyes widened when she recognized the voice behind her. She turned to see the beautiful older woman standing in the garden and wearing a light gray dress. Joanie was stunned as Kaya joined her on the bench and peered out at the exuberant scene before them.

"Don't worry, there will be no interruptions at this reception. The wedding was beautiful, by the way."

"Kaya? What are you doing here? How is this even possible?"

"Since I'm no longer a Seer, I've been able to branch out a bit. I can't remember the last time I got to see not only a wonderful event but also experience it. The floral scent of the garden, the sweet smell of grass, and that delicious aroma, what is that?"

"Thomas's wife, Lenna, opened a catering business. She's an amazing cook. You should go make yourself a plate. There's plenty."

"Thank you, but I can't stay long." Joanie took a shaky breath and steadied her composure.

"Alright, lay it on me. What's wrong now?" Kaya giggled.

"Nothing is wrong. In fact, everything is quite right…well…as right as it can be in such a complicated world. I never thought I would see the day when it would happen, but you can feel it too, can't you? All it takes is one look at the sky to know it. The universe is buzzing with energy. Balance has been restored. You should be proud of yourself, Joanie. You all should be."

"Before, when we thought Dominic was the Ultimate Evil, I could still sense it. I was in denial, but every instinct was telling me it wasn't over. I don't feel that anymore. It's truly over, isn't it?" Kaya smiled warmly at her.

"The Naturas have fulfilled the prophecy. You can rest easy, knowing that Absolution has been accomplished. What will you do, now that you are no longer trying to solve cryptic messages or battle dark forces?"

"Chris and I are going to actually have that honeymoon it feels like we've been planning forever. We're going to Maui. I even plan on taking some surfing lessons with him while we're there. I have a feeling we'll both be pretty good at it. Vic and John are heading to Sweden first and then traveling across Europe before checking out Central America. After the school year ends, Stacie and Randy are going to Morrocco. None of us have really gotten to travel much, so we figure we all might as well go see the world for ourselves."

"The world is a big place. You should definitely explore it."

"That's the plan. Chris and I are coming back to Anderson, at least for a while. I really like running the antique store. I'm going to expand it and add a bookstore as well. I've spent so much time away from home that I'm looking forward to figuring out how to make it my own again."

"Well, you have an eternity to do that, so take your time. You don't have to get it all back in a year."

"Not that I'm complaining or anything, but I'm kind of surprised we're still immortal. A part of me figured after we defeated Gedeon our powers would be returned to some force of nature or something."

"I assure you, the energy that flows within you is yours and yours alone. Never doubt that. Besides, it never hurts to have a force of good available." Joanie eyed her curiously.

"Available for what? What aren't you telling me? Why are you really here?"

"I don't blame you for being paranoid, but I assure you this is a joyous time, and all is right in the world. You don't have to believe me, though. Close your eyes and feel it for yourself." Joanie's eyes slid shut. She let the sounds of the party slip into the background and focused on the faint buzz of energy swirling around her. She inhaled and let the euphoric feeling wash over her.

"The universe is balanced once again, and it is only such because this world is practically buzzing with forces of good. It is necessary and you have saved humankind from the brink of extinction." Joanie arched an eyebrow at her.

"But?" she questioned. Kaya giggled.

"No 'but.'" Joanie eyed the original Seer again and slowly nodded.

"Okay…"

"However…"

"There it is," grumbled Joanie.

"The universe is vast, Joanie, and contrary to what humans need to believe to feel safe in it, this is not the only planet with a species that must choose between good and evil from time to time. Good doesn't always win the battle, but that is what keeps the balance."

"So, what does that mean for us?"

"It means you have nothing to worry about. I have seen your future and I assure you the Naturas have created a lasting force of good on this planet. That doesn't mean that force could never be challenged again in this eternity. After all, balance is what keeps the universe going. The fates will always have their way."

"Kaya, are you sure..."

"Stop worrying, Joanie. This world is as it should be. Go forth and be the good you want to see in it. Fare thee well." Kaya stood up to leave, but Joanie called to her again.

"Will I ever see you again? Now that you're no longer the Seer, is this it?" Kaya gave Joanie a wink.

"I'll never be far. I never have been." With that, Kaya headed back into the garden. Chris jogged over to her and pulled Joanie up to him. He frowned as he looked around the garden.

"Are you okay? I was trying to call you over, but you seemed to be distracted and talking to yourself."

"I wasn't talking to myself. I was talking to..." She surveyed the area and a small smile crept onto her lips as the wind blew and euphoria washed over her.

"Never mind; it doesn't matter." He gave her a curious look.

"Are you sure everything is alright? You seemed to be deep in conversation. Did you have a vision? Is there danger? Is the Ultimate Evil..."

"It's over, Chris. I promise."

"How can you be so sure?" She looked up at the sky as the sun began to set and the stars illuminated the vast atmosphere.

"Because the fates always have their way." Before he could question the comment, she captured his lips in a sweet kiss. He pulled her closer and became lost in the woman he loved. The world around them faded into the background. The sound of his brothers' heckling soon found them, however, and Victoria and Stacie's catcalls made the couple pull apart.

"Come up for air, you horndogs. It's not that type of party," called Victoria. John chuckled as he nodded in agreement. Joanie and Chris shook their heads in amusement at the teasing of their siblings and Joanie slipped her hand in his.

"Come on, handsome. Let's go celebrate."

"With pleasure, *tesoro*." Chris and Joanie headed back to the dance floor to join in on the celebration, and Joanie laughed when Victoria and Stacie pulled her over to them as her sisters danced. Chris shook with mirth when John tried to show Randy a dance move he learned from a new social media app he downloaded, and Randy assured him he knew how to dance. In that moment, Chris felt a wave of serenity fall over him as he watched his wife dancing with her sisters and his brothers teasing one another. His smile widened when Ethan and Gabriella joined them on the dance floor. The former Guardian pulled his wife closer and danced to the upbeat tempo. Zayneb and Maya managed to get Carlos and Reo onto the dance floor as well. However, it did not take long for the couple to focus in on one another while their friends danced around them. Zayneb noticed Chris smiling at her and her wife, and he laughed when she pulled him over to their group. They all gravitated to the middle of the floor, where their guests were enjoying the music as well.

"I didn't think you danced," he called over the music. Zayneb winked at him.

"Only on special occasions, like this," she assured.

"You're truly getting to see her in rare form," added Maya. Chris began to dance with the Praevians and grinned from ear to ear when Joanie wrapped her arms around him from behind. He turned in her arms and gave her a twirl. The couple shared a smile before looking around at the boisterous group. The euphoria was palpable, and Joanie sighed happily when Victoria's head fell back in laughter. The adoration John had for his bride was evident in his eyes as they rhythmically moved to the beat and embraced the moment. Joanie and Chris both decided to do the same and all thoughts of Kaya's presence ceased for the Seer. As dusk set in and the white string lights around the backyard illuminated the lawn, Joanie truly felt carefree. For the first time in Joanie's life, she felt like everything was as it should be, and she couldn't wait to spend an eternity with the people she loved.

o o o o o o

The End

o o o o o o

Made in the USA
Columbia, SC
24 June 2024